THE BEAUTIFUL HARPIES

With all my love to Penny and Cody.

My appreciation to Stephen Jones (aka Babybird) and his alter egos for his/their musical inspiration over the years.

And, many thanks to Alix for championing this novel with great enthusiasm, and Afaf for her editing brilliance in making sure it gets to publication in better shape than I could ever do on my own.

THE BEAUTIFUL HARPIES

by

Cameron Scott Kirk

First published in paperback special edition, 2023
By Cybirdy Publishing Company
101 Camley Street, London NIC 4DU

This book is sold subject to the condition that it shall not, by way of trade, digitalisation or otherwise, be lent, resold, hired out or otherwise circulated without the publisher's prior consent in any form of binding or cover other than that in which it is published and without a similar condition being imposed on the subsequent purchaser.

Cameron Scott Kirk has asserted his right to be identified as the author of this work in accordance with the Copyright, Designs and Patents Act 1988

Cover design by Joze Groselj
Illustrations by Anwot
Edited by Afaf Shour
Printed by Hobbs the Printers Ltd

This book is typeset in Minion, Proxima Nova and Copperplate
A CIP record for this book is available from the British Library

ISBN: 978-1-7396637-5-9

THE BEAUTIFUL HARPIES

Cameron Scott Kirk

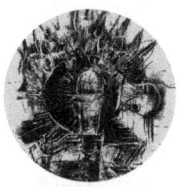

PROLOGUE

"Jewellery," the older woman called to the younger as she passed by, "jewellery for such a fine beauty, such a pretty young thing."

The old crone's brittle voice somehow penetrated the laughter of children, the clashing notes of musicians and the shouts of street hawkers all thronging the market square.

The younger woman stopped, and her striking green eyes roamed over the items laid out on a sackcloth. Brushing a strand of long black hair behind her ear, she said, "I can afford no jewellery nor desire it."

From the back of her cart, the older woman cocked her head, giving her the aspect of a crow perched on a fence. "A cloud of sadness follows you among the merriment. You alone are different. What I offer will lighten your heart."

"My heart is made of stone. It cannot be lightened."

"Do not be so sure. I have something special, something for one such as you." The old woman reached within the folds of her black cloak and produced a thin band of metal, a bracelet which seemed to glow from within, changing hues in her hand. First silver, then deep blue, then purple and then crimson.

The younger woman stared, transfixed. "It's ... beautiful. I've not seen anything like it."

"No one has," the old hag said, "at least no one around here or no one still living. This metal is ancient and comes from exotic lands that only the truly insane can envisage. Despite my frail appearance, I still have the strength and skills to shape this into anything you desire if its current form does not please."

The woman peered at the bracelet. "Can you ..."

The noise of the festival seemed to fade away, leaving the two of them alone in the universe. "Yes, child? Can I what?"

"Can you engrave a name into this?"

The old one smiled and crooned, "Oh, yes. Yes, I can, for no further cost. Consider it a favour for a friend. What name do you wish scripted?"

The green eyes of the younger woman met the sunken eyes of the older. "Bessie," she said.

CHAPTER 1

Wives

Recognizing that the wickedness of women is greater than all the other wickedness of the world, and that there is no anger like that of women, and that the poison of asps and dragons is more curable and less dangerous to men than the company of women, we unanimously decree for the safety of our souls no less than that of our bodies and goods, that we will on no account receive any more sisters. **Conrad of Marchtal, Clunic Abbot at Marcigny.**

The cool evening wind hissed in the pine trees. The river gurgled, and the waterwheel creaked. Inside the millhouse, gears groaned and turned slowly.

Mary Brown tied off a large sack of flour and dragged it across the floor to join several others. She patted at the golden bun of hair tied atop her head, causing a fine pale powder to puff into the air. Mary put one hand on her hip and arched her back. She ran her other hand across the swelling beneath her apron and yawned. The sun had gone down behind the shoulder of the mountain, and the light was fading. One more bag and the day's work would be done.

A noise attracted Mary's attention, something outside, loud enough to be heard over the river and the gearwheels. Her husband leaned over the balustrade in the grain store above, a quizzical expression on his face. Willard Brown was in his late twenties, but the freckles around his nose gave him the look of an eternally gawkish teen.

"Did you hear that?" Willard called down to his wife.

Mary nodded. "I heard something." She eased her way past a large horizontal cog and peered out the window. "It's Tom. Tom Gallagher."

Tom stood on the stone walk bridge over the river, his hands cupped about his mouth as he shouted again.

Willard frowned. "Tom? What's he doing here at this hour? What's he saying?"

"Can't hear a word of it," Mary said, "but he doesn't look happy."

Willard descended the creaking wooden staircase and, without breaking stride, patted his wife on the rump. Mary aimed a kick at him, but Willard was already on the stairs to the ground-floor kitchen.

"Oi!" Mary shouted after her husband. "There'll be none of that when the child is born. Hands to yourself, you lecherous devil."

Mary leaned out of the window as Willard strode out into the early evening air and approached the man on the bridge. The two shouted to be heard above the sounds of the hissing water, yet from this distance, she had no way of making out what they were saying.

Tom was half a head taller than Willard, his mop of black hair tossed about in the chill evening breeze. He thumbed at the bow on his back, then pointed towards the farmlands below. The same finger now swivelled and pointed up the mountain road towards the darkening forest. Something had agitated the bowyer. Tom had a good business fashioning bows, arrows and crossbows for the townspeople of Dysael, and some of his customers were among the well-to-do of the city. Mary couldn't imagine why he'd be up here after sunset.

Willard made a 'wait here' gesture and rushed back inside the millhouse. Mary went downstairs to meet him. She found her husband reaching above the fireplace for his axe.

"What's going on?" Mary asked. "Where are you going with that?"

The freckles above Willard's nose wrinkled as he frowned. "Elsie's gone. Tom thinks a wolf has taken her."

Mary put her hands to her mouth. "Elsie? Gone? Oh, my goodness. But … but there are no wolves this far down. She's probably just walked into town."

"Not at this hour, not without telling Tom." The miller fumbled the axe, and it clanked to the stone floor.

"Don't be an idiot, Will. It's getting dark, and if there are wolves about, you're no hunter. You'll get yourself torn apart or chop your own fingers off, at the very least. Tom's a skilled bowman. Let him go."

Willard shook his head, though he was clearly reluctant to leave. "That's heartless, Mary. I can't turn my back on Tom when he needs my help."

Mary put her hands on her hips. "It wouldn't be the first time you've turned your back. Not your business. Isn't that what you said?"

Willard winced as if struck across the face. He glowered at Mary. "Don't speak of that. We promised. We *all* promised."

Mary's face flushed red beneath the thin powdering of flour. "Just you be back before dark. We have grain arriving early in the morning. Early, do you hear?"

"Lock the door, my little baker's loaf."

Little baker's loaf. Willard called her that because her golden-brown hair resembled a freshly baked loaf of bread, especially when tied up on her head and dusted with flour, as it often was. Mary had never liked the term but didn't have the heart to tell him, and it was too late now. He's called her that forever.

Willard strode outside and to the rear of the millhouse. He released a latch on a small kennel, and a dog burst out, wagging her tail so fervently that the animal's lean torso twisted this way and that.

Willard pushed the dog away as she jumped on him. "Settle down, Jess. We're going up into the trees, girl. I trust that you will see us there and back."

Willard and Jess crossed the bridge to join Tom. The miller and the bowyer moved swiftly up the road, the excitable Jess leading the way.

Mary had never liked the dog, always traipsing mud inside. It was a thankless task keeping the millhouse clean, but she now wished that her husband had left Jess with her. It was all very well rushing off to save another man's wife, but his own? Nary a second thought. If there *was* anything out there, wolves and the like, Mary was now defenceless. She shook her head and scolded herself for her foolishness. Elsie had simply gone out for a walk. She took off her apron and went outside. By the wall of the millhouse, the overspill from the waterwheel buckets fed a long stone basin. She released her golden-brown hair from its tight bun and dipped her face and head into the cool water. She wrung her hair out and, with a glance at the empty road and the lengthening shadows of the trees, went back inside before she caught a chill.

A cup of tea, yes, that would settle her nerves, but her mind was racing, her fingers trembling. Fool husband. He wasn't the kind of man who could just go gallivanting off into the forest at night. More likely to break a leg than not. Look how he'd fumbled the axe. Will was no hero, his responsibility lay in the millhouse, with his customers, with his wife and the child on the way. The wind started to whine and whistle at the door and window. This was bad. This was very bad.

Mary rubbed her swollen belly and addressed the unborn child. "Your father is a ninnyhammer and no mistake." A kick of agreement fluttered beneath her fingers.

The miller's wife lit a lamp against the encroaching darkness and cursed her husband again. Of all the times to be running off. Couldn't see your hand in front of your face in half an hour.

Something splashed in the water outside, loud enough to be heard over the creaking gearwheels. Probably a rock rolling into the river. Just a rock.

Another sound pricked at her ears. A shout or scream? Or was it the howling of a wolf? Mary scurried to the window. Darkness was beginning to spread like slow black flames through the trees on the mountainside. The skin on her arms prickled. She drew the bolt on the door and turned to examine the small kitchen. A cup of tea, yes.

CHAPTER 1 Wives

She would stoke the embers and put the kettle on.

Mary used a poker to stir the ashes in a small fireplace. She blew on a small ember, and it glowed. A tiny flame licked at a splinter of kindling, growing until it burned hungrily. Satisfied that the fire was reborn, Mary placed a small block of wood on the flames and hung a kettle on a hook over the growing heat. She sat down, listening intently.

The internal gearwheels of the millhouse creaked, and the cold water rushed through the millrace outside. The dark shapes of the buckets rose and fell at the window with a regular, mechanical rhythm. Life in the millhouse usually lulled Mary into a trance. She had found the sounds peaceful after the initial settling-in period two years ago. But they did not lull her tonight. The paddles were now ominous shadows at her window, and the sounds of the river and the gearwheels seemed to hide the telltale indications of something far more menacing. She wished for quiet. Was that Jess barking? Were Will and Tom returning already? Had they found Elsie?

Mary hitched the hem of her skirt and hurried upstairs. From the second floor, she could see little of the forest road winding upwards into the trees. She climbed higher, up to the grain store. The window here was nothing more than sackcloth over a rectangular opening in the side of the millhouse. She pulled the makeshift curtain aside and leaned out into the cool air. Mist clung to the top of the darkening tree line. She could just make out patches of white water over rocks in the river below.

A shadow under the window moved, something clinging to the stone walls. The thing reached up and clasped Mary's wrist in a cold, clammy grip.

"Come with us," it whispered.

Pain and shock electrified Mary. She screamed. Her screams cut through the creaking of the gearwheels, overpowering the rushing water of the river below.

Her screams echoed all the way up the mountain.

CHAPTER 2

The Gates of Hell

Dangerous things lurked in the shadows. Wolves, bears and other beasts of strange design. There was no telling what was out there, but *something* had come down out of the woods and attacked his Mary.

"Are you alright, Willard?"

Willard blinked. He tore his eyes from the still dark and sinister tree line. Greg Downing was looking at him from the back of his cart, concern on his whiskered face. The carter had arrived with a load of grain before the morning sun and was busy unloading it.

"Sorry, Greg. I was lost in thought."

"Hate to hurry you along," Greg patted a sack of grain resting against his legs, "but I have another delivery before the sun makes the shoulder of the mountain. I can't be dawdling."

Willard nodded, grabbed the sack of grain and heaved it across his shoulders. He carried it inside, where Mary sat knitting at the kitchen table, head down and silent. She hadn't spoken a word since the night Elsie Gallagher had disappeared. Tom and Willard had returned to the millhouse to find her frantic, inconsolable. She was babbling and making no sense. The following morning, she had woken, and nothing more could be got from her. Willard sighed and carried the sack to the storeroom upstairs, his heart heavier than any bag of grain. He returned to the kitchen and touched his wife's cheek before rejoining the carter outside.

"Willard, are you expecting anyone else this morning?" Greg Downing was pointing down the road at two stocky horses, both duns, identical in size and colouring: sandy coats, black manes and tails. The riders, however, could not have been more disparate in appearance. As the horses ambled closer, the contrast between the two became even more apparent: a woman dressed in a black mantle, white tunic and coif, signifying her as a nun. She was overweight, her cheeks puffy. The other figure was a man in black leather breeches and vest—a big, lean fellow with a sober expression.

Willard heaved another sack of grain over his shoulders and went inside. He did not welcome any more disruptions and hoped that the two riders would pass by. When he returned, he found his hopes drowned. The big man was tying off the horses as the fat nun flapped her way across the stone bridge. She was waving and smiling, engaging Greg Downing in conversation, but Willard could not hear what they were saying over the perpetual roar of the river. He approached the ruddy-faced nun and the bemused carter. The nun turned her attention to Willard and spoke with enough enthusiasm to make herself heard over any noise.

"Ah, hello, sir. It's a beautiful day. I was just saying to this fellow," she gestured to the carter with a pudgy hand, "that the millhouse is a brilliant example of rustic grandeur, man and machine working together seamlessly, technology and nature wonderfully counterposed. I would love to return with my easel and watercolours at a later date." She cleared her throat. "For now, I have business with Willard Brown, the miller. That man is you, I take it."

Willard nodded. "I am the miller."

The nun pointed to her ear. "Can we talk somewhere a little quieter? A beautiful scene, but rather loud."

Willard turned and walked to the back of the millhouse. The nun followed, and they were soon joined by the bodyguard, or so Willard assumed him to be. The man was big, over six feet, with not an ounce of fat on him. His red-stubbled face radiated cold, his eyes were narrow and his nose hawkish beneath ginger eyebrows. Willard experienced an odd mental image of the big man sitting on the forearm of the nun like some expertly trained hunting falcon. He shook the image from his mind and folded his arms. He welcomed neither falconer nor falcon.

Willard cleared his throat and said, "Mary wishes for no more disturbances. She's not well."

The nun put her hands together in a prayer-like gesture. "I am Sister Kempson of the Holy Sisters of Conviction. This," she waved to her big falcon, "is Garth. I apologise for the intrusion. You and your wife have many duties that keep you busy. However, it is imperative that I speak to Mary Brown."

"As I said, she is ill. Needs her rest."

The nun was not to be discouraged. "Mr. Brown, you may be aware that seven women have mysteriously vanished from the city of Dysael. Elsie Gallagher is, by all reports, the first of these vanishings. We have been informed that Mary witnessed something on the night of Elsie's disappearance. This makes your wife a vital cog, if you will," the nun whirled her finger in a circular motion, "in our investigation."

Willard frowned. "Seven? I … I had heard of five."

"The numbers are rising, Mr. Brown. Hence, the importance of our task."

"You've come for naught. Mary hasn't spoken since the night Elsie disappeared. You're wasting your time."

Sister Kempson raised her eyebrows. "Are you suggesting that your wife is currently mute?"

"Aye. Was I not clear? She needs peace and quiet 'til she finds her balance and her tongue again. The last fellow who came by upset her something terrible."

Sister Kempson frowned. "The last fellow? I know nothing of any other fellow. I have come to speak to your wife in the official capacity given to me. I am charged, you see, with finding the missing women."

"That's what he said."

"He? Who?"

"The man what came by yesterday. Charged, in an official capacity, he said."

Sister Kempson's smile came out a little sickly. "I assure you that the man in question is not part of any authorised investigation."

"He insisted that he was."

The nun glanced at Garth. The big man shrugged. Turning back to the miller, Sister Kempson said, "I think we're setting off in the wrong direction. I have paper and chalk. Perhaps we can tease out some representation of what Mary saw the night she became mute. This would help me to—"

"She doesn't want any more visitors. She's not well."

"I understand, Mr. Brown, that your wife has suffered a terrible shock." The fat nun raised her hands apologetically. "However, this is not a request you may deny. The people of Dysael have petitioned the bishop. *I* am the answer to that petition and have all legal rights to carry out my duties."

The miller scowled. He wished to simply turn and walk away.

"I promise," Sister Kempson went on, "that I shall not harm your wife. On the contrary, consider this a therapeutic transaction, a form of spiritual solace. I am a nun, after all, and am trained in these things. I believe Mary needs me as much as I need her. We will both be better off for the interview."

The waterwheel turned, and the river rushed by in the millrace. The morning skies were brightening, the shadows in Willard's mind receding. Perhaps it might be a good thing for Mary to have a sympathetic presence. He'd tried, himself, to comfort her, to get her to speak again, but did not know how to reach her. He felt helpless, and Mary's unresponsive state had begun to scare him. Perhaps this woman could do what he could not. Willard sighed and gestured for the nun to follow him inside.

The miller's wife sat in a chair in the kitchen next to the unlit fireplace, a dog at her feet. The animal perked up as the miller, the nun and the bodyguard entered the kitchen. Mary simply continued gazing at the hands resting in her lap, her knitting having fallen to the floor.

Sister Kempson immediately recognised the signs of mental trauma, the dull, almost catatonic state in which the miller's wife sat. The dog whined and put its head back on its paws, looking up at the nun mournfully, as if to suggest that it, too, understood something was terribly wrong with its mistress. *Marvellous animals, dogs*, Sister Kempson thought. *Empathetic.* It was time to test her own skills at empathy. She had to be gentle with this woman or risk provoking her from catatonia to mania.

"I am Sister Kempson," the nun said gently. She slowly picked up the knitting and put it aside. She sat in a chair and placed a white parchment and a piece of black chalk on the kitchen table. The miller's wife raised sleepy eyes in an ashen face. Her hand moved to her swollen belly. Sister Kempson smiled. "The millhouse is wonderfully picturesque, quite a sight coming up the road."

"I must attend to the grain," Willard Brown said.

The nun swung around. "Yes, yes. You do that. Garth can help you." She raised an eyebrow at the big man, and he followed the miller outside. Sister Kempson turned back to Mary and whispered conspiratorially. "You know, some of the sisters at the convent do talk such drivel, meaningless nonsense about the weather and food and such. I like food but would rather consume it than talk about it. I often find myself longing for the company of a man as I have heard that they are the more … pragmatic sex, if that's the term. But Garth, the big ginger fellow in here just now, speaks so infrequently that I still have little idea what goes on inside a man's head. Perhaps it not for a woman to ever truly understand the mysteries of the masculine gender, eh?"

Mary Brown stared at the nun with a morose expression. One of her eyelids seemed to droop.

"We are taught to sketch at the convent," Sister Kempson said. "I have a talent for it, God forgive me for my pride. I shall make some rudimentary lines. May I?" Sister Kempson held the stick of black chalk over the paper. Mary Brown nodded weakly, but at least there was a glimmer of a reaction in the woman's eyes. The nun made a few swift strokes of the charcoal. "You keep your house beautifully clean, even with a dog and all the grain coming in and the flour going out. I do wonder how you manage it."

The nun prattled on idly as she continued to gracefully sweep the black chalk over the white paper. She turned the parchment to admire the lines and perspective and to give Mary the best view. The miller's wife gazed at the impression of her home in black chalk. The nun touched her cheek in an absentminded gesture, as if wondering which addition to make to the sketch, and, in so doing, left a smear of dark chalk on her plump cheek.

"I forgot to bring my yellow," Sister Kempson said. "It adds a wonderful contrast."

Mary Brown stared at the smudge of black on the nun's face. She took one hand from her belly and pointed to it. Sister Kempson feigned ignorance, and the miller's wife leaned forward to wipe the black chalk from the nun's cheek. Her fingers were cold and trembling. Sister Kempson reached up and grasped the fingers in her own. "You're cold. You poor woman. You must stay warm, for yourself and the baby. Let me start a fire."

Mary shook her head and guided the nun's fingers down to her belly. The swelling, too, was cold to the touch. Sister Kempson slid forward off her chair, placing her other hand upon the woman's enlarged body. Cold. So cold. A thought chilled the nun's mind just as the flesh of the miller's wife chilled her fingers. Sister Kempson leaned her head against the woman's belly and listened. No heartbeat. Not one. Not the miller's wife nor that of the child.

"They have opened the gates of Hell," Mary whispered.

Sister Kempson jerked her head away and looked up. "What did you say?" The miller's wife appeared not to have spoken, her eyes glazed over once more, dull. "Who has opened the gates of Hell? Mary, can you tell me who is responsible for the missing women? Elsie, Elsie Gallagher, you knew her. Can you tell me who took her, where she is now?"

Mary Brown did not respond. Sister Kempson dragged the sketch off the table, placed it in the lap of the miller's wife and flipped it over. "What did you see the night of Elsie Gallagher's disappearance?" The nun offered the black chalk, but Mary seemed not to see it. Suddenly the miller's wife jerked in her chair and clasped her belly, her face screwed up in pain. The dog began to whine.

"Oh, my goodness." Sister Kempson heaved herself to her feet and ran outside.

Willard Brown whirled about at the sudden appearance of the nun. "What happened? Did she speak to you?"

Sister Kempson blinked in the early morning sunlight. "Yes, she did. Briefly."

"What did she say?"

The nun did not respond. Garth looked on, concern on his face. "Are you alright, Sister?"

"I … I'm fine. Mr. Brown, I need water, warm water and towels. I think your wife is … in difficulty."

The miller gawked. "The child is coming?"

"I … I can't be sure. But something is wrong."

"Wrong? No, no. She's upset by recent events, but she's alright. The baby is healthy."

The dog barked from inside the millhouse. Then, it let out a long, mournful howl that chilled the blood. Everyone stood motionless, exchanging glances. Willard Brown reacted first. He ran into the millhouse, Garth right behind him. Sister Kempson hitched the hem of her habit and huffed after the two men.

The miller screamed. The dog stopped barking. When Sister Kempson reached the doorway to the millhouse kitchen, she stopped and gasped.

They have opened the gates of Hell.

Blood everywhere, splashed and sprayed on the table, over the walls. A limp, gelatinous foetus on the cold stone floor, umbilical cord leading off into a pool of gore. The dog licked at the dead infant with flattened ears and wide eyes, as if she knew this to be forbidden but could not resist the salty tang. Mary Brown was gone; the kitchen window had been flung open.

The miller shrieked again, and the dog backed away, tail between her legs.

"What have you done?" Willard shouted, turning on the nun, eyes wide, face enraged. Sister Kempson opened her mouth to reply but could not utter a sound. The miller lunged at her, and Garth knocked the man unconscious with one blow.

"Not in his right mind," Garth said. He ran outside and around the back of the house where the kitchen window opened onto the grassy river embankment. The dog twisted in circles by the body of her senseless master. Sister Kempson stepped through the viscous fluids, slipped, regained her balance and poked her head out of the window.

Something was dragging itself from the water on the other side of the river, thirty yards away. Despite the clarity of the early morning light, the thing remained indistinct. It was pale pink, its body flexile, as if the creature were constructed entirely of the webbing between the tendons of a goose's foot. A boneless, flapping thing, yet somehow human.

The nun pointed. "There!"

"I see it," Garth said.

Garth looked quizzically at the nun, who nodded and said, "Go!"

The big man set off running across the footbridge. The creature had by now made the shadows of the trees across the road and disappeared. Garth vanished into the same trees a few moments later.

Sister Kempson turned, surveyed the obscenity smeared around the kitchen and made the sign of the cross. Something on the table caught her eye. She came closer to examine it. An image had been scrawled on the paper in black chalk beneath the flecks of blood. Sister Kempson leaned forward and peered at it.

CHAPTER 3

The Woodsman

The thing moved fast. Garth had only caught a glimpse of it, but in that moment, the creature had seemed more suited to water than a hillside forest. It had emerged from the river and made for the trees, appearing an ungainly thing on land but somehow accelerated upwards and out of sight into the denser bush.

Garth knelt and examined one of the thing's footprints. It was unlike anything he had ever seen. It resembled, if possible, that of some web-footed animal like a duck, though larger. He shook his head in wonder and moved further up the mountain. Droplets of water and blood quivered on the fern fronds, some sliding down the length of the leaves to fall to the rich earth. The creature was injured, or it was the blood of the miller's wife. It was impossible to know. The thing had not carried the body of Mary Brown as it came out of the water; perhaps the strong currents had swept her away.

Garth followed the footprints until the water disappeared and the droplets of blood became more intermittent. Upwards he climbed into the pine-scented heights. He had been following the trail for a good half-hour when he heard the rustling of undergrowth from somewhere up ahead. Garth pinpointed the source of the sound and made a mental map of the trail of footprints thus far. The thing, he realised, had veered to the right. If he cut across the terrain at an angle, he could make some ground on … whatever it was. Garth leapt over a felled tree and sprinted into a small depression, a drainage channel cut into the hillside and up the other side. The gradient here was steeper, but he scrambled upwards like a stag in flight. He came upon a small ridge. No sign of the thing, yet a fern moved a dozen yards away, indicating the recent passing of a large object into the shaded trees just beyond it. He was close now. A dozen yards.

Garth's breath came hard and heavy, but he was far from spent. The forest was no enemy or obstacle to him. He'd been born a stone's throw from the end of civilisation, on the border of the True Wilds, and as soon as he'd learned to walk, it was not civilisation he had tottered towards.

Less than a dozen yards. Garth was quick. Quicker than this thing, he was sure of it. A scent of something came to him, and like the footprints, this was unlike anything he understood: a salty, sickly odour, the hint of a great ocean.

The trees grew closer together, blotting out the morning sun, creating pools of shadows and cool, eddying draughts. The pungent smell of moss and pine filled Garth's nostrils: the smells of home.

He slowed down as his eyes adjusted to the dimness. The trail of bizarre footprints disappeared. Garth scanned the intertwining branches overhead, suspecting an ambush. Nothing. This made no sense. He stopped and listened. No sounds. The skin on his scalp tickled, and the hairs on his arms stood up. The creature was here among the shadowed trees, no doubt, but it had stopped running. Waiting for him. *Careful now, Garth,* he thought. *You are the hunter. Do not become the hunted.*

The ground was a carpet of needles and cones, ferns and aromatic wild ginger, but something else lay a foot in front of him, something metallic. Garth knelt and used a long twig to brush aside the pungent pine needles, revealing sharp-toothed metal jaws open and poised to crush the leg of any large animal or man: a trap, recently placed by the looks of it. Anger flowed through the big man. These traps were indiscriminate tools, outlawed in Dysael and for good reason. He cursed. He couldn't afford to ease his pursuit, but nor could he run at the same pace, for this trap would not be the only one of its kind nearby. If he ever got his hands on the bastard that laid this, he'd make sure to imprint upon the man the finer points of trapping law.

Garth tiptoed through the fern and ginger. Upon making clearer ground, he cursed again. He had lost the creature's trail. For want of a better plan, Garth continued to ascend, hoping to stumble once more upon its tracks.

He made his way to a ridge and looked back down over the treetops. The patchwork fields, misted with evaporation fog, gave way to the city of Dysael beyond them. Some said Dysael was a marvel of modern architecture and offered all the comforts of the new technological age. Garth couldn't see it. Looked like any other city to him. The box-like wooden houses built one upon the other gave no room to breathe. The city seemed shrouded with a darker mist than that of the fields: the gloom of human squalor and misery. Garth de Silva had spent his life in the rain and the wind and trees, had gone further into the depths of the True Wilds than any of the older woodsmen who'd taught him of its secret ways. He'd missed out on some things, true. Never slept in a nice bed, never washed his face with warm water, never wiped his arse on soft paper. He didn't care about any of that. He didn't desire any of the luxuries in Dysael below. Fancy big town. Not for him. Except maybe the soft paper. Might make a nice change from scratchy leaves.

The woodsman turned away from the city and moved up the mountain, listening, sniffing the air. He must have been at five hundred feet or so now, the first hints of thinner air in his lungs, breath coming harder. The trees closed in again, and the shade-loving wild ginger began to carpet the forest floor once more, its aroma and that of the pine disguising the salty scent of the creature.

The clank of something metallic. The sound of an animal whining softly, high-pitched like a dog in pain, but quiet. Garth slid his long hunting knife from its hip sheathe, the tip of the blade ending in a wicked gut hook. Movement in a depression up ahead. Garth avoided dry foliage and stepped only on soft earth to dull the sounds of his approach. Looking into the depression, Garth blinked in surprise.

CHAPTER 3 The Woodsman

The thing lay on its back, trying to cover itself in dead pine needles and leaves, its leg crushed within the maw of a trap, bloodied bone splintered, tendons flayed. But this creature no longer resembled the pale pink thing that had emerged from the waters below. It was covered with hair, like a dog or wolf, and yet the leg within the maw of the trap was different, as if transplanted from a different body: the last remaining vestige of the water creature. Garth could not understand what he was looking at. The creature tried to crawl away from him, but it was pinned. The pain must have been tremendous, but it clenched its jaws and did not cry out.

Garth raised his hunting knife, and then the creature whispered one word. "Please."

Human eyes in an alien face. Garth hesitated. "By the Green Gods, what are you?"

The thing shook its head, in too much agony to speak. Garth did not move for several moments. Finally, he bent over, slipped his hunting knife between the serrated blades of the trap and pushed down and away. At the same time, he compressed the springs at the side of the trap with his foot, using all his sixteen stone to release the maws of the device. With a grinding click, the jaws snapped open, and the thing crawled away.

"Stay where you are," Garth warned.

The creature complied, panting. Blood covered its oddly animal yet still human torso. The thing seemed to possess flat breasts. The creature raised a long, hairy arm and pointed behind Garth.

Garth turned and saw the arrow too late. The metal-tipped projectile whizzed past his ear and thudded into a large spruce tree, sending out splinters. If the aim had been better, Garth would have been too dead to roll away, but roll he did. A musket ball exploded and chipped away at the bark of a tree mere inches from his head.

Bows and muskets. What had he come upon now? Trappers?

"I'm no bear, stupid pricks!" Garth shouted from behind a tree. "Hold your fire!"

Another musket ball tore a chunk out of the bole of the spruce.

Garth peeked around the tree. The strange creature had gone. He jerked his head back as an arrow buried itself in the earth an arm's length away. He took another risk and poked his head low around the tree trunk: three men, hiding behind trees at twenty-five yards, one bow and two muskets. Bastards. Had they attacked him to allow the creature its freedom? No, they hadn't seen it, of that, he was sure. Hadn't been close enough to see the thing hiding in the depression. This was simply shit timing.

He couldn't stay here. The men would close the ground and have him at their leisure. A counterattack, then. One bow and two muskets, both firearms expended. He could do it, but he had to move now. He rushed out from behind the tree and sprinted.

Garth hated muskets. They were all the rage, however, among cowards, cunts and kings. The big man thundered behind another tree, intending to outflank his assailants as they reloaded. If he had miscalculated and missed a fourth assailant, he was a dead man.

Mary Brown was gone, possibly swept away by the angry downhill currents. The carter had freed his horse from the cart and ridden into Dysael to bring the constable, the coroner, the Night Watch, anybody.

Sister Kempson walked the road but could see no sign of Mary's body in the water. She regretted letting Garth run off after the thing that had attacked the miller's wife. Their first duty was to Mary Brown, and if there remained any chance of finding her, then it would be best to have Garth's strong hands to pull her from the cold waters.

The nun shivered at the memory of the millhouse kitchen and the blood smeared across the floor and walls, the tragic gore-slicked foetus, almost a fully formed infant. The miller's wife could not have survived such an attack. There was too much blood.

The river reached the flatlands of the farms bordering Dysael. The river widened, and the rushing water eased its pace, gravity no longer adding its impetus. Still no sign of a body, dead or otherwise.

With a heavy heart, Sister Kempson turned and trudged back up the road to the millhouse. She glanced occasionally at the trees lining the road on one side, the river on the other. If the creature returned, she would have neither Garth nor the carter for protection.

Sister Kempson froze. Willard Brown strode down the road towards her, his dog at his heels. The last time the man had been conscious, he had lunged at her before Garth intervened. She could see the bruise on the man's face even at this distance. The nun took a deep breath. If he attempted to do her harm, she would not be able to outrun him. Too much soft living, the other sisters had told her, and not enough exercise.

Sister Kempson was not completely defenceless, however. Beneath her habit tunic was a long knife. Hardly a chaste accoutrement for a bride of Christ, but she was not ignorant of the ways of men. Garth had insisted she take it, and she had not refused. If the miller came at her again, she'd stab him in the chest and answer to God later.

The miller raised two open hands. "I won't hurt you," he said. "I'm sorry." The nun let out a long breath and waited for the man to come closer. "Any sign of my Mary?" Willard asked.

"No, I'm sorry."

"We're both sorry, then. Where's your big falcon?"

Sister Kempson frowned. Was the miller referring to Garth? She pointed up into the trees.

Willard Brown's shoulders slumped. He nodded and continued walking, scanning the river for his wife. Sister Kempson shook her head sadly and headed back up the road. As she approached the millhouse, the morning light began to change hue, hinting at the arrival of early afternoon.

The nun averted her eyes from the bloodied infant as she entered the kitchen. She took the parchment from the kitchen table and walked back outside. On one side of the parchment was her own sketch of the millhouse kitchen. On the other side was a rough outline, beneath flecks of blood, of something that looked like an anvil. Why had Mary Brown scribbled the image of an anvil? Sister Kempson let out the breath that she had been holding, closed her eyes. Something nagged at her, something about the anvil. She opened her eyes and let them run over the wooded mountainside. Garth was up there somewhere. He could look after himself under normal circumstances—no man was more adept in the wilds—but these were not normal circumstances. The Devil was at work here. Fire and brimstone. *An anvil.*

Sister Kempson and Garth had come to the millhouse that morning looking for some answers, a clue to guide them in their hunt for the missing women. Sister Rose Kempson of the Holy Sisters of Conviction had found more than she could have possibly bargained for. She scanned the woodlands on the mountainside again. She needed Garth back, alive. She needed her *falcon* back.

Garth gritted his teeth in anger. It was one thing to lay a bear trap. He might even have forgiven a near miss from an inexperienced hunter mistaking him for an elk. But it was another matter altogether to announce himself as loud as church bells and still end up dodging arrows and musket balls.

One of the bastards was pumping his ram rod down the long barrel of his musket, cartridge paper still sticking to his whiskered lips. And there was the defect in the modern weapon: a laborious reload. The thin man was crouching behind a felled tree, his rough beard all over his face and neck in patches, as unkempt as a frontier whore's fanny.

Garth hurdled the tree, which was, in fact, moss-covered remains of a toppled smokestack, remnants of industrial activity high on the mountain long ago. Scattered red bricks were visible under the moss and lichen. It would be a simple thing to stumble on them, but Garth didn't stumble. The wide-eyed musket man abandoned his futile attempt to reload and swung the weapon like a club. Garth ducked and drove his shoulder into the man's stomach, lifted his legs and sent him sprawling to the forest floor. Garth was well within his rights to gut the prick, but he settled for a vicious headbutt, not so hard as to knock the scrawny man senseless.

Garth held his hunting knife across the man's throat. "Up. On your feet."

As Garth hauled the man up, the other two men stepped warily out from behind trees a few yards away, pointing a musket, now reloaded, and a bow, arrow nocked. Garth hoped that Bow and Musket valued the life of the man he now used as a human shield.

"Drop your weapons, or I'll cut his throat," Garth said. The two men hesitated, and Garth whispered into the bearded man's ear. "You've got a face like a hairy quim. Do you know that? If you survive this day, shave." The man sneezed and blood spurted from his broken nose. He whined in pain.

"Unhand that man," the fellow with the loaded musket said. Garth eyed him up. Black moustaches waxed to tips; a thin goatee finely pointed on the chin. The man's manicured facial hair proved a stark contrast to that of the scraggly runt clasped against his chest.

Garth snarled. "You fired on me even after I announced myself. That is not the mistake of a simple poacher or trapper. I call that attempted murder."

"We are neither poachers nor trappers," the finely groomed musket man replied. He had pointed boots of the kind currently fashionable among the effete, but the boots were not suited to the bush and, along with his ridiculous facial hair, made the man look like a fop. "We are hunting the man, or men, responsible for the abduction of several local women. In our zest to apprehend the villains, we may have innocently mistaken you for one of the perpetrators."

Garth kept his bleeding shield close. "Is that so? On whose authority do you undertake this task?"

"We represent the Consul of Dysael Barristers, North Quarter. I demand you release that man immediately."

Garth snorted. "You're lawyers?"

"I am trained in the law but execute powers of a different office in this matter. I am Constable Vincent E. Thackery." He gestured to the short, stocky bow man beside him. "This is Night Watch Sergeant Robert Jones. You hold a knife to the throat of Night Watch Sergeant Terrence Frood. The king and the common law have called us to action. To harm any of us will result in your hanging. Release the sergeant. This is your final warning."

Garth sneered. "What does the E stand for?" Constable Thackery just stared. "The E," Garth repeated, "in your name. Earl? Earnest? Ermine? Something equally pompous, I imagine."

The moustachioed man frowned and said with some distaste, "Ermine is a weasel, I believe."

Garth raised his eyebrows. "Is it?"

"It doesn't stand for anything. It's an appendage."

Garth barked his laughter. "An appendage? What, like an extra cock or something?" He grabbed Frood roughly by the hair and held the knife tight against the sergeant's windpipe. "Listen to me, Constable Vincent E. Thackery. My name is Garth de Silva, and I am in the employ of the Holy Sisters of Conviction, who seek the same missing women you do. Where you serve your scumbag king, the sisters serve the bishop, probably no less of a scumbag but not my concern. Any harm done to me will not only result in your hanging but in the eternal damnation of your souls." Garth released the broken-nosed sergeant and kicked him up the arse, sending him sprawling at the feet of his colleagues.

Garth put his hunting knife back in its sheath and said, "How's that for an appendage?"

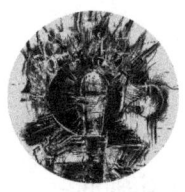

CHAPTER 4

The Sketch

Blood spatter marked the parchment. Blood and mother's fluid. The image scrawled in black chalk beneath the dark red gore was barely visible.

Constable Vincent E. Thackery looked up from the paper into the face of the portly nun sitting on the opposite side of the kitchen table. She sat patiently, awaiting a reaction. Thackery examined the floor and walls of the millhouse kitchen, a kitchen that he had visited only the day before. It looked quite different now. The entire room was stained with the same unpleasant materials as the parchment. Despite the horror of the scene, the waterwheel and the gearwheels continued to turn, and the miller was even now upstairs, seeing to the grinding of the grain. His customers would not wait, he had said.

"Shouldn't someone clean that up?" Thackery said, gesturing at the floor and walls in distaste.

Sister Kempson raised one eyebrow. "I should do it by virtue of being a woman?"

The constable cleared his throat. He had briefly examined the tiny, bloodied and broken corpse of the infant before Coroner Stimpson had bundled the thing into blankets and placed it in his cart. He struggled to get the image out of his mind. "I don't care who does it. It's an eyesore."

"Perhaps we can talk outside if you find yourself discomforted."

Thackery bristled at the term 'discomforted'. It was meant as commentary on his lack of fortitude. He ignored the nun and squinted at the roughly drawn sketch again. "It's an anvil. Clearly an anvil."

"I came to the same conclusion."

"Why would Mary Brown bother to sketch an anvil?"

"That's the question. What can you tell me of this matter?"

Thackery eyed Sister Kempson suspiciously and countered with his own question. "Who did you say you represent?"

"The Holy Sisters of Conviction."

"I mean no offence to you and your august office," Thackery said, "but abductions, disappearances and now an attack on an innocent woman, these things do not belong under the purview of an assortment of nuns. I am the chief constable of North Quarter, a position of some authority. The investigation belongs with me and the men of the Night Watch."

The nun folded her arms. "The Holy Sisters of Conviction answer to the bishop, and therefore we, *I* in this case, carry his authority."

"The state of Dysael deals in civil law," Thackery countered. "You have no power here, nor does the bishop."

Sister Kempson frowned. "I think he would be both surprised and displeased to hear you say that."

If the nun thought she could threaten him, then she had another thought coming. Time to counter her arrogance. "You say that this woman, Mary Brown, was taken beneath the very noses of you and your man?"

The nun shifted uncomfortably on her chair, much to Thackery's satisfaction. Her reply was defensive. "I was out of the room but for a moment."

"I see. I fear the worst for the other women."

"We have no evidence to suggest they, too, have suffered violence."

The constable glanced around the room. "I can hardly agree. This matter is now a homicide investigation and, as such, shall be conducted, I say again, under the auspices of the King's Law."

The nun sat up straight. "There is more than one version of the law."

"Not in North Quarter. You and your man have proven yourselves incompetent. Stand down and leave this to the professionals."

The nun tutted disdainfully. "I won't engage in a tiresome argument as to the legalities of the matter, Constable Thackery. I am authorised by the bishop and that is all you need to know. I see no reason why we cannot pool our resources. After all, we both seek the safe return of the missing women. Why should two good Christians clash over this?"

"My personal beliefs play no part in my duty. I am an officer of the law first and foremost." The finely moustachioed man held up the bloodied parchment. "I will be taking this as evidence." Before the nun could object, he stood abruptly and swept outside.

Thackery could still make out Coroner Stimpson's cart in the distance, rolling its way down the road to Dysael with the small corpse on board. Garth was leaning against the millhouse wall, his arms folded over his chest, glowering at the two night watchmen, Jones and Frood, who glared back, at a safe distance of course. The smaller of the two sergeants still dabbed at the pulpy mess of his broken nose. Garth pushed himself off the wall and approached the constable as the other man neared his horse.

Thackery reached for the rapier at his hip. "Stand back."

Garth narrowed his eyes. "That's the nun's drawing. Give it back."

Sister Kempson smiled and waved the big man away. "It's alright, Garth. I have allowed the constable temporary possession of the sketch. We have agreed to share resources for the betterment of all."

Thackery cast a sharp glance at Sister Kempson before shoving his way past Garth. The nun had a cheek. Two fat ones, in fact. Thackery would be damned before he would allow any interference in his investigation. This woman would prove a hindrance, no doubt, and he couldn't afford any delay. Seven women abducted and the eighth clearly murdered. Most likely, *all* of them were dead. This was not the mundanity of a housewife or two running off with her lover. This was a brazen attack on moral decency and the law, and if there was one thing Constable Vincent E. Thackery of the Consul of Dysael Barristers could not abide, it was a lack of respect for the law.

The constable mounted his horse, Jones and Frood following his lead. The nun, a beatific smile on her face, stood between Thackery's horse and the footbridge, blocking him entirely on purpose. He had to reign in his instincts to run her down and instead edged his horse around the fat woman.

Thackery sniffed as he spoke down to the nun. "I say again, this is a matter for common law, not canon. Do not interfere."

He kicked at his horse, and the animal sped off at a speed not quite justified except by the anger now brewing at the front of his skull. He kicked again at the flanks of his horse and cursed. He would be damned if he'd allow a representative of the church to complicate his investigation, and he'd be doubly damned if he let a *woman* stand in his way.

CHAPTER 5

Blacksmiths

Constable Vincent E. Thackery of the Consul of Dysael Barristers stroked wax into his moustaches and glanced casually through the grimy windowpane of his third-floor office. He thought he'd requested the window cleaned. Whoever hadn't done the job was going to get the constable's boot up his backside. Thackery frowned and squinted closer at something in the muddy street below. He cursed under his breath. It was the fat nun and her bodyguard, she stumbling along like an overweight, disoriented foal, and he stalking grim-faced beside her. The previous day had been Thackery's first encounter with Sister Kempson, and he very much hoped it would be the last.

Had a full piss pot been at hand, Thackery would have taken extreme pleasure in opening the window and throwing its contents over the two of them. But his office did not contain a piss pot. It contained his framed lawyer's certificate on the wall, a large open book in a glass case in the centre of the room and two chairs, one on either side of his large pine desk. But no piss pot, more's the pity.

A knock at the door brought an irritated sigh from the lawman. "Enter." Thackery did not turn for several moments. When he did, three men stood on the other side of his desk.

Constable Thackery lowered his lean frame into a chair and gestured for the men to do the same. He was gratified when they looked awkwardly at each other. The men, members of various craftsmen guilds in North Quarter, made a show of politeness, offering the only remaining chair to the other, each refusing, offering to the next man and so on in ever ridiculous circles. It was a farce. Constable Thackery almost laughed out loud. Finally, a tall, bony man took the seat and removed his green felt hat.

"I am Guild Master Bruce of the metalworkers' association," the man said. He went on to introduce the other two fellows and the guilds each represented, something or other about tailors or textiles. Thackery wasn't listening. The vision of Sister Kempson and her hired muscle trudging in the streets below intruded upon his thoughts.

Guild Master Bruce was rambling on, but Thackery cut him off. "Why did you petition both the king and the bishop in the matter of the missing women? This nun, Kempson, is an irritation and, more than that, a legitimate interference. How am I to do my duty when she muddies the investigation?"

Bruce cleared his throat, rather sheepishly, Thackery thought. "We have legal rights to do so," the guild master said.

Thackery raised an eyebrow, thrust himself to his feet and approached the glass display case. "Don't talk to me of legal rights. Do you see this?" He leaned over the open book with its yellowing pages. Bruce nodded that he did, in fact, see it. "This," Thackery said, his fingers lingering over the glass, "is the law, a charter written up fifty-two years ago by my grandfather, enforced by my father and now entrusted to me. Despite the rare addendums to the document, it remains practically the same now as it did all those years ago. *This* is the law, gentlemen."

Bruce rubbed his thumbs over the rim of his felt hat. "With all due respect, Constable, several women went missing before you or anyone else deigned to get off your arses and pursue the matter. We wouldn't have gone to the bishop if we'd had satisfaction through other channels."

Thackery didn't like the man's attitude. Less sheepish now, more arrogant without the right to be so. "The law gets off its arse when it's good and ready. These things take time. Disappearances, in isolation, do not necessarily initiate action, but I would not expect a layman to understand this."

"Isolation?" Bruce harrumphed. "We've had seven women go missing in the last month. Eight now, apparently. The miller's wife, or so we hear."

Better not to mention that Mary Brown was most probably dead. "Those trained in the law, such as I," Thackery said, "look for patterns, which take time to formulate and are not evident to the eye of an untrained professional. One doesn't rush in haphazardly."

The guild master bristled. "Seems no one is bothering to rush in at all, not from your side of things, at least."

"Do you know any of these women personally?"

"No, but our guilds rely on the toil of honest men and women. We can't have our workforce and their families disrupted in such a fashion."

"Hurts your bottom line, does it?"

"It hurts a lot of things, Constable. People are scared, and rightfully so. In our defence, we did not expect a … woman. A priest or two to come and soothe frayed nerves, do a little enquiring, yes. None of us are happy with the nun."

This news mollified Thackery somewhat. "Yes, well, we can all agree on that, then. Get another petition organised to have the woman returned."

Bruce shifted uncomfortably and shared embarrassed glances with the other two guild masters. "One does not throw the bishop's offer of assistance back in his face."

Thackery snapped. "The bishop doesn't care! He wouldn't send one fat nun if he did! He's fobbing you off. Kempson is going to make a fool of herself, and nothing could bring me more joy, but she'll ruin my investigation in the process."

Bruce turned his mouth down and gave a subtle shrug. "As I said, if something had been done sooner, we wouldn't have gone down that road."

Thackery gritted his teeth. "Need I remind you that your guilds run with the blessing, nay the direct beneficence, of city government in North Quarter. This nonsense is apt to fray the cordiality tying the whole arrangement together or increase taxes at the very least."

The guild master's eyes narrowed, his tone darkening. "You can't threaten us. That relationship goes both ways. If you can't find the missing women, then there's no harm in letting the nun have a go."

Thackery threw up his hands. "This is not a bloody game of rounders. She can't just *have a go*. I am the authority here, and I say—"

"One man is not the law."

Thackery had heard enough. "Get out before I find you in contempt of my grandfather's constitution."

"You can't find me in contempt outside a courtroom."

The bastard was right, inflaming Thackery further. "Get out!"

Muddy streets and rotting timber. Pools of rainwater and piss. Sister Kempson trudged through the slop, lifting the hem of her habit in a futile attempt to keep it clean. Garth reached out to steady the nun as she slipped. Not for the first time, he worried that she was out of her depth. The woman never complained, in fact, approached her assignment with great enthusiasm, but she was, after all, a nun in the world of men, corrupt men operating within corrupt, violent systems. Still, his was not to wonder why a single member of the convent had been chosen for this task. He had his own job to do: assist the nun and keep her alive in doing so. Simple, no complications.

Some of the larger buildings in Dysael were six stories high, taller than the spruce on the mountainside. They seemed to lean at disconcerting angles over the men, women and children in the muck-filled streets. Garth stayed close to Sister Kempson, eyeing the warped structures warily, ready to pull her to safety should one of them choose to topple over on the unsuspecting nun.

Civilisation. Culture. Education. The city had it all, or so they said. Garth didn't see much of it, but he did see three filthy street urchins laughing as they came to a splashing halt and flashed their floppy little pricks at Sister Kempson. Garth cursed and swung a large boot at them. The urchins scattered and were gone with more shrieking laughter.

"Sorry about that, Sister," Garth said. "Little shits today have no respect."

Sister Kempson puffed with exertion as she trudged through the mud. She waved away Garth's concerns. "I'm a nun, Garth, not an angel."

Garth wasn't quite sure he understood the reply but shrugged it off.

Steam issued from a large, low-roofed building further down the street. A sign over the door proclaimed this as the Burridge Smithy.

Sister Kempson reached out to knock on the door, but before she could do so, Garth said, "I saw something up on the mountain yesterday when I ran into Thackery and his men. I was close to the ... thing."

The nun's chubby fist was poised at the door. She cast a sideways glance at Garth. "What did you see?"

Garth hesitated. "Something odd, difficult to explain. Let's attend to this matter first. I'll tell you as soon as I can ... find the words."

The nun nodded slowly, as if unsure what to make of Garth's sudden confession. She knocked on the door, which remained closed. Garth moved past her and pushed the door open. The smithy hissed and clanged with industry, steamed with sweat and smoke. It looked much like the two other smithies they had visited that day, though smaller: a two-man crew, one hammering away on a large anvil, the other holding a sword to a grinding stone. The fire burned low in the firepit, but the heat assaulted the nun and bodyguard, watering eyes and searing throats. The acrid stench of working men hung heavily in the air. Both blacksmiths wore leather aprons but little else, their torsos and arms sheened with perspiration. Weapons rested in a rack: swords, pikes, spears. Neither man had noticed them.

Garth put two fingers in his mouth and let out a piercing whistle. Sister Kempson clasped her hands over her ears. The man at the grinding stone stopped pumping the pedal, stood to his full height and removed his protective goggles. He held the half-sharpened sword in his hand and did not put it down. He had a large bushy beard sprinkled with metal shavings and was of similar height and build to Garth, his chest and shoulder muscles well-developed.

The bodyguard weighed the smith as a potential threat, as he weighed all men, and decided he could take the man if he had to. The other fellow at the anvil was younger, blond and clean-shaven. A hairless chest, though no juvenile: early twenties, wiry, faster than the older man, though with less stopping power. The younger one frowned with singed blond eyebrows at the sight of Garth and the nun. Garth could take him too. He couldn't, however, take them both at the same time, not without some luck.

The nun cleared her throat. "My name is Sister Kempson of the Holy Sisters of Conviction. I have some questions, gentlemen." The two blacksmiths simply stared. Sister Kempson fanned her ruddy face with her hands. "Bloody hot in here, isn't it?"

Garth cast a sideways glance at Sister Kempson. Were nuns supposed to use that kind of language?

The older man smiled, the grin almost lost in his bushy brown beard. He placed the unfinished weapon in the rack. Taking a cloth, he cleaned his hands and led Sister Kempson and Garth to a back room. The heat didn't penetrate here with the same force, and Garth gratefully sucked in a lungful of cooler air.

"I have many orders awaiting completion," the bearded man said, "and little time to sharpen that blade before it cools."

Sister Kempson made noises about not delaying the man overly long. Then she said, "You are the Mr. Burridge whose name appears over the door?"

"Aye, I am George Burridge."

Sister Kempson wasted no time getting to the point. "Mr. Burridge, what do you know of Mary Brown?"

"The miller's wife?"

"The same."

"I know Willard Brown, a friend I'd like to say, but have had little to do with his wife. No man should have anything to do with another man's wife." The blacksmith looked from Garth to Sister Kempson again. "What is this all about?"

"Mary Brown was abducted yesterday. Most likely murdered." The blacksmith's mouth dropped open. He shut it and whispered something under his breath. The nun went on, "Can you tell me who might want to harm Mary Brown and the other missing women?"

"Missing women? How many, now?"

"Surely you have heard, sir, of the other seven. It has been the talk of the town. Mary Brown is the eighth."

The big blacksmith shook his head in wonder. "Eight women, you say?" His eyes darted to something behind the nun and the bodyguard. Both turned to see the younger man standing there buttoning up a white, sweat-stained shirt. "Douglas, get back to work."

"Nine," the young fellow with the singed eyebrows said. "Nine women taken. My Bessie was the first. Bessie Partridge. I am Douglas Partridge."

The nun glanced at Garth, who frowned and shook his head. The name Bessie Partridge did not appear on the list of the disappeared.

"What do you mean 'the first'?" Sister Kempson said.

Douglas Partridge's blond curls were flattened to his forehead with sweat. "Before the others," he said. "My Bessie disappeared before the others. Before Elsie Gallagher."

"Why, then, is your wife's name not on the list of missing women?"

"I didn't report her as missing."

Sister Kempson's brows tightened. "Why on earth not?"

"I thought she just run off. We'd been having arguments, bitter ones. She seemed on the verge of leaving so many times. Sometimes it was good between us, but those times dwindled away." He shrugged with a pained expression. "I … I just thought she run off. But now, what with all the others, I cannot be sure. Perhaps she was the first victim."

The older blacksmith had been listening to the exchange with a stony face. The man's skin had begun to prickle with the cooler air in the back room. Something in his demeanour set Garth on edge.

"You must visit Coroner Stimpson immediately," Sister Kempson said. "Your wife's disappearance must be made a matter of public record."

The young man looked to the older blacksmith, who nodded and said, "Go see Stimpson."

Young Douglas Partridge bowed his head and turned away. When he had gone, Sister Kempson turned to the bearded blacksmith. "What do you make of his wife's disappearance?"

George Burridge sighed wistfully. "Douglas is overthinking things. Bessie weren't happy. I think she's run off. I understand that this happens to some men, their wives just up and leaving with no warning."

"I can assure you that Mary Brown didn't just run off."

The blacksmith shrugged. "The two might have naught to do with the other."

"Then why did Mary sketch an anvil?"

George Burridge raised two thick brown eyebrows. "She did?"

"Yes, that's why we are here. Before she disappeared, Mary Brown sketched an anvil. Can you explain that?"

The smith rubbed at his face with a cloth, small metal shavings falling from his beard. "Strange things in strange times. I cannot explain any of it."

"And your own wife?"

George pointed to the smithy. "I am married to the firepit and the bellows. I have no traditional wife as you would understand it."

"I am married to God. I think I understand."

Burridge nodded and said, "Then you also understand that I must return to my wife, for she gets upset if I am away too long. I bid you both a good day."

To Garth's surprise, Sister Kempson, her face still flushed from the heat of the smithy, ambled off the muddy streets and into a public house.

"Would you like an ale, Garth?" she asked. The air in the pub was sour with booze and body odour. The floors and walls were dark and mildewed, the room so gloomy that the filthy ale glasses on the tables and serving counter did not give any glint of reflected light. The nun didn't seem to mind the dour, oppressive atmosphere. She strolled to the bar and leaned against it like a seasoned drinker. She raised her eyebrows at Garth expectantly.

"I don't drink," the big man said.

The eyebrows ascended closer to God. "I thought all men drink to excess, as often as they can, especially men like you."

Garth snorted. "Why would you think that?"

The nun gave Garth a playful punch on his arm. "You're a large, rough and tumble fellow. Adept at cutting down trees, starting fires, wrestling forest animals and all that. I naturally thought you would take liquor."

Garth wanted to laugh. It had been a long time since he'd wanted to do that. It built up behind his mouth, then dissipated. Still, the temporary urge felt good. "Drink makes a man soft. I've seen better fighters lose to inferior because they were drunk. Won't happen to me."

"Well, I won't be getting into any punch-ups today, I hope." Sister Kempson turned to the publican, who stood waiting, his expression as gloomy as the interior of his premises. "I would like beer, good sir." The man nodded and moved away.

Garth scratched at his hawkish nose. "Anyway, I thought nuns couldn't drink."

"We take vows of poverty and chastity, not abstinence from alcohol. I can have a tipple provided someone else pays for it and doesn't attempt to get in my undergarments afterwards."

Garth's face reddened. "You don't talk like a nun."

"What do they talk like?"

"I don't know."

"It seems we both have preconceived notions of what the other is. Perhaps we should start with a clean slate. What do you say?"

Garth watched Sister Kempson pass a coin to the barkeep as he slid the beer towards her. "What happened to your vows of poverty?"

"I have been allowed a little stipend for this mission, with express instructions to spend it wisely." The nun took a sip of beer, wiped her mouth and sighed happily. "I believe this is spending it wisely."

The urge to smile came again and faded just as quickly. Garth scanned the sparsely populated room, looking for threats. The only man with any physical wherewithal about him was the barkeep, and he did not have the attitude of a fighting man, at least not right now.

The nun suddenly threw a question at him. "What do you make of this Bessie Partridge business?"

Garth frowned as he recalled the body language of the older blacksmith. "Burridge was lying. I think they both were."

"Lying about what?"

"I can't be sure. But something passed between the two of them."

"Come now, Garth. You were hired for your masculine instincts. I'm a babe in the woods when it comes to men. I rely on you for your savvy. You are my … falcon in the world of muscle and sinew, of bristling facial hair and short male tempers. What do you sense?"

Falcon? Why had she called him that? Garth tapped at the countertop. "Secrets."

"Of what nature?"

"If I could get one of them alone, I'd find out."

"Are you referring to violence?"

"I am referring to violence."

The fat nun raised her index finger off the beer glass and waggled it. "The church does not employ someone to perpetrate such on its behalf. Your job is to prevent violence from overtaking me. We don't dish it out."

"You may have missed news of the holy crusades in the old world, Sister."

She waved him away. "That was a long time ago and misguided. What is our next course of action?"

Garth had not bothered to sit down at the counter but did so now. The three-legged stool creaked under his weight. "Tom Gallagher, the bowyer. We should speak to him next. Throw the name Bessie Partridge in his face and watch his reaction carefully. But I suspect that you have already decided on the same."

"I have. We shall interview each husband in turn and look for patterns, particularly in reference to Douglas Partridge's wife. Yes, this new information may prove valuable." Sister Kempson winked at Garth. "I feel we are making progress."

"We have gotten nowhere."

The nun sighed. "Garth, a pessimistic attitude doesn't help. I have been entrusted with a great responsibility. Many wish me to fail. Many *men* wish me to fail. I must prove that a woman, that a *nun*, is capable of practical solutions in times of trouble. People are losing their faith in the bishop, in the church. It falls to me to restore it, at least in these parts. I don't need you in my ear telling me we've 'gotten nowhere.'"

The urge to order an ale crept up on Garth. "You take much upon your shoulders, Sister Kempson. I see no easy resolution to all this. Arsehole E. Thackery will ruin you if you fail, and he will try to ruin you even if you don't."

"Then I must succeed and succeed well, if I live long enough."

Garth ground his jaw against the urge to drink. "You'll live. That's my job. But I cannot vouch for the outcome of your efforts here."

"Tom Gallagher, you say?"

"Yes. We have nine women missing, now, yet nine husbands remain behind, unharmed."

"You suspect the husbands?"

"I suspect everyone and so should you."

"Willard Brown had nothing to do with his wife's ... abduction?

Death? We can both testify to that."

"Maybe. Just give me a few minutes alone with someone, anyone."

"No. I've made my feelings on that quite clear."

"Suit yourself. Your head on the chopping block."

"Confession under duress is outlawed."

"News to me."

"We live in a progressive age, Garth. Have you not noticed?"

The weedy smell of piss hung in the air: one too many a drinker had lost control of his bladder at some time in the past and it hadn't been cleaned up properly. "Oh yes, a progressive age. And when this is all over, you'll find me long gone, back to the True Wilds where I belong. Better the bush than this stinking place."

"Garth, you're not telling me something."

"Me?"

"What of the events on the mountain yesterday? What did you see in your pursuit of the creature that attacked Mary Brown? You hinted at something back at the Burridge Smithy. If it is pertinent to our investigation, then out with it."

The urge to knock back an ale sharpened. "I thought confession under duress was against the law."

The nun looked around the room. "Hardly duress. A quiet drink in a public house."

Garth lowered his voice. "This may not make much sense, but …"

Sister Kempson leaned in to receive the conspiratorial whisper, but when it did not come, whispered back. "Well, spit it out, man. But what?"

"I came upon the creature in a beartrap. I was as close to the thing as I am to you now. Thackery and his buffoons attacked me at that very moment, allowing the thing to escape. But it had changed."

"Changed? In what way?"

"Its body … I can't explain it other than to say it … morphed from one creature to another."

CHAPTER 5 Blacksmiths

Sister Kempson sipped her beer. "Fascinating."

"But that's not what I want to tell you."

"No? What could be more startling than the revelation of a shapeshifter running the hills of Dysael?"

"I don't think it attacked Mary Brown."

Sister Kempson put the beer glass to her mouth, her dark brown eyes wide. She slurped, then smacked her full lips together. "Then what took the poor woman?"

Garth had to resist grabbing the glass and taking a long drink. "I think ... I think that creature did not harm Mary Brown. I think it *was* Mary Brown."

CHAPTER 6

Husbands

Tom Gallagher did not answer the knock at his door. The bowyer's hut sat in a small field at the edge of the city. Sister Kempson wandered around the back of the man's house. Two circular archery targets had been set up thirty yards away, and one of them had arrows embedded in it. Several other arrows, in different stages of fletching, lay strewn over the trampled grass beneath the nun's feet.

Sister Kempson picked up an arrow shaft and examined it. She glanced at Garth standing nearby. He was a solid man by build and had proven himself equally dependable in spirit. Garth was her falcon, she had come to think of him, sharp-eyed and keen of talon. A stolid hunting companion. However, he seemed to be showing signs of an incomprehensible mental breakdown. The man had suggested that Mary Brown had torn her own infant from her womb, transformed into an aquatic monster and run from the millhouse. Nonsense, really, but she trusted Garth as far as she trusted any man, which was not to say her circles of influence contained many of the masculine gender. But he was a good one, from what she knew of men.

She presented the unfinished arrow to Garth. "Can you tell me how long ago the bowyer was here?"

The big fellow took the shaft and stared at it. "And how do you expect me to do that?"

"Perhaps you can judge the freshness of the blade marks on this item or smell when it was cut." With a bemused expression, Garth ran the shaft under his nose as if it were a fine cigar. He took a deep breath and exhaled. Sister Kempson waited. "Well?"

"No fucking idea."

The nun turned away, feeling foolish. "I thought you were a woodsman."

"Don't get angry."

"I'm not angry." She *was* angry, but mostly with herself for making the apparently ludicrous suggestion. The nun approached the window and peered inside, not the most respectful approach, and Lord forbid she should see the man in his private moments, but something had to be done. The bowyer's hut possessed a bed, workbench and stove but not the man they sought. Sister Kempson shrugged and turned away. "We move on to the next name on our list, the next husband."

Garth cleared his throat. "I suggest we choose the next based on geography. Meaning the closest one, or we'll be running around town in circles."

"A practical suggestion. Well done."

"Only common sense."

"Still, well done."

Garth simply stared. A moment of awkwardness passed between them.

The big man turned toward the targets and the concentric circles painted on them at the far end of the field and then frowned at the bowyer's hut. "Something's not right," he said. Garth approached the small house and, without warning, aimed a powerful kick, smashing the door off its hinges.

"Garth! Goodness me, what are you doing?" The man simply shrugged and disappeared inside. Glancing around to see who may have witnessed the brazen intrusion and thankfully finding no one, Sister Kempson tentatively followed.

The industrial district of Dysael North Quarter reeked. It stunk of tannery piss, wet dog and open-pit communal lavatory. But nothing smelt as sickeningly malodorous as the catgut spinner's workshop. Half a street away, the foul, sulfuric miasma emanating from the small string-maker cleared the air of every other stink.

Vincent E. Thackery held an expensive cotton scarf across his mouth and tried not to retch. The catgut spinner's wife was among the seven women mysteriously abducted, eight counting the miller's wife, if that was, indeed, an abduction and not a slaughter. It was, therefore, his duty to interview the catgut spinner, his obligation to the law overriding any personal distaste he might have for the nature of the working-class people it protected.

The constable swung his boot at a malnourished dog that sniffed too closely at his heels. He found the animal's scrawny hide, and the skeletal creature scurried off with a yelp, kicking up mud as it ran.

"What's the man's name?" Thackery said from behind his scarf.

The very stocky, and very pale, Sergeant Jones had stuffed cotton balls up his nostrils. He looked ridiculous. "Hickson. Eugene Hickson, sir."

"Let's get this over with," Thackery said. "I can't stomach this place much longer."

Sergeant Frood seemed the only one not struggling with the vile smell. Perhaps a broken nose had its advantages. The scruffy-bearded man knocked at a door of flaking sickly green and pushed his way inside. Thackery and Jones followed.

The catgut workshop was a precursor to Hell. Buckets of liquid guts had been tipped over, spilling bulbous lamb entrails across the floor. Cracked basins dripped a lethal concoction of sulfuric acid and alkaline substances. Animal fat was smeared across filthy benches. The product of this demonic abattoir, long lines of catgut string, stretched between two large separating poles on one side of the workshop. The catgut spinner, himself, was absent.

"Jesus Christ," Thackery croaked, gagging. "How does anybody work in such conditions?"

"People do like their violins," Sergeant Jones said, plucking at the tightly wound catgut with stubby fingers.

"You're no musician, Jones. Leave that alone. Frood, check the back." Thackery had several more husbands to interview today and was eager to be gone. He hardly expected to find the other working-class men inhabiting better conditions, yet nothing could be worse than this. Something about the general disarray of the workshop set Thackery's nerves on edge. This stinking chaos could not be part of a day's normal operations.

He removed the musket from his back and gripped the polished wooden stock in one hand and the cool iron barrel in the other. The weapon was primed but would be a danger to use in close quarters, particularly with the collection of chemicals about the place. Still, he felt reassured with the weapon in his grasp. He'd had a small bayonet attached to the underside of the barrel for close quarters fighting and so pointed it around the workshop.

Sergeant Frood shrieked. Thackery whirled around but could not see the scruffy man.

"In here!" Jones shouted, disappearing into a hidden niche at the back of the workshop. Thackery ran after the sergeant into a dark storeroom.

The constable struggled to comprehend what he was witnessing. Sergeant Frood hung suspended in the air, feet dangling, his fingers clutching at his own throat. Sergeant Jones was grappling with an assailant, the man's broad back momentarily obscuring his opponent. Jones absorbed a kick to the balls and went down, revealing a small, hooded figure in a dark cloak.

Thackery lunged forward, stabbing with the bayonet. He pierced the shrouded figure through the shoulder and it shrieked. Thackery heard a whipping sound and turned his head. A single line of catgut string sliced through the air, possessed of a life of its own. He ducked and narrowly avoided having his head removed by a cello E string but dropped his musket.

Thackery lashed out with the heel of his left hand and snapped the cloaked figure's head back, sending the assailant sprawling to the floor.

Frood's neck was entwined in a catgut noose, his face turning purple and his eyes bulging. Thackery cursed. He could not restrain the cloaked assassin without letting the sergeant choke to death. The constable grabbed a small stepladder and leapt upon it, taking Frood's weight. Jones was slowly getting back to his feet.

"Stop him!" Thackery called, but the cloaked figure sprinted from the storeroom. Blood dripped on the constable's face from the cut in Frood's throat. "Wire cutters! Cut the bloody string!"

Suddenly, the catgut string released Frood of its own accord, and Thackery collapsed under the weight of the sergeant's body. The two men came tumbling down on top of Jones. Thackery's head hit the storeroom floor with a thud. The room began to spin, and an aching tiredness overcame him. Before he blacked out, Thackery saw the catgut spinner's body in a corner of the storeroom, the man's naked torso wound around again and again with slicing catgut, the stomach cut open and spilling guts, the head cut clean off and sitting upright beside the torso, staring wide-eyed and open-mouthed. Thackery blinked, trying to stay awake.

Then, a blanket of sulfur, no longer repugnant but oddly soothing, came to smother him.

The bowyer's one-room hut was vacant. Garth checked under the bed and examined every corner of the room. He approached a wall proudly displaying the bowyer's tools: hatchet, clamps, saws, hammers and finer blades.

"Perhaps he's in town buying supplies," Sister Kempson said.

Garth shook his head. "Anything a bowyer requires is in the woods. He might be off up there among the trees, but I doubt it. Something's setting my skin to crawling."

Garth peered out the window and, a moment later, strode purposefully outside. Sister Kempson struggled to keep up with his long steps as the woodsman-cum-bodyguard headed off down the field.

"Where are you going, Garth?"

Garth didn't slow down. "The women were all married. Every one of them, each without children. Why are only married women without children being taken?"

"But Mary Brown," the nun puffed, "was with child."

"No, no. Unborn," Garth said, coming to a halt in front of the target with the arrows piercing it. "Unborn at the time of its death. Mary did not have children in the strictest sense of the word. There's a pattern here, somewhere."

Sister Kempson came to stand beside him, breathing hard. "I think you draw too clean a line between the born and the unborn. A child is a child. This one a girl, I believe."

Garth shuddered. "Was she? I didn't have the courage to look at the poor wee thing."

"Why are we standing here?" The nun turned back to the bowyer's hut. "Any clue to the man's whereabouts probably lies back there."

Garth pointed at the boss, the tightly compacted straw target used for archery practice or testing arrow flight. Sister Kempson followed his finger.

Blood dripped from several metal points piercing the target from behind.

Garth and Sister Kempson rushed around behind the boss. Tom Gallagher had been struck through the torso with several arrows; one had pierced his eye and come out the back of his skull. Each arrow combined to pin the bowyer to the reverse side of the target as if he were a butterfly on display. Tom Gallagher's mop of black hair shifted gently in the breeze. His jaw hung loose, his pierced eye a gelatinous pulp, the other eye casting an accusatory stare at someone, perhaps at the nun and her bodyguard for arriving altogether too tardily to save his life.

Sister Kempson began to pull at the arrows. "Get him down, for God's sake."

Garth merely stepped back, shaking his head and scanning the field for signs of the assassin. "He's dead, Sister. Leave him be."

"What is happening here, Garth? What is happening in this town?"

Garth shook his head again. He pulled Sister Kempson away from the corpse. "Leave it for the coroner. Learn what you can from it."

"Learn? What can I learn from this? This is madness." The nun's voice was threatening to break into hysterical shrieking.

"Breathe. This is your job. Breathe. Examine the man's body. Look around you. This is your job."

The frantic nun calmed somewhat. "Yes, yes. What can we learn from this?"

"It's not suicide."

"Even I can tell that. Do you have any useful suggestions?"

"I do not wish to sound callous, Sister, but this is an opportunity to prove yourself competent. My job is to keep you alive, and you're currently breathing. My competency is beyond question. Yours is not. You have been assigned to find the missing women, and now," he pointed at the corpse of Tom Gallagher, "this. Find out who did this, for the Green Gods know these events are connected. Do your job or go back to the Holy Sisters of Conviction and live out your days in the peace and quiet of the convent and let me live out mine far away from here."

Sister Kempson stared at Garth, somewhat taken aback by the man's blunt outburst. "Alright," she said. "Alright. I have regained myself. Who would want to kill Tom Gallagher?"

Garth looked annoyed. "I don't know."

"I'm not asking you," Sister Kempson said. "I'm thinking aloud. His wife was taken, the first woman taken."

"The second."

"Yes, I haven't forgotten Bessie Partridge, but Elsie Gallagher is the first woman *officially* reported missing." The nun tapped her fingertips together, pitter patter, pitter patter. "Consider the facts," she said. "Mary Brown is frightened out of her wits by something on the same day that Elsie Gallagher vanishes. Then six more women go missing before Mary Brown becomes …" Here Sister Kempson glanced awkwardly at Garth. "… the eighth to disappear.

CHAPTER 6 Husbands

Then we learn of Bessie Partridge. And now this." She put her hands on her knees and leaned over to examine the cold cadaver of Tom Gallagher. "My skills run to a careful observation of the living, Garth. I can tell nothing from a dead man." She paused and then said, "Except one thing."

Garth waited, but no answer seemed forthcoming. "Which is?"

"This cannot be coincidence, as you have said." The nun's voice grew in excitement. "The remaining husbands are in grave peril and must be warned."

Sister Kempson turned and ran, and Garth had to put in effort to haul the fat nun in.

CHAPTER 7

The Ratcatcher

Huge vats formed a metallic, steaming colonnade across the brewery floor. On elevated walkways, children stirred busily at the acrid-smelling mixture within the vats.

Anderson Jack dabbed at the perspiration at the sides of his widow's peak. It was hot down here on the brewery floor, but it had to be hellish for the children on the platforms working over the vats of boiling malt and liquor. A small boy, face sheened with sweat, waved at him from on high, and Anderson Jack waved back.

"This way, Mr. Anderson. Mustn't dawdle."

Anderson hurried on after the large figure of Mr. Augustine Prost, the brewery owner and purveyor of his own product. The man had a beer gut to rival the vats lined up along the factory floor; capacity: one hundred and fifty-six gallons by the looks of it. The man possessed immense wealth and, more to the point, was about to hand a good portion of his riches over to Anderson.

Augustine Prost opened the door to a small clerical space at the back of the factory. He ushered Anderson inside. A small child sat on a chair, glum-faced, his right foot bootless and wrapped in bloodied bandages.

"I think you should see this before you go down," Prost said. He gestured for the boy to remove the bandages, and the boy obeyed, doing so with several pained winces. Anderson leaned in to get a closer look at the child's foot, which was missing three toes and a large chunk along the side of it. The child whimpered and began to cry.

"Voracious little bastards, aren't they?" Prost observed. "Took half Craig's foot off before he woke up. Gareth had his ear torn in half, and Clive got nipped on his codger. None of the boys want to go back down there. Can hardly blame them, but I want lads watching the barrels. I have thousands of pounds of product down beneath us, currently unattended. I've had arson attacks, threats on my life from those ridiculous social reformists. Bloody idiots want to take children's livelihoods from them before they've even started. I've got through all that, and I won't be sunk by some filthy rodents. Well, can you do it, or do I get someone else in?"

Anderson Jack put a finger to his pointed chin and shook his head in dismay at the damage done to the boy's foot. He tut-tutted and turned to the frowning liquor magnate. "Can I do it? Course I can. They don't call me Jack the Rat for naught."

Prost nodded and reached within his fancy vest. He handed a bag of clinking coins to Anderson. "Half now, other half when it's done."

Anderson felt the weight in his hands and suppressed a smile. The half was more than he had expected the whole to be. The whole, then, would be pleasing indeed. "Give me two days, sir."

Prost nodded. "Very well, but if those sharp-toothed bastards puncture one barrel, you don't get the bonus."

Bonus? This job was turning out better than he had expected. "Show me the way, good sir."

Prost cleared his throat. He appeared uncomfortable for a moment and then said. "I ... uh, I heard about your wife. Terrible business. Her and the others."

Anderson sobered up, the money forgotten briefly, but only briefly. "I live in hope that my Keira returns and we hunt together once more. She cooked a beautiful rat, did my Keira."

Prost rubbed at his jowls. "Yes, very, ahem, romantic. Alright, follow me."

It was dark as a crypt down in the cooling cellar of the brewery. Anderson Jack didn't mind, for it was in the nature of a ratcatcher to poke around the dark places. The air smelled of beer and ale, which were distinctive entities to the trained drinker, both comforting. He'd have an ale or two after this job; Lord knew he could afford to live in the public house for a year, what with all the money Prost was giving him. The brewery owner had, unsurprisingly, declined to join Anderson in the cellar.

Anderson placed the lamp he carried in his right hand on the cold cellar floor. He placed the cage in his left hand down beside it. He opened the cage, and the ferret shot forward silently into the darkness. He'd have as much trouble getting the vicious ratter back into its cage at the end of the day than in actually killing the rodents, rodents which he, himself, had slipped into the external drainpipes of the brewery a few months before. They had apparently multiplied in number and taken the brewery cellar as theirs by right. The boys watching the beer and ale barrels had suffered some heinous injuries. Anderson didn't quite understand that. The rats he'd planted here hadn't been of the vicious variety, and Anderson knew rats, knew them inside and out. They were his bread and butter in more ways than one. No, no, Anderson carried no blame for the boys getting bitten. Could even be some other rats, the nasty type, had gotten in after he'd released his. In which case, he ought to be careful.

Anderson put on his gloves and made sure his leather biting apron was firmly attached to his waist. He slipped a sack off his back and loosened the string tie. A small dog, Anderson's trained terrier, poked its head out of the sackcloth. The ratcatcher smiled and lifted the dog free. Anderson picked up the lamp and moved forward, the dog at his feet. Beer barrels of various sizes loomed into the light of the lamp and disappeared behind like icebergs viewed from the porthole of a large passenger ship sliding through cold, black waters.

The crawl spaces. Between the walls or in cracks and crannies. That's where his ferret would find the nest and send the rats fleeing into the path of his terrier, and the dog would pounce on them and break their necks with trained precision. Failing that, he would use arsenic and melted cheese traps and return in a day. But the ferret and terrier were his preferred formulae, for he could then sell the unspoiled rats on to the butchers and tanners.

Scuffling in the darkness ahead, his ferret, giving head to its primal instincts, scurrying around sniffing out rodents. The animal was frantic to find them, judging by the incessant scratching. Suddenly, a rat careened into the lamplight, and his terrier went to work. The small dog leapt after the rat, both rodent and canine disappearing into the darkness. A half-squeak later, the terrier returned with a dead rat in its jaws. Anderson smiled and patted the dog on the head before slipping the rat into the sack.

With the money he made from clearing the cooling cellar, combined with the profit from the dead rats, he could afford to go a-courting after Ella, the candlemaker's widow. Keira wasn't coming home, and a man needed a wife, a living one, that was. One way or the other, Keira Jack was gone. Perhaps he could have her declared legally dead and marry Ella. It was the only practical thing to do under the circumstances.

The sound of a door creaking open behind Anderson. The ratcatcher jerked his head around. Had Prost come down to check on his progress? If so, the man was premature as there was much work left to do. "I won't be done 'til well after sunset," Anderson said into the darkness. No reply came. Perhaps the man had only poked his head downstairs. Anderson Jack shrugged and returned his attention to the cellar. Another rat came hurtling into the pool of lamplight, and the terrier snatched it up and shook it viciously, breaking its back and clamping off its air supply. In a few seconds, the second rat joined the first in the sack. Things were going well, a rat-a-minute well.

Footsteps, not his own, shuffled somewhere in the darkness. He held out the lantern and swung it around in a circle. "Who's there?"

Shadows loomed and leered across the cellar floor, over the nearby barrels. Anderson's terrier sat on its haunches, its ears pricked up, head cocked to the side. The dog, too, had heard something.

"Who's there?" Anderson asked again and again no response came. The ratcatcher considered scurrying from the cellar but the thought of losing his pay, and his pride, kept him motionless.

Then, a woman in a grey cloak walked into the light of the swaying lamp. She was barefoot, a dangerous practice in a cellar of rats. Her head was bowed, the cowl covering her face, but the figure was a woman, feminine in its outline. Anderson took a step backwards, and the lamp's light no longer illuminated her clearly. The woman took another step forward into the stronger light, and this time, Anderson did not take a backward step.

"You shouldn't be down here, miss," he said, squinting at her. "Specially not without shoes. There are rats. I've … I've got work to do. Dangerous work, miss. You'd best be off."

The woman pulled back the grey hood of her cloak, but her long black hair continued to obscure her face. When she spoke, Anderson's blood ran cold.

"You," she said, "have work to do. Dangerous work. As have I. But a woman's work, they say, is never done." Her voice was low, almost baritone, unusual for a woman, but it wasn't the timbre of her voice that set Anderson's heart to racing. It was the fact that he knew the voice. The terrier trotted towards the woman and sat at her feet, the dog, too, having recognised her.

She brushed long black hair from her face and Anderson Jack stared into the green eyes of his wife. The ratcatcher could barely breathe. Relief, joy and a small, unobtrusive twinge of disappointment plucked at him. "Keira, you've come back. Where …? Where were you?"

"In Hell," Keira said. "I was in Hell, Anderson, my dear, and you put me there."

Anderson didn't understand. He approached and clasped her to his chest. Keira's arms stayed at her side. He stepped back and tried to read her face. No emotion in the green eyes. She was cold, hard … determined.

A shriek cut through the cellar and Anderson flinched. Keira remained impassionate. Another tremulous squawking. The terrier began to growl. Then, Keira did something odd. She waved her hand over the dog's head, and it fell silent. The terrier licked its paw contentedly.

Anderson's ferret scurried into the lamplight. Blood coated the animal: its hide ripped and torn. It lurched unsteadily and collapsed at Anderson's feet, blood streaming from its nostrils. It shuddered and died.

Anderson leapt back from the animal. "Jesus wept." The light from the lamp seemed to be growing weaker, the darkness crawling closer, nibbling at the edges of the lamplight, absorbing it. He glanced at the dead ferret. These rats were more savage than he had bargained for. "Keira, I think we need to get out. I'll ... I'll leave traps, but we should not linger."

Keira did not move. The living darkness encroached, biting at the lamplight, closing in on Anderson. "In sickness and in health, dear husband," Keira said. "Was I not an obedient woman? Was I not loyal? Did I not fulfil my obligations under contract? Was I not ... what is the word for it ... *a wife* to you?"

Anderson's skin cooled. He was sweating, and the draught in the cellar began to chill him. "There is no time to talk of this. We must be out of here." A thousand rats scuttled into the far edge of the lamplight. Anderson gawked in panic as more rats than he had ever seen crept closer in tiny, measured steps.

"A wife," Keira repeated. "The most noble of all professions. Dangerous work, that. Dangerous to mind and body."

Anderson backed away, holding out the lamp to slow the rats. "What are you talking about? We must flee!" He whirled around, trying to remember where the door was.

Keira shook her head, long black hair framing green eyes. She pouted. "Tut, tut. No, Anderson. Nowhere to flee. We're all just rats scrambling over each other. One falls only to have another take its place. You can't escape your destiny." She waved her hand and the floodgates opened. The rats rushed, screeching at the ratcatcher.

Anderson Jack ran. He stepped on rats, waded through a sea of them. He stumbled but did not fall. They crawled up his legs, under the biting apron, nipping at thigh and buttock, the soft flesh at his waist. Some scrambled as high as the back of his neck, where they tore small chunks from his flesh. He could not find the door. The lantern fell from his hands, and he slipped and fell. He shrieked as the rats went to work.

They ate him. They ate him raw. They ate him with no condiments or salt. They ate him with no commentary on the savoury nature of his flesh. They ate him with no malicious intent, no hatred in their tiny hearts.

The malevolence here belonged to Keira Jack and Keira Jack alone.

Keira smiled and patted the terrier on the head. She lifted the small animal into her arms and disappeared into the darkness.

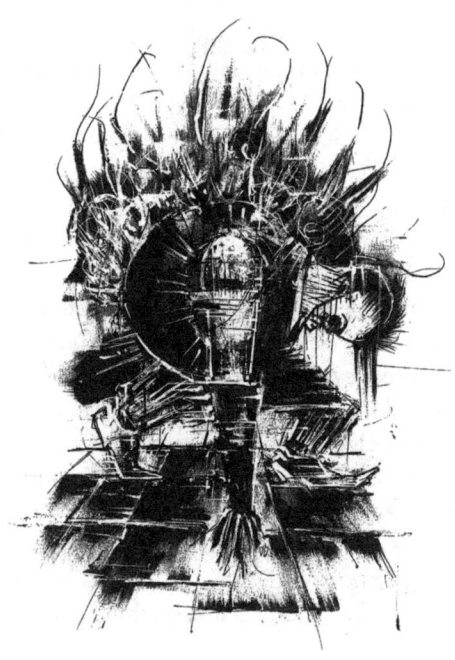

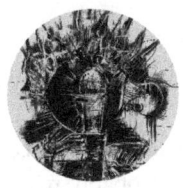

CHAPTER 8

Speak for the Dead

Peter Stimpson drew back the sheet and stared at the latest corpse delivered to his autopsy table. The tall, gangly coroner gave a wordless shake of his balding head and turned to the young man standing beside him. The youth flicked his eyes over the corpse but did not gaze upon it for long. Not a good sign. If the lad wanted to be a coroner, he'd have to develop a stronger stomach than that. Still, in this case, Peter could hardly blame the fellow. In thirty years as a coroner, he had never seen anything like it.

"Where was this man found?" Peter asked.

"A brewery cellar, sir," the young fellow responded.

The older man put his hands on his hips. "Well, what do you make of it, Anton?"

The young coroner-in-training swallowed hard. "Rats, sir. Gnawed by rats."

Peter leaned in to study the corpse more closely. The body had not merely been gnawed; it had been *devoured*, the flesh practically stripped from the bone, and the bones themselves showed evidence of bite marks. The man's eye sockets were empty, his cheeks and the soft cartilage of his nose also absent. The rodents had torn the hair and skin from his skull. Macabre, quite macabre. Anton was struggling to maintain his breakfast, judging by the occasional retch coming from the youth.

"I believe cause of death is unarguable," Peter said. "There'll be no need for an autopsy. What else can you tell me about the man and his circumstances?"

The coroner's apprentice took a piece of paper from his jacket pocket and peered at it, probably relieved to look at something other than the grotesque corpse. "Anderson Jack by name, local ratcatcher by profession. Recently employed to deal with a rodent infestation at the Prost brewery. Little else is known about him at this point. Both our clerks and the coppers are attempting to contact next of kin."

"The Night Watch, Anton. Don't call them *coppers*, not in earshot of Constable Thackery anyway. He'll have your guts for garters." Coroner Stimpson placed the white sheet over the obscene cadaver. The man's name seemed familiar. *Anderson Jack*. Something crawled at the nape of Peter's neck, something uncomfortably akin to tiny rat feet. "We must contact his family immediately."

"He has no children, apparently, and we are unable to find his wife."

"Wait a moment," Peter said. Jack. *Keira* Jack. The coroner pointed to something, and the younger man followed his finger. Upon the wall was a collection of outdated tools, including a rusted bone saw, several callipers with oddly curving handles and a trephining drill. Above them was a sign, now faded, which read *Speak for the Dead to Protect the Living*. But it was not these that the coroner pointed to. Peter approached the wall and tore a note that had been pinned under the display of autopsy tools. He scanned the paper and handed it to Anton.

The young man read down the list of names on the note, and his eyebrows raised as he read one entry. *Keira Jack, ratcatcher's wife.* The young man nodded to the corpse under the sheet. "His wife?"

"Highly unlikely to be anyone else. That explains why no one has been able to contact her. She is missing, abducted possibly." The coroner rubbed at the grey stubble on his cheeks. "He's not going to like it, but I think she's right."

The younger man was puzzled. "Who, sir? Right about what?"

"Right about them," Peter said, gesturing to two other bodies lying under sheets nearby. He walked briskly from the morgue, the apprentice coroner at his heels. Raised voices became apparent halfway down the gloomy corridor, and by the time Peter and Anton reached the coroner's office, the raised voices had become a full-blown shouting match. It was mostly Constable Thackery doing the shouting, of course, but Sister Kempson wasn't backing down.

"This, surely, cannot be coincidence," Sister Kempson said. "Tom Gallagher and Mr. Hickson the catgut spinner are killed within …" She turned to the coroner as he entered. "… a day, less?"

Peter nodded. "I calculate their deaths at no more than sixteen hours apart." The coroner was about to add the death of Anderson Jack to the discussion when the excitable nun went on.

"Clearly, we have a new series of crimes. Or, more to the point, the same crime now affecting the male counterparts of the missing women."

Thackery wasn't having any of it. "Two deaths do not make a pattern," he sneered. "Any assumptions at this point would be folly, plain and simple. You know what they say about assumptions."

"Nonsense," Kempson countered. "Both Elsie Gallagher and Charlene Hickson are among the missing women. Their husbands are now dead, murdered. There is a connection, don't you see? It would be foolish to ignore what is clearly an obvious—"

"I see no connection, and I am no fool," Thackery spat. "The husbands are illiterate tradesmen who have no doubt made enemies of some other churls. Death and murder are commonplace among the working classes." Thackery pushed himself off the coroner's desk on which he had been sitting. He made a cease-and-desist gesture, chopping both hands through the air. "There is nothing mysterious about the fact that men of a low nature are subject to more visceral crimes. Happens every day, does it not?" Thackery looked at the coroner for confirmation.

"Ah, well, about that, I—"

"We cannot ignore the facts," Sister Kempson said, cutting Peter off. Not a very Christian gesture for a nun and one that irked the coroner. "Something very untoward is going on here in Dysael."

The constable put two fingers to the purpling bruise on his forehead and winced. "Sergeant Frood is in the hospital with his head nearly severed from his shoulders. Jones here—" He waved a hand at the Night Watch sergeant standing in the corner. "—received a jolly good kick to the balls, and I have taken my lumps as well. Something is certainly going on, I agree, but I won't be side-tracked by whatever idiotic notions you're putting forward."

The big bodyguard growled from the other corner of the room. "Show a little more respect for the sister."

The nun frowned. "That will be enough, Garth. I can fight my own battles."

"Be a good dog and sit," Thackery said. Garth snarled at him in a very dog-like fashion.

"It is important," Sister Kempson said, "that we share information. If we can piece together enough of the clues that are presenting themselves, then, collectively, we may have a chance of finding the women and preventing any further deaths. The husbands must be protected, put under guard. Immediately."

Thackery sighed angrily. "I don't have the resources to babysit every Tom, Dick and Nigel in town. Do you have any idea of the projected costs to the city coffers? There is no *death list* of husbands in Dysael. Balderdash."

"I disagree," Sister Kempson shot back. "These men must at least be forewarned so that they may take precautions to protect themselves."

"Against what? Your theory is nonsense. This is a serious business. If you in any way muddle my investigation, I'll have you placed under arrest and don't think I won't. I've done a little digging on your Holy Sisters of Conviction. An order founded by former prostitutes, or so I am led to believe. You wouldn't have been a whore in your youth, by any chance?"

Garth stepped menacingly towards Thackery, but the nun waved him away. Peter sighed. The prostitute comment was a low blow, even for Thackery. The man was a prick. *Like father like son*, the coroner mused.

"If I could get a word in edgewise," Peter said. "There's something—"

"You have no legal right to pursue your investigation here," Thackery said. Apparently, Peter could *not* get a word in edgewise. The constable and the nun were so busy tearing pieces from each other that the coroner had become quite overlooked, in his own office no less. Thackery blustered on, "You're seeking public favour and money for your order, for redevelopment or whatever it is you people are after. You've come to Dysael to sway everyone with a benediction here, an innocuous blessing there. I'm not buying any of it."

"Nuns cannot offer blessings. That is the role of a priest," Sister Kempson said, correcting the constable on the finer points of religious hierarchy.

"I don't care. You're not welcome here. You're a charlatan."

Sister Kempson stiffened. "It is true that I have been chosen to represent the Holy Sisters of Conviction, and we are hoping to raise both funds and public goodwill for our work. There is nothing inherently wrong with that. It is important to help people in need, and that kind of help doesn't cost nothing." She frowned and folded her arms. "I find your attitude entirely cynical, Constable Thackery."

"And I find you a pompous windbag who is sailing close to the edge of the law. I say again—"

Coroner Stimpson had heard enough. He guided young Anton outside and whispered in his ear. The young fellow nodded and walked briskly back to the morgue. A few minutes later, he returned with a table on wheels and pushed it inside the office. Sister Kempson had her back to the body under the sheet, but Thackery saw it and stopped, another threat intended for the nun frozen on his lips. Sister Kempson turned around, a quizzical expression on her face just as the coroner removed the sheet from the grotesque corpse of the ratcatcher.

"Jesus Christ," Thackery said. "What is that?"

"Who, is the pertinent question," the coroner said. "Now that I have your attention, let me introduce Anderson Jack, ratcatcher."

"Why are you showing us this?" Thackery scowled.

"He's one of them," Sister Kempson whispered. "Isn't he?"

"He's one of them," the coroner confirmed. "This man is husband to Keira Jack, who is on the list of missing women. This makes three."

Sister Kempson turned to Constable Thackery and raised her rounded chin.

"Coincidence," Thackery said, though he didn't sound convinced by his own statement. He remained quiet for a moment. Finally, he said, "Shit it all." He turned to Sergeant Jones. "Get down to the Law Courts and get a duty roster together. We must track down the remaining husbands of the women on that list. Get extra men down the industrial district tonight if we can spare them." Jones nodded and left the coroner's office. Thackery frowned in distaste and pointed to the corpse on the table. "Could you take that away?"

"Certainly," the coroner drew the sheet over the body of Anderson Jack. "Messy business, eh?"

"More so by the minute," Thackery said, staring at the white sheet. "The ratcatcher torn apart by rats, the catgut spinner sliced into pieces with his own catgut and the bowyer stuck full of arrows." He sighed. "Alright, Sister Kempson. You may be onto something."

"I'm glad you are seeing reason. I suggest that we work together."

The constable stroked his fine moustaches. "Just because you're right doesn't make you any less insufferable." With that, Vincent E. Thackery swept from the room, leaving Sister Kempson shaking her head in exasperation.

The coroner thought he heard the nun whisper something under her breath. It sounded like 'arrogant prick'. But that could not be right, not earthly curses from a nun. Surely not.

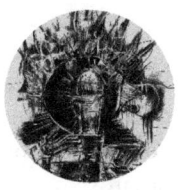

CHAPTER 9

The Lamplighter

Bolt your door and bar your windows. Stay at home, they said. There was a list of potential victims, they said. A list of women's names, but Death had dipped his pen in a differently gendered ink, and the list now included the husbands: three of them down in the bone house awaiting interment, each name a counterpart to one of the missing women.

And *his* name was on the list. Paul Hardcastle, humble lamplighter, was on the list because his wife was one of the missing. It made no sense. Who would want to hurt them? Paul had known all three of the dead men: Tom Gallagher, Alexander Jack and Eugene Hickson. Had known their wives too. At first, the blokes were just casual acquaintances down in the street or the public house, but then … well, you get to know a man when you share a secret. Yes, he knew them, and he was next, apparently. The Night Watch didn't know who was coming for Paul or why. But someone had a mind to murder him; that much was certain.

Stay at home, the Night Watch had told him. Paul had laughed, not because he didn't believe the warning. He laughed because his profession required his presence on the streets. How could a lamplighter stay at home and still make a wage? He couldn't afford to miss one day, not one. It was a good job, steady, as long as the sun set every evening. Not well-paid, but steady. He had debtors, needed to get out there and light wicks at the end of every single day and snuff 'em out in the morning. If he stayed at home, he was as good as dead anyway, dead like a flame starved of air. The Night Watch sergeants at his door had seemed concerned but not so concerned as to assign an officer to accompany him on his rounds, no, not that concerned. Bastards.

And so, he walked the streets alone. Paul Hardcastle was a lean man, almost flat, as if he'd come out of the womb under immense pressure. He carried a knife in his boot and something else, something that might save his life if *they* tried to jump him in a dark alley.

Paul decided to light the lamps a little earlier than usual today. He wasn't keen on hanging around after dark. The only impediment to a quick day's work was Knockers Lane, which required a new supply of oil for the empty reservoirs, and that would mean the use of a stepladder. Still, it was only one street, the other lamps on his round merely requiring a lit wick and that he could do with little effort. He should be done by seven if he hurried. It would be almost dark by seven, and he would be far from home, but what choice did he have? Life didn't just stop, not even when Death came calling. You just had to put your head down and get on with it. He cursed under his breath. He hadn't done anything wrong. Didn't deserve to be hunted down and murdered.

Paul stopped at the intersection of a cobbled avenue and a gravel side street and peered behind him. Was someone following him? There were plenty of people still out and about as it had been an unusually fine day, bright cloudless skies, only the hint of a chilling breeze. The cobblestoned main avenues had less muck than usual, the side streets of gravel almost free of puddles. People strolled leisurely, going about their business, unconcerned at the prospect of a sudden assassination. He envied them their illusion of safety.

One figure in a long cloak had been following him for a city block, sure of it. Paul put his boot up on an iron fence, pretending to examine it for damage, long enough to allow the stranger in the cloak to stroll by. The lamplighter surreptitiously tracked the stranger until he had passed from view. Just a stranger, then, out on some errand. His mind playing tricks, that's all. Nothing to fear.

CHAPTER 9 The Lamplighter

Get the job done and get home. Start with Knockers Lane, just down the street.

The sun rarely fell upon the gravel of Knockers Lane, a narrow connection between two larger thoroughfares. Half-timbered buildings lined the quiet street, their skeletal cage-like structures containing dirty white wattle or daub walls.

Twelve lamps. He had to fill the oil reservoirs of twelve lamps along the street, and then he'd be back onto the more populated roads and safety in numbers. It was not yet early evening. Surely, his lurking assailant or assailants would not dare attack him during daylight despite the lack of passers-by on the lane.

Something poked him in the small of his back, and he whirled about with a cry on his lips, but when he saw the lad standing there, crooked cap at a careless angle across his forehead, Paul exhaled in relief.

"Don't sneak up on me, Jake. Gave me the death of fright."

Jake, a bucktoothed boy of about thirteen, gave a bemused shrug and pointed to a stepladder leaning against a nearby lamppost. "As you asked for, Mr. Hardcastle. I shall meet you at the other end to collect the ladder." Jake turned to go. The lamplighter looked up and down Knockers Lane. Not one soul walked the small street. It was too quiet.

"Wait, wait. Come with me, Jake. You can hand the oil up to me."

"But I have other business, sir."

"I'll pay you. Just until we get to the end of Knockers Lane. We'll be done in less than forty minutes, lad. Only got a dozen to fill." The boy shrugged and nodded. Paul cursed his own anxiety, and yet the company of someone, anyone, even a stringy youth like Jake, made him feel better. The villains wouldn't hurt a child, would they?

By the time Paul had removed and filled the first oil reservoir and set the wick alight, clouds had come in over the gabled roofs of the half-timbered buildings on Knockers Lane, creating a close, foreboding atmosphere. It was unusually dark for the time of day. Still, day it was, and no one would attempt to murder him in, if not broad daylight, then a diffused one.

Jake scratched at his nose. "Any news of your wife, sir?"

Paul eased the ladder against the bars of the second lamppost. He shook his head. "Not a peep. I fear Helen's gone, boy." He didn't mention the murders of the husbands, the warning given to him by the Night Watch that he could be next; the boy would most likely scarper and leave him alone. Paul climbed six rungs and opened the glass lamp case. He reached in and removed a tin tray.

"Alright," Paul said, leaning down. Jake tipped a portion of oil from a canister into the tray. "Easy, lad. Not too much. We have ten more." Something heavy fell from the inside pocket of Paul's coat. It landed at Jake's feet, and the boy, with a puzzled frown, bent his knees to pick it up. "Don't touch that!" Paul warned. He carefully placed the oil reservoir back into its case and hurriedly stepped down.

"What is it?" Jake asked.

"A hand cannon, boy. A gun. Very dangerous." The lamplighter blew dirt from the flintlock pistol and put it back in his inner pocket. "Very dangerous, best left well alone by a young pair of hands. You hear me?"

"Aye, sir."

Jake watched as Paul used the long-handled wick lighter to light the lamp. The lad glanced anxiously up and down the street. Paul's frayed nerves and the appearance of the snub-nosed pistol seemed to have afflicted the boy with a case of jitters.

"Storm coming," Jake said with a chattering of teeth.

Damned if the boy wasn't right. Dark clouds broiled, descended. A wet, salty breeze blew down Knockers Lane. Half an hour ago, it had been a sunny late afternoon. Paul's breath steamed in the suddenly frigid air. "Come on. Let's get this street lit up against the encroaching night. People need to see the ground beneath their feet when they are abroad after dusk. It's a public service; what a lamplighter does, you see? We are a friendly light in the darkness, a ray of hope against … against …"

"Against what, sir?"

"Never mind. Come on, I want to be done with this street."

The lamplighter and his young assistant refuelled and lit several more lamps. Halfway down Knockers Lane, Paul ascended the stepladder to the next glass lamp case and opened it. In the gloom, he did not see the window open above him. He did not see the large jug of oil tipped from the window, but he felt the thick liquid splash over his head and shoulders. He screeched and slipped from the stepladder. Jake backed away and narrowly avoided having the older man crush him. Paul spluttered and shook his head, wiped at his face. He couldn't see, had swallowed some of the oil and was choking on it.

Jake pointed open-mouthed. "Sir, sir. A person comes."

Paul's eyes were gummed together. He frantically wiped the oil from his eyes and squinted. Holy Hell, a cloaked figure was coming down the lane at him with a lit torch. But the oil … if the flame touched the oil on his person, he would—

Realisation struck him. This was it. *This* was the attempt on his life. Paul fumbled blindly for the flintlock pistol within his jacket. The man carrying the burning torch approached. Paul pointed the pistol, and the man stopped dead in his tracks.

"Don't you come near me with that flame, fucker. Stay back!"

Young Jake looked from lamplighter to the figure threatening to turn Paul into a human candle. "What's happening?"

"Get the Night Watch! Run for the coppers, boy!"

And Jake ran. Paul couldn't follow, for as soon as he turned his back, the torch would be thrown at him. But the boy was safe. Paul Hardcastle, humble lamplighter, had saved the boy in a noble gesture. He was not a man who deserved to die; anyone could see that.

"I've … I've done nothing wrong," Paul stammered. "I am innocent."

The figure with the torch simply stood there, the face obscured by shadows within its hood. "It's not what you did, Paul. It's what you didn't do."

The lamplighter gasped. He knew that voice. It could not be. "Helen?"

She pulled back the hood. Helen Hardcastle stared at her husband. Her brown hair was parted down the middle, like two waves reaching her jawline in a way that accentuated the roundness of her cherub-like face. "I have no desire to do this," she said, "but it must be done."

Paul didn't understand. He didn't understand anything. "Put the torch away," he said. Helen hesitated, and for a moment, the lamplighter thought he was saved. "Dearest, put it down. Come home. I do not know where you have been these last weeks, and I care nothing for the whys and wherefores. I've missed you. Come home."

Helen raised her hand to throw the torch, and Paul pulled the trigger. Flint struck lock. A spark flashed, and the musket ball exploded from the muzzle. Helen fell, the burning torch clattering harmlessly to the street. The ignition powder from the flintlock caught among the oil on Paul's coat, and his sleeve burst into flames. The lamplighter shrieked and waved his arm frantically, but within seconds, his entire coat crackled with fire. The skin on his face curled like paper burning in a blazing hearth. He screamed in agony but could not remove his ill-fitting jacket.

Several windows began to open. The shouts of women and men melded with the pained cries of the lamplighter as he hurled himself against a wall and fell to the ground. Doors opened, and residents attempted to douse Paul in what little water was at hand, using even piss from their pots. But it was too late. The lamplighter was a smoking, stinking corpse.

Helen Hardcastle groaned in pain amid the darkening shadows. A figure in a hooded cape knelt at her side. Keira Jack put her hand to Helen's abdomen, and blood coated her fingers.

"On your feet," Keira said. "We must go."

Helen winced. "It hurts, Keira."

"Get up. We must get you back to the house."

"I can't."

"If you are caught here, you're done for, do you hear me? I know it pains you, but we cannot linger. Come."

Keira helped Helen to a sitting position. The injured woman moaned, but Keira showed no mercy, pulling Helen to her feet. Keira moved in under Helen's shoulder, and the two women set off down Knockers Lane as the Night Watch began to arrive with wet whistles and drawn swords. The two women were ignored by the neighbours who came to peer at the hissing cadaver of the lamplighter, ignored by the lawmen crunching down the gravel street.

Ignored except for one woman: an old widow who had been among the first to glance out of her open window and, despite her age, one of the first down to the street below.

"Is she alright?" Old widow Granger asked Keira as she and Helen stumbled past.

"She's fine, dear," Keira said. "Do not trouble yourself."

Widow Granger reached out and laid a hand on Keira's shoulder. "I think you should wait for the doctor." There was an air of suspicion in the way she stared at Keira and Helen.

"I'm alright," Helen said through gritted teeth.

The old woman babbled on and followed them down the lane, drawing attention to them. Keira grabbed the old woman and hissed in her face. "If you don't fuck off and mind your own business, your toes will be eaten off by hungry rats this night."

The old widow nearly fell over in shock. She backed away.

Keira and Helen trudged further down the street and turned right onto a larger road. Foot traffic had thinned with the onset of the early evening and the storm clouds, but there were still people around, unaware of the drama on Knockers Lane. The two women walked as upright as they could to avoid attention, just two friends, arm in arm, walking down the street.

"Bit rough on the oldster, weren't you?" Helen breathed painfully.

"Meddlesome old biddy. People interfere when their attention is not required, when it is safe, but when you need it, when there's a risk to their own welfare in helping you, well, it's never there, is it? Never there." Blood began to drip from within Helen's cloak to the street. The growing darkness hid the drops. Keira stretched her head around and gazed back down the street. "We must not be followed, but you are injured, and I fear we have no time to take the maze. It is directly home we go, regardless of the risk."

Helen shook her head. "No, if we are discovered, all the girls are doomed. I ... I won't be responsible for that. Leave me here. You go on."

Keira ignored Helen and supported her down the street. They turned left through another narrow lane with its tightly fitted, half-timbered buildings, almost a replica of the street upon which the lamplighter had burned to death. Every few paces, Keira would look back to make sure none followed them. Helen grew heavier on her shoulder, and Keira knew that the woman was ailing, slowly collapsing in on herself, dulling, dimming like the waning light of dusk.

"Let me rest," Helen whispered painfully. She sat heavily in a shuttered and darkened storefront doorway.

Keira knelt and frowned. She put her hand to Helen's stomach. "Expunge the bullet from your body."

"And just how am I supposed to do that?"

"You're the healer, love, not me. Just push it out. Close your eyes, concentrate." Helen did as Keira asked. "Can you feel it?" Keira whispered. "Find it and push it out. Here, where my hand is." Several people walked by but ignored the two women in the doorway. Helen groaned and twisted, and then Keira felt a small metallic object slip into her bloodied fingers. She held up the rounded lead ball. "You've done it, girl." Keira held a rag to the wound. "Take a moment, catch your breath."

The sounds of running feet came slapping down the lane. Keira wished to be away, but Helen needed a moment before the power within her sealed the wound. Now that the pistol shot had been removed, Helen should recover speedily. The footsteps receded; Keira and Helen remained undetected.

Sure enough, the bleeding slowed, and the hole in Helen's side began to close. Keira helped her companion stand, and they waited until the narrow street was empty before moving off into the shadows. The oil lamps of this street, and many others, would remain unlit tonight. As a result, darkness would reign and, if Keira Jack had any say in the matter, would continue to do so for many nights to come.

CHAPTER 10

Mrs. Sandhurst's Home for Fallen Women

A key urgently inserted into a brass-plated lock. A door opened onto a hallway lit by the light of a fire coming from the sitting room on the right. Keira and Helen attempted to pass by quietly, but a woman suddenly appeared from the sitting room. She was in her fifties with greying hair and wore a pearl necklace and a check skirt of the style popular with much younger women.

"I wish to speak with you both," Mrs. Sandhurst said. "Come inside."

Keira and Helen exchanged glances before following the older woman into the comfortably furnished sitting room. A small continental toy spaniel perked its ears up from where it sat on the armrest of a plush divan near the fire.

The older woman turned to the two younger. "I must inform you that I am aware of what is going on."

Keira's heart skipped a beat. "Going on, ma'am? What do you mean?"

"I refer to your comings and goings at odd hours and …" Mrs. Sandhurst trailed off when she noted the bloodstains on Helen's shoes. "Whatever has happened to you, Helen?"

Helen stuttered. "It's … I'm … I …"

"Eve's curse," Keira said. "She was late getting her rags. No need to concern yourself, Mrs. Sandhurst."

CHAPTER 10 Mrs. Sandhurst's Home for Fallen Women

The landlady shook her head and sighed. "I honestly don't understand younger women today. Please don't sit on the divan until you've cleaned yourself up." The landlady addressed Keira and said, "I don't want whores in my house. I have sympathy for your situation, but you must understand that I risk my reputation by offering you lodging. One can only go so far, help so much."

"We are not whores," Keira said. "Not me, nor Helen nor the other girls."

"The hours you keep would suggest otherwise."

"You need not concern yourself with that. It's all quite innocent."

"Innocent?" Mrs. Sandhurst raised plucked eyebrows. "You'll excuse me if I am not assured." She reached out and patted her toy spaniel, the animal closing its eyes in pleasure. At that moment, a woman in a nightdress walked barefoot into the sitting room. Keira smiled and winked at the olive-skinned woman, and the woman smiled back.

"Are we, Elsie?" Keira said.

Elsie Gallagher brushed a strand of curling black hair from her cheek. "Are we what?"

"Whores. Mrs. Sandhurst misunderstands us. I was just telling her that we are not whores."

Elsie's dark brown eyes twinkled. "No, Mrs. Sandhurst. We are not whores. We do not entertain gentlemen in our rooms, or anywhere else for that matter."

"Ever again," Keira added.

Elsie nodded. "Ever again."

Mrs. Sandhurst's forehead wrinkled in confusion. "Well, I can't take any more of you off the streets. I'm losing money. I'm not a charity. One must make a living."

Keira folded her arms. "We pay for our lodgings, Mrs. Sandhurst. You have lost no custom."

The older woman cleared her throat. "I'm just not ... I think we need to discuss the arrangement. Perhaps there is somewhere else you can go."

"We have nowhere else."

"I'm sorry," Mrs. Sandhurst said coldly. "I simply can't have you here anymore."

"How's Mr. Barker?" Elsie asked suddenly.

Mrs. Sandhurst's pearl necklace clicked as she jerked her head around at the question. "Eh? Mr. Barker?"

"Your gentleman friend," Elsie smirked. "He what comes to visit weekly."

The landlady frowned. "He is well."

"Oh, very well, from what I hear."

Mrs. Sandhurst fingered her pearl necklace. "What are you suggesting? That I conduct myself improperly? This is my house, and I may entertain guests of my own choosing in the fashion of my choosing, which is not a privilege extended to you or the other girls, who are merely boarders."

Elsie turned to Keira and grinned. "I heard her sucking on old Barker's codger last night. He was having a whale of a time. They both were." Elsie pointed to her ear. "I couldn't help but hear it. Mrs. Sandhurst was making noises like the prize truffle pig that hit the motherlode."

The landlady's face turned red, but the knuckles grasping her necklace turned white. She breathed sharply and looked from one woman to another. "Out on your ear, all of you," Mrs. Sandhurst spluttered. "Outrageous … such impertinence, in my own house."

"Mrs. Sandhurst is becoming jittery again," Keira said. "I would like a more docile version of our landlady."

Mrs. Sandhurst frowned. "What did you say?"

Elsie Gallagher, smiling and holding her hands out peaceably, approached the older woman. "I apologise, Mrs. Sandhurst, for the insult to your character just now. You are well within your rights to have your fun, especially at your age. Lord knows you don't have too many more years of pleasure left in you."

Mrs. Sandhurst took a step backwards, but Elsie stepped close and laid a hand on the older woman's greying hair. Mrs. Sandhurst flinched, her head jerking backwards. She stumbled. Elsie grabbed her to prevent her from falling and guided the woman to the divan, where she slumped beside her toy spaniel. The dog looked at its mistress with a cocked head.

Blood dripped from Mrs. Sandhurst's nose, and she dabbed at it absentmindedly. She blinked at Keira, Elsie and Helen and said, "Oh girls, you're back. I didn't hear you come in." She gazed at the fire and said no more.

Elsie gave the woman a handkerchief and helped clean blood from her fingers and nose. "I cannot do this many more times," she said, "or I risk permanently damaging her mind, and as much as I dislike the bitch, that is not a punishment befitting the crime."

"I understand," Keira said. "We do not remain here much longer." She waved a hand over the toy spaniel's head, and it eased itself into the lap of its mistress. The dog cocked a leg and pissed all over Mrs. Sandhurst's check skirt, the landlady seemingly unaware, for now. "*That* is a punishment befitting the crime."

"Are you alright?" Elsie asked Helen.

"I'm alright," the cherub-faced woman said, touching her stomach. "The pain is gone. I am healing."

"Good. We mustn't lose a sister. Is it done?"

Helen nodded. "It is done. Paul is dead."

Elsie looked to Keira. "Who's next?"

Keira did not answer but moved out of the sitting room and up the stairs, which did not creak, not once. Old Sandhurst may be a conceited, hypocritical cocksucker, but she ran a well-maintained house. Keira opened the first door at the top of the stairs and entered a room with a low ceiling and four beds, two resting against either wall. It was dim, the only light filtering down from a small window in the roof.

The lack of light did not bother the woman who sat on the edge of the bed nearest the door. She had short, spiky red hair. In her hand, she held two dice. She threw the small objects into the air, and when they reached the apex of their ascent, they did not fall but rather rotated slowly on their axes in the gloom.

Keira marvelled at the sight. "Impressive. But you should get some rest, Charlene."

"Can't sleep," Charlene Hickson said.

"What's the matter, love?"

"I keep seeing Eugene's face when the catgut began to cut into his throat. That look, you know? When he saw it was me."

"Are you feeling guilty?"

Charlene shrugged. "Had to be done. We are chosen."

Keira nodded. "Yes, we are. You did the right thing. How's your shoulder?"

Charlene rotated her left arm around in its socket. "Right as rain. The officer's little pecker did no permanent harm."

"Good. Sleep. I'll ask Elsie to soothe your thoughts so that you may rest."

Charlene let the dice fall into her hands. "No, no. I don't want her in my head. No offence. Lovely lass, but I just don't want her rumbling around up there." Charlene pointed to her temple. "You know?"

"Alright."

Keira left Charlene and made her way to another bed in the room, where a woman was lying on her side. Keira sat gently and put her hand on the coverlet, pulling it back slightly. Despite the failing light, the woman's hair was a vibrant golden brown, tied in a bun atop her head. She was not sleeping. Keira could sense it.

"Helen has done hers," Keira said. "It is time. Time for you to do yours."

The woman lying under the heavy wool coverlet did not speak. Keira pulled the blankets down further, revealing a bare arm. She ran her hand over the arm, the warm, smooth flesh.

"I am not ready," the other said.

Keira pulled at the shoulder and turned the woman onto her back. She lifted her nightshirt to expose the scarring across her abdomen. "It is your turn," Keira said. "They have unleashed Hell. We are the hounds, the bitches, come to do the damage, come to serve up justice."

The woman in the bed whispered anxiously, "They have a bride of Christ. Her name is Sister Kempson. And the big man. He is not like the other men. He's different. He …"

Keira shushed the woman and rubbed at her belly as if she could erase the scars there. Her eyes glazed over with memory. "Harpy, old Anderson used to call me," Keira said. "*Shut your mouth, you nagging harpy*, he used to say. So be it, husband. Not the hounds of Hell, then. We are the Harpies." Keira blinked the memory away. "Don't worry about the big fellow, love, or Sister Kempson. We will strike them down should they get in our way. Do not be afraid."

"I'm not afraid, but he … the man could have killed me, yet he … he let me live. He's not like the others."

Keira frowned. "He's a man. He's like all the others. Listen to me; I have no desire to kill him or the nun, but we must not hesitate if they interfere. Do you understand?"

The golden-haired woman in the bed nodded. "Yes, I understand. When? When should I do it?"

"Three nights hence. Perhaps a week. There is no hurry. I want him to consider what is coming for him. I want to give them all time to stew in the juices of their own fear, as we did." Keira reached up and released the woman's golden-brown hair and let it fall across her pillow. Keira caressed her face.

"Why did it take my baby?"

Keira's hand froze on the other's cheek. She frowned and swallowed. "It didn't," she said. "That was … a natural …" Finally, Keira shook her head. "I don't know. Perhaps … I don't know. Sleep now." Keira got up and left the room.

When the woman in the bed was alone, she rolled over and pulled the coverlet around her shoulders once more. Moonlight filtered through the skylight. The golden-haired woman stuck her hand out from under the blankets and watched as it transformed from a human hand to a webbed foot of some aquatic creature, then to a hairy paw like that of a large dog and finally, a cloven goat's hoof. She sighed and closed her eyes, the hand returning to normal.

It was so hard to sleep without the sounds she had become used to. Hard to sleep without the rushing river and the creaking gears.

CHAPTER 11

The Butcher's Warning

Jess howled at the quarter moon rising over the shoulder of the mountain. She sounded so mournful that Willard Brown opened the cage and allowed her inside the kitchen. Mary wouldn't have approved, but Mary wasn't here anymore.

Jess settled beside the fireplace, her head resting on her paws, her eyes gazing sadly at the miller. Willard sighed and ran his fingers over the kitchen table. "She's not coming back, girl. It's just you and me now."

The last sack of flour had been tied off for the night. Willard went outside and bathed his face in the water basin. The dark tree line blurred with the oncoming night. He dried his hands and returned inside to light a small candle from the modest fire. He placed it in a holder on the kitchen table and glanced around the room. The bloodstains on the kitchen floor and walls were barely visible now; he had scrubbed for days, at every available moment. Barely visible but still present to a knowing eye, and Willard's eye was all too knowing. He shuddered and patted his knee. Jess came to him, and he caressed her head and neck. The dog was the only true solace left to him, his last real friend now that Mary had been taken.

Willard rubbed at his chest and shoulders. His muscles ached, still not accustomed to the extra work they had to now take on without Mary lending her toil to ease his own. The waterwheel continued to turn, and the gearwheels upstairs rotated more freely without grain to grind. It was quiet, as quiet as it ever could be in a millhouse.

Jess trotted to the door, sniffed and scratched at it, eager to get out, which was odd so soon after being let in. Willard slid a kitchen knife into his belt and approached the door.

"I wouldn't do that, sir." The man who spoke was young, barely out of his teens. The steps to the storeroom above creaked under his weight as he descended to the kitchen. Private Freddie Burns of the Night Watch rubbed at his eyes. "Stand back from the door, sir. Anything untoward is my duty to investigate."

Willard stepped back and allowed the younger man to cautiously open the door and poke his head outside. Jess bounded past the private, startling him. The young fellow was further startled when Willard rushed outside after his dog. Jess began to cross the stone bridge to the mountain road and the dark trees. Willard called her back, but either she couldn't hear him or the call of something else spurred her onward. Private Burns ushered Willard back inside, casting fearful glances at the shadows in the trees as he did so.

"Get inside, sir. 'Tis not safe out after dark."

Jess disappeared into the enveloping blackness of the mountain woods.

Jess sensed something out in the dark, but it was not unfamiliar, this presence.

A twig snapped somewhere. Jess pinned her ears to her head and trotted towards the source of the sound. Light glowed in the millhouse window below, but Jess moved away from it. Up ahead, something crept among the dark shadows. Jess stopped and sniffed. Familiar but intertwined with the other scent. The before and after states mixed. The thing moved between tree boles, hard to make out, but darkness was no enemy to Jess. She was not yet so domesticated that she had lost her ability to track, to hunt. Dulled, perhaps, her senses dulled, yet sharp enough.

She recognised the gait of the thing and did not recognise it. Intertwined, the before and the after. It was descending towards the millhouse, stopping occasionally to peer between the tree trunks. Danger, there was danger here. The desire to flee surged through her, but Jess padded softly in a parallel line to the creeping thing. She decided that she would make herself known. Jess whined and the thing stopped moving. It turned towards her. Jess froze. Time flowed backwards.

The creature sat on its haunches and whispered, "Come, girl."

Jess moved closer. The hands that caressed her coat were familiar. The woman had come home. A surge of joy ran through Jess. They stayed together, the woman and the dog, until the moon appeared through the branches overhead.

The woman finally shook her head. "Go back, Jess. It is your home but no longer mine." With a sigh, the woman moved stealthily back up the rise, melting into the shadows between the dark trees. Jess wanted to follow but did not. She was confused. She had to go back to the man, for he was waiting. But why did the woman not come? Jess padded down through the trees back towards the light in the kitchen window.

The knock at his door took Willard by surprise. It was an authoritative pounding, not the apologetic rapping one might expect from a caller at such an improper hour. From the fireside, Jess lifted her head, only having just returned from the darkness among the trees. Willard fumbled for the long kitchen knife at his hip, reassuring himself that the blade was still there, but it was Freddie Burns who opened the door.

The man standing there was no stranger to Willard. He was of average height, had a stocky frame and mutton chop whiskers of light brown from ear to mouth. The man frowned at Private Burns, and the private frowned back.

"It's alright, Freddie," Willard said. "I know this man. He is a friend. Hello, Jock. What brings you at this hour?"

"Can I come in?" Jock said, his voice deep and rough. Those who knew Jock Burgess understood that this was less a request than a command.

"Aye, of course." Willard peered past Jock and saw three men dismounting from horseback, their shapes barely outlined by the light issuing from the kitchen. "And your men?"

Jock shook his head and continued to eye the young Night Watch sergeant suspiciously. "They shall keep watch outside. Who's your friend?"

"Private Freddie Burns, this is Jock Burgess."

"Pleased to meet you, sir," Freddie said as he stepped back to allow Jock ingress. The man with the mutton chops did not return the private's cordial greeting.

Willard approached the fireplace and dropped a small log on the fire. "Three men, Jock?"

Jock Burgess turned his mouth down and took a seat at the table. "You can't be too careful these days, Willard. You can't be too careful." Jock unbuckled his sword and leaned the scabbard across his lap.

"Is the sword necessary?" Willard asked. Jock pointed out the long kitchen knife at Willard's hip. Willard gave a wry smile. "As you say, can't be too careful."

"May we speak in confidence?" Jock murmured. Willard looked towards the young private, who nodded and walked back upstairs. When he had gone, Jock said, "Are you making money, Willard?"

Willard joined the other man at the table. "I make ends meet. Odd question to be asking, Jock."

"Odd times, Willard. Making ends meet, well, let me tell you that's not enough, son. Take myself. The butchery business is good, good enough for me to afford those men outside. I keep 'em with me every moment. You would do well to do the same, and I'm not talking about that fellow upstairs. He's too young. You need hardened men."

"Why would I need hardened men?"

"For fear that you'll end up like the others."

"The others?"

"Come on, Willard. Stop pretending ignorance. Eugene, Tom and Anderson, of course. Their deaths aren't random." Jock licked at dry lips. "There's been a fourth. Paul Hardcastle is dead."

Willard sat stunned. "What? Paul, too?"

"Aye. They lit the poor bastard up like a pagan bonfire last night. Burned him alive." Willard merely stared, and Jock snapped his fingers in front of the miller's eyes as if to awaken him from a trance. "Someone wants us all dead, Will. Do you have something to drink? My nerves are playing up."

Willard mechanically opened a small storage cupboard and brought out a bottle of cider and two mugs. He placed them on the table and sat down again, dazed. The butcher poured himself a mug of cider and took a long, lusty drink.

"Four," Jock repeated, holding up the equivalent number of fingers, as if Willard did not quite understand the import of what he was saying. "*Four* of us murdered."

Willard frowned. "Is this business connected with Mary's ... with the disappearances of our wives?"

Jock turned his mouth down. "Aye. Not too much of a stretch to assume that. First the women, now the men." Willard's blood ran cold. The conversation took a stilted turn, and neither man spoke for a few moments. "You need men," Jock said finally.

"That won't be necessary. I have Jess and Private Burns, and I have my axe and knife. Besides, I don't think we are in danger."

The butcher shook his head. "You still don't get it, Will. First, the wives and now, the husbands. It's no coincidence, believe you me. No coincidence. We are hunted men. We're on a list, a death list. You'll need more than a kitchen knife, a dog and that wet behind the ears fopdoodle upstairs to protect you."

Willard shuddered. *A death list.* "Who is doing this?"

"No bloody idea. Not yet, anyway. I have a man down in the Law Courts, but the coppers don't know what's going on. One fact remains as true as the freckles on your face. *Someone* wants us buried, and the bastard has got half of us already".

"What are you going to do, Jock?"

"I'm warning those that remain alive. I can't do much more than that. Coppers are useless, so we look after ourselves. Consider yourself warned." The butcher thumbed outside. "And I'm keeping those fellows with me at all times. I suggest you find some real protection, Willard, and soon because you're on that list, just like I am."

CHAPTER 12

The Dripping Man

Shivering in the early morning damp, Yohan Schuman knocked at the warped and rotted door. He knocked again, and a bleary-eyed fellow in a nightshirt and cap opened the door.

"Wassat? Who's there?" the occupant said.

Yohan sighed in exasperation. Every morning, the same confused question uttered in the same confused tones by the same confused idiot.

"It's me. It's always me."

"Oh, is that you, Yohan?" The other man blinked several times and looked up and down the alley. "I 'spose you're here for the dripping."

"I'm not here to suck your cock, Yurl. Course I'm here for the dripping."

Yurl grunted a 'wait here' and disappeared inside. A few moments later, he returned with a small bucket. Yohan took the bucket and tipped the soap-like contents into a larger version he carried, making sure to scrape every spoonful of the dripping into his container. He reached into his trousers and handed over a thin coin to the thin man in the nightcap. Yurl gave an empty smile, held the coin up by way of farewell and closed the door on Yohan.

The dripping man walked slowly along the edges of the street. He soon found traces of animal fat in the gutters running beneath a small pub, mixed in with urine, faeces and other things of a less savoury nature. Making sure that he was unobserved, Yohan knelt

CHAPTER 12 The Dripping Man

and began to ladle the noxious glop into his bucket. He should probably boil it before selling it, but decided doing so was too much trouble. It would be fired up in cooking pans anyway. No harm done to anyone.

Yohan Schuman trolled on down the street, eyes on the gutter all the way. This was his second bucket of dripping this morning, most of it impure but indistinguishable from the real thing. Cork Strickland, owner of the Cleric's Long Plum, would pay a fine price for the animal fat, and Yohan needed the money. He needed it badly. It was time to get out of Dysael and go far away.

Yohan passed by the butchery owned by Jock Burgess, one of several that the successful butcher owned in Dysael. The dripping man stopped and stared into the darkened shop windows. No animals hung there, no ducks, no rabbits, no sheep shanks. No signs proclaiming the special cut of the day. But come dawn, the windows would be dressed, the shop would open, and the public would clamour for the choicest cuts and the cheapest pieces of gristle. Yohan felt a pang of envy. Jock Burgess was doing well. He had money, enough to buy protection: three men to attend him wherever he went. *Three*, mind you. Yohan shuddered and looked up and down the streets. He, himself, was a man of little means, had nothing to protect him except his own wits, but even they wouldn't go too far. It was luck he needed. And money. He had to get out of town and quick.

Four men dead. Word had spread. Four men, now. Jock the butcher, despite his gruff and aggressive mien, well, he was scared too. Yohan could tell it in the man's eyes when he had come to warn him. Four dead and four left standing, but Jock would be alright— his money would see to that. And the bastard had dripping to spare, yet never let Yohan near it, at least not for free. Yohan stood in front of the butcher shop and spat sharply up against the window in a moment of self-pity and resentment.

A clattering, as if an empty bucket had been kicked over, came from the end of the street. Yohan peered off in the direction of the sound. The streets were empty before the sun's rising. The drunks had gone home or were sleeping in places likely to give them the death of chill. No one still in their right mind walked these streets except the dripping man, and Yohan wasn't entirely sure that he was in his right mind. A cat screeched from somewhere behind him. Yohan whirled around, nearly spilling the contents of his dripping bucket. His breathing became harsher in his throat, nerves chilling. He cursed himself for a fool. Nothing there. Besides, who would want to assassinate a dripping man? For what possible gain? He had nothing of worth. But Yohan knew this was not about money. This was about something else.

He scurried off down the street, curtailing his search for dripping, legitimate or otherwise. He had tested his luck too far already tonight.

Footsteps behind him, unmistakable. Yohan's knees weakened. He willed them to stand strong, to support the rest of his body as he trotted through the streets. His trained eye spotted the telltale signs of animal fat in a nearby gutter, and his equally adept nostrils confirmed the suspicion. Yohan did not stop. Something was following him, had latched on to his scent as he had the fat in the gutters, lurking in the darkness. He had to get home behind locked doors. Yohan had sharp eyes, but he could make out nothing behind him, yet it *was* there. It was there. He didn't need sharp eyes to know it.

The bucket of dripping slowed him down. He contemplated throwing it aside and running as fast as he could, but he might as well offer up his own neck to the blade. Without money, he was a dead man. The dripping was his means out of Dysael.

A cloaked figure stepped out from the shadows several feet in front of him. Before he could scream for help, a woman's voice said, "Hello, Yohan."

The fear in his breast quietened, but only a little. Impossible. She was gone. The owner of that voice was gone. The hooded figure removed the cowl. Hair in black waves framed a porcelain face and large brown eyes.

"Yes, dearest Yohan," the woman said. "I am returned."

CHAPTER 12 The Dripping Man

Yohan dropped his bucket of dripping. "Sage, my darling. Where have you been? They told me ... everyone said you were taken."

Sage Schuman stepped closer. "I *was* taken, Yohan. Taken, murdered. Reborn."

"Murdered? I don't understand." Yohan cast a frantic glance behind him. "We can talk of this later. Something is pursuing me, us. We must run, run for home."

Sage shook her head. "No, we have no home together. Not anymore."

A flash of anger. She'd run off and returned, only to tell him that she had no intention of coming home? Then, a cold chill ran down his neck and spine, a chill of understanding.

"You," he said, stepping away from his wife. "It's you."

Sage reached out to him, as if to deny the implicit accusation, as if to ask him not to go. But Yohan had not erred. She had come to kill him. Yohan saw his wife with new eyes. Sage became a different being, unrecognisable to him. To look upon a soul that you have loved only to know that this person means you harm. The transformation shocked him, froze him to the spot even though his mind screamed for him to run.

"I'm sorry, Yo," she said, using the pet name she saved for him in their private moments, such an obscene name upon her lips now that she had murder in her heart.

"I've ... I've done n ... nothing wrong," Yohan said.

"Bessie Partridge begs to differ."

Yohan shook his head again and again. "Oh, no, no. I didn't have nothing to do with that." Sage was a small woman, but her physical presence terrified him now; she seemed to loom large over him. "Nothing to do with it."

She repeated, "Bessie Partridge begs to differ." Sage held out her hand and revealed a small bubble floating above her palm, and within the bubble, tiny flames swirled.

Yohan stared. "What's that?"

Sage blew on the bubble, and it began to float towards him. His instincts rallied. Yohan reached for the bucket at his feet and threw the dripping at Sage. When the dripping touched the floating orb, the bubble exploded in flame, superheating the fat and sending it towards Yohan in searing shards. Yohan shrieked as the scorching substance sprayed across his face. Sage staggered backwards, arms raised to ward off the hissing lard.

Running footsteps echoed down the street. "Arrest that woman!"

Constable Thackery was sprinting towards them, Sergeants Jones and Frood right behind him. Yohan desperately scraped sizzling fat from his scorched face and stumbled towards the three men, towards salvation.

Sage turned and ran.

Yohan reached out to Thackery, a plea to save his life on his lips, but the constable just shoved the man to the ground and careened after the fleeing woman.

Thackery hurtled after the assassin. He'd been close enough to recognise the figure as female but not close enough to apprehend her. He was gaining on the villain. Jones was at his side, but Frood was falling back, the smaller man still recovering from his own recent brush with death, his neck a mass of red scars from the catgut that had almost strangled the life out of him.

A bubble floated in the air ahead of him: a glowing bubble of red heat, the same kind used against the dripping man. Thackery dodged it as it exploded. A searing pain bit at the nape of his neck, but he kept right on running. He had no time to marvel at the supernatural orb. He had to take the assailant down. There would be no more murders on the streets of his city.

A second figure appeared from the shadows of a low wall, another female, judging from the gait, similarly robed and cowled to the first attacker, though taller. The two women ran side by side, cloaks billowing behind them. The first rays of the morning sun began to filter over the rooftops, sheening the cowls of the two running figures in a ruddy glow. The tall one raised her one hand to the morning sky. A large blackbird swept down and clawed at Thackery's eyes. Throwing up an arm, the constable stumbled and nearly fell. Another bird, a thrush, swooped at Jones, clawing at the squat man's face and cutting the bridge of his nose. Jones squealed and fell, splashing into a puddle of filthy water. Thackery didn't stop. Behind him, the constable heard the screeching of a third bird mixed in with Frood's curses, the scrawny man subjected to a similar attack. The large blackbird that had assaulted Thackery plummeted down for a second attempt at plucking his eyes out.

Globes of fire and now birds bent on murder. What supernatural events were unfolding? These fiends, these witches, could not be allowed to escape. Thackery carried a rapier and struck out at the blackbird with the weapon as it came diving at him, and he pierced a wing. The bird shrieked in almost human-like pain and crashed to the road, but not before it took a piece of Thackery's cheek and a section of his finely manicured moustache with it.

Ignoring the stinging at his face, the constable pounded on down the streets, *his* streets. *His* city. What gall, what outrageous nerve on the part of these women to think that they could just go blithely about the business of murder with impunity. No. They would learn to fear the Law, to fear Vincent E. Thackery, and no dark magic, no beaked and clawed foe would prevent him from running down his quarry.

The two fleeing figures entered a dead-end alley formed at one end by a high-slatted fence. Upon coming to the fence, the women turned and, surprisingly, raised their fists in the pose of bare-knuckled fighters. Thackery slowed, catching his breath. He stopped, and Frood joined him a moment later.

"Leave her alone," the taller woman said, her face still covered in shadows beneath her hood.

"This woman," Thackery said between heavy breaths and gesturing at the shorter of the two, "is under arrest for attempted murder. Any further trickery, any sorcery, and I'll run you both through." He pointed his rapier at the taller woman.

Frood screamed in pain and astonishment as a hissing cat jumped from nowhere and latched onto his face, tearing and clawing at the scrawny man's features. Jones arrived and pulled the insane feline from the thin man's head, booting it away into the shadows.

"Very well," Thackery said. "I gave you fair warning." He stepped in and lunged with the rapier, but the cloaked woman moved with inhuman speed. She swung around and aimed a kick at Thackery's groin, but the constable, too, was quick. He moved away in time to avoid a crushing blow to his fruits.

Vincent E. Thackery had never fought a woman before. Part of him was abhorred at the thought, but these females possessed unnatural abilities and, if Thackery was right, had already murdered several men.

Sergeant Frood, his face a scratched and bloody mess, and Sergeant Jones moved in on the other woman. Suddenly, the taller broke away from Thackery and leapt onto the top of the fence, an astonishing jump of eight feet. Frood and Jones stared in amazement. The woman balanced on the balls of her feet and reached down to haul her companion up and over the fence.

Thackery cursed the useless night watchmen as he lunged. He cast aside his rapier and clamped onto the assassin's legs as she ascended the fence. He held on with all his strength.

"Help me, you stupid bastards!" Thackery screamed.

Together, the three men pulled her off the fence and to the cold, wet dirt of the alley.

"Keira!" she cried, reaching out.

But the taller woman was gone.

CHAPTER 13

Losing Face

Thackery scowled into a small, handheld mirror. He ran his fingertips over his torn moustache and the scratched and tender skin beneath it. The skin would heal, and the moustache would grow back, but it was the audacity of the whole thing that aggrieved him, and, if he were to admit it, he was unnerved by the supernatural powers that both women had displayed that morning.

Thackery placed the mirror on the desk and strode purposefully from his office. He made his way down a flight of stairs and followed a long corridor that ended in a solid oak door. He knocked once, and the lock rattled as a key turned and the door opened. Sergeant Frood stood there, and if Thackery was displeased at the damage done to his own features, he was thankful he didn't look like the night watchman. The taller woman had set a feral cat on Frood's face, and between the ferocious animal and the catgut that had nearly taken his life and left horrendous garotte marks across his throat, the sergeant was hideous beyond that which nature had already gifted him.

"Do we have a name? Has she said anything?" Thackery said.

"She's said nowt', Constable," Frood croaked in a husky whisper. The man's voice box had not escaped the catgut unscathed.

Thackery brushed by the smaller man and walked past several holding cells, each with iron bars from floor to ceiling. They all remained vacant, except one, about which several night watchmen milled. The sole prisoner was strapped to a chair, her hands bound with leather strips and tied behind her, an uncomfortable position and one that caused the woman much pain. Her dark robe was gone, replaced by a filthy white prison gown.

"Well?" Thackery addressed the stocky Sergeant Jones as he entered. "You've had her for an hour. I want some answers."

"She's not talking, sir."

"Then make her talk, damn it." The constable turned his attention to the other men. "Out. Only Sergeants Frood and Jones to be in here with the prisoner. Back to your duties. She isn't the only villain in North Quarter. Get those empty cells filled."

When the night watchmen had left, Thackery examined the slightly built woman. "Why did you attempt to murder the dripping man?" The woman did not move her eyes from the cell floor. "Where is he, by the way?" Thackery said to Jones. "Where is the dripping man?"

"He's with the doctor, sir. His face got burned."

Thackery touched his mutilated moustache and again thanked his lucky stars the damage done to him was superficial. "Bring him here."

"Yes, sir." The stocky night watchman backed away and left the cell.

Thackery eyed the prisoner. "We are going to get some answers from you, one way or the other. I suspect that this is not your first dalliance at murder. I warn you that if you maintain your silence, you will be held accountable for the deaths of four men and an attempted fifth. Do you understand? A confession may ease things for you somewhat." The prisoner said nothing and continued to stare at the cell floor. "Don't make us bring out devices of confession."

A woman's voice came from the doorway to the holding cells. "If you are referring to torture, Constable Thackery, a forced confession is illegal. You, of all people, should know that."

Thackery cursed under his breath as the fat nun and her dour-faced bodyguard entered the holding cells. Thackery addressed Frood. "What is she doing here? Who let her in?" The night watchman gave a limp shrug.

CHAPTER 13 Losing Face

"Seeing that I *am* here, Constable," Sister Kempson said, coming to stand in front of the half-moustachioed lawman, "you may address me directly."

"Very well. What are *you* doing here? This is a matter for the constabulary, as I have said several times. You have no jurisdiction here. Piss off."

Garth stared at Thackery's mangled moustache and pointed to his own upper lip. "Been shaving, mate? Missed a spot."

Thackery controlled his voice. He wouldn't allow the ginger thug to rattle him. "Both of you, if you don't get out immediately, you'll end up in matching cells. Do you hear me?"

"We have every right to be here, Constable Thackery." Sister Kempson passed a rolled parchment to the constable, which he unfurled suspiciously. The constable frowned and squinted at the flowing script. He ignored most of it, except the signature at the bottom. Signed by the bishop himself. Thackery wanted to tear the parchment to shreds and throw it in the woman's face. He held himself back and settled for angrily thrusting the document against the nun's ample bosom.

"I must reiterate," Thackery said between gritted teeth, "that I need no outside help."

"I disagree. One should never refuse help, particularly when one needs it."

"But I don't need it."

"If you are unhappy at cooperation," Sister Kempson went on, "then I suggest concurrent investigations. We try not to step on each other's toes and yet share information. Are you agreeable to this?"

The constable fumed but was powerless to object now that the portly nun had provided heavyweight documentation. "As you say," Thackery said coldly.

"Who is this woman?" Sister Kempson said, coming forward to observe the bound figure in the cell.

Thackery wanted to scream in frustration. With every ounce of his self-control, he said, "We don't have a name yet, but this morning, I apprehended this person in the very act of attempted murder. Without my intervention, a fifth man would now be under the care of Coroner Stimpson."

"Marvelous," the fat nun said. "You have done well." Was there an undertone of mockery in her voice? "Can you provide details, Constable?"

No. Fuck off, he thought. The constable shifted his weight and cleared his throat. "She ... she showed unusual abilities. I can only conclude that she is a witch."

The nun stared. The bodyguard stared. Even Frood stared, and the idiot had been there.

Sister Kempson spoke after an uncomfortably long silence. "A startling claim, Constable. Could you elucidate on these *unusual abilities*?"

He would rather not. Thackery sighed and indicated the woman bound to the chair. "Balls of ... floating heat. She somehow produced bubbles of exploding flame, as ludicrous as that sounds. And the other one speaks to birds, commands them to her bidding. No, not just birds. There was a cat as well. Christ, she may very well command the entire animal kingdom for all I know."

"The other one," the nun repeated. "What other one?"

Thackery's heart went cold. He didn't like admitting to failure. "Another suspect ... escaped." That damned uncomfortable silence again. "But I got one of them," Thackery added.

"Yes, yes," the nun nodded. "One of them."

The silence continued. The nun was judging him on his failure to apprehend the second assailant, refusing to credit him with the capture of the first even though he had succeeded where Kempson and Garth had failed. Not a word of that, though. Bitch.

"Perhaps the woman can have her hands freed," Sister Kempson said. "To bind her in this way seems unnecessarily cruel."

The constable wanted to slap the nun. "Have you not heard a word I have said? This woman is a witch. She summoned the heat bubble with the use of her hands. That is why she is bound and will remain so."

"Let us not speak of witchcraft," Kempson said. "We don't wish to alarm the populace before we have the facts. As an executor of the law, you would no doubt concur that evidence is required. Firm evidence."

"I have all the evidence I need," Thackery said as he touched his scratched face. "I am a witness to the events in question."

"You say there is another like her?"

"At least one. I am not convinced that this woman," he said, gesturing to the bound prisoner, "murdered the catgut spinner. And it was not the other woman we encountered this morning. She was much too tall. Therefore, I can only conclude that we have multiple assailants."

"This information must be discreetly guarded," Sister Kempson said.

"Hah. You fear panic among the ignorant and uneducated."

The nun smiled without mirth. "You speak of your people with much disregard."

"Not *my* people," Thackery countered. "Most citizens of Dysael are peasants of varying classes. It is *the Law* that I respect."

Kempson raised a finger as if to expose a flaw in Thackery's logic. "And yet, in your avid policing of the law, you protect the citizens of Dysael. An irony, don't you think?"

Thackery sneered. "That is a natural consequence of a man's duties, yes, but of little concern to me."

"Well," the nun sighed, "one must admire the results of your actions, if not the intent. Still, we require evidence before putting this woman up as a witch."

The constable's voice sharpened in irritation. "Don't you people preach of the dangers of the Devil and his minions? Are you not here to forewarn us and protect our immortal souls? Here is the evidence." He once again gestured to the prisoner. "The very proof of what the Church is supposed to be fighting, and you seem rather eager to deny it."

The nun clasped her fingers together and said, "Constable Thackery, I urge you to caution. We must use our faculties of reason and logic."

"He's right," Garth said suddenly. "I've seen it too. I've seen one of them."

Thackery turned on the big ginger bodyguard. "What do you mean? One of *them*? Who?"

Garth's face now resembled the colour of his hair: he was clearly embarrassed by his imminent confession but went on anyway. "A shapeshifter, up in the mountains, a woman." The prisoner raised her head slightly. Garth went on. "One moment she was a ... web-footed creature, and then ... a wolf, or parts of it."

"You cannot be sure, Garth," the nun said quietly. "You cannot be sure of this."

"I saw it," Garth said. "I believe it was Mary Brown."

Thackery gaped. He did not like Garth, but the fellow's story confirmed Thackery's suspicions, at some cost to his own credibility. Thackery was still not sure he believed Garth despite the supernatural events he, himself, had witnessed that very morning.

"They have opened the gates of Hell," the prisoner said.

All eyes turned to her. Thackery's skin prickled. Just then, Sergeant Jones entered the holding cells with the dripping man, Yohan Schuman. The woman in the cell lowered her head, her hair falling over her eyes. The dripping man took in the assorted important personages in the cell and became cowed. He fidgeted and rocked from foot to foot, his face splotched with angry burn marks, but the pain in his eyes went deeper than any physical injury. He stared at the woman in the cell.

"Do you know this woman?" Thackery asked the dripping man.

Yohan Schuman blinked and turned his sad eyes towards the constable. "I know her." He did not go on.

"Well, man? Speak up. Who is she?"

The man's lower lip trembled. "Her name is Sage, Sage Schuman, and she is my wife." The constable, the nun and the bodyguard looked at each other, as if one of them might just understand what was happening and why.

Anger surged within Thackery. None of this made sense, and he loathed ignorance in others and doubly so in himself. Sergeant

CHAPTER 13 Losing Face

Frood broke the silence and addressed his commanding officer in his husky whisper.

"What the fuck's going on, sir?"

Constable Vincent E. Thackery found himself disconcertingly unable to answer that question.

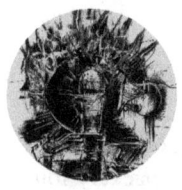

CHAPTER 14

Brotherhood

Sister Kempson cast an eye over the book in the glass case: she recognised it immediately as the founding charter of Dysael law, a charter written up by Thackery's own grandfather, or so she had heard. Thackery was proud of the Book of Law, perhaps a little too proud. Yes, there was nothing more precious to the moustachioed constable than Law and Order and his family's role in its creation and implementation.

Perhaps that was why he was going a little too hard at the dripping man.

"I shall ask you one more time," Thackery said, pointing a finger at the cowering man in the chair. "Why did your own wife attempt to murder you? A woman who was reported as missing, supposedly abducted, until this morning. She returns from … wherever she has been to orchestrate your destruction. Why? I suggest you be forthcoming, or I shall drag you back downstairs and throw you into the same cell and let her finish the job."

Yohan Schuman had his head in his hands, his body hunched. Garth stood threateningly behind him, Thackery confrontationally in front. Sister Kempson remained off to the side, not wishing to add to the interrogative atmosphere pervading the constable's office. Yohan was clearly in distress. Apparently, the attempted assassination of his person at the hands of his wife was not something he had been prepared for. She supposed no man ever was.

CHAPTER 14 Brotherhood

"You see this fellow behind you?" Thackery said. "Turn around and look at him." The dripping man twisted around to cast a fearful glance at Garth. "He," Thackery said, "is an expert at skinning a man alive, and he's itching to take that knife from his hip and start peeling you like an apple."

Garth glowered at Yohan, going along with Thackery's ruse. It was gratifying, Sister Kempson thought, to see the two boys playing together nicely for a change.

"I ... I don't know. I swear," the dripping man pleaded. "My beautiful Sage wants to kill me, do me in. I can't believe it. She was always so sweet. I can't ... I just don't understand. Have sympathy for my plight; have pity on me, sir."

"I have none, not when you're lying," Thackery said matter-of-factly. "I smell untruth upon you. I am the Law here in Dysael, and I am about to find you guilty of obstruction, a charge that comes with a lengthy prison sentence.

"Obstruction?" Yohan splayed his fingers in supplication. "But I don't even know what that means."

"You're getting in my pissing way! Is that clear enough? I have a killer to catch, several killers, apparently, and I won't have you arsing about holding me up. Confess, you lard-collecting bastard."

"Confess to what? I am the victim here, ain't I?"

The dripping man looked genuinely confused. Sister Kempson was about to step in and object on his behalf when Garth met her eye and shook his head. The nun sighed and let the drama play out.

Thackery raged on. "Four men are dead, several women are missing, at least one of whom is an apparent assassin. Poor old Sergeant Frood nearly had his head sliced from his shoulders, Sergeant Jones has been battered from pillar to post, and my moustache looks fucking awful!" The constable grabbed the man by his shirt collar and started shaking him. "Confess!"

The dripping man blubbered something unintelligible. Then, he shouted, "Murder!"

Thackery released the man and stepped back. He frowned. "You may have misunderstood me. I want to learn something fresh.

We are all aware of the murders currently doing the rounds. I want to know who—"

"No, no, you don't understand," Yohan said. "Listen. It all started with a murder. All of this. I see it now. I've been thinking on it. It started with Douglas Partridge, don't you see?"

"I see nothing. Who is Douglas Partridge?"

"Blacksmith's apprentice," Garth said before the dripping man could sniffle a coherent response. Thackery looked at the big man with a quizzical expression.

Thackery turned to the nun. "What's he talking about?"

"Apprentice to George Burridge," Sister Kempson said. "You may remember the sketch of the anvil."

"Mary Brown's sketch?"

Sister Kempson nodded. "Yes. If you'd followed that up as you should have, then the name Douglas Partridge may mean something to you."

Thackery stared. "*As I should have?* I thought we were supposed to be sharing knowledge. Concurrent investigations, not stepping on toes and all that. What's all this about a blacksmith's apprentice?"

Sister Kempson arched an eyebrow. "I had just assumed that with Mary Brown's sketch in your possession, on *loan* mind, that the image may have led you to George Burridge and Douglas Partridge." She paused and added, "I would have thought."

Thackery cocked his head. "That sounds very much like an accusation of ineptitude on my part."

The nun shrugged. "Well, I can hardly help what it sounds like, can I?"

Thackery mumbled something about *temerity* and *his own office* and turned back to the dripping man. He bared his teeth. "Alright, so what about this Douglas Partridge? What does he have to do with anything?"

"He started it all, the bastard. Doomed us all. He opened the gates of Hell."

The gates of Hell. Sister Kempson's blood ran cold, and she shivered at the familiar phrase.

CHAPTER 14 Brotherhood

The constable almost shrieked at the dripping man. "I'm going to slap you if you don't start making sense."

Yohan stuttered, "I ... I think it's time to ... I need to show you."

"Show me what?"

The dripping man snorted bubbles of snot. "Bessie Partridge."

"My dear fellow," Sister Kempson said. "Bessie Partridge is missing. The first of the women to be taken, in fact."

Yohan shook his head. "Missing forever more. She's dead. Buried in a shallow grave outside town. Murdered."

The nun gasped. "By whom?"

Yohan's voice tremored with emotion. "By Douglas Partridge, her husband."

"What? But ... but why?" Sister Kempson became flustered. "How...? Why was this not reported?"

Thackery, his brows furrowed, swatted the nun's question out of the air and then stroked his one good moustache. "No, no. That is not the pertinent question." He pointed at Yohan Schuman with a steady finger. "The question is how has the murder of one woman resulted in the death of four men?"

"We ... I can't say."

Thackery clenched a fist under Yohan's nose. "You'd better bloody say. Your own life is under threat. The only people that can save you are in this room, and we can do little to protect a man who protects his secrets to his own detriment."

Yohan stammered, "But ... we are all ..."

"You are all what?"

"Guilty of silence. God help us, we are guilty of silence."

"Speak plainly, fool."

"I knew of Bessie's murder. So did the others, but we said nothing about it."

"The others? Who? Who knew of the murder of Bessie Partridge?"

"Do you really have to ask?" Sister Kempson said. Frowning, the constable swung around to stare at her. The nun walked to the desk and picked up the paper containing the list of missing women.

She held it up. "Tom Gallagher, bowyer, husband of Elsie Gallagher. Anderson Jack, ratcatcher, husband of Keira Jack. Eugene Hickson, catgut spinner, husband of Charlene Hickson. Paul Hardcastle, lamplighter, husband of Helen Hardcastle. Must I go on?"

The frown slowly disappeared from Thackery's face. "No, I don't think you must." He turned back to the dripping man. "The women on that list aren't missing at all, are they? They're out there somewhere, lying in wait and murdering their husbands as some sort of ... vengeance against those who knew of Bessie Partridge's death and kept it a secret."

Yohan shuddered. "I ... it seems that way, sir. It seems that way."

Sister Kempson glanced at the paper. "There are three more men in danger. Willard Brown, miller, Jock Burgess, butcher, and Stephen Cox, cider maker."

Thackery shook his head. "Those men are alive and well as far as I know. I have not had a coroner's report bearing those names."

"They're dead men anyway," Garth said quietly.

Thackery scowled. "Not if I have any say in the matter. And Douglas Partridge, the man who has supposedly set this whole thing off? What of him?"

"He'll be last," Garth said.

"How would you know something like that?"

Garth folded his arms and growled, "Cos that's what I'd do. Make him know what's coming. Leave him time to grow his fear. His death will be the jewel in the crown."

"I spoke to Douglas Partridge a matter of days ago," Sister Kempson said. "You must bring him in. He's at the Burridge smithy."

Thackery nodded. "I'll get a man on it."

Yohan had tears in his eyes. "The ladies wanted to have young Douglas Partridge up in front of the law, but the men hushed them down. George Burridge said it was a mistake. Douglas didn't mean to kill her. He said it would ruin his future. So we all agreed to stay silent on the matter. But ... we've gone and cut our own throats. We've cursed our own futures. We have no future. They're after us."

The dripping man sniffled and wiped a forearm across his nose. "Me own wife came for me. Me own wife."

Thackery shook his head in wonderment. "How does your wife come to manufacture bubbles of heat from her bare hands?"

The dripping man's eyes grew wide in fear. "I have not seen that before. That is not my wife, not *my* Sage. She's changed. Something's gotten into her."

"Obviously." A cold look came over Thackery's features. "Evidence of your fanciful story, I need evidence. Take us to the grave of Bessie Partridge."

CHAPTER 15

Bessie Partridge

She was buried among the pale pink marshmallow flowers. A small patch of earth, where the flowers grew younger, signified the place where Bessie Partridge lay.

Yohan Schuman's hands trembled as he stood at the foot of the heavily shaded grave, around which gathered Constable Vincent E. Thackery and Night Watch Sergeants Jones and Frood. Both sergeants carried shovels. Garth towered over the grim-faced Sister Kempson, and above them all towered the spruce trees. This place was not high on the mountainside, yet took a good hour's trek from the farmlands below. The ground was always damp here, and the marshmallows bloomed all year. The wet, spongy ground underfoot meant that it was not a good place to light a fire or have a picnic. It was not even a good place to bury a body, perhaps that least of all.

"Did she receive any prayers for the dead?" Sister Kempson asked.

Yohan shook his head. "None. We was in a hurry, you see."

"She must be exhumed and replaced in consecrated ground," the nun said.

"Not before Coroner Stimpson has examined the body," Thackery said, "though I fear he will have little to work with." The constable nodded at Jones and Frood, and both men reluctantly moved forward to begin the process of uncovering the unfortunate woman. "How long has she been here?"

The dripping man glanced around uneasily, as if another attempt on his life lay just beyond the trees. "Four months, perhaps longer."

Garth turned his back and moved away from the grave. Sister Kempson didn't blame the man. The corpse would have decomposed badly in the swamp-like conditions. Garth radiated strength, but every man, even the teak-tough woodsman, had his moment of weakness.

"How did Douglas Partridge kill her?" Thackery said.

Yohan Schuman flinched at the question. "Knocked her in the head. I saw it. Just a simple backhand. She fell and didn't stand again. Douglas didn't know his own strength. It weren't the first time he'd done it. Didn't seem a heavier blow than any other. Just bad luck."

"Stop making excuses for the man," Garth said. Yohan swallowed and remained silent.

It did not take long before Jones looked up and said, "Found her, sir."

"Gently, Sergeant. Put away the shovels." Thackery rolled his own sleeves up and joined the two sergeants in clearing moist earth from the body. Sister Kempson wouldn't have picked that. She had thought the constable cold, aloof, the kind of man to allocate duties, particularly the unpleasant ones, and stand back and see them administered. Perhaps she had misjudged him.

Yohan turned away and bumped into Garth, who was standing right behind him.

"Watch, you bastard," Garth said. "Open your eyes and watch your handiwork."

The dripping man whined something about having nothing to do with Bessie's death, but he watched all the same. He vomited when Bessie was pulled from the mud.

"How do you intend to murder your husband, Samantha?"

The question was posed with an innocent air, as if it did not imply violence and death. Samantha Burgess, the butcher's wife, winked and disappeared beneath the cold surface of the pool, only to reappear with a splash a moment later behind Jasmine Cox, the cider maker's wife.

Samantha placed her hands on Jasmine's milky white shoulders, leaned in and whispered in the other's ear, "Haven't decided yet, but I've been thinking on it." Her hands crept up to the side of Jasmine's throat. "Might just throttle him in his sleep."

Jasmine turned and laughed as she brushed water from Samantha's thick, curly brown hair. "Sam, you can't do that. That would be wrong. Jock's a butcher. He must be done in a way that suggests his trade." Jasmine excitedly raised a finger. "I have it. Gut him and hang him in his own shop window. Now, that would be just right." She laughed. "I think I'll drown Stephen in his own cider or make him drink it 'till his belly explodes. It's not just the deed but the manner of it, you see?"

Samantha nodded. "You're right, Jaz. I just have no imagination to do it the way the others have."

"You'll think of something, Sam. Keira was wonderfully clever to suggest we do them in this fashion. First, Elsie gets in the bowyer's head, sedates him, and then she shoots him full of arrows. Brilliant. Keira sets the rats on the catcher. Helen lights up her husband brighter than the midday sun. Just wonderfully clever."

Samantha nodded. "Don't forget how Charlene sliced her man up with the catgut."

"How could I forget?" Jasmine opened her blue eyes wide. "Charlene is amazing. Controlling objects like that. She's powerful."

"We all are, Jaz," Samantha said, moving closer and kissing the pale woman on the lips. "We all are." Jasmine returned the kiss, and the two women slipped beneath the surface of the shaded pond before bursting out of the water in a laughing embrace.

A twig snapped in the trees surrounding the mountain pond, and both women jerked their heads towards the sound. Something or someone was approaching through the pine. Samantha and Jasmine exchanged sober glances and disappeared beneath the water once more, but this time silently so as not to disturb the surface of the pond.

A figure in a cloak and hood broke through the line of heavily shaded trees and came to stand before the pond. The figure observed the barely rippling waters, seemingly waiting for something to break the surface. The ripples faded, and the sheen of the high mountain waters remained unbroken. The figure reached beneath its cloak, taking out a long knife. The stranger held the blade at arm's length in the air and said, "Hold, Samantha, or I'll cut your throat. Your tricks do not work on one such as me."

Water patted softly among the pinecones a yard from where the figure stood, though the skies were clear of rainclouds. A moment later, Samantha Burgess appeared naked and dripping wet where a moment before she had been invisible. The stranger's blade was poised at Samantha's throat.

"Steady," Samantha said as she held up her hands.

Keira Jack removed her hood and took the blade from Samantha's neck. "Who's in there?" she said, nodding to the pool and putting the blade away.

Samantha turned towards the pool and shouted, "You can come out, Jaz. It's Keira."

Jasmine emerged from the water, gasping for air. "Oh, Keira," she said between breaths. "You gave us a fright."

"We got your message to meet," Samantha said, drying herself on a small towel. "Why all the way up here? Why are we leaving old cock-struck Sandhurst's house?"

"They have Sage," Keira said.

Jasmine put her hands to her mouth and gave a small cry. Samantha stared at the ground and said, "Shit. Shit, that's not good."

"We are no longer safe in the boarding house," Keira said.

Samantha looked up sharply. "You think Sage will talk? Tell 'em who and what we are?"

"I don't know, but they'll damn well try and make her. Where are the others?"

Samantha pointed off between the trees. "At the old timber mill, like you asked."

"Get dressed, you two. We need to talk, all of us."

The butcher's wife nodded and reached for her clothes. Jasmine stepped lithely out of the pool.

Keira stalked off in the direction of the abandoned timber mill, but she stopped and turned. "Is Mary among them?"

Samantha nodded. "Aye. She's there. We all are except …" She shook her head sadly. Keira turned and walked away.

"She don't look happy," Jasmine said, coming to stand beside Samantha. "And not just 'cos they got Sage."

"No," Samantha said, observing the ratcatcher's wife moving through the trees. "Keira Jack ain't happy at all, and that augurs bad for someone."

The abandoned timber mill stood in a clearing of young pine trees. Men would not return here again until the trees had reached their full maturity, or perhaps they would never return at all. It had been several years since logging operations had moved further down the mountain to a more convenient location, yet the timber mill stood strong against the encroaching tendrils of nature. The roof was mostly intact, as were the four walls, though the structure of the building displayed creeping vines like the varicose veins in an old widow's leg, and the weight of its own existence had caused the entire edifice to sag. The dismayed shouts of several women bounced off the warped timber walls and rusted metal blades inside the timber mill.

Jasmine Cox and Samantha Burgess, their hair still damp, sat shoulder to shoulder on a floor that had not seen fresh sawdust for many years. Their shouts mixed in with those of Charlene Hickson and Elsie Gallagher, sitting on an uncut log nearby. Helen Hardcastle was less forceful in her unhappiness, muttering to herself and shaking her head. Beside Helen, Mary Brown simply sat cross-legged, her face pale.

"Calm yourselves, my beautiful Harpies," Keira Jack said, holding up her hands. "Calm down."

"Poor Sage," Charlene called, running her hands through her short, spiky red hair. "What are we to do?"

"We get Sage out," Elsie said.

"But they are onto us," Jasmine said. "We must leave Dysael."

"We can't abandon Sage," Elsie countered.

"Jaz is right," Samantha said. "It would be foolish to stay. They have exposed us."

"We're not going anywhere," Keira said. "Quiet everyone. Let me speak." All eyes fixed on the ratcatcher's wife. She placed her hands on her abdomen as if to settle the butterflies madly circulating there. "We served our husbands for years, sacrificed for them as dutiful wives are expected to do and got nothing in return but heartbreak and betrayal. All that shall now be requited in blood. We've done four of the pricks, but our work is not finished. We'll do them all, and Douglas Partridge shall be the last."

"But they're looking for us," Jasmine said, her fingers fluttering over her chest and throat in anxiety. "You said so yourself. They know who we are."

"They can't stop us if we are united," Keira said. "They'll be leery, true, but they don't know what we are, what we're capable of. The odds are still in our favour. But we need to be in the city to carry out our work. We can't stay up here, and we cannot return to the boarding house."

"How do we remain undiscovered?" Samantha said. "They'll have our descriptions by now."

"We'll just have to go somewhere they'll never look for us."

"And where's that?"

"The Yard. We'll be close enough to strike from there but far enough away to remain unnoticed."

"The Yard?" Samantha looked around at the gathered women. "But that place is … it's poisonous. Nobody goes there."

"So no one will look for us there."

"I'm not one for running," Elsie said, "but have you thought this through? Sam's right. The Yard is toxic. It's slow death to any who dwell there."

Keira put her hands on her hips. "We are chosen. We are protected. Nothing will harm us in the Yard or anywhere else."

"What about Sage?" Elsie asked.

"She's heavily guarded. We'll get her out if we can, but if not, we'll do hubby on her behalf. That's the best we can offer Sage. Yohan probably thinks he's safe now. He's not, the fucker. In the meantime, we work together on the others. The miller is next." Keira glanced at Mary. "We're behind schedule on that one. Mary does the deed any way she sees fit. Then we do the butcher and the cider maker, Samantha and Jasmine's men. That leaves the blacksmith. Remember, Douglas Partridge is mine. No one harms the man except me. I'm going to murder that bastard, and when I do, my lovely Helen will bring him back from the brink of death, and I'll kill him all over again, a hundred times."

Helen Hardcastle nodded. "I'll make sure he doesn't die too soon, Keira."

"That's my lovely lass. Alright, make your preparations. Mary, I wish to speak with you privately." Every woman cast a glance at Mary Brown. "Stop gawking and get a move on," Keira said. "I want bedding, food and other supplies on a horse and cart heading for the Yard tonight. Procure them now. Hide yourselves in heavy cloaks. Go nowhere alone but always with a partner. Off with you now."

The women left the timber mill, where only Mary and Keira remained.

Keira's voice was heavy when she finally spoke. "Why is Willard Brown still alive?"

"There were men guarding him." Mary did not meet Keira's eyes.

The tall rat catcher's wife circled Mary Brown before sitting down beside her. "Your gift is exceptional among us. You are unstoppable, Mary. I control animals, can direct them to do my bidding, but you, you can *become* any creature that you have ever laid eyes on or an amalgam of such. You have the speed of an elk, the power of a bear. Nothing can stop you except the will to see it done." Keira examined the other's face. "Do you have the will to see it done?"

CHAPTER 15 Bessie Partridge

Mary continued to stare at the cutting room floor. "I cannot help but think."

"Think of what?"

"The child I lost."

Keira crossed her arms and sighed quietly. "You are looking at this the wrong way. You are freed. The child is the yoke that would have seen you tied to the plough of an unjust union. You are freed from the man, from all bonds that held you."

"I do not feel ... free. I feel resentment."

Keira whispered low but fierce. "You cannot say that, Mary. Not here, not among any of us. Those are dangerous words. I do not know just what power we possess, but I know that it listens. It *listens*, do you understand?" Keira's voice resumed its normal authoritative baritone. "You must guard against these traitorous thoughts." Keira patted Mary's knee. "My love, there is no place in our world for children, for as much as we are the hunters, we are also the hunted. Ours is no life for a child. We cannot be impeded. We must run when the need arises. The child would have been the death of you, can you not see? This power and freedom we now enjoy come at a price."

Mary looked away. "I was not consulted."

Suddenly, Keira bared her teeth in anger. "Nor was Bessie when she was put in the ground! Poor Smudge, murdered and cast aside like supper scraps. And then those bastard men came together to protect one of their own. We are simply doing the same. Your husband is as guilty as any of them, as guilty as Douglas. He must pay. You know this."

Mary bowed her head. "I know it."

"Then kill Willard! No more excuses. It's your turn. If you are not with us, you weaken us, and I'll not have us weakened. Do you understand?" Keira got to her feet. "Do you understand?"

Mary nodded. "I understand." Keira stared for a moment before walking away. When she had gone, Mary placed her hand over her belly and whispered, "I was not consulted."

CHAPTER 16

Douglas Partridge

George Burridge used tongs to carefully extricate the metal from the searing embers and place it on the anvil. He picked up his hammer and held it under the pimpled youth's nose. "Strike now. Forge a weapon fit for our customers." Jeremy winced and pulled his face away lest he find his nose broken.

"Temper both sides of the blade evenly, boy," George said, "or you'll end up with a lopsided sword, and no one would be willing to pay for that. Watch me carefully. Keep the stock flat against the anvil." With an expert rhythm, George hammered at the glowing blade. "First, you shape it, flatten it and then bevel the edges. It's monotonous work, long and hard, but it frees the mind." Jeremy did not look as if he wanted his mind freed. The boy glanced around the smithy, distracted. George fumed. He didn't have time for a scatterbrained apprentice. "Are you paying attention?"

Jeremy picked at his acned cheek. "I'm sorry, Master Burridge. I just, uh … it's just that …"

"What? Out with it."

Jeremy nodded behind George. The blacksmith turned to see two men standing a few yards away, observing the master and apprentice. George sighed. Another unwelcome visitation, too many of those recently. He handed the hammer to Jeremy. "Do as I have shown you. I will return soon." He left Jeremy tapping at the glowing metal. "Hit it harder, lad," he said over his shoulder.

The two men followed George into the cooler back room. The

sound of hammer on metal could be heard at irregular intervals from the main smithy floor. *Rhythm, boy, get into a rhythm*, George thought.

The blacksmith folded his arms and stared at Jock Burgess. "Why are you here? We all agreed to keep our distance from one another."

"You haven't heard then?" the butcher said.

"Heard what?"

The other man spoke up. Stephen Cox was tall, but the curvature of his upper spine bent him forward, as if he were embarrassed by his height and sought to mitigate it by hunching over. "They know who's after us," the cider maker said. "They have Sage."

George frowned in confusion. "Sage? Who is Sage?"

"Yohan's bloody wife, that's who," Stephen said.

The blacksmith blinked. "Oh, they found her? She's alive? That's good news."

"It ain't good news," Jock said, scratching at his mutton chop whiskers.

"But if they can find Sage, then the other wives may still be alive. Your own women may be returned to you."

"Oh, they're alive all right," Jock said. "And they're returning. It's *them* who've been knocking us off."

George looked from one man to the other. "What?"

"The law grabbed Sage," Jock said, "right before she could murder Yohan. Caught her in the very act."

George frowned. "Why would she want to do that? That doesn't make sense."

Jock growled and folded his arms. "Don't it? I'm starting to suspect otherwise."

"Aye, think about it," Stephen said. "It's the women doing the men. Not just that, but apparently, wife does husband. It's *that* personal." The tall man looked around. "Where's Douglas? Who's the kid inside?"

"That's Jeremy, my new apprentice. Douglas is … he's, uh …"

"On the run," Jock finished George's sentence. The butcher eyed the blacksmith suspiciously. "You *knew*."

"Don't know what you're talking about," George said.

The butcher flicked Stephen on the arm. "Come on, I need a drink."

Stephen removed a shoulder bag, placed it on the floor and removed a large, stoppered ceramic jug. Neither Stephen nor Jock seemed concerned at the lack of drinking vessels. They simply passed the container between them. Jock offered the cider to George.

The blacksmith took it slowly, his thoughts tripping over themselves. "Why are your wives attempting to murder you?" He took a slug of Stephen's newest batch of cider. It was rough, but George Burridge was a rough man and did not flinch as he swallowed.

"Attempting? They're more than just bloody attempting. And why? You still haven't twigged, son? What do we all have in common? What ties us together?" George looked away. He did not want to mention Bessie Partridge. Jock mentioned her anyway. "Your former apprentice is what. The fact Douglas murdered Bessie is what."

"And the fact we all knew about it," Stephen added, taking the cider. "They've all gone mad. Mad as march hares, and now they blame us. Sage has … she's gone … strange."

George stared at the cider maker. "What do you mean *strange*?"

"She tried to kill Yohan with magical balls of fire," Stephen said. "I know it sounds bonkers, but that's what Yohan told us."

"Balls of fire?"

"Yohan swears."

George shook his head. "But … how?"

"We don't know how!" Jock exploded, cider and spittle on his chin. "But they're doing it, by God, they're doing it. Tom, Anderson, Eugene and Paul, all dead. Yohan, nearly gone. Who's next? Where's Douglas?"

George shrugged. "I don't know. I've had the coppers asking after him, and I'll tell you what I told them. He scarpered, night before last. That's all I know."

Jock's eyes narrowed. "Bullshit. Where is he, George? All our lives depend on this."

"On what? What are your intentions for Douglas, Jock?"

"We hand him over. Give him to the wives. It was him that murdered Bessie. It's him what should pay. The rest of us might be allowed to live, then."

George shook his head. "Won't stop 'em."

"Why not?"

"If it was only Douglas they wanted, they'd have gone after him first. No, they want all of you."

"All of *us*," the butcher corrected. "*You're* included."

"I'm not married. I have no lunatic wife seeking my destruction."

"Come on, you bastard. You protected Douglas, just like we all did. You're protecting him now. You're on the list and make no mistake about it."

George nodded and let out a long breath. "Aye, no doubt I am."

"What are we going to do?" Stephen said. "Jasmine ain't come for me yet, but I know she will. Only a matter of time." He tried to take another swig of cider, but Jock roughly grabbed the jug from his hands and gulped at the apple liquor.

Jock cleaned his mouth on his sleeve and handed the cider to George. "I ain't running," he said. "I got my fellows outside. Three men, hard men, and they've kept me safe so far. I ain't going to die. Thackery is onto the mad bitches now, and all I have to do is wait until he gets all of them."

"Aye, it's alright for you," Stephen said. "I can't afford bodyguards to trail me around every hour of the day. How about you, George?"

George handed the cider back without taking a second drink. "Only thing I can afford is that young idiot in the forge room."

"We must run," Stephen said. "Like Douglas. Where is he? Perhaps we can all flee together."

George eyed the tall cider maker warily. "I don't know where he is, and even if I did, I'm not telling you so that you can offer him up for slaughter."

"But you're quite happy for us to have our throats cut," Jock growled.

George turned on the butcher. "Careful, mate. Don't come here bringing accusations and blame."

"If there is any blame to bring, it falls hard on you, George. Hard on you."

Jock Burgess was right. Douglas Partridge hadn't appeared in the dock for the murder of his wife because George had pleaded with the men to get the wives onside and keep it hushed up. Pleaded that Douglas wasn't a bad man, had simply made a mistake, a tragic mistake. It wasn't going to benefit no one to have him put away for murder, George had said. Yes, indeed, the master blacksmith had lobbied hard on the apprentice's behalf, and the men had agreed and forced the wives into a silent contract. The wives were coming for him, too. No doubting that.

George shrugged and sighed. "Take care of yourselves, lads."

"That's it?" Stephen whined. "Take care? What are you going to do about this, George?"

"Nothing I can do, Stephen. We all get what we deserve."

Stephen appeared on the edge of full-blown hysteria. "We're being lined up and knocked off like … like, God, I don't know. You have to do something, George."

"Find Douglas," Jock said. "Hand him over to those demons, or I'll find him and kill him myself."

George bristled and stood tall. He glowered at the butcher and, between clenched teeth, said, "Careful the next words that come out your mouth, Jock. Careful now."

The butcher backed away. "Come on, Stephen." Jock placed the cider on the floor and dragged the taller man from the room. "Enjoy the booze, son," Jock said.

And then the butcher and cider maker were gone.

Jeremy stopped at an intersection to make sure he was not being followed. It was dark, the streets quiet. Everybody that had a home was now firmly in it, behind locked doors, probably.

Jeremy scratched at his acned face. Master Burridge had told him not to scratch, even when it drove him mad. You'll only make it worse, the big, bearded blacksmith had warned.

But what man could resist scratching a persistent itch, especially when unobserved? Jeremy certainly couldn't. He worried away at the acne until he realised he had no idea where he was. Dysael was not Jeremy's hometown, which made Master Burridge's mission for him all the more difficult and confusing. Why not do this himself? But Jeremy hadn't asked. It never paid to question the boss.

For some reason, the master had insisted that Jeremy take no map with him. The apprentice had memorised the path sketched out for him, or at least he thought he had. Did he turn left or right here? Jeremy recognised the large building opposite him: a drapery by day, whorehouse by night. Master Burridge had specifically mentioned the whorehouse. Jeremy licked his lips and wondered just how far his first wage as a blacksmith's apprentice would take him. He had no interest in curtains; his proclivities lay with the night-time offerings, yes, of *those* he might partake.

How much would he earn? The master had grumbled something about quality of workmanship and its value in coin. Jeremy wasn't sure what that meant other than he would be paid what he was worth. In that case, he hoped the whores in Dysael were cheaper than those at home.

Left, yes, he remembered now. Left here. Halfway down the next street, Jeremy stopped and looked around. He slipped the bag off his shoulder, rummaged through it and removed the stoppered flagon of cider. He ran his fingers over the cork and began to pull at it. What man, after all, could resist scratching a persistent itch, especially when unobserved? With another surreptitious glance about himself, he took a slug of cider.

"Yarrgh, it's askew, boy! I'll give you a keel hauling!"

A previously unseen drunk lurched from the shadows, and Jeremy partially soiled himself. The drunk reached for the cider, but Jeremy slapped the man's hands away. The drunk stumbled, fell on his face and did not move.

"Christ's codger, you gave me a fright, you old bastard."

The drunk did not respond. Jeremy stopped up the cider flagon and swung a kick at the man's ribs. It connected solidly, but still, the old drunk lay motionless. "That'll learn you to jump from the shadows."

Jeremy scurried away, leaving the drunk unmoving and bruised.

❋

Douglas Partridge was not a murderer.

Douglas had seen murderers on the gallows: mean-faced, rough-looking fellows. Murder twinkled in their eyes like joy in the eyes of children when spying a new toy. But Douglas was not that type of man. He had never meant to murder Bessie. He hadn't even meant to hurt her. An accident, that was all. A freakish accident. He'd had too much of Stephen's cider, true, and he'd let the drink blur his better judgement. That was all. Blurred judgement.

Douglas shivered. It was cold in the farrier's loft. The furnace below had quietened for the evening, and the updraft of warmth no longer bathed him. He was grateful for the hay and the blanket, but he wished the farrier would replace the wooden slats in the loft so that the chill night breeze could not find him. Three nights now, three cold nights tucked away in a farrier's loft with only a bucket to piss in. He supposed he should be grateful that old Jackson had let him stay. The farrier hadn't been happy about it, but he owed George Burridge a favour, apparently, and his lodgings served as the reciprocation of that favour.

No hammer clanged on metal. It was dead quiet, the workshop below empty. When the knock on the door came, it seemed amplified by silence. Douglas sat up in fright. He peered through the cracks in the boards but could not make out who was standing in the darkness at the door. The knock came again, more impatient this time. Rap a tap tap. Douglas hesitated and then clambered down the ladder to the workshop floor. He approached the door and put his ear to it. The knocking had ceased.

"I've come with food," a voice said quietly on the other side.

CHAPTER 16 Douglas Partridge

"Master Burridge sends me to find you."

Douglas attempted to open the door before he realised it was locked and he didn't have the key. "Come to the window," he whispered. A pimpled face appeared a moment later. Douglas released the catch and opened the window. "Who are you?" Douglas asked.

"I'm Jeremy, the new apprentice. Who are you?"

New apprentice? Douglas suppressed a pang of envy and resentment. He supposed he could not blame George for replacing him so soon. "Never mind who I am. What news from Master Burridge?" Jeremy lifted the sack and squeezed it through the window. Douglas eagerly accepted the sack and opened it. Bread, dried fruit and something else. Douglas unstopped a ceramic jug and smelled it. Cider. He took a swig. There wasn't much left, but it was welcome. "What news?" Douglas asked again.

"Master Burridge says you're not to come out. He said ... he said you must beware the wives."

Douglas frowned. "Beware the wives? What does that mean?"

"I don't know. All he said was that they are returned and seek revenge, the wives, that is. He specifically told me to tell you about the wives. Also ..."

"Also what?"

"If you do not hear from him in another few days, you are to get out of Dysael at the first opportunity."

"Get out? Your message makes no sense. Where am I to go?"

"I don't know. He didn't say. I have delivered the food and message. It's cold out. I must get back."

Douglas Partridge peered from the window at the receding figure and tried to understand the message just given to him. The wives are returned and seek revenge? The missing women have reappeared? But they were dead and gone. No, not true. The only one he knew for certain was dead was his own wife. The others had simply vanished. Douglas did not like where this train of thought was taking him. He drank deep of the cider, locked the window and ascended once more to his cold bed. He finished the cider before he took his first bite of solid food. He had, however, lost his appetite.

He lay back on his straw mattress and stared at the gabled ceiling. What had Jeremy said at the last? "Get out of Dysael at the first opportunity." That was the plan, then.

Douglas had to flee Dysael.

CHAPTER 17

Afternoon Tea

Vincent E. Thackery stroked his damaged moustache and leaned forward to peer at the document on his desk. "Am I the first to see this?" he asked.

Coroner Stimpson sheepishly cleared his throat from the other side of the desk. "Sister Kempson was waiting outside my door the moment I finished writing it," he said.

Thackery slammed both fists on his desk. "Damn it, Peter! I'm the senior constable in charge of this case. All official documents, therefore, go through me first." Thackery brusquely removed a pair of reading spectacles from his desk drawer and placed them at the fine point of his nose. He waved at the only other chair in the room, and Coroner Stimpson sat. Thackery picked up the document and examined it for several minutes before finally removing his spectacles and holding the report up. "There's not much to this, Peter. Cause of death is indeterminate. That's a little wishy-washy for my liking."

Coroner Stimpson shrugged. "The condition of Bessie Partridge's body does not allow for certainty. She had a broken nose and pelvis, but I cannot tell you if they are pre or postmortem."

Thackery sighed and let the document fall to his desk.

The coroner shook his head in a gesture of amazement. "Incredible. Wives returning from the dead, or at least an extended absence, to murder their husbands. It's an unbelievable tale."

The constable furrowed his brows and stared icily at the coroner.

"It *is* an unbelievable tale but not one you've heard from me. The nun has been opening her mouth when it should be shut."

"I was able to glean some details from her, yes."

Thackery drummed his fingers on his desk. "That woman is going to create public unrest with her deliberate disregard for confidentiality."

"I'm the coroner, Vincent. I hardly think I qualify as a source of public unrest."

Thackery ignored him and glanced towards the large book under glass in the middle of the room. "This entire matter is a flagrant abuse of the constitution. The bishop and his idiotic minions will only hinder my investigation. People are already starting to ask questions about the nun's presence. It's unsettling, for *me* most of all." The constable leaned forward and picked up the report again. He didn't bother to replace his glasses but merely squinted at the paper. "According to this, the victim's maiden name was Wagner. Why is the name *Wagner* familiar to me?"

Stimpson puffed air from his cheeks. "Keira Jack possesses the same maiden name."

Sitting up in his chair, Thackery said, "Keira Jack? The ratcatcher's wife? These women are kin?"

The coroner nodded. "Sisters. Keira is the elder by four years. It's all in the report."

Thackery pursed his lips and flicked through the document again. After a moment, he stood and approached the large book containing the minutiae of Dysael law. "Do you know what that means?"

"No. What?"

"Motivation. The spur for a crime." Thackery nodded to himself. "Yes. The big sister seeks to avenge the little. We now have the who and the why, and perhaps the how and when of it."

The coroner came to stand beside the constable. "How do the other women and their husbands play into this? It was Douglas Partridge who did for Bessie, apparently. The other men have nothing to do with it."

Thackery shrugged. "Don't all women band together in their secrets and shame?"

Coroner Stimpson frowned. "We are speaking of murder, not sorority."

The constable turned away from the glass case and strode towards the door. Over his shoulder, he said, "In this case, it's turning out to be the same damn thing."

"What are you going to do with Sage Schuman?"

The constable didn't answer as he sped down the corridor.

Sergeant Terrence Frood wheeled a table into the cell occupied by Sage Schuman and, with a theatrical flourish, whipped a white cloth from it, revealing a series of vicious bladed implements. Smirking, the sergeant picked up a ludicrously curved and serrated knife.

Sage leaned as far away from the knife as her bonds would allow. "You touch me with that, and your name will be on the list," she spat.

Sergeant Frood used the bizarre blade to point at the red garotte marks around his throat. He croaked, "Was I on the list when you tried to kill me the last time? Seems a man don't have to do much to get on it, least where you witches are concerned. If I'm already on, what do I care?"

Sage shook her head. "I never hurt you. That weren't me. I got nothing against you."

Frood tut tutted. "One of you tried to kill me. I don't care which one. You're all in it together. Where are the others? How many of you lurk out there in the shadows? And how did you get your freakish powers?"

"I ain't talking. Done enough talking."

Frood didn't quite understand that last part. The woman had said bugger all during her incarceration. Hadn't done anything that could vaguely be called talking. She would talk though, very soon now. The boss hadn't let Frood off the leash yet, but it was only a matter of time before the implements of torture came into play.

Constable Thackery bustled into the room and headed with swift footfall towards the cell containing Frood and Sage.

"You might want to cover that up," Thackery said, pointing at the table.

Frood heard voices coming from the hallway outside and recognised at least one of them: the fat nun, back again. The scrawny sergeant quickly covered the table just before Sister Kempson swept into the room, accompanied, as ever, by her big bodyguard. Frood snarled under his breath. The two were relentless. Just when he thought they'd gone ...

"What is that?" Kempson said, gesturing to the table with the white cloth on it.

"Afternoon tea," Thackery said. "Would you like some?"

"I'm no fool, Constable. I don't need to see under that to know what you're thinking. Confession under duress is no longer allowed by law."

"As you have so succinctly pointed out in the past, madam, there is more than one type of law."

Sister Kempson folded her arms. "Unacceptable. I insist on speaking to the woman."

Thackery shook his head. "That witch is likely to murder you if you get too close. For your own protection, I must once again deny your request."

The nun held up a rolled parchment that Frood could have sworn did not exist a moment before. "If you insist that I run around getting documentation for my every action, Constable, I will continue to do so." Thackery sighed and stepped aside. "You don't wish to read the document?"

"I'm sure it's in order," Thackery said, waving the nun into the cell. "You seem the punctilious type."

"I wish to interview the woman alone."

Thackery pointed at Garth in surprise. "Without him?"

"That is correct."

Thackery turned his mouth down. "Alright, then. At your personal risk. I take no responsibility for whatever befalls you."

CHAPTER 17 Afternoon Tea

Garth was obviously discomforted by the nun's decision, which pleased Sergeant Frood. The night watchman wished for more than just discomfort to befall the big man. He still owed the bastard for the broken nose, and he owed one of those harpies for his sliced-up throat. And he owed another one of them for setting the cat on his face. He owed a lot of people for a lot of pain, and somebody was going to pay soon. If the fat nun didn't get any answers, it would be his turn, and he had no intention of holding back because the subject was a woman. No intention at all.

"Everyone out," Thackery said.

"God is forgiveness, Sage."

Sage Schuman looked up. Black hair fell in waves over tired brown eyes in a pale face. "Pardon, Sister?"

"God is forgiveness," Sister Kempson repeated.

Sage nodded slowly. "Is he? That's nice of God. Very decent of him. Perhaps his forgiveness extends to loosening these ropes about my wrists. They pain me."

"I'm sorry, Sage. I can't do that." Sister Kempson glanced towards the door and lowered her voice. "I know about Bessie Partridge. I understand the terrible distress that must have caused."

The prisoner's big brown eyes cleared and narrowed. "*Distress?* Pretty word, totally inadequate. Say agony and rage and you're getting closer. Bessie was a good friend to us all."

"But God forgives."

"You keep saying that. Means nothing to me."

"Why do you want to hurt your husband? Because Douglas murdered Bessie? That seems … an excessive and misplaced attempt at justice. I also know that Bessie was sister to Keira Jack, and her death must have affected Keira more deeply than the others. A terrible crime, but God forgives."

Sage smiled wanly. "Forgiveness is a currency that not all can afford. Some people's hearts are just a little more frugal than those of others."

"But forgiveness is the only currency that matters. And God has enough for everyone. God forgives, you see."

Sage suddenly thrust herself at Sister Kempson and snapped, "Keira Jack don't!" The nun jerked backwards and nearly fell off her chair. Sage raised her head high. "Keira Jack don't forgive, and nor do the rest of us, not anymore. Enough. Enough with telling lies, keeping secrets for them. No more cleaning up after those useless bastards."

Sister Kempson composed herself and settled back on her chair. "You speak of your men."

"Not *our* men, and we are not their women. Free now, all of us."

"Murder is not the answer. You must not seek vengeance or take the law into your own hands. With His grace, all this murder and death shall come to an end."

Sage stared unblinking into the nun's eyes. "There you go, babbling on about God again. I am accused of witchcraft. Tell me, will God come down from on high and forgive me for that? Am I to be set free if I confess and give the others up?"

Sister Kempson did not respond.

"Didn't think so," Sage spat. A slow smile crept across the prisoner's face. "Would you like to know a secret about God? I've got a good one."

Sister Kempson frowned. This woman, an attempted murderer, could teach her little about God, but then again, everyone knew Him in different ways. "Very well."

"Come closer," Sage whispered. "This is only for the ears of another woman. Come nearer."

Sister Kempson had not forgotten Thackery's warning. "No."

Sage feigned a disappointed expression. "You hurt me, Sister. Thought we were mates."

"What do you wish to say, Sage?"

"Only this." Sage smiled wider. "God don't have a cock and balls. God bleeds once a month and has a fucking vile temper. Come join us."

CHAPTER 17 Afternoon Tea

Sister Kempson felt something flutter in her chest. "Join you? In murdering innocent men? I cannot do that."

"Innocent, my moist fanny. You listen to me. You'll need us one day, Sister. You live in a man's world, and it's only a matter of time until one of them takes something from you. Or everything. They'll take your body, take your pride and your freedom as a matter of course. Then they'll break your mind. The bishop, the king, the coppers or just some drunken bastard climbing in your window one night. Only a matter of time. They'll take you at their leisure and pleasure. You are powerless. Come with us and things will be different. Come with us, and you will have the power to defend yourself. And more."

"I don't want power."

Sage bared her teeth. "That's only 'cos you've never had it. Once you do, you'll see."

"Come now, Sage. There's still time to save your soul and those of the others. Tell us where they are. Forego the evil in your hearts. Repent."

"Fuck that. I like how I am. I won't go back."

Sister Kempson sighed. "I can't help you if you don't help me."

"I'm not asking for your help, but you're too blind to see that you need ours."

The door to the holding cells opened, and Thackery, Frood and Garth jostled for entry.

"Unless you have significant information," Thackery said, popping through the doorway like a squeezed pimple, "it's our turn to interview the prisoner." Sergeant Frood smirked behind the constable.

"They'll come for you too, Sister," Sage whispered, "just as soon as you show signs of true rebellion. You wait and see."

"No torture," Sister Kempson said to Thackery.

The moustachioed lawman gestured to the table with the white cloth. "Don't worry. Frood's absolutely shit tea makes torture unnecessary. Now, get out."

❈

Peering from a window, Sergeant Terence Frood tracked the fat nun and her big ginger companion down the street. When he was sure that they had gone, *truly* gone, he removed the white cloth from the implements of torture.

He leered at Sage as he picked up an object resembling a pair of scissors with pincer-like blades. "Time for tea, bitch."

Frood had no idea just how the odd-looking implement should be deployed. He was an amateur torturer, at best, but he did have a knack for obtaining confessions from even the hardest men. He would just have to use his imagination.

He held the scissors under Sage's nose. "Right. My turn. We have followed due course of law but to no avail. This is what your stubbornness has brought you. Don't say we weren't fair. Gave you a chance to talk to us and the nun, but you hocked our kindness back in our faces."

"Bring her back in," Sage said. "I'll talk. Changed my mind."

Frood smiled. "You can't delay this any longer." He scratched his rough beard and said, "I've never done a woman before."

"That's cos you're fuckin' ugly."

Frood tried to clamp the scissors on Sage's nose, but she twisted her head away. The sergeant put the scissors down and picked up the torture cap, a device designed to keep the victim's head stationary. Sage struggled, her hands still bound tightly behind her back, but she could not stop Frood from slipping the cap over her head. He attached two leather straps to buckles embedded in the cell wall and tightened them. Her forehead and chin were strapped, and her head held fast.

"Seems a shame to ruin such a pretty face," Frood said, staring down at her. "You could have done better than become a dripping man's wife, a fucking lard collector's bit of snatch."

"I agree with you, Sergeant," Sage said through clamped jaws. "But I didn't know then, did I? I would have done better if I'd known the power I had."

"Power? What power?"

"The power of my cunt. How about you and I have a bit of fun? I'll give you such a knee trembler as you've never 'ad."

Frood frowned, pursed his lips and looked around. "Eh? In here?"

"Anywhere you like, lambkin. I like a bit of rough, and if I'm doomed, I'll have a last shag before I'm done. Providing you'll have me."

Frood thought about it, his lust beginning to rise. Then, he shook his head. "I'm not an idiot. You'll probably vice-grip my old boy and try to escape. No, no, we want answers." He held up the odd pair of scissors. "Me and him, we want answers."

CHAPTER 18

Burning Down the House of Law

"They're torturing her. I know it." Sister Kempson sat, scowling, propped at the end of a bar like a sailor looking for a fight.

Garth nodded and watched the bride of Christ drinking a flat ale. "Most likely," he said. "Nothing you can do about it. Had your turn, and she didn't talk."

"Torture is an illegal means of obtaining a confession. The church does not condone such practices. The world has progressed. Society has moved on."

Garth snorted. "Society? Sage Schuman is to be hanged as a witch. Your precious church won't do a thing about that. Civilisation is a lot less civil than it pretends to be. The bishop and Thackery are just two sides of the same demented coin if you ask me."

"Do you hate everyone, Garth? You make out as if you'd be happy spending the rest of your days in the wilderness, but I wonder if that is the truth. Surely, even *you* have a reason for being, a cause that inspires you to go on, to get out of bed every morning."

The big man shrugged. "I have no cause and mistrust those who do."

Sister Kempson nearly coughed up her ale. "Which is virtually the entire populace. Your attitude makes little sense. You can't believe in nothing."

"You don't sit where I sit."

"Without a cause, what are we? Meaningless vessels of earthly desire and empty gratification."

Garth gave a slight shake of his head. "I do not wish to discuss this."

Sister Kempson took another mouthful of ale. She seemed to be almost bristling with aggression, an odd aura to get from a nun. "What are you hiding behind that austere countenance, Garth?"

"Nothing. Stop picking. You're getting drunk and argumentative."

Sister Kempson sat up stiffly on her stool. "I'm a nun. I don't think I *am* drunk or argumentative."

"If you say so."

"Alright, I'm a little drunk. But I'm not argumentative. I'm … I'm …"

"You're frustrated," Garth offered.

"I'm useless. I have failed utterly here, achieved nothing." The nun's bottom lip protruded in an oddly childish gesture of unhappiness.

"Don't be so hard on yourself," Garth said. "We know that the wives were not abducted. We know they have it in for their husbands, and we know why. That's progress, and much of it down to you."

Sister Kempson shook her head. "I am the architect of none of these developments. Thackery apprehended Sage and saved a man's life in the process."

"He got Sage because you told him where to look. Without you, Thackery would still have his head up his own arse, blinded to any other reality than what his insides look like."

The nun brightened somewhat. "He is a dislikeable man, isn't he? He struts around like a preening peacock, the law his feathers." She paused. "We must return."

"Return where?"

"To the Law Courts. We must insist that Sage Schuman receive a fair trial and that she is not subjected to torture."

Garth sighed heavily. "Just finish your drink. Nothing you can do about it. Anyway, they won't let you back in."

Sister Kempson pushed herself unsteadily to her feet and headed for the door. "We'll see about that."

"You'll get yourself locked up."

"They wouldn't dare arrest a nun."

Garth wasn't so sure. Arresting a nun seemed just like the kind of thing Thackery would do, with malicious pleasure.

※

The Law Courts, home for the Night Watch and the Consul of Dysael Barristers, was a large three-story structure that could be accessed via a courtyard off Hamilton Avenue. The main entrance within the small courtyard was manned twenty-four hours a day, and on this occasion, the guard happened to be Private Henry Joad of the Night Watch.

Henry had just turned twenty-one and aspired to be a barrister, but as was the case for all practitioners of the law in Dysael, an indentureship of three years in the Night Watch preceded any advancement into jurisprudence.

Today marked one year of service. Henry sighed. Two years to go. He was still a private assigned to the most mundane of duties, standing idly at the entrance to the Law Courts being foremost among them. The two years remaining on his apprenticeship seemed like an eternity. Nothing interesting ever happened on duty. No malefactor would dare attempt to gain ingress to the Law Courts, would, in fact, pay good money to stay out of the place. Who in their right mind would attempt to storm a building containing anywhere as many as fifty officers on duty at a given time?

Three women approached the private. They wore long cloaks against the sharpening winds. The tallest of the three removed her hood. She had long dark hair and deep green eyes. "Good sir," she said, "I am busting for a pee. May I use the privy?"

"Sorry, miss, only staff allowed inside. There's a public toilet further on down the street."

The second woman withdrew her hood to reveal an olive complexion. She put her fingers to her temple. She stared at Henry, and he felt an uncomfortable warmth flush the skin of his forehead.

"I would also like to relieve myself," the second woman said. "You be a gentleman and show us the way."

Henry blinked several times. He supposed there would be no harm in allowing the ladies inside. They were not criminals. Yet … what had Constable Thackery said about women? Something in the way of a warning. But not *these* women. No, Henry was quite sure that the constable's warning did not extend to these women.

"Of course, ladies," he said. "Follow me."

Keira Jack, Elsie Gallagher and Samantha Burgess followed the young soldier inside. The sight of a guard leading three cloaked and hooded women through the narrow hallways of the Law Courts attracted stares from other men, but Private Henry Joad seemed to have the situation under control and so his fellow officers did not intervene, which was just as well because Elsie could only control the mind of one man at a time.

At a quiet point in the corridor, Elsie whispered, "Take us to Sage Schuman."

"But I thought you wanted to use the privy."

"No, we want to visit Sage Schuman, remember?"

"Oh yes. I remember. Upstairs, come this way." The young private frowned and looked up and down the hallway. "Wait a moment. Where is the other one?"

"The other what?" Elsie asked.

"There were three of you just now. I see only two. Where's the other one?"

"You are mistaken. We are but two," Elsie said, gesturing slowly to herself and Keira. "Only two, remember?"

Henry blinked and rubbed at his temple. "Yes, sorry. Of course. This way." The young private did not notice the crumpled cloak lying on the floor as he led them towards the stairwell.

At the top of a flight of stairs, the group bumped into Sergeant Robert Jones. The squat man frowned at the guard and his small entourage. "Private Joad, what is happening here? Why are you not standing guard at the entrance?"

"Guests to see the prisoner," Henry said.

Jones' scowl deepened. "No one is allowed in there without—" The scowl relaxed, along with the man's body, as he slumped to the floor. Samantha Burgess became visible in all her nude glory, standing over the unconscious Jones with a blackjack in her hand.

Keira put her hands on her hips. "Yes, yes, we all like your tits, Sam, but get you disappeared, quick. We ain't done here."

Samantha Burgess vanished once more. Private Henry Joad seemed unconcerned at the assault on his senior officer or the sudden appearance of a naked female wanted for conspiracy to murder.

"What do we do with him?" Elsie said, pointing at the unconscious Jones, a bloodied welt appearing on the back of the man's head.

Keira scanned the hallway. "Nowhere to hide the body. Leave him. We won't have but a minute before someone finds him. Move, girls."

Garth hurried after Sister Kempson, but the woman's righteous anger, no doubt fuelled by the booze, gave an extra spring to her stride. The Law Courts were two blocks from the pub, and Garth stayed close to the nun lest she should stumble and fall on the hard cobblestones. Sister Kempson was not in the best state of mind. Garth had never seen her so determined, but that wasn't going to sit well with Thackery. He hoped the nun wouldn't do anything stupid and make his job all the more difficult.

The sky was roiling grey, and a chill wind whipped at clothes and hair. People scurried this way and that to avoid the sudden change in the weather, to get home before the inevitable downpour arrived. Sister Kempson and Garth approached the Law Courts and entered the ground floor unobstructed. Garth looked around. Should be a man stationed at the entrance. Perhaps he'd gone for a piss. Once again, the nun outpaced him in her eagerness to confront Thackery.

CHAPTER 18 Burning Down the House of Law

An exclamation came from above, and Garth leapt up the stairs to find Sister Kempson standing motionless at the beginning of a hallway, at her feet the figure of a man lying prone on the floor. Garth froze.

"Why is that man sleeping in such an odd place?" Sister Kempson asked.

Garth recognised the unmoving form of Sergeant Jones. He knelt and checked the man's pulse. Still alive. Garth stood and grabbed Sister Kempson by the shoulder. "I'm getting you out of here. This is a mistake. Time to go."

"No, Garth. I have a mission here, a purpose and I will see it through."

Shouts in the distance, a battle taking place in the narrow confines of the holding cells. Garth's instincts told him to run, to get the nun out, but she brushed him aside and hurried down the corridor.

Constable Thackery appeared from the floor above and collided with Sister Kempson. "What's going on?" he said.

Thackery, Kempson and Garth rushed into the holding cells. Several men lay scattered about the floor. Sage Schuman was free of her bonds and walking towards them, her face bruised and blood dripping from her nose. At her side were two other women. Strangely, Sergeant Frood led the way, his rapier swinging from side to side as if he were carving a path in the air for the three women to walk through.

Thackery withdrew his own rapier and shouted at his man. "Frood, what are you doing? Do not allow them to escape!" The scrawny man's eyes were glazed over. Garth had seen the look before in the eyes of people influenced by a travelling mesmerist: a dreamlike state in which the participant forgets everything and becomes a puppet for their master.

Frood poked at Thackery with his rapier, but the constable easily sidestepped the strike. "Frood, don't make me hurt you."

"Get out of our way," Keira Jack snarled. "Just step back and allow us to pass."

"Wait, wait, there is no need for violence," Sister Kempson said.

All eyes turned to the nun, and Garth took the opportunity to step forward and punch Frood in the face, knocking out several teeth and sending him senseless to the floor.

The nun looked at Garth in disbelief. "Garth, what are you doing?"

Keira smirked. "No violence? I don't think your man is listening, Sister Kempson. They rarely do, in my experience." A siren sounded from somewhere close by. Keira cursed and pointed at Garth. "Do him."

Elsie put her fingers to her temple, and Garth felt something crawling around at the front of his head. He was about to step forward to interrupt the mental assault when Sage Schuman did something with her hands, waving them over each other. Two glowing orbs of red and pink swirling flame appeared above her palms. The three women seemed unaffected by the heat, but Garth, Sister Kempson and Thackery had to step backwards.

Elsie took her fingers from her temple, the tendrils of thought withdrawing from Garth's mind. "Can't reach him," she said.

"We don't have time for this, "Keira said. She turned to Sage. "Light this place up."

Sage Schuman raised her hands, and the glowing orbs shot up and splintered, setting fire to the ceiling.

A young soldier burst into the holding cells. He raised a musket, and Garth pulled Sister Kempson out of the firing line. Elsie put her fingers to her head to invade the man's mind, but it was too late. The soldier fired the musket with a loud bang. The musket ball flew harmlessly over Keira's head, the muzzle having jerked skywards a split second before the shot was fired. The soldier looked at his weapon in confusion only to find it leaping out of his hands and the butt end swinging viciously into his face. He fell to the floor unconscious. Garth's jaw dropped, but he closed it a moment later when something brushed against his arm: there was an invisible assailant somewhere in the room, as impossible as that seemed. Thackery must have understood the same thing, for he shouted a warning to the men rushing into the holding cells as the fire began to spread along the ceiling and walls, but the men only looked at the floating musket in confusion and fear.

The musket swung towards Thackery, but he ducked. Sister Kempson took the blow to the side of the head and cried out in pain as she fell. A switch flicked in Garth's head. He had one job: protect the nun. One duty, no complications.

Garth lashed out, and his fist hit something soft and fleshy. The invisible figure went down, unconscious, her naked body now visible over the sprawled body of Sergeant Frood, the two appearing a battered husband and a bloodied wife resting in the aftermath of violent sex.

Keira's eyes turned to Garth, and she shrieked. "You big ginger bastard! You fucking hair of Judas! I'll kill you for that!"

Garth stood over the dazed Sister Kempson in a protective stance and pulled out his hunting knife. Thackery was shouting something about the witches giving themselves up, but these women weren't going to give up anything.

Garth growled, "Leave the nun be. I have no quarrel with you." The flames continued to spread along the ceiling.

"Then get out of our way," Keira spat.

"I'm not stopping you."

Thackery shouted, "You will not let these women walk out of here!" He grabbed a blunderbuss from a man standing nearby and pointed it at Keira. "Garth, you will assist me in the arrest of these women!"

"I'm tired of people shouting at me," Garth said, helping a dazed Sister Kempson to her feet. "This is between you and the ladies." Timber began to creak, threatening to collapse, the heat intensifying until it stung at eyes and throats, the very air on fire. Garth hauled Sister Kempson outside, shoving aside several members of the Night Watch as he did so.

As he was helping the nun downstairs, he heard the deep boom of the blunderbuss.

❈

Things were not looking good for Keira Jack and her girls.

Samantha had been knocked out cold. Elsie, her powers almost exhausted, was unable to control the prick Thackery, who had a blunderbuss pointed at Keira's chest. Add to that, the building was coming down around them in flames. The men of the Night Watch had backed out of the door, the heat driving them away, but Thackery just stood there, a grimace on his face. Why didn't he run? The heat began to penetrate Sage's protective bubble, and Keira was now struggling to breathe. It had to be Hell on earth for the constable. Why didn't he run?

Probably because the bastard was mad. That's why.

"This is a house of Law!" Thackery shrieked. "You come in here bold as brass, under my very nose and think you can get away with it?"

The air shimmered with heat. If they didn't get out now, they would all die. Not even Sage could protect them from the flames. Keira leapt forward, and Thackery, the last man left in the holding cells, fired the blunderbuss.

Elsie screamed and Keira whirled around. Sage was lying on the floor, a smoking hole in her chest. Sage's protective bubble dissipated, and the true power of the flames struck them. Keira pulled Elsie down to the cooler air. To stand now would mean death. Thackery was gone, the heat overcoming even his rage.

Keira fumbled at Sage's throat. There was no pulse, but Keira wasn't about to give up. Helen could reach her if they could just get Sage out in time. Keira pointed to the unconscious form of Samantha. "Wake Sam up. Get in there and wake her up."

Elsie put her fingers to her temple, but nothing happened. "I'm exhausted," she said. "I don't have the power to reach her."

"Reach her or we're all dead."

Elsie squeezed her eyes shut and trembled with effort. A moment later, Samantha stirred and opened her eyes. That was good. The flames had immersed the exit. That was bad. Staying low, Keira dragged the unresponsive Sage to the barred window, which was yet free of flames. Elsie and Samantha crawled along the floor right behind her. Keira Jack reached up and wrenched the bars from their concrete foundations. She stared at her own hands in amazement.

"How'd you do that?" Elsie whispered.

"How are we doing any of this? Can you reach Sage?"

Elsie shook her head. "She's too far gone. To wake her would mean death, even if I could. Only Helen can help her now."

Keira cursed. "Come on, jump. No time left."

They leapt to the street below, where a crowd had gathered to witness the blaze engulfing the Law Courts. The crowd gasped at the sight of several women, one of them naked, falling from the window. Elsie and Samantha broke ankles, and Keira shattered her hip and several ribs in clasping Sage to her and trying to cushion her fall. The ankles, hip and ribs would heal, but they could not run with an unresponsive Sage. The men would be upon them in mere moments.

"Look," Sam pointed. Several armed soldiers were pushing their way through the crowd towards them.

Keira touched Sage's throat once more. Cold. But not dead. Whatever powers they all shared protected Sage yet. But Keira wasn't willing to risk the other girls, not any further than she already had. It pained her, but there was no other choice.

"I'm sorry. We must leave her," Keira said. "Run."

Samantha closed her eyes and vanished. She assisted Elsie to her feet, and the two women stumbled, supporting each other, into the crowd, only one of them visible and the other very cold.

Keira cast one last glance back at the burning Law Courts and snarled. They'd failed Sage despite their best efforts, but this wasn't over. Thackery and the big red-headed one, what had the nun called him? Garth. Yes, Garth. Those two bastards were now officially on the list.

Keira kissed Sage's forehead and, ignoring the pain of her shattered hip, ran.

CHAPTER 19

Harlots and Haberdashery

The Law Courts no longer smouldered and smoked. The building had collapsed in on itself and pooled in ashen sludge as the rains intensified.

Vincent E. Thackery had every right to be sullen as he gazed upon the wreck of the former centre of moral and legal virtue in Dysael, North Quarter. The fact that he was viewing the destroyed Law Courts from the second-floor window of a nearby drapery cum whorehouse, now commandeered as a makeshift centre of operations for the Night Watch, only added to his outrage. He wasn't the only one in a foul mood. The working girls had complained about being kicked out until Thackery had promised them limited use of the upper floors in the late hours of the day, but for now, his men needed a place to conduct business. He tried to ignore as best he could the squeaking of beds and occasional grunts in the late evening hours coming from the upstairs floor.

He'd had to reprimand Frood and Jones several times as the two men attempted to barter for sexual favours from the harlots as they lounged about in their off hours. Idiots. Both were lucky to be alive as Thackery had singlehandedly dragged the unconscious men from the blazing building. He had, tragically, been unable to return in time to save the Thackery Book of Law. It hurt to know it had gone up in flames. Yet he carried that Law within him; he was the living *embodiment* of that Law, and this gave him some

CHAPTER 19 Harlots and Haberdashery

consolation. Still, he suspected Frood and Jones did not appreciate the sacrifice he had made.

And to add to everything, he had been forced into yet another tiresome meeting with the nun.

"You cannot hang Sage Schuman," Sister Kempson said. The nun's fat backside was deep in a depression in an old divan in the middle of a circular, draughty entrance hall. Drapes lay rolled in pigeonholes around the walls, and items of haberdashery scattered the floor, but no one was purchasing curtains today, not with the place full of angry soldiers and disgruntled lawyers. The divan upon which the nun sat had lost some of its stuffing, probably because it had seen a good deal of humping over the years, and though it had ample room for another to sit upon, even one as large as Garth, the bodyguard preferred to stand at one end of the once luxuriant couch.

"You're quite right," Thackery sniffed. "There will be no hanging. We intend to burn her as befitting a witch."

Sister Kempson shook her head vigorously. "You can't do that, either."

Constable Thackery pinched the bridge of his nose with his thumb and forefinger and closed his eyes. "Why the fu …" He sighed, calmed himself with great effort. "Why not?" Thackery sat at a makeshift desk, a thin and cracked bench that had probably seen as much fucking as the divan.

"Because she is barely alive. She hangs to life by the slimmest of threads."

Thackery threw his arms wide. "Which only attests to the aberrant and abhorrent nature of the woman. She should be dead! I shot her in the chest with a fully loaded blunderbuss. Whatever supernatural powers these women possess, it seems that an unwillingness to die is among them." The nun had her hands on her knees, a normally demure position for a lady, yet this woman was anything but demure: she was a stubborn, argumentative pain in Thackery's arse.

"It is sadistic to condemn a woman to death while she lays in a coma," Sister Kempson said.

Thackery stared in exasperation. "Then what do you suggest?"

"That she be allowed to recover."

Thackery threw an ironic smile at the nun. "You accuse me of brutality, and yet you recommend a slow and painful recuperation before an execution. That is macabre and, if I may say so, unnecessarily cruel, even for me. Mrs. Schuman is scheduled to be burned at the stake tomorrow morning, and it will be so. There can be no dispute."

"The bishop has not yet signed off on the deed."

Thackery slapped the desk with both hands. "Hah! He doesn't have to. He would not wish to be seen protecting this woman or any of the others who are responsible for *literally* burning down the Law and murdering men in the streets. The people want justice, and they shall get it. We can't let these women run loose. Sage Schuman's guilt is beyond question. Even you, madam, cannot argue otherwise."

Sister Kempson tried to stand, but the divan provided no solid foundation from which to launch herself. She flailed about for an embarrassing few moments before Garth reached down and pulled her to her feet. She put her hands behind her back and began to pace the floor. "We must seek to understand them. To make enemies of these women would be dangerous."

Thackery folded his arms. "Too late for that. I won't negotiate with murderous witches."

"Can you stop calling them witches? Besides, they are not all confirmed to have killed men."

"Poppycock. Those who haven't yet slaughtered their husbands are no doubt planning to do so. From the descriptions provided to us, we know that Keira Jack and Elsie Gallagher were at the Law Courts. A third woman was with them but was invisible. *Invisible*, mind you. Only God knows whose wife that was. When Sage Schuman is dead, Keira Jack will be hunted down and sent to Hades, the others swiftly to follow. This is war."

Sister Kempson stopped pacing and spoke quietly. Thackery had to lean forward to hear what she was saying. "I believe there is something more going on here than just murder."

Thackery frowned, sat back and snorted. "*Just* murder? You trivialise the crime."

Sister Kempson seemed as if she were about to sit on the divan once more but thought better of it. "That's not what I mean. Where did these women get their powers?"

"The Devil for all I care."

"I think we are missing the wider view."

"What wider view? What are you getting at?"

"Clearly, something has affected these women."

Thackery clasped his fingers together on the desk. "I'm not disagreeing with you. You are suggesting a disease of the mind, perhaps?"

"I'm not sure. But this may not end with these women."

The constable shook his head at the foolishness of the suggestion. "Is there something in the water? Is that it? Is every man in Dysael to suspect his wife? To sleep with a knife under his pillow in fear that she is waiting for the chance to murder him? That's nonsense. Insanity. How can society function if a man and a woman cannot trust each other? We can't. There *is* no society. What you are speaking of is nothing short of the end of civilisation as we know it, at least in Dysael. I maintain that this is simply an isolated incident. Alright, several isolated incidents, but it is not an epidemic of betrayal and spousal murder. This will end with the deaths of Keira Jack and the others."

Sister Kempson paced again. "You have countered me at every turn, constantly thrown my ideas back in my face, and yet I have been proved right on many occasions. I tell you now that until we understand what has happened to these women, killing them may not be the end of it. Sage Schuman is an opportunity to learn, to understand. If we study her, we may prevent the likes of her from happening again."

Thackery got to his feet. "No. She's too dangerous." He waved a hand towards the ruined Law Courts across the street. "We've all seen that."

"Then I insist she has a fair trial."

"She's had her trial."

"What? When?"

"Last night. Evidence was presented from both sides."

"But she was in a coma."

"She had legal representation provided by the state, at the state's expense, I might add."

"Why was I not informed of this?"

"You were not part of proceedings."

The nun's face reddened in outrage. "This is nonsense. You make a mockery of the law you so proudly represent."

"That's enough of that. I'll not have you come in here and tell me how to conduct—"

A knock at the door interrupted the constable's flow. Sergeant Frood entered the room, his ruined face now missing two front teeth courtesy of Garth's fist. As a result, he spoke with a newly formed lisp. "Sage Schuman is awake." Frood cast a venomous glance at Garth, who simply winked back.

Thackery nodded. "That settles the matter. Her burning takes place tomorrow morning as scheduled. Let's hope a flaming pyre can achieve what a blunderbuss could not."

CHAPTER 20

Hounds and Harpies

The burning of a witch pleased people in different ways. Some came to witness the law in action and to feel safer because they themselves abided by the word of God and would never suffer the same fate. It gave them a warm, secure feeling. Others came for the simple entertainment of it. These were the ones that cheered and nibbled sweetmeat even when they did not know who was being burned or why. Some came because they wanted to see someone, anyone, suffer. To them, the action was a cosmic redressing of the balance, a salve to their own wounds and disappointments.

No one ever came to wish goodbye to a friend or lover. Those people, generally, stayed away or said their goodbyes in the wings.

Yohan Schuman was conflicted. He had loved his wife, as far as love went. But in the moment that his wife had attempted to murder him, to turn him into nothing but human dripping and dead man's lard, well, feelings of love could change to something else, couldn't they?

The wind chilled Yohan, despite the thronging crowd about him and the long woollen cap over his face and ears, which he wore partly to disguise his identity. He had come to witness the execution of his own wife, and he simply did not know how he felt about it. Relief, probably, was the overwhelming sensation, if he were to be honest. Relief that the coppers had intercepted Sage before she could murder him. Relief that she wouldn't have the chance to finish the job.

In a show of comradeship, Jock Burgess and Stephen Cox stood with Yohan among the gathered townsfolk. Jock patted him on the arm, and though the butcher was a gruff man, he spoke with some sympathy.

"This has to be done," Jock said. "She tried to kill you, and if it is established that Stephen's wife and mine seek our deaths, that they are infected by Satan, then they must be burned too."

Stephen Cox put his arm around the dripping man's shoulder. "We're with you, Yohan. All in this together."

It was a show of solidarity from the butcher and the cider maker that made Yohan feel better, until he realised that it had been a show of solidarity that had got them all into this situation in the first place.

"We should have let Douglas hang," Yohan whispered. "Instead, it's come to this." Neither Jock nor Stephen answered him, and the crowd continued to jostle the three of them, seeking a better position from which to witness the death of the witch, oblivious to the presence of the accused woman's husband among them.

Yohan didn't want to stand too close to the pyre, didn't want Sage to see him or give him an accusatory stare as they set her on flames, but the crowd surged in eddies, and the three men were pushed forwards. Looking around, Yohan could no longer see Jock's bodyguards in the mass of people.

Sage Schuman appeared in a filthy white gown, her hands tied behind her back and two burly officers on either side of her small and fragile form. She stumbled along an elevated walkway, hunched over as if in great pain. Her hair had been shaved, and the sight of it struck Yohan a blow. She looked so different. The nun, Sister Kempson, walked behind her to the platform containing the unlit pyre and a half dozen night watchmen standing at attention. The kindling of the pyre shifted this way and that in the chill breeze as Sage approached. The cleric conducting the execution wore a black kerchief over his mouth and nose, hiding his identity to prevent any chance of retribution. Yohan didn't think anybody was likely to seek revenge on the cleric, not when the charges were read out and they included burning down the Law Courts, attempted murder and suspicion of consorting with the Devil. No, indeed, the only person here today with the remotest reason for calling a halt to proceedings was Yohan Schuman, and he wasn't about to utter a word.

After the charges had been called out, the condemned was given the opportunity for last words, as allowed by Dysael law, but not before the flaming torch that would set the pyre ablaze had been lit.

The crowd stilled as the small woman raised her head, the flaming torch held high behind her. Her face was bruised, and Yohan felt a pang of something. Guilt? Sympathy? He couldn't place it. Sage looked to Sister Kempson and the fat nun leaned in to receive the whispered words.

The nun appeared embarrassed as she approached the edge of the platform and cleared her throat. The crowd stilled. "I speak on behalf of Sage Schuman, who is unwell and has asked me to do so." Yohan wondered why the nun would risk her reputation in assisting Sage. He certainly wasn't prepared to do so. Sister Kempson cleared her throat again and said, "Ahem, Sage Schuman would like to say that … she is requesting a … spiritual divorce."

Some in the crowd laughed, and Yohan frowned. That didn't seem right. No matter what had happened, she was still his wife. The nun didn't have the powers to grant that, did she?

Sage said something else, and Sister Kempson leaned in once more. The nun shook her head, apparently unwilling to announce Sage's next utterance. Sage scowled in anger. Yohan glanced at Jock and Stephen, the two men waiting, along with everyone else, for Sage Schuman to utter her last words through the nun.

Suddenly, Sage Schuman shouldered the nun aside and stepped forward to the edge of the platform. Two burly guards moved in so that she could not bolt for freedom by leaping off the edge. But Sage did not attempt to escape. She stopped, took a breath and spoke, her voice surprisingly strong and resonant.

"You've all thought about stabbing the bastard," Sage said. "Rolled the thought round your minds. Come on now." She looked out over the gathered throng and smirked. "Not one of you ain't contemplated setting him on fire while he lay drunk and a-snoring, don't deny it, ladies." A murmuring broke out among the men in the crowd; the women were quiet, and several shared surreptitious glances with others of their gender. Sage smiled more broadly. "Well, I have a revelation for you all. God won't mind one little bit. Go ahead and get yourselves free. Tonight."

The hangman made a throat-slitting gesture, and the two guards stepped forward to cut Sage off before she could sew further discontent among husbands and wives. Sister Kempson shook her head sadly and walked away. Sage Schuman was tied to the pyre, and the men doing so did not perform the task gently.

Yohan's stomach turned upside down. Sage had just urged the womenfolk of Dysael to murder their husbands as they slept. It was true, then. Sage was gone. The Sage he knew was dead already, the burning about to take place irrelevant.

The cleric said a few words and set the flaming torch to the kindling. Flames began to lick at the feet of Sage Schuman in a hungry crackle.

Jock Burgess waited for the screams of agony, but they did not come. Even when her body became embalmed in shimmering flame, Sage Schuman uttered not a sound. The crowd hushed, a collective entity listening for the death shriek of the witch.

The only sounds were dogs barking from somewhere nearby, their yipping and yapping increasing in intensity. Jock frowned and looked at Yohan. The dripping man's eyes were locked on his wife. The crowd began to murmur, some shouting out in disappointment at the lack of pleas for mercy, their expectations of brutality disappointed.

Jock couldn't see his men. Had they skived off somewhere? Bastards wouldn't be getting their day's wages if they didn't show their ugly faces in the next minute. The barking and howling of the dogs mixed with the equally animalistic screams of the crowd now baying full-voiced for blood. The good people of Dysael wanted their pound of burnt flesh.

The crowd jostled Jock, and he almost punched a nearby gap-toothed knave in the face. Jock didn't like his person to be touched. He pushed back, trying to clear some space around him and Yohan. Where was Stephen? The tall cider maker had gone, perhaps dragged off by the crowd like a leaf in an eddying stream. The sound of the barking dogs increased, drowning out the shouts of the blood-mad crowd. Something was wrong here. Jock's spine tingled a warning. Where were his men?

He grabbed Yohan by the shoulder. "We need to get away from here." Yohan did not respond; perhaps he couldn't hear Jock. The man just continued to stare at his wife, now blazing in flames. "Yohan, we need to go!"

Keira Jack stood several yards behind Yohan Schuman and Jock Burgess. They could not see her among the crowd. No man paid attention to her, for she was no one, no one of import. But she would be someone of note, oh she would be, very soon now. The ratcatcher's wife sneered. Men were such idiots. They should have known from their first encounter with Sage that she had the power to control fire and was now embalmed in a protective shield against the flames. But it would not last. Sage had to be nearly exhausted.

Keira closed her eyes. *Hang on, Sage,* she thought. *I cannot get you out, but just hang on until you witness your retribution. Hang on, my love.*

Dogs, filthy street mongrels and expensive pure breeds. Dogs, big and small, skeletal runts and fat pets given more care than some children. Dogs of all shapes, sizes and social classes came hurtling as one into the square and careened, tongues wildly flapping from slobbering mouths, towards the raised platform as if the Lucifer of Dogs pursued them. The animals circled the throng of people and leapt up onto the platform, the short-legged ones scampering up ramps at the back. Some in the crowd laughed at the canine capers.

Then, each dog threw itself into the fire engulfing Sage Schuman.

The crowd hushed, astonished at the sight.

People screamed when an army of flaming hounds leapt off the platform and into their midst. They shrieked and knocked each other to the ground, stomped over each other to avoid the arrowhead formation of dozens and dozens of burning, howling dogs as they hurtled straight for Yohan Schuman.

The crowd parted, and Yohan stood there, unmoving and open-mouthed as the animals closed on him.

Jock whispered, "Jesus Christ." He ran as Yohan disappeared under a landslide of burning dogs. Yohan shrieked once and no more, now engulfed in slavering tooth and searing flame.

Keira watched Jock stumble as he sought safety. Then, he saw her, and his eyes widened in horror. Keira pointed a finger at him. *You're next.*

The cleric ordered the fire doused and examined Sage, who breathed yet in ragged short gasps. He waved a hand and several soldiers stepped forward and began hacking at her, chopping, gouging. Sage's struggle ended when the men cleaved her head from her shoulders. Sage had suffered torture and a gunshot to the chest at point blank range, she had suffered fire and now finally, finally they had killed her with long cold metal blades. But she hadn't gone easy.

None of the Harpies would go easy.

The dogs burned to death, forming a pyre of smoking canine corpses over the shredded and singed body of Yohan Schuman. Fat from the dogs sizzled and melted together to form pools of hot lard. The dead dripping man oozed fat along with them. Jock Burgess wandered around in circles. Breathlessly, he dropped to his knees and vomited.

Keira nodded to herself as she ran down the back alleys. The message had been delivered. They couldn't stop her. The Law couldn't stop her. Thackery and his men couldn't stop her. She could not be pacified, and Jock was next.

The mutton-chopped bastard was next.

CHAPTER 21

Disobedience

If anyone wanted to murder Willard Brown, they were taking their time about it. Private Freddie Burns had been stationed in the millhouse for over a week. The nights up in the grain store were cold and noisy, what with the constant grinding of the gear wheels and the rushing of the water in the millrace outside. The days were dull, uneventful. Freddie spent his time trailing around behind the miller, following him here, following him there, up the stairs as Willard unloaded bags of grain, processed the contents and tied up bags of flour. Up and down, up and down. The life of a miller was hardly an exciting one, and it was laborious. Private Burns had considered abandoning his watchdog duties to help Willard with his work, but he had been told that patience was key and never to let his guard down, so he had allowed the miller to toil alone and felt some guilt for it.

Yes, indeed. If anyone wanted the man dead, they weren't in a hurry to see it done. But that didn't mean it wasn't going to happen. Word had come up from Dysael of the death of another man, another husband on the list. This one had been attacked by rabid dogs, apparently moments before his wife had lost her head in a public execution. By all reports, the whole thing had devolved into carnage. People were too scared to walk the streets. Freddie had better be on alert, his superiors had said. Two more men had arrived to bolster the guard on the miller, but two men were all the Law could afford to spare. All available resources were now being directed into a manhunt, or in this case, a witch-hunt.

Thackery had brought in dog handlers from out of town, and the hounds were now accompanying Night Watch officers door to door. The Law fully intended to flush out the remaining women, to hunt them down and destroy them. The whole thing was madness: housewives turned monsters, abroad and intent on murder. Freddie could recall nothing like it in all his years, as brief as they had been.

The young private had got into the habit of taking a cider with the miller before turning in, and so, as darkness spread, Freddie and Willard sat at the kitchen table chatting while Jess lay near the fire. Outside, patrolling the walk bridge, were the two new soldiers recently arrived from the city. Those men would not sleep tonight.

"I don't need *three* men watching me," Willard said. "I don't even need you, no offence, Freddie. My Mary is dead, and even if she isn't, she's no killer."

Freddie sipped his cider. "Are you sure on both counts? Things have turned bad in the city, another man down. There's genuine reason to believe you are in danger."

Willard scratched at the freckles around his nose. "Less sure than I'd like to be. I hope I'm wrong about her being dead, but …" He sighed and shook his head. "It's hard to believe the tales of … well, you know."

Freddie nodded. "It's hard, alright, but my superiors believe it, so I'm obliged to fall in line with their opinions on the matter. I'll be here until they say otherwise."

Willard shrugged. "Fair enough."

Not for the first time, Freddie experienced a pang of sympathy for the miller. He seemed like a decent bloke, not the type of man that anyone would want to murder, least of all his wife.

"It's a bad business," Freddie said. "The whole thing, gotten out of hand. I have married friends who admit to watching their backs around their wives. Can you imagine your own wife wanting to kill you?" Freddie's face reddened, and he cleared his throat. "Well, I suppose you can. Sorry."

"That's alright, Freddie. I can't imagine it, myself, honestly. I know what they're saying, but I just can't. If you knew Mary, you'd understand." The miller paused and sipped at his cider. "I met her when we were both, oh thirteen, fourteen. She's my best mate, not just my wife. Or she was. I just don't know what to think. I can't believe she's gone, and I certainly can't believe she's … she's returned to do me harm."

Freddie was about to reply when a light rapping came from the door. The two men exchanged glances. Neither of them had heard the guards outside challenge the newcomer. Freddie got to his feet as quietly as he could and drew his sword. He put a finger to his lips and edged towards the door. Jess did not seem alarmed at the late intrusion. She simply sat on her haunches by the fire and looked expectantly at the door.

"Let me open it," Willard whispered. "This is silly."

Freddie shook his head. The last thing he wanted was to give the assassin, if an assassin it was, a clean shot at the miller. It did not occur to Freddie, in his youthful enthusiasm, that an assassin rarely knocked on the front door. Freddie flung the door open, his sword poised to strike. The firelight illuminated nothing but a rectangular patch of well-trodden earth outside the millhouse kitchen door. The nape of Freddie's neck prickled. He walked outside and could not see the two other men.

The stairs to the second floor creaked, and Freddie turned to see a woman standing on the treads. She wore a dark green cloak with the hood pulled back and her hair glowed golden in the firelight.

"Mary," Willard whispered. He took a step towards her.

"No!" Freddie shouted. "Mr. Brown, get back!" Freddie leapt past Willard and raised his weapon.

Mary Brown, for it could only be the miller's wife, held out both hands in a gesture of non-confrontation. "I mean no harm. I simply wish to speak to my husband."

Freddie hesitated. She seemed reasonable, seemed *normal*. But the words of his superiors had been imprinted upon him with severity. Do not trust them; do not give them a chance. Do not believe them, for they mean to kill. Freddie swung his sword at the woman's unprotected legs. The world exploded in a bright light and turned upside down, and then quietened to darkness.

Willard stood motionless, the chair he had used to club Freddie about the head hanging limp in his hands. Mary Brown looked from the unconscious private to her now unprotected husband and smiled.

I am about to die, Willard Brown thought.

Mary remained on the stairs. When she finally moved, she did so with a fluid grace as she stepped down onto the kitchen floor.

"Take me to her," Mary said. She patted Jess on the head as the dog came quietly to her. "I will see the place where she lies."

At first, Willard was confused. Take her where? To whom? And then he understood. Willard had grieved alone, but now, perhaps, it would be good to share that grief. He pointed to the unconscious form of Freddie Burns. "The Night Watch are out in force. They're hunting you and the others. You must hide. You must flee Dysael."

"I understand and thank you for the warning. Take me to her."

"Alright. It's a short walk. We'll need a candle."

Willard lit a candle from the fire and walked outside. The two newly assigned soldiers had vanished. He did not ask Mary what had become of them as he led her across the walk bridge and up a path into the dark trees. They came to a small glade of pleasant grass at the far end of the clearing, a place where Willard and Mary would often come for picnics on the finer summer days. Mary knelt at a white cross embedded in the earth and gently ran her fingertips across the name written on it: Victoria Brown: their daughter.

Mary spoke quietly, and Willard could barely make out her words. "I will choose my own way. No more being subjected to the whims of others. I take myself back, and I take you back, little one. I am your mother, always, no matter what they say or the length of time your heart beat. These are unimportant measurements of love. I know this now." She placed her fingers to her lips and then touched them to the name on the cross. She sat there for a long time, and Willard could think of nothing to say though he searched desperately for the right words. Finally, Mary stood and turned to him. "You cannot stay here, husband. When she finds that I have not obeyed, she will come for you. They will all come for you."

"You refer to the missing women, the wives."

"I do, and in particular, I speak of Keira Jack. She is the force that drives them. She will not tolerate disobedience. When she discovers that I haven't carried out my task, she'll kill you herself, and then she'll do me. We must flee."

"But this place is my … our home."

"*I* am your home, Willard. Is that not true?"

He nodded. "Yes."

"Then get yourself prepared. Though it pains you to leave our child and home, we must go tonight." Mary turned back to the cross. "But her spirit will attend us, for when all flesh is gone, the spirit prevails. This is another truth I have learnt of late. Come, Willard."

They walked down the path and returned to the millhouse. Willard collected necessary provisions for a … well, he did not know how long they would be on the road. "Where will we go?" he asked.

"Far away. Far away from millet, grain, flour and toil. Away from murder. To a quiet place."

"Freddie has a horse. It's around the back."

"Then saddle it, for we ride."

Willard frowned. "Jess can't keep pace with a horse. She's too old."

Mary rubbed under the dog's chin. "I must confess to not always having loved this animal, but I have no intention of making the poor creature run or walk. That shall be my task. Jess will ride with you."

Willard screwed up his freckled brow. "But you cannot … how do you propose to keep up?"

Mary looked away. "I'll keep up. Do not ask me how. There are many things that you would struggle to understand, that I, myself, struggle to understand." She turned her eyes towards his. "Just know that I am still your wife. I am still your Mary, no matter how I may appear changed. Just … just have some faith in me."

Willard nodded slowly. "Alright, Mary."

The woman stared at him. "Do you not wish to embrace your wife, Willard? Or do you believe what they have told you about me?"

He did not move. She seemed colder, changed. She even spoke differently, more eloquently, if anything. If what they said was true, then she *was* changed and not for the better. But she hadn't murdered him. Not yet.

Willard gave voice to the question that had been bothering him. "Where are the two men that were outside?"

Mary sighed sadly. "You doubt me. You think me … a threat? A murderer?"

"No, no, I just …"

"Follow me."

For the second time that evening, husband and wife entered the bracing evening air. Willard followed Mary to the back of the millhouse. She stood over the two motionless forms of the guards lying together in the shadows. Both men breathed, noisily in fact, as if snoring deep in slumber.

"Satisfied, Willard?" Mary asked.

"I had no doubts."

"Then embrace me." She extended her arms wide, and he slowly hugged her. In the old days, he would have allowed his hands to roam down her back, perhaps even given her a cheeky slap on the buttocks.

He dared not do so now.

"Did you miss your wife, Willard?" she whispered in his ear.

"Of course, I did, my little baker's loaf."

"Don't call me that again. I have always found it condescending." Mary slapped Willard hard on his rump and pushed him away. "Now, saddle the horse."

CHAPTER 22

Fast Horses

Douglas Partridge was getting the hell out of Dysael. It had been several days since Master Blacksmith George Burridge had sent his new apprentice with the warning about the wives. "Run if you don't hear from anyone in the next few days," Jeremy had said, "and don't return to the smithy." There had been no word since that time, and so Douglas had decided to flee.

Yet George Burridge was not only Douglas' employer but also his friend. Douglas could not just abandon the man, even at the risk of his own life. And so, Douglas, the entirety of his life's possessions in a sack over his shoulder, crept through the streets of Dysael by the light of a waning moon. He would find George and say goodbye. He couldn't leave without saying goodbye. It was the least he could do.

It was a chilly night, but Douglas was sweating, his blond curls matted to his forehead. Was he ill with fever? Or was it a soul sickness fuelled by guilt?

The Burridge smithy appeared out of the shadows. It was a place he had spent many working hours, many happy hours. He had just been apprenticed to George Burridge when he first met Bessie. His future looked bright, so she had agreed to marry him. It had all looked so bright. Why had he thrown it all away in a reckless moment?

The moon was high, the street empty. Douglas crept towards the door, the spare key still in his pocket. A sign had been posted on the door proclaiming a new owner and operator of the smithy, effective immediately. Douglas gaped. George Burridge had sold up and moved on? That made no sense, for the man loved his work and was wedded to the forge room and molten metal as surely as any mortal man was wedded to a mortal woman. For what possible reason would he sell up? Was Douglas himself to blame?

Douglas inserted the key into the lock, and it activated the tumbler. Apparently, the new owners had not had time to fit a new lock. The door creaked open, and he entered the smithy. Douglas sighed at his own foolishness. This was fruitless. George was gone; this was a dangerous waste of time. Just one last look around before he said goodbye.

Something stabbed at him from the shadows. Douglas jerked his head back and kicked out. A strong hand grasped his ankle, and the forge room turned upside down. Douglas twisted through the air and crashed into the cold stone wall of the furnace.

George Burridge stared down at him. "Shit, Douglas. I told you not to come here." The younger man shook his head in a daze and raised a hand. The senior blacksmith hauled him to his feet. "Sorry, lad. I didn't know it was you. Dark in here."

"Why have you sold up?"

George sighed and brushed metal dust from the younger man's clothes. "It's time to get going. I wanted to collect you earlier. I'm sorry for the delay, but I think they're watching me. I couldn't lead them to you. However, you're here now, so none of that matters. We ride out of this place, together."

"I don't understand. Why must we flee? Who is watching you?"

George turned away and ran a calloused hand through his hair. "The law executed Sage Schuman yesterday, but not before Yohan was murdered. It's all turned sour, lad. We must escape."

Douglas simply stared. "Yohan? Who killed Yohan? And Sage? I don't understand."

"No time to explain. I fear they're closing in." George locked the front door and headed for the smaller room in the back. "Come on, lad. We'll climb out the window and just pray they don't have eyes on us."

CHAPTER 22 Fast Horses

❋

George Burridge shivered in the cool night air, his breath curling up to intersect with that of the younger blond man riding beside him. George had sold up his shop and, with the money, bought two fine horses. In times of trouble, a horse could be the difference between life and death, and yet, for all the years of toil in the smithy, two horses, as fine as they were, seemed little in the way of recompense.

George glanced across at his younger companion. In all the confusion of recent events, it would be easy to forget that Douglas Partridge was wanted for the murder of his wife, Bessie Partridge. Fortunately for Douglas, the constabulary had their hands full with witches, murderers, arsonists, the loss of the Law Courts and the mass suicide of many respected citizens' pet dogs. George Burridge had not attended the execution of Sage Schuman in the town square the day before, but he'd heard about the chaos and madness, of how Yohan had been torn apart by a flaming pack of hounds and Sage had been beheaded, the only way to finish her, apparently. Another husband and wife torn asunder.

But that mattered little now. Douglas was a hunted man, hunted by both the Law and the Wives. George was determined to get the younger man out of Dysael. They would start a new shop somewhere, anywhere, if they could just stay alive, but that would be no easy task.

The Night Watch were out in force, and very few citizens, apart from thieves and drunks, were willing to risk life and limb walking the streets in the wee small hours, not in these most dangerous of times, not when there were man-hating harpies abroad lurking in the shadows.

Not one soldier or commissioned officer in the Night Watch hindered their progress as they clip-clopped through the dark streets. The Night Watch was on the lookout for only one gender, and it didn't have a ballsack.

Several times, Douglas whispered questions, but George hushed him. They could talk more freely when they were out of the city and on the open road. He could not risk one word that would draw attention to them, could not afford to be recognised in any shape or form. Both their lives depended on getting out unnoticed. The main gate loomed in the silvered moonlight mist. Nearly there. Nearly free: a final blow of the hammer and the blade would be ready for the tempering stone.

Questions were asked, but the guards at the gate asking them were jittery, looking over their shoulders for the real threat.

"Business on the road, business in Dunedin," George said in response to the perfunctory questions.

"That's a long ride," the guard responded, and George nodded. The guard waved them through, and they walked their horses out into the cool, dark air. Half an hour out on the road and Douglas let loose with a torrent of questions. George smiled. He could speak now. He sighed, letting the tension ease out of his body.

"Settle down, Douglas. One question at a time."

"I have so many. You said that the missing wives have returned seeking revenge and that Yohan is dead. His wife Sage is dead."

"That is all true. Jock and Stephen seem to think that …" George trailed off, then sighed heavily. He didn't want to say it, didn't want to bring up a past best left buried, but the boy had to know. "They think Bessie's death has sparked all this madness. The wives are back to kill all those with a hand in it."

Douglas nearly fell out of his saddle. "But … but I alone am responsible for Bessie's death."

"That's not how the wives see it. You are best well away from Dysael."

Douglas looked stricken with misery. "I am … I am responsible … for all of it? For you selling your smithy?"

George was about to deny it, to make an excuse for selling his workshop, to take at least some of the guilt from the boy's shoulders, when he heard hoof fall on the road behind them. His body stiffened, and he held his hand up to silence Douglas. Horses, moving fast.

"Ride, boy." George spurred his horse into a gallop, and Douglas followed.

CHAPTER 22 Fast Horses

Horses, the difference between life and death. George prayed that the horses under them were worth the good money he'd paid for them.

George and Douglas thundered down the road in the darkness, their only light that of a waning gibbous moon behind scudding clouds. Such light would have been sufficient for horses at a gentle walk, but they were riding at full pelt, and a fall at this speed would result in severe injury or death. To stop and allow the riders behind them to overtake them, however, would result in protracted death and insidious amounts of pain.

There was only one choice: ride like Hell.

And they rode as if Death was behind them, grinning and snapping at their heels, for she *was*. Neither blacksmith was more than a competent horseman, yet the horses beneath them surged and seemed to leave the ground, such was their power. If George was going to die this night, at least he hadn't bought a dud horse. At least he hadn't done that.

Hope coursed through George as his horse powered over the dirt road. They were increasing the distance between them and their pursuers. They were going to make it. Hope came a cropper when he heard Douglas cry out behind him. The young man hit the road with a sickening thud. George hauled his horse in and whirled around. Douglas lay motionless on his face. In the distance, five horses and five cloaked riders cut through the mist.

It was Douglas they pursued. George could turn and run, and he'd probably make it. He cursed and drew his sword from the scabbard on his horse's flank. He dismounted and stood over Douglas as the five hooded riders pulled up hard.

George swung his sword through the air. "Take me, you bitches! Leave him alone!"

Jock Burgess pulled back his hood. "We're taking both 'o you, George. And who the fuck are you calling a bitch?"

CHAPTER 23

And Think of Murder

Bridget could not remember the precise moment she stopped loving her husband. It was a collection of moments, she supposed, small arguments or simply cold silence that had a cumulative effect, an erosion, if you would: a slow weathering away at her happiness over the long years.

She could, however, remember the exact moment she wished Cranford dead.

He'd strangled her with his rough hands up against the bedroom wall. It wasn't the first instance of abuse, but this time was different. This particular act of violence had come out of nowhere. He wasn't even drunk. Anger blazed behind his eyes as he grasped her throat and squeezed. The flame of his rage ignited the small spark of retribution behind Bridget's own eyes. Cranford's mistake, she thought when she regained consciousness on the bedroom floor, was not finishing her off.

Over the next few days and weeks, Bridget fantasised about killing Cranford in a variety of ways. There was, of course, the issue of money to consider. Without Cranford's wages as a carpenter, life would be very difficult to afford. She had no children to worry about. That was something at least: she hadn't brought innocents into the world to suffer at the hands of the mentally unstable Cranford or endure deprivation without the man's money. She was both relieved and sad. Childless at the age of twenty-eight, Bridget wondered if it was too late to have children with another man, if any would have a simple laundress. But first, she had to do away with Cranford and not get caught doing so. If she was to have any chance of a new life, she had to rid herself of the man she had called her husband these past nine years and make it look like an accident.

But she was inexperienced in this kind of thing. Had no idea how to carry the act out.

"I have heard you wish your husband murdered."

Bridget turned at the sound of the voice. There, on the street, an old woman in a black cloak stood gazing at her. The aged crone had a warty, hooked nose poking from the shadows of her hood. She removed the hood and shifted from foot to foot, her head tilted to one side, giving the overall impression of a blackbird listening for earthworms just below the surface of a freshly turned field.

Bridget blinked twice and scanned the street. She couldn't see to the end of it for the fog. The other laundresses hanging up clothes were shrouded in a mist, those further down the street invisible altogether. Every available line stretching across the road was replete with clothes hanging out to dry, a feckless task on this dreary and damp morning.

"I'm sorry, but I think you have made a mistake," Bridget said.

"Have I?" the old crone replied with raised eyebrows.

Bridget tied back her wild auburn hair, but it refused to be tamed and immediately fell back around her long, pale face. "I don't wish no one harm," Bridget said.

"Your hands are dried out," the old woman said, taking Bridget's hands in her own. "It's all that lye and starch. Poor wee thing. You don't have the necessary hands for murder. Supple hands, that's what's required. Supple hands for murder. But I know who possesses them."

Bridget looked up and down the street again. The other washerwomen were wringing out clothes and making room to hang them on the lines. No one seemed to be aware of the old woman or the discussion taking place, but if there were any coppers within earshot, such talk would have her bailed up down in the cells quick smart, considering the current climate.

"Really, I thank you, but I don't wish harm on my husband."

"Come on, dear," the old woman tut-tutted, "your bruises are yellow, some are blue. It's not a one-off, is it? The kicks and punches, the throttlings. They'll keep coming until he kills you. I've seen it before."

Bridget's heart hammered at the base of her throat. Was this the opportunity she had been desiring? She leaned in and whispered, "I have no idea how to go about it. You … will you …?"

"Not I," the old woman said, a smile playing at her crinkled mouth. "Long past it, I am, Lord bless you. But if you walk down this street and think it nice and clear and loud, they will hear you."

"Think what? Who will hear me?"

"Think of murder, dear, and *they'll* hear you. Particularly if you carry this." The old hag reached out an open hand. In her wrinkled palm rested a necklace formed from tiny metal beads.

"What is it?" Bridget said, taking the necklace, each metallic bead glowing a different colour.

The old woman stepped back. "A bond. A binding. It is solidarity. They have taken it upon themselves, you see, to give aid to women just like you. Heroines, they are. Shining knights on the bleed." The old woman cackled to herself. "You'll see. It's war now."

Bridget fingered the necklace, and a sense of peace settled on her. For a moment, she forgot about the old crone, and when Bridget tore her eyes from the necklace and looked up, she was gone. Bridget placed the strange necklace around her neck and walked dazedly down the street. A few of the laundresses watched her as she passed. One called out her name, but Bridget did not reply.

She had murder on her mind and had to think it loud and clear.

Keira liked to remember Bessie before she was murdered.

She remembered the playful, laughing, stupid girl who had blossomed into a playful, laughing, stupid woman. *My sister*, she thought. *My little Smudge.* Dead and buried among the pale marshmallow flowers. Bruised, battered, broken. Dead.

Elsie had asked why they hadn't returned to dig her up and give her a proper burial once their powers had come to them, once they had taken control. The dead are dead, Keira had replied. The rotting corpse that lay buried among the marshmallow flowers bore no relationship to Bessie. It was a dead thing and best left alone. The only reason anyone buries anyone else is to make themselves feel better. To medicate the feelings of pain, remorse, guilt. Whatever.

Keira didn't want to feel better. Let the horror and anger burn forever.

Elsie laid a hand on Keira's shoulder and whispered, "Careful. Don't get too close. Not even you could survive a fall from this height."

Keira blinked and shook her head free of morbid musings. She looked down into a swirling fog that obscured the ground far below. A few feet away, Charlene Hickson stood at one end of a slanting roof. At the spiky redhead's feet lay a thickly coiled rope, and attached to the end of a rope was a metal hook like the end of a harpoon.

Keira Jack and Elsie Gallagher approached Charlene as she knitted her brows in concentration.

"Can you do it?" Keira asked.

Charlene took a deep breath. "I reckon I can. Are the other girls ready?"

Elsie put a hand to her temple and looked out into the rolling sea of mist. She nodded. "They are ready."

"They'd better be," Charlene said. "They won't have much warning afore it comes at 'em. Thick as shit soup up here."

Keira grabbed the end of the rope without the hook and tied it off to an exposed beam in a gap in the tiled roof. "Now, Charlene," Keira said.

Charlene took another breath and waved her companions back. She squeezed her eyes shut, clenched one fist and raised it into the air. In a violent motion, Charlene opened her hand and brought her arm down, bending at the hip to allow her arm to snap down and behind her. The hook disappeared out into the fog as if shot from a cannon; the rope trailing behind snaked through the air in a series of whip cracks dulled by the moist atmosphere.

Then, the rope trailed off and down. A miss.

"Damn it," Charlene said. "How far off was I?"

As Keira and Charlene began to haul the rope in, Elsie once again put her fingers to her temple. A moment later, she opened her eyes. "Samantha believes you must aim to the right five feet and extend your range another ten feet."

Charlene grunted as she hauled on the rope. "Ten more feet. I'll squeeze it out. I can do ten more feet."

Once the rope had been gathered and furled on the rooftop, Charlene picked up the hook and pointed it in the desired direction. Then she lay the object down, maintaining its orientation, shook her hands out and rolled her head around her shoulders like a prize fighter about to step into the ring. Keira and Elsie offered words of encouragement.

"Alright, stand back," Charlene said.

This time, Charlene clapped once, twice, and on the third, the hook shot out into the air, but this time, the rope did not eventually dip or fall. It stopped and hung suspended. Charlene whooped, and Keira patted her on the back. Keira turned to see a wince of pain cross Elsie's face.

"What is it?" Keira asked. "What's wrong?"

"Something." Elsie pointed down into the fog. "Someone down there is … I feel as if the hairs are being pulled from my scalp one by one. It is a call. Someone calls me."

❈

CHAPTER 23 And Think of Murder

Bridget stopped, and the fog closed in about her. She could not recall how many streets she had walked, how many corners she had turned down. She was quite lost and alone as no other footfall had mimicked hers for some time. She seemed the only person in the world, abandoned in a sea of mist. Then, a sound through the thick air, echoing off unseen brick walls.

"What is your name?" a voice said, a woman's voice just beyond the mist.

"I am Bridget."

"Your full name, if you would be so gracious."

"Bridget Susan Hayes."

"And your husband?"

Bridget inhaled sharply. "Cranford Hayes."

A tall woman with long black hair stepped out of the fog. "I am Keira Jack, and I murdered my husband. You may have heard of me."

Bridget nodded. "I have heard the name. You are a wanted fugitive."

"Hah. Fugitive implies the act of fleeing. We do not flee. What do you want, Bridget?"

"I … I … uh …"

"She wants her husband, Cranford, dead." Bridget started at the new voice. An olive-complexioned woman joined Keira. "My name is Elsie. I heard your thoughts."

Bridget's eyes widened. "My thoughts? My goodness." Bridget swallowed hard. "Aye, I want Cranford gone."

"It can be done," Elsie said.

Bridget looked from one woman to the other. "You do not wish to know his crimes?"

Elsie shrugged. "He is unworthy, or so you believe. That is all we need to know."

"Where did you get that?" Keira asked, taking a step closer.

Bridget looked down at the necklace over her coat. "An old woman gave it to me not more than two hours ago. She told me to walk the streets until you found me."

Keira and Elsie exchanged glances. "Describe her," Keira said.

"Old and wrinkled. She had a wart on her nose. Reminded me of a blackbird, the way she held herself, but I could not say other than that."

Keira frowned and said, "Where can we find your husband?"

"He is a carpenter down at Bentley Pearson, in Teak Square."

"Do you have any preference as to how it is done?"

Bridget shook her head. "No. Only that … only that it appears an accident, and … he doesn't have to suffer. I just want to live without fear again. What do you charge for this task?"

"There is no fee," Keira said. "You may consider what we do a public service. But what will you do for money when he is gone?"

"I am a washerwoman. I have something set aside."

"Whatever money you have is not enough. It will be a hard road for you. The world is not kind to a young widow, a washerwoman no less."

"A hard road is better than a dead-end street."

Keira tilted her head. "I understand. But you do not have to be so lowly or lonely."

"I am a washerwoman, soon to be widowed. I do not see how I could be anything else."

"Come with us." Keira waved her hand at herself and Elsie. "Give up your work and live in commune with your sisters."

"Forgive me, but I do not wish harm to any other man except my husband. I do not think I would be suited to your kind of life."

Keira shrugged. "Very well. If you ever change your mind, just walk the streets and think of murder. Now, Bridget, you find yourself in the Yard, and that is not a safe place for one such as you. I suggest you leave immediately." Keira Jack and Elsie Gallagher backed away and disappeared into the fog.

The last thing Bridget heard was Keira's voice dancing through the mist.

"And remember what I said, love. Should you need us again, just walk the streets and think of murder."

CHAPTER 23 And Think of Murder

❊

Cranford Hayes was an experienced carpenter, ten years in the trade and all that time working for the same company, Bentley Pearson, down in Teak Square. He arrived early one morning to continue work on various tables and chairs that comprised the stock products of Bentley Pearson, and somehow, Cranford managed to drive a nail through his wrist and bleed to death on the workshop floor.

Upon discovering his body, his shocked and horrified workmates observed that Cranford was never early. What was more, it was odd that after suffering the tragic accident, he had made no attempt to call for help. He had simply laid down on the spot to die.

Many wondered if Cranford's death was, in fact, a suicide. There were whisperings of something else, but without evidence, the coroner swiftly signed off on an unfortunate workplace accident. Cranford's wife, Bridget, received a small amount of money from Bentley and Pearson, a gesture that was by no means obligatory under law, but the company felt it fitting to assist the grieving widow of a man who, by all accounts, was a hardworking and solid individual.

Coroner Peter Stimpson signed two other death certificates that morning: both tragic workplace accidents. By the time the fourth one came in, the coroner hesitated in signing his name to anything.

"How many did you say, Peter?" Constable Vincent E. Thackery asked, looking up from the papers on his desk.

"Four. Four accidents in one day."

"Well, well. The working classes are proving to be rather clumsy today, but an accident is no reason to get me involved."

"Four in one day doesn't strike you as odd?"

Thackery sighed and sat back in his chair. "Many things, of late, strike me as odd. What are you suggesting?"

"Wouldn't be the first husband to be murdered in Dysael this year, would it, Vincent?"

Thackery sat up stiffly. "Now, wait a minute. This is unrelated to

Keira Jack and her band of murderous harpies. They have it in for their husbands, no one else."

"Unrelated? That's what you said about the last batch of murdered men."

"Good God, are you saying that these madwomen have started to kill innocent men at random?"

Peter sighed and scratched his long jaw. "I'm not sure about the innocent or random parts, but the sooner you stop Keira Jack and her harpies, the better for the married male populace of our fair city."

CHAPTER 24

Profit and Pragmatism

A gas lamp illumined a long table with a spotless white tablecloth. Jock Burgess had closed his butchery early today, as he had for the last two days, and the cutting room had now been transformed into a parlour for entertaining. Empty meat hooks hung from the ceiling, and a dozen chairs had been positioned around the long butchery workbench now serving as a dining table. Strips of cooked meat lay cooling on silver plates, and bowls of fruit lay evenly placed along the length of the table.

Stephen Cox paced the room with a jug of his finest cider. He wore a white silk shirt and bent his tall frame at the hip to carefully fill each of the dozen mugs on the table to an equal level. He rubbed at his pointed chin as if estimating whether his guests would be pleased.

Douglas Partridge and George Burridge sat in positions of great esteem at either end of the long table, the place reserved for guests of honour. The fact they sat bound and gagged somewhat blighted that esteem and honour.

"Do you think they'll come tonight?" Stephen asked.

Jock scratched at his mutton chop whiskers as he glanced once more at the large double doors leading to the pitch-black slaughter yard at the rear of the butchery. The doors stood wide open and invited the cool evening breeze tinged with the blood and shit of various dead animals. They also invited something else, something that had not arrived these last few nights. It was the waiting that unnerved Jock. He couldn't stand the waiting.

Jock smoothed down his fancy crimson doublet. "I don't know, do I? Stop asking. They'll come when they come."

George struggled to speak past his gag, twisting his head and grunting something unintelligible. Jock had no intention of removing the gag to allow George to say anything. The butcher nodded to one of his bodyguards, and the man slapped George on the back of his head hard enough to cause blood to trickle from his nose and over the gag.

"Don't let him bleed on the tablecloth," Jock said. The bodyguard roughly wiped George's mouth and beard and held the cloth against the blacksmith's nose. "We must keep things presentable for our lady guests," Jock added.

The irony of Jock's statement was not lost on him, considering what lay under the clean, white tablecloth: the bloodstains of the butchery workbench were ingrained and could never be scrubbed away, but a casual visitor would never know of the horror and death to which the table attested.

George was foolish enough to attempt to speak again, and Jock's bodyguard backhanded him across the face. Jock sighed and waved his man away.

"Shut your mouth, George, before you get your brains skittled. I've heard it all. You think me a fool. You say that we are all doomed, and that your sacrifice and his," he gestured to Douglas, "will avail me nothing, but I'm a man who views the bright side of things. I'm a pragmatist, George. That's what I am. A pragmatist." Douglas just sat there with a gormless expression on his face, and Jock turned on him. "Fucking idiot boy. All of this is on your head."

George grunted again, and Jock's man moved in, his fist raised. Jock intervened and pulled the blacksmith's bloodied gag down around his bearded throat. "Fuck's sake, George. This had better be good, or I'll bash you myself."

"I want a drink," George said, his dry lips sticking to his teeth. "I just want a drink, Jock."

"That we can do," the butcher said. "Stephen, get the man a drink." Stephen looked from one mug of cider to another. "Come on, son,"

Jock said impatiently. "They're all the same, unless you've poisoned one of them." Stephen's long, angular face seemed to melt as he looked at Jock. "Jesus Christ," Jock said. "You haven't poisoned them, have you? It won't work on them harpies, you fool. You'll get us killed."

"No, no," Stephen said. "I ain't poisoned them."

"Then give George a bloody drink."

"And Douglas," George said.

Jock nodded. "Aye, alright. And Douglas. One last drink for old times' sake, eh?"

"Old times' sake," George agreed.

Stephen held a mug to the lips of first George and then Douglas. Both men drank greedily. Jock took a long drink himself. If he was going to die, better to die drunk. After all, when Death's dark mistress came calling, you wouldn't turn down a final drink if she offered you one. How many men knew exactly when the Grim Reaper's missus was coming for them? For most, it was a surprise, an unpleasant one at that.

"We could all still run," George said. "Together, we'd have a chance."

Jock pointed a finger in George's face. "That's your last chance, son. Any more talk like that and you're gagged, permanently. Do you understand me? You weren't there. You didn't see what they did, what Keira Jack did. She gave me the evil eye, George. Set those burning mongrels on Yohan and stood there, calm as you like, pointing the finger of Death at me. No one can stop her. Not the law and not you. I don't have a chance if she wants me dead, not a chance."

George shrugged. "Not like you to give up, Jock."

"I haven't given up. She wants *him*." Jock stabbed a finger at Douglas. "And you, probably, but *him* for sure."

"She wants all of us," George said, blood trickling from his mouth. "We're all dead."

Jock opened his mouth to shout George down when the front shop doorbell chimed. Startled, he whirled around. Stephen stood slack-jawed, staring back at him.

"Thought we locked the shop door," Stephen said.

"We did," Jock said. "Shit, they're here. Everyone, stay calm. Positions."

Jock's three bodyguards formed a semicircle around him. Stephen backed away from the door leading to the shop, gulping at his mug of cider. He bumped into a fiddle leaning against a wall, and it toppled over with a clacking sound. Jock finished his cider in one swig and gently placed the empty cup on the table, eyes on the door.

Elsie Gallagher appeared at the door leading to the front shop. The gas lamp gave her olive complexion a greenish tinge. She wore a fine white mantua: a woollen gown with a train and matching petticoat.

"I have heard," Elsie said with a half-smile, "that there is to be a party."

Jock cleared his throat and waved Elsie inside. "Aye, a party. A dinner and a do. You always did love a do, Elsie."

The half-smile blossomed into a full one. "Oh, I do love a do, Jock. You're not wrong."

"Have you come alone?"

As if to answer the question, Charlene Hickson and Helen Hardcastle glided out of the darkness of the front shop to stand on either side of Elsie. All three women wore dresses of a similar cut. Charlene's gown was the same red as her short, spiky hair. Helen wore a black gown, and her eyes were circled with kohl, giving a more insidious aspect to her normally cherub-like face.

"Welcome, ladies," Jock said as he bowed. "It's lovely to see you all again. Lovely, lovely."

Elsie curtsied. "Hello, Jock. Hello, Stephen."

Stephen blurted, "Is Jasmine with you? Where's my Jasmine?"

"Doing her face. She'll be along shortly." Elsie turned back to Jock. "Who are your handsome friends? Are they coppers?"

"Oh, no, no." Jock gestured at his bodyguards. "No, they're uh ... *private* friends. The law is not here. You have my word. I sent them away, insisted on it. It's just us."

CHAPTER 24 Profit and Pragmatism

Elsie's smile flicked off like a burning candle wick snuffed out between thumb and forefinger. She turned her eyes to George and nodded in his direction. George nodded back, a grim expression on his bearded face. She next looked at Douglas. "Hello, Douglas." Douglas Partridge's response was muffled by the gag in his mouth. "I notice, Jock," Elsie said, "that you do not ask after Samantha. Could it be that you do not miss your own wife?"

"Yes, of course I miss her, but ... I ... I know she is somewhat upset with me."

"Upset, yes. I think that is fair to say. She is upset, as we all are."

"I'm starved," Charlene said. "Do you mind if I tuck in?"

"Go ahead," Jock said, "but are we not welcoming more guests?"

Charlene licked her lips. "The others will be along soon. I'm sure they won't mind if we start without them." She waved her hand, and a small cluster of pale green grapes rose from a bowl and rotated in the air. Jock's men shifted uneasily behind him. Jock grimaced and hoped they wouldn't do anything stupid. He'd told them to be ready for anything, told them not to flinch or show any sign of weakness, but they were spooked all the same and looked at each other, wanting to run or strike out. *Don't do neither, you bastards,* he thought. *Just stay still and wait.*

A single grape broke off the bunch and floated into Charlene's open mouth. Several more followed until the sprig was exhausted. She wiped the juice from her lips on the frilly sleeve of her fine dress.

"Do I stink, Jock?" Charlene asked suddenly.

Taken aback, Jock stuttered his reply. "N ... no, Charlene. Not ... you look lovely. All you ladies look lovely."

"Such a gentleman, but I do not refer to my appearance. Eugene was a catgut spinner, and he stunk somethin' awful. I was always afraid that, though I did not spend time in the workshop myself, the obscene reek would cling to me, a gift from my husband, if you like."

Jock stretched a smile across his mutton chop whiskers. "No, no, Charlene. Not you. Eugene was ... well, he stunk like rotten farts, didn't he? But you? No, never. Not that I noticed."

Charlene smiled and fanned at her throat. "Well, that is a relief, I must say. A woman has her pride, you know."

"Oh, I know. I know. As does a man."

"Particularly men, don't you think?" Elsie said.

"Oh, yes, particularly," Jock agreed.

George twisted in his chair. "Let me out of these ropes, Jock."

Jock didn't turn to answer the blacksmith directly. His eyes remained fixed on the three women. "I can't do that, George. Quiet now. We're all getting along fine."

George shook his head. "They're here to kill us, Jock. This is a farce."

"Shut up, George!" A moment later, Jock gave a sickly smile as he patted down his doublet. "I'm sorry for the outburst, ladies. George and me see this whole thing differently."

"Boys not getting along?" Elsie said. "That's a shame. Still, a difference of opinion should not come between friends."

"Exactly," Jock said. "Exactly. We're all friends here, aren't we?"

Elsie flicked her smile back on. She put her fingers to her temple and looked at Stephen. The cider maker's long face remained blank for a moment, and then he pulled his penis from his fancy trousers and began jerking at it.

"What the fuck, Stephen!" Jock roared. "Put it away!"

Elsie snapped her fingers, and Stephen, a shocked expression on his face, hurriedly stashed his cock back in his breeches. Elsie, Charlene and Helen laughed.

Elsie had made him do it, but Jock was furious with Stephen anyway. He was about to remonstrate with the cider maker when Samantha and Jasmine, hand in hand, walked casually out of the darkness of the slaughter yard and into the room. Both women wore gowns of a matching blue-silver.

Jock's bodyguards turned and put their hands on the hilts of their swords.

"Steady," Jock whispered. "Steady." He stepped forward, his arms out wide. "My darling," he said to Samantha. "My darling wife, I know what you want, what you all want. Poor Bessie, it was a terrible shame what Douglas did to her, and I now see, with a clarity born of a … of a … chagrined heart, that we were wrong to hush it up. We should have listened to our wives. Here he is," Jock said, gesturing to Douglas, "the man you've all been after, and, to sweeten the bargain, the man who wanted to protect him. Yes, we have George Burridge for you as well. Stephen and I have come to a realisation, you see. We … we have repented. Haven't we, Stephen?"

Stephen merely cowered against the wall, staring at the milky white face of his wife, Jasmine Cox. "Yes," he said in a small voice. "We have repented. We have."

Jock rushed on, "I love you, Samantha, my darling. I want to make this right. Tell me how we can make this right."

Samantha waved an arm around the room, and though the sleeve of her dress was visible, the hand at the end of it was not. "My jolly Jock," Samantha said. "What a feast you have put on. Let's eat and be merry for a while."

Jock's skin crawled in horror at his wife's missing hand, but he nodded vigorously. "Excellent idea. Excellent. Stephen, play us a tune, man. Play us a tune!"

Stephen fumbled for the fiddle and placed it under his chin. He was normally an excellent fiddler, yet his fingers trembled, and he missed the notes. All the time he played, his eyes were held by those of Jasmine as she chewed on a strip of meat.

Helen and Charlene picked up mugs of cider. Helen sniffed and nodded. The two women sipped daintily at the liquor. Samantha and Jasmine joined them, and the four women clicked their mugs together. They held their drinks towards Jock and his men. Hurriedly, Jock grabbed another drink and bade his men follow suit, and the four men and four women clinked their ciders together in a friendly gesture.

The only woman not drinking was Elsie Gallagher. She ate an apple while looking from one man to another. Something itched in Jock's skull, like a butterfly frantically flapping on the inside of his forehead, looking for a way to get out. The butcher ignored the flitting and scratching in his mind and took another long drink.

Stephen began to find his rhythm, and the merry sounds of the fiddle raised Jock's spirits, eased the dread in his heart, or perhaps that was the cider. For whatever reason, Jock breathed more easily and allowed himself the merest glimmer of hope, hope that he would not be slaughtered like just another animal in his own butchery.

And then *she* came gliding out of the darkness and ruined everything.

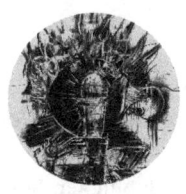

CHAPTER 25

A Do at the Butchery

Keira Jack prowled into the slaughter room, her long black hair tied back, her long dress the same springtime colour as those eyes. Stephen stopped playing the fiddle. Jock's bodyguards froze, mugs halfway to their mouths. Keira's sharp gaze met everyone in the room until it fixed on Douglas Partridge.

Jock realised he had a mouth full of cider and swallowed it. The sound of his gulping seemed too loud.

"Play," Keira said. Stephen merely stared. "Go on, play for us."

Stephen's next few notes sounded like a goat bleating as it was gutted. Jock cringed, but Stephen pulled himself together and played something that was at least tuneful, if not as mournful as a funeral hymn. God damn, Stephen. Play something light.

The tune sped up, and Stephen changed key. It was a jollier song now. Jock breathed again, and the women began to drink and chat amongst themselves.

Keira approached Elsie, and the two women touched foreheads, exchanging softly spoken words hidden beneath the sounds of the fiddle. Jock sidled closer to his men and sipped at his cider, making sure to keep Keira in his field of vision in case she should suddenly snap and come at him like a rabid dog.

For want of anything else to do, Jock kept drinking. He considered making small talk with his three bodyguards to maintain the pretence of a jovial atmosphere but couldn't think of a single thing to say. His men were in no mood to chat anyway, for despite the outwardly civil sheen to the gathering, they sensed violence and death. These men were ready to fight. Jock just hoped it wouldn't come to that.

Something nagged at the butcher. Someone was missing. With a start, he realised that Mary Brown was not present, nor was her husband. Jock had sent word to Willard, but the miller had not showed up. The only other absent wife was Sage Schuman, for obvious reasons. But where was Mary Brown? Murdering her husband at that very moment? It didn't matter. The only life Jock was interested in saving was his own. It was every man for himself now.

Stephen was getting into his work: the jig he played sped along at a frantic lilt, his face reddening with the effort. The manic expression on his sweaty face made Jock shudder, as if the fiddler were not entirely in control of himself, like a coachman whose horses had got away from him on a precarious cliff road. Samantha and Jasmine grabbed each other and began to whirl around the room. Helen and Charlene laughed. Keira continued to whisper in Elsie's ear.

The unease that Jock had tried so hard to drown in cider pricked at him, returning with vim and vigour, chattering in his head. Stephen squeezed his eyes tightly shut and grabbed onto his fiddlestick, his knuckles white. Samantha and Jasmine continued to dance madly in each other's arms, spinning and flinging each other away only to close in again. Helen, her eyes glistening within the circles of kohl, began to clap in time with the music, and Charlene joined her.

Jock became dimly aware that George was repeating his name. He ignored the blacksmith. *Too late, George*, he thought. *I know it's madness. But this will end the way it will end. The fates are cast.*

Samantha grabbed Jasmine by the head and roughly kissed her with a passion that Jock had never seen in his wife before, certainly never expressed to him. She liked women? How had he never suspected? Jasmine returned the kiss with great gusto, sucking and licking at Samantha's mouth and tongue. Charlene let out a lewd whistle and giggled. Something broke inside Jock.

CHAPTER 25 A Do at the Butchery

"Samantha!" he shouted. "You're still mine, and I expect you to behave as such! I'll not have a depraved slut as a wife!"

Stephen stopped playing as if he had been released from a spell. He dropped the fiddle, stumbled backwards against the wall and slumped to the floor, gasping for air. Jock closed his eyes. He hadn't meant to say it. Why had he said it? He'd fucked them all.

Keira Jack moved away from Elsie, green eyes on the butcher. "Thank you, Jock," she said.

Jock did not turn to meet her gaze. "Why ... do you thank me?"

"I thank you because I am sometimes confused by the thoughts that run through my own head. I thank you for speaking the truth on behalf of all men everywhere and making my task easier, particularly on my conscience." A perplexed frown came over Keira's face, and she examined her fingernails. "I think that a husband ofttimes does not value his wife for any other reason than what she makes him."

Jock grasped for a mug of cider, but they were all empty. "Makes him what?"

"Makes him a man."

"I don't understand."

"We are all simply reflections for someone else." Keira approached George. She stood behind him and lowered herself to one knee. She opened her mouth and leaned in, baring her teeth. Jock cringed, expecting the blacksmith to scream in agony, but Keira bit clean through the twine binding George's wrists to the chair. Jock's knees nearly gave out as Keira spat fine threads of twine from her teeth. George rubbed at his hands. He did not stand up.

"You're free to go," Keira said.

"You'll kill me as soon as my back is turned," George said without emotion.

Keira leaned in and snarled in the blacksmith's ear. "You may believe me when I say, George, that if I wanted you dead, you would see it coming and your eyes would be wide open. You may leave."

Jock spluttered, "Bu ... but ... why? I expended much effort to get him here. Surely, he is ... why?"

Keira straightened. "I hold no grudge against George Burridge."

"What? But … are you mad? You destroy us one by one. Why not him?"

"What is his crime?"

"He … he protected Douglas after the man killed your sister."

"And my brother-in-law will die. But my sister's death is not George's doing."

"But … it's *none* of our doing. Bessie's death had nothing to do with any of us except Douglas."

Keira approached Stephen and looked down at the panting fiddler. "You're wrong, Jock. George's loyalty lay with his friend. I do not begrudge him that. But where should *your* loyalty lie? And *his*?" She pointed at Stephen. "Where does a husband's first loyalty lie?"

Jock suspected he was beginning to understand. "With … with …"

"Say it, Jock. Is it so difficult to utter the words?"

"With his wife."

Keira nodded. "Just so." She turned to George. "Get out of here, now. I will not offer you another reprieve."

"I won't leave Douglas."

"You see?" Keira said to Jock. "Loyalty. Just be careful where you place it."

"You're insane," Jock said. "You murder innocent men simply because they have wives?"

Keira shook her head in annoyance. "You're not listening to me." She approached the long table. Suddenly, Keira whipped the tablecloth from the surface, sending empty mugs and plates of meat clattering to the floor. "Hop up here, Stephen."

George held out a hand still rubbed raw from his recent bonds. "Wait, you don't have to do this."

"Place your weapons on the floor," Keira said to no one in particular. One of Jock's men threw his sword on the bloodstained floor. The other two looked sideways at the first. The man had a pained expression as he rubbed at his temple.

"All of you," Keira said. From a second scabbard, a sword lifted

CHAPTER 25 A Do at the Butchery

without a finger being laid on it and floated to fall with the first sword. The third man swallowed hard and placed his sword with those of the other two men.

"Are you gentlemen married?" Keira asked. All three bodyguards nodded. "Then, I suggest you go home and eat some fanny." The three men looked at each other.

"Don't go," Jock said. "You must stay."

"Go now," Keira said. "Your fate is yet undecided. Your deaths will take place at a future place and time, and I will not be there to either orchestrate or witness them. If you stay, I will do both." The three men backed away.

"I paid you handsomely," Jock shouted. "Do not go!"

"Close the door on the way out," Keira said. "And remember what I said about eating your wives' cunts. I'll know if you don't." The three men turned and ran, closing the door to the slaughter yard behind them. Jock shouted after them, to no avail.

Keira beckoned to Stephen. "Get on the table, Mr. Fiddler."

"Don't do this, Keira," George said.

"You do not have to stay to witness any unpleasantness, George," Keira said. "You'll wish you hadn't. On the table, Stephen." Stephen whimpered but got to his feet and eased his long frame on the table. "Charlene, love, if you wouldn't mind strapping our lad down."

"I've got it," Charlene said. The tablecloth rose into the air and tore itself into strips, which wound their way around Stephen's torso and legs and then under and over the table, restraining him.

"Jasmine, love," Keira said. "How do you want to do him?"

"I want to do it the way you all did," Jasmine said, edging her way closer to her husband. She ran her hands up and down his torso as if he were a new and very expensive horse. "I want to take his profession, the only thing he ever loved more than me, and fucking kill him with it."

Keira smiled. "Cider the bastard to death."

"But how?" Jasmine asked.

"Force it down his throat, drown him in a bucket of it, pump it up his anus. Whichever pleases."

"Oh lord, Keira. You're just so imaginative. I can't think of half the things you do."

"It's a gift, love. Now, get in there and have some fun."

George stood to his full height. "Don't do it." He walked around the table to stand beside Douglas. He put a reassuring hand on the younger man's shoulder. "You don't need to do this."

"You can't stop us," Keira spat. "For all your strength as a man, you are the bottom of the barrel now. Each one of these girls in this room could tear you apart, each in their own way. Piss off."

"Stephen doesn't deserve this. Nor does Douglas."

Keira closed the distance between herself and George Burridge. The blacksmith must have seen the look in her eyes, for he raised an arm across his face, but it did not stop Keira. She lashed out with nothing but her bare hands and cut the big man's forearm to the bone. She kicked him in the balls, and his guard lowered momentarily. The next strike sliced George's throat. Blood sprayed over Keira's dress, over Douglas's face and shirt, over the floor, over the walls. George grabbed his throat and collapsed, gurgling to the floor, his breath rasping through a torn windpipe.

Jock's heart was pounding in his chest as he whispered, "Fuck, fuck, fuck," over and over. Douglas was twisting and turning in his chair, screaming incoherently, his eyes brimming with tears.

"Don't cry, dearest brother-in-law," Keira said. She leaned her blood-spattered face close to Douglas. The apprentice blacksmith turned his head away, but Keira grabbed him roughly by the jaw and brought his face back to hers. "You didn't cry when you dropped little Smudge. You didn't. Not one tear. Not in front of me, anyway. You fucking bastard, you cunt. George is dying and you're next. You'll see. But I'll fucking do you slow. Years, it'll take me. Years."

Helen laid a gentle hand on Keira's shoulder. "There is still time," the small, cherub-faced woman said, the whites of her eyes stark in contrast to the black makeup around them.

"We're out of time," Keira whispered, her gaze still fixed on Douglas.

"We're not the villains here," Helen said.

"How many of you feel this way?" Keira asked, stepping back and glancing around the room.

"We do the husbands. It's what we agreed," Elsie said.

"And anyone who stands in our way?"

"Case by case, ain't it?" Elsie shrugged.

Keira stood over the body of George Burridge and nodded to Helen. "Alright, then. If you are all decided. Fix him up."

Helen knelt by George's side. She reached out and grabbed the blacksmith's trembling shoulder. "He's far gone," she said.

"Can you reach him?"

"Aye, I can reach him."

Jock edged his way towards a discarded weapon on the floor while all eyes were on Helen and George. Surprised that he had got this far without anyone noticing him, Jock grabbed a sword and lunged at Keira.

But, of course, Keira Jack was not to be caught short on her bleed without a rag.

George Burridge woke and cursed his bed. The mattress was as cold and hard as a sheet of ice, and though he was not a man who cared for luxuries, this was ridiculous. He'd have to pay for a better mattress and damn the expense.

But he was not lying in his bed. He was lying alone on the cutting room floor of Jock Burgess' butchery. George sat up and blinked. His eyes gummed together with … something. He reached out and grabbed the edge of the table as nausea sloshed around in his guts. Hauling himself to his feet, he took a moment to recover his senses.

He wished he hadn't.

Jock Burgess hung cold and naked from a meat hook, his body slick with blood, his ribs exposed and entrails hanging from his stomach. Plates on the table lay evenly placed with raw cuts of meat and organs taken from the body of the butcher himself.

George put his hands on his knees and vomited. He wiped his mouth and saw the headless corpse of Stephen Cox under the table. George reeled away, looking for the door. The skull of the cider maker sat upturned at one end of the long table. It had been scraped and cleaned and now contained a shallow pool of the headless man's very own cider. The women had been drinking cider from Stephen's skull and eating Jock's raw flesh. George retched, having nothing left in his guts to throw up.

They were mad, utterly, hopelessly mad, all of them. George retched again and stumbled for the door. He clutched at his throat, remembering the damage done to him by Keira Jack. His neck was intact, though tender. They had spared him, healed him and let him live.

They had not spared Jock Burgess or Stephen Cox.

And Douglas, where was Douglas? He was not among the dead. Had they spared him too? No, Keira Jack had taken Douglas so that she could kill him slowly, without interruption and at her leisure. His death would outdo even tonight's depravity. It would be a death of unimaginable agony. Douglas was damned.

He was damned, and George could do nothing about it.

CHAPTER 26

Dead Metal

Madam Hathaway adjusted her large tits, pushing each one up to sit higher on her chest, exposing the twin swellings above her lace corset. The brothel owner performed this action with an appalling lack of discretion for a woman in her mid-forties. Constable Thackery marvelled at her utter disregard for common decency. No doubt she'd dressed like one of her whores explicitly to make him uncomfortable. Sergeants Jones and Frood, standing to attention by the door, exchanged glances and suppressed laughs.

"Are you kicking us out?" Madam Hathaway said, the beginnings of a snarl about her garishly painted lips.

"Hardly, madam, hardly," Thackery replied. "I term it a *relocation* for you and your girls. I have men coming in from West Quarter, courtesy of Constable Walters, and they'll need a place to bed down. Reinforcements, you see. We all have to make sacrifices."

"That's my desk you're sitting behind, all lordly and superior."

"It *was* your desk. The arrangement thus far will no longer do. The desk, like the entire building, has been requisitioned full-time to serve the Law."

"Yeah, well, we serve the city's cocks, a service not less important than yours."

Thackery's eyebrows raised. "I think you overestimate the importance of your industry's contributions, madam."

"Fancy words. You can't kick us out. We've got rights."

The constable spread his hands. "Look on the bright side. More men in town equate, if you'll do the arithmetic, to more potential customers. I'll happily steer the new gentlemen in your direction should they desire … leisure activities. Let me know where you choose to set up premises. I understand there are quite a few vacant shops around town. Now, if you'll excuse me, I am a very busy man. I have a witch-hunt to conduct."

Madam Hathaway raised her head haughtily. "We've been set up here since your father was in office, and he would never—"

"Enough, enough." Thackery waved a hand at Frood and Jones, and the two men escorted an outraged Madam Hathaway out of the door, one on each elbow. The ageing bawd found time to throw a few sailor's curses at the constable before the door closed behind her.

Thackery sat back and smiled. One down, one to go. Sister Kempson had outlived her usefulness. Christ, she never *had* any usefulness to begin with, but at least the woman was now aware of the fact. She should be here any minute. While he waited, Thackery glanced once more at the letter from Constable Walters in West Quarter. Walters was a buffoon, but at least he'd agreed to send men, South and East Quarters apparently understaffed and facing their own problems. Walters, however, wasn't the kind of man to send aid with no expectations of reciprocation. Thackery now owed Walters a large favour, and Thackery hated owing people favours.

Ah, there was the knock he had been waiting for. The door opened to allow Sister Kempson and her hired muscle ingress. Thackery caught the arse end of a few more curses from Madam Hathaway, who was apparently putting up quite a fight as she was dragged downstairs.

Garth retreated to a corner to lean menacingly in it. Thackery gestured for the nun to take the seat recently occupied by the bawd and was struck by the counterpoint between the two women: one a plump brothel manager, the other a plump bride of Christ. Oddly, the two women were less different than might be expected in both demeanour and attitude.

Thackery brushed the thought aside, lifted a box from the floor and placed it on the desk.

CHAPTER 26 Dead Metal

"Consider this," he said, pushing the box towards the nun, "a parting gift. A shame that things had to end this way, but there's just no controlling a spiteful woman, or several of them."

Sister Kempson blinked. "What is this?"

"Sage Schuman's worldly possessions, or at least what she was carrying on her when apprehended. Surviving relatives of the husband get the rest. She bequeathed these items to you. The Law states that a woman's last wishes, even those of a witch, would you believe, must be obeyed, and I have obeyed. There aren't many who gave a sideways shit for Sage Schuman's legal rights, but the Law is the Law. I'm sure you appreciate my efforts."

"Oh yes, Constable Thackery. Always. Why did she ... choose me?" Sister Kempson peered into the box.

Thackery blew air from his puffed-out cheeks. "I am unsure. Perhaps your attempts to save her soul were appreciated, if fruitless. It doesn't really matter." The constable leaned back in his chair. "You know, we've butted heads on occasion, but I bear no ill will. I hope that we part on good terms."

"Am I going somewhere?"

Thackery shifted uncomfortably in his chair. "You can't be staying, surely? Not after the debacle in the town square. You have failed in ... whatever it was you were sent here to accomplish. I know that sounds harsh, but how else can I put it? There's no more defending these women. No more saving of souls. Martial Law is in effect. I have men coming in from West Quarter, qualified men. That's how bad things have gotten. I'm recruiting from outside my own jurisdiction, a shameful loss of face for me, but I have little choice in the matter, and we must all make sacrifices. Your time here is over. For what possible reason would you wish to stay? Your efforts, commendable efforts, have come to an end."

The nun sighed, and Thackery waited for the inevitable counter, the acidic retort, the contemptuous scoff, but it never came. He was almost disappointed.

"You're right," she said, finally. "I have failed." Sister Kempson took a shawl from the box and stared at it. She put it back and removed a thin metallic bracelet. Sister Kempson rested the object in one pudgy palm. The band had been fashioned from an unusual metal: it had a soft lustre and perceptibly changed colours: blues, reds and oranges, no one colour remaining for long. The nun seemed drawn to the object and said nothing. Even Thackery struggled to say something appropriate as he, too, gazed at the bracelet.

Sister Kempson dreamily uttered, "I wonder where Sage got this?"

No one answered. Thackery did not answer. The large lump of a man lounging in the corner did not answer. Thackery supposed that the big man would be pissing off along with his mistress. He hoped so.

Thackery cleared his throat. "Well, if there's no other business, this is goodbye. A bittersweet parting but a necessary one."

The nun blinked and seemed to snap out of a trance. "Yes, I bid you good day." She dropped the bracelet into the box, gathered it and ambled from the room, Garth at her heels.

Thackery leaned back in his chair and closed his eyes. This was proving to be a good day. Two thorns had been removed from his backside in swift succession, and now all he had to do was track down and kill the rest of the harpies. Then, perhaps, life might return to normal, and the Law would reign supreme once again.

How he longed for the day.

Sister Kempson drank an entire mug of ale without uttering a word or even looking up, an unusual occurrence for the normally garrulous nun. Her sullen demeanour even began to draw odd looks from the other customers in the pub. It was clear to anyone with half a heart that she was depressed. Garth could sense it. He was not, under normal circumstances, the most empathetic of people; in fact, he did not often spare a thought for his fellow man. Someone had once called him a *misanthrope*. When Garth had learned the meaning of the word, he had simply shrugged and conceded that the word was a good one, a solid word, apt, and he would remember it and carry it with some amount of pride. "I'm a misanthrope," he would admit. "I don't care for your troubles. Fuck off."

But he sympathised with the fat nun. Sister Kempson had been gutted by the death of Sage Schuman, gutted by the fact that she hadn't been able to save the woman, physically or spiritually, or even find out what motivated her. She couldn't stop the deaths of either the husbands or the wives. Sister Kempson was a lost child in a world of demons, but at least she would be safe now that she had decided to return to the Holy Sisters of Conviction. She would go back to the convent to live out her days in peace and, in so doing, absolve Garth of his responsibilities as her bodyguard. He would be free to return to the True Wilds again, free of responsibility to anyone other than himself.

Sister Kempson burped and hurriedly covered her mouth. Garth smiled. The nun was a good person, as far as people went. He couldn't say the same for Thackery and his men, nor Keira Jack and her ladies. Garth was pleased that Sister Kempson would be right out of it, out of danger, out of the crossfire between two forces, each as insane as the other. The convent was the only place that made sense. It was the right place for her.

"I am not returning to the convent," Sister Kempson said suddenly.

Garth frowned. "Eh?"

"I feel a sense of ... something unaccomplished."

Garth shook his head. "Thackery's a complete prick, but he was right when he said there's nothing more you can do here. This is war now, war between the Law and the Ladies. You can't do anything about it. You shouldn't be here. Things are bad, but they are going to get a lot worse."

"How could you know that, Garth?"

"That's the one thing I *do* know. These women aren't going to just fade away, and Thackery isn't going to let them. They see each other as the enemy. This is no place for a nun. You can't save anybody. It's gone too far."

"You sound just like him."

"As I said, the man is a fopdoodle, but he—"

"Yes, yes, I know. No place for a naïve nun."

Garth sighed. "You were never meant to succeed here. You cannot blame yourself."

Sister Kempson slowly screwed up her brows. "What do you mean I was never *meant* to succeed here? What are you suggesting?"

Garth hesitated. "Do not take this the wrong way, but …"

"But what?"

"You were not given the resources to … a solitary woman thrown into the deep end. You … you …"

"Garth, what are you trying to say?"

"If the bishop had been serious about this whole thing, you wouldn't have been assigned this task alone."

"I am not alone. I have you."

Garth threw up his hands. "Yes, alright. I just think we find ourselves unprepared for what we have encountered here. It is time to withdraw." Sister Kempson went back to dreamily supping her second ale, which had been presented without asking for it. "You're drinking too much," Garth observed. "The barkeep isn't waiting to serve your next beer. Not a good sign for a nun, I would suggest."

"My dear Garth, I'll think on what you have said over this drink."

A glint of light caught Garth's eye. "What's that?" he said.

"What's what?" Kempson responded innocently.

"Are you carrying the dead woman's bracelet?"

The nun looked down and pulled Sage Schuman's bracelet from a habit pocket. "Yes. I like the glow it produces."

Garth rubbed at the red growth of his stubble. "I don't know much about nuns, but I know they don't carry jewellery around."

"I won't have it for long. I'm just … contemplating it."

Garth shrugged. "If you say so."

"It has Bessie Partridge's name on it." Sister Kempson held up the band, and Garth peered at it. In small script on the inside of the band was the name *Bessie*.

The big woodsman recoiled. "You're in possession of a dead

woman's bracelet with the name of another dead woman engraved on it. Makes my skin crawl."

Sister Kempson seemed unaware of Garth's discomfort as she slipped the bracelet back into her pocket. "Anyway, I won't go," she said. "I have made my mind up. I am staying in Dysael."

"Please, Rose. This is not a good idea."

Sister Kempson stared at her ale and said softly, "You may not address a nun by her given name alone."

"I'm sorry, but you shouldn't be drinking a face full of booze, nor hanging around this place, or wearing a dead woman's jewellery. Sister Kempson, you must get out of Dysael."

"I can't, Garth. If I run now, I'm admitting defeat."

"There's nothing shameful about defeat."

"But I still feel I can serve some purpose here."

"What purpose? The wives are beyond helping. They have nothing but murder in their hearts. You've tried, to your credit, but they won't sway from their path, and you'll only get yourself killed getting in their way. You're also likely to get a bullet in the back of your head from Thackery, and he'll call it a mistake in public and be grateful in private. This town is condemned as far as I'm concerned. You're better off getting right out of it, as far away as you can."

"You make a lot of sense, Garth."

"Aye, I do. So, pack up your things and let me escort you back to the convent."

"You've been longing to get out of this place since we arrived."

"I won't deny it, but that's by the by."

Sister Kempson sipped thoughtfully at her ale. A large shape at the periphery of Garth's vision caused him to reach for the hunting knife at his belt. He relaxed when George Burridge approached them.

"May I join you?" George said.

Sister Kempson nodded. "Would you like a drink?"

George sat down beside the nun. "Aye, I'll take a beer." Garth shook his head angrily. The last thing Sister Kempson needed was a drinking companion. "They took Douglas," George said. "Murdered Jock and Stephen but took Douglas. I think they mean to torture him before they eventually kill him."

Sister Kempson's puffy face turned white. She drank a little more, but it didn't add any colour to her cheeks. "That's dreadful," she said. "I ... I'm sorry. I wish there was something I could do."

"There is," George said, sipping at his beer, which had arrived swiftly, probably already lined up for Sister Kempson. "You can help me. You can get Douglas out before it's too late."

Garth nearly hauled the blacksmith from his seat and dragged him out the door. The nun was on the cusp of leaving Dysael, and now this idiot was encouraging her to stay.

Sister Kempson sat straighter on her chair. "Why do you think I can be of assistance?"

"Because you're the only one who deals in forgiveness. The only one. It is only forgiveness that can save Douglas."

"No," Garth said, unable to bite his tongue any longer. "Sister Kempson must return to the Holy Sisters of Conviction. Nobody is interested in forgiveness, not here."

Sister Kempson raised a hand. "Steady on. Let the man speak."

"I won't. I've heard enough," Garth said angrily. "You are my responsibility, and your welfare falls upon me. I'll not have you wandering around Dysael on any more idiotic crusades. This is over, for you at least."

"I think you've quite forgotten your place, Garth. Yes, you are to guard against dangers to my person, but also to go where I go. You do not have the authority to terminate my mission here. Only the bishop may do that."

Garth slammed his hand down on the counter, causing both Sister Kempson and George Burridge to flinch. "I can't protect you anymore! There are too many threats from too many sides. This situation is beyond anything I can control. If you go on, you go on without me."

Sister Kempson spoke quietly. "I need you, Garth."

Garth grimaced and turned away. He kicked an empty chair, and it flew into a table occupied by two elderly drinkers, rocking the table and spilling both their ales. The men stood, cast frightened glances at Garth and scurried from the tavern. The publican growled and made menacing noises about lost income.

Garth turned to the burly barkeep and said, "I'll have an ale." The man grunted, pulled an ale and presented it to Garth. He drank it with vicious intent and turned to Sister Kempson, who was staring wide-eyed. Garth then glared at the blacksmith. "Why," he said. "Why the hell do you think the sister can help you, and don't give me any bullshit about forgiveness."

"She's the only person the wives don't despise," George said. "I overheard them talking when I was ... I was out cold, but I think I heard them talking. Sister Kempson can get in without them harming her. I can't trust anyone else. If I tell Thackery what I know, he'll blunder in and get Douglas killed."

"What do you mean tell Thackery what you know? What do you know?"

George Burridge fingered the scars at his neck. "I know where they are," he said. "I know where to find them. I think."

"How," Garth blurted, "could you possibly know where to find them?"

"They carried a scent upon them."

"Scent?" Sister Kempson said, leaning in closer to the blacksmith. "What scent?"

"A tang that any man who works with metal would recognise. The scent of dead metal."

"Dead metal?" Garth scowled. "What are you talking about?"

"You'd know it were your livelihood tied to smithing," George said. "I think they're down in the Yard."

"What's the Yard?" Garth asked.

George rubbed at his beard. "The abandoned industrial district in the heart of the city."

"Extraordinary," Sister Kempson said, "that you have located them from your olfactory senses alone."

"Aye," Garth said angrily, "a little too extraordinary for my liking.

I have a pretty good nose myself, and this smells very wrong. I urge you again, Sister, to pull up stakes and get out of Dysael. Do you hear me?"

Sister Kempson nodded. "I hear you."

"Please, Sister," George said. "I beg you to help Douglas."

"Shut up, man," Garth snarled.

"Garth, put a civil tongue back in your head," Sister Kempson said. "Can you not see that Mr. Burridge is in pain?"

"I see it and don't give a shit. He and his crew made their beds. I don't wish to sound cruel, but maybe Douglas is getting what he deserves."

George pushed aside his chair and stood to his full height. Garth squared up to the big blacksmith, and the two men glowered at each other.

"Gentlemen," Sister Kempson said. "Violence solves nothing. I would have thought that would be apparent by now. Put your aggression back in the box."

"Douglas does not deserve torture and a slow death," George said, his voice tremoring. "You didn't see what they done to Jock and Stephen. Cut strips from them, gutted them. Cut Stephen's head off and drank from his skull. There were still bits of flesh and hair hanging from it." Garth frowned and blinked several times. "They're animals," George went on. "Douglas did wrong. I know he did. Bring him back and let the law take its course, but he doesn't deserve what those women are planning for him. It's probably already started, and I cannot imagine …" The blacksmith trailed off and slumped back down in his chair. He lowered his head and put his hands over his eyes.

"Good Lord," Sister Kempson whispered. She looked from George to Garth and back again. "Mr. Burridge, let me discuss this with my colleague. I'll approach you at your smithy with my answer as soon as I have decided what my course of action will be."

George looked up hopefully. "I'm staying with Adam Jackson, the farrier on Thornton Street. I've sold up my own shop. Find me there as soon as you can, please."

CHAPTER 26 Dead Metal

George Burridge walked from the pub with his head held low. The nun went right back to her ale without a word. Garth sipped at his own drink, but it did nothing to ease the growing concern in his head and heart. Sister Kempson had said that the bishop was the only one with the power to call her home, but what the nun did not know was that Garth had, indeed, been gifted that exact authority by the prelate, without the nun's knowledge. It was a final ace up his sleeve that he was reluctant to play. Rose Kempson had the whole city of Dysael against her, the law in particular, but had managed to maintain her dignity if not her confidence. He'd rather not remove what powers of self-governance she had left. If the nun had any sense, she'd make the decision to get out on her own. Surely, she saw the sense in leaving.

Garth snorted into his beer and said, "Dead metal. Never heard such a stupid thing."

Sister Kempson said something about retiring early for the evening to ponder her next move. Garth escorted her to her room and bade her good night. He slept on the floor in the adjoining room, as was his custom. He slept light, as was his custom. He awoke before the sun the next morning, as was his custom. And he checked on the nun, as was his custom.

Sister Kempson was not in her bed. She had arisen sometime in the night to steal away so quietly that she had not alerted Garth.

And that was anything but customary.

CHAPTER 27

Teeth on a Leash

Roy Barker whistled quietly as he strode purposefully down the street. He was feeling fit as a fiddle for a man in his middle years—or early late years if he were quite honest with himself. Not even the darkening clouds and biting winds could erode his cheerfulness this evening, for Roy Barker was on his way to have sexual relations with a randy widow.

Roy grinned to himself. There was nothing better than coitus with a randy widow. Barbara Sandhurst was an absolute animal between the sheets. It had been many years since Roy had managed to bed a younger woman, but he was damned sure no woman in her teens or twenties rutted quite like the esteemed Mrs. Sandhurst. She did things no decent woman should do. Roy burst into another bout of whistling.

There was her house now, a large two-story affair with several upstairs bedrooms in which Mrs. Sandhurst rented rooms to women down on their luck. Something about making love to Mrs. Sandhurst in a house populated by women pleased Roy, almost as if he was an exotic emperor from faraway lands, the ruler of a small kingdom containing his private harem.

Roy checked that none of the tenants of the boarding house were coming in or out before he inserted his private key into the brass lock plate. Only boarders were supposed to have a key, but Roy didn't particularly care if he was discovered in the act of entering the premises. None of the girls really had a say in the matter, and after

CHAPTER 27 Teeth on a Leash

all, Barbara Sandhurst had provided him with the object herself. Still, he felt an illicit thrill run through him, as if he were sixteen again and creeping in the back window to shag the washerwoman in the pub scullery before the doors opened for the day.

He stepped into the hallway and was immediately disconcerted by a cloak stand lying sideways on the floor near the front door. Mrs. Sandhurst ran an immaculately tidy ship, and this aberration was most unlike his paramour. He heard a scuffling coming from the sitting room on the right and poked his head inside. Mrs. Sandhurst sat on the divan, her wrists bound with a leather belt and her mouth stuffed with a rag. Her eyes were wide as she stared at Roy.

Roy's first thought was that he had caught Mrs. Sandhurst in the act of 'courtly romance' with another man, but that was absurd. Not here in the sitting room, surely not. An unseen figure from behind the door reached out and grabbed Roy by the lapel. The room spun around as he was hauled bodily across the carpet and flung at the feet of the whimpering landlady.

"I say," Roy said, sitting up, "what is the meaning of this?"

The man standing over Roy spoke with a rasp. "Shut up, old man. Night Watch business. That's all you need to know. Get on the sofa and keep quiet."

Despite the force with which Roy had been hurled across the room, the man responsible was not large, though he was ugly. He had scratch marks and red scars over his face and neck, where a scraggly beard grew in asymmetrical patches. Roy sat beside Mrs. Sandhurst, who wore her customary check skirt and patted the crying woman on the knee. "There, there, Barbara. There, there."

A dog barked from somewhere upstairs, immediately followed by the screams of several frightened women. A thumping in the hallway above shivered through the ceiling. What on earth was going on up there? Shouts of men mixed in with the shrieks of frightened women and the snarling of at least two dogs, big ones judging from the baritone rumble of the animals. Footsteps came downstairs, and a man entered the sitting room.

"We have them cornered, Sergeant Frood." The newcomer looked at Roy and gestured. "Who's that?"

Sergeant Frood scratched at his uncooperative beard and said, "Dunno. Don't care. Tell Graham not to unleash the dogs until Thackery gets here. But if they try anything funny, let the animals go."

The man disappeared, leaving Sergeant Frood with Roy Barker and Barbara Sandhurst. The Night Watch officer brusquely removed the gag from Mrs. Sandhurst's mouth, and the woman inhaled sharply in pain. "Quiet now. I ask the questions; you furnish answers. What are the names of them upstairs?"

"Excuse me, Sergeant Frood, was it?" Roy said. "I must insist that Mrs. Sandhurst's hands be unbound. She is a woman of upstanding quality, and this treatment of her is quite—"

Frood backhanded Roy across the face. Lights burst in Roy's vision, and a bruise formed instantly on his cheek. "I'm not talking to you. Shut your mouth." The sergeant turned back to the landlady. "Names. Who's up there?"

"I ... I don't know, not off hand. I'll have to check the register."

"Come now. You don't know who boards on your own property?"

"My memory is ... has been patchy of late."

"An unlikely story. I say you are harbouring fugitives from the law, a charge that carries a heavy penalty."

The landlady's eyes widened in fright. "Fugitives? But ... I don't understand."

Blood began to trickle from Mrs. Sandhurst's nose. Anger rose in Roy, and despite the blow to his face moments before, he spoke up once more. "How dare you assault this woman? I'll have you thrown out of the constabulary. Outrageous. Your superiors shall hear of this, mark my words."

Frood blinked and stepped back. "I ain't touched her. But you, I'll smack again if you speak out of order." The sergeant frowned at the blood flowing from the landlady's nose. He unbound her hands and offered a handkerchief. She dabbed at the blood.

"It's alright, Roy," Mrs. Sandhurst said. "Just another nosebleed, that's all. Don't anger this man. He's clearly unbalanced."

A moustachioed man burst into the sitting room. Roy recognised him as Chief Constable Thackery. The city official took in the scene and raised an eyebrow at Frood, who gestured upstairs. Before Roy could protest their ill treatment, Thackery was gone.

❉

Constable Thackery leapt up the stairs. He came to a landing upon which stood six burly men at an open doorway. The men were all West Quarter fellows, three of whom were specialists in handling dogs. The three held leashes of large mastiffs at least as powerfully built, in canine terms, as their masters. The dogs were pulling against their leashes, but their handlers would not allow them to enter the room. At Thackery's feet, a small fluffy white spaniel lay twisted in death, mauled. Its throat was a mass of torn flesh, the small animal's dead eyes open and its tongue hanging from its head.

One of the dog handlers turned to Thackery as he approached. Sergeant Graham was a large man with a large jaw, almost oversized, giving him an unsettling appearance, as if he were closer in biology to his dog than his fellow humans. He must have noticed the wary looks Thackery was giving the mastiffs.

"They're alright, Constable Thackery," Graham said. "They are under control. You need not fear."

"Why?" Thackery said, pointing at Mrs. Sandhurst's dead pet. "I can hardly believe that animal offered a serious threat to anyone."

Graham shrugged nonchalantly. "Got in the way. My boys need their fun."

"It was unnecessary," Thackery said. "Remember, Sergeant Graham, at the first sign of anything untoward in your animals, you put a firearm to their heads. One of the witches controls animals, that has been made clear to you."

Graham nodded and patted his dog. "Aye, sir. But I promise you, no woman will supersede my authority, witch or not. I raised this lot from pups, and they know no other lord. I am their master.

They will not turn against me."

"You're new in North Quarter, Sergeant. Just remember what I said. I'm not having a piece of my arse nipped off by your dogs."

Thackery edged his way past the dogs and their handlers and peered inside the room. Four women huddled together, clasping at each other and gazing fearfully at the snarling mastiffs. The oldest must have been in her sixties, the youngest no older than seventeen. Thackery recognised none of them.

"For Christ's sake," Thackery said. "This is not them. Any fool can see it's not them."

Graham frowned. "My boys are onto the scent, and they do not make mistakes."

"I don't care what your dogs think. These are not the women we seek. Have you not been provided with accurate descriptions?"

"Well, they've been here then, sir. My boys got a jolly good sniff of their clothing that was provided. My boys don't make mistakes."

"So you keep saying." Thackery tweaked a moustache and, without a word, rushed back downstairs. He found the landlady weeping on the divan. An elderly man was attempting to comfort her. Frood stood over them both.

The older fellow looked up and said, "Mrs. Sandhurst has received quite a shock. Is all this kerfuffle really necessary?"

"Your name?" Thackery asked.

"I am Roy Barker."

"And your relationship to Mrs. Sandhurst, that is her name, yes?" Thackery turned to Frood, who nodded.

"I'm a friend, paying a social visit," Roy said.

Blood dripped from the woman's nose, a bloodied handkerchief in her hand testament to the bleed's unwillingness to stop. Thackery glared at Frood.

"I didn't touch her," Frood said, raising his hands.

Thackery noted the bruise on Roy Barker's face. "What about him?"

Frood shifted his weight. "Aye, I belted him."

"There's a little too much uncontrolled violence going on here today, Sergeant. Let's keep this civilised while we can." Thackery addressed the landlady and her associate. "I apologise for this whole fracas, but we have good cause to be here. We are seeking a group of murderers, *murderesses* in this case. Foremost among them is a woman by the name of Keira Jack. I believe she is the chief inciter of the terrible events happening in Dysael of late. Others go by the name of Elsie Gallagher, Helen Hardcastle and Charlene Hickson, to name but a few. Do they reside here, or have they done so at any point in the past? Do these names mean anything to you, Mrs. Sandhurst?"

The landlady seemed dazed, as if the invasion of her boarding house by the constabulary had left her bereft of intellect. "I … uh, those names sound familiar, but I can't be sure. I have many women come through, and my memory… " She raised a hand to her temple. "I've been suffering headaches, you see."

"Do you keep a register?"

"Yes, I do, but I can't seem to recall where I put it." Barbara Sandhurst dabbed at her bleeding nose once more.

"And you, Mr. Barker? Do you know these women that I have named?"

"I do not acquaint myself with guests in the house. I simply visit my dear friend." Here, he patted the woman on her knee. "Most of the boarders tend to keep to themselves at any rate."

Thackery glanced at Frood. "Find the register." As Frood stalked away, Thackery added, "Don't destroy the place in the process, Sergeant."

Mrs. Sandhurst gasped and looked up suddenly. "Where is my Nubby?"

Thackery frowned. "Nubby? Who is this Nubby?"

"Nubby, where are you?" Mrs. Sandhurst attempted to stand but sank back on the divan and put her head in her hands.

"Who is Nubby?" Thackery asked Roy.

"Her continental toy poodle," Roy said. He cast a sad sideways glance at the landlady. "The love of her life, fair to say." He put his arm around her shoulders and then rubbed her back.

Thackery grimaced. He didn't mention that the love of Mrs. Sandhurst's life lay upstairs with its throat torn out. If she laid eyes on the ruined carcass of her pet, she wouldn't be any good to anyone for the rest of the day, and Thackery needed answers. "We'll have men search for the dog later. Probably hiding under a bed somewhere, do not fret. Right now, I need to know where Keira Jack and her insane harpies are hiding. Those women upstairs are the wrong lot. Where's that damn register?"

Mrs. Sandhurst struggled to her feet and stumbled. "Nubby? Come here, boy." She began to totter for the door and the stairs.

"My dear Mrs. Sandhurst," Thackery said, taking her by the elbow and guiding her back to the divan. "We shall attend to the matter of your dog shortly. A few more moments of your time. Perhaps Mr. Barker can make everyone a cup of tea. I assume he knows where the kitchen is?"

"Yes, yes. Of course." Roy Barker pushed himself off the sofa and, with a final concerned glance at Barbara Sandhurst, shuffled from the room.

Frood entered the sitting room a moment later. "Can't find any register."

Thackery swallowed a curse. He blinked and stared at Frood. Blood dripped from the scrawny sergeant's nose. Thackery pointed at it. "Your nose is bleeding," he said.

"Again?" Frood no longer had a handkerchief, having given it to Mrs. Sandhurst, so he wiped his bloody nose on his sleeve.

Thackery frowned and looked from the sergeant to the landlady and back again. "How long have you been having nosebleeds, Frood?"

"Ever since that bitch Elsie Gallagher got in my head."

Thackery nodded to himself. Sergeant Graham was right about his dogs. They had, in fact, caught the scent. The harpies had been here, most certainly, but had fled.

But the Law was onto their scent now. There would be no escape.

❇

Helen Hardcastle found herself in unexplored territory. The foggy streets had the tinge of familiarity but only in the way dreams are familiar and yet utterly foreign at the same time, half-remembered and half fever dream. Her feet padded silently on the street made of a clear stone, a kind of gauzy hard rock. She was barefoot, yet the roads did not cause distress to her feet. Chilled them, yes, but otherwise left them unharmed. Structures, some intact but most in a state of crumbling ruin, loomed out of the mists. The streets appeared indistinct, maze-like.

He was going deeper, of this there could be no doubt, but still, there were only the two of them, and it should not be taking this long to find him. Helen's breath rasped icy raw at the back of her throat: the air was so cold and growing colder. She had to locate him soon, or he may find his freedom in the pale and misty avenues of this ethereal city.

A stone skittered somewhere in a courtyard containing what looked to be a collapsed church. Something moved on the exposed beams of the upper floors of the structure. Entering the courtyard, Helen surmised that the only way to get to the upper levels of the church, if it was indeed a church, was to clamber up the broken walls. Helen hitched her black gown and then gave up on the idea of protecting her fancy dress. She needed two hands to climb, and the dress would just have to take its licks and dirty up. Not that it mattered, not here, at any rate.

She climbed, hand over foot, like she had as a tomboyish young girl climbing the apple trees in the orchards around Dysael. She came to a dusty but sturdy plank and caught her breath. Something whimpered from the dark corner of the partially collapsed room. Stepping across groaning planks, Helen slowly approached a small figure huddled in the corner. The child, a young boy, had his face in his hands. He turned, exposing damp blond curls. As his hands lowered, his bottom lip trembled.

"Who are you? Please stay away."

"Steady," she said. "It's only me. It's Helen. I've come to take you back."

"Take me back? Take me back where? I can't ... I can't remember where I am or where I came from."

"That's alright, don't worry, lad. I can explain everything. Just take my hand, and we'll go back together." Helen reached out to the boy. "You don't want to say here cold and alone, do you?"

"Are you my mother?"

Helen shook her head. "No, I'm not your mum."

"Is she waiting for me?"

Helen hesitated and eventually decided on the truth. "No, your mum's not waiting for you. You're not a child in the other place. Don't you remember?"

"I don't remember."

"Come on. It's cold. You'll catch your death out here. You don't want to die, do you?"

"I want my mum. I want ... I want ..."

Helen raised an eyebrow over a dark kohl-rimmed eye. "Yes? Who do you want? Come on, Douglas, try to remember. Who do you want?"

"I want my Bessie."

Helen smiled and made a come-hither gesture with her fingers. "There you go. You can come back now. Just take my hand."

Douglas reached out and tentatively took Helen's fingers.

And the moment he did so, he screamed.

Douglas Partridge screamed. He screamed in agony. Blood blurred his vision so that he could not see anything except Keira Jack standing over him. He struggled against the bonds holding him, and beneath the chair pooled ichor and sputum, his bodily fluids. Several rags had been tied about his shirtless body at various places to stem the bleeding. He hurt everywhere, his face, head, hands, legs, his penis burned, and even his organs ached. He gasped for breath. Keira Jack held some kind of metal tool in her hands, indistinguishable from the blood coating her fingers.

Douglas screamed again.

CHAPTER 27 Teeth on a Leash

Helen Hardcastle stood by, breathing hard, looking whiter than her usual pale self.

"What took so long?" Keira said, wiping her hands onto her green ball gown.

Helen leaned forward, puffing, hands on her knees. "He's going deeper into the abandoned places of his mind. He was hard to catch this time."

"Don't tell me that. We've only just started. He can't be escaping me inside his own head. I won't have it. You need to get him back every time he tries to cross over."

"How many times have you killed him now?" Charlene Hickson asked from nearby, her arms folded over her chest. Charlene was the only other person in the small room. One wall was formed of canvas, which fluttered in a whistling wind.

"That makes five," Keira said. "And what's it to you? You feeling sorry for the bastard?"

Charlene shrugged and turned away. "Not me. Just asking is all."

Keira turned back to Helen as Douglas gurgled and spat blood. "Don't let him get away, love. He owes me a lot more pain yet. This ain't over 'til I say so."

"I won't, Keira. I'll find him. No matter where he goes, I'll find him."

"That's my lass." Keira leaned in over Douglas and pulled his head back by his short blond hair. "Did you hear that, Douglas? You can't escape me, not even in death. There's nowhere you can go. You're mine until I've burnt out every fibre of pain your body has to give. Every last bit of your soul I shall squeeze from you in drops of sheer, brutal pain. My only wish is that you healed the way we do and that I didn't have to be careful with your fragile body. Truthfully, I don't *want* to be careful with you. I want to tear you to shreds, but you couldn't handle it, Douglas, and I'd have my fun only once. You're not man enough to take the hiding I really want to dish out." Keira kissed Douglas' forehead, and blood smeared her lips. She smiled as she held the gory object of torture under Douglas' nose.

"Here we go again, love. Here we go again."

CHAPTER 28

The Space Between

Willard cradled Jess on the back of the horse he had stolen from Freddie Burns. Poor Freddie. Willard had whacked the Night Watch private a good blow with the kitchen chair. He hoped he hadn't done any long-term damage to the young man's head or spine. Freddie wasn't a bad fellow, but Willard couldn't let him strike at Mary. Freddie simply hadn't understood the situation. Mary was not there to hurt either of them, but the young private hadn't understood that.

Willard and Mary were now on the open roads outside of Dysael, the city several leagues behind them. Jess didn't like it up on the back of the horse, but they had a long distance to cover, and she wasn't a young pup anymore. Mary walked in front of them, an unhurried stride that somehow kept her always ahead of the horse. Odd that a woman walking with a languid sway could keep pace with a horse, in fact, keep ahead of it with ease.

The skies were cool but clear, as free of clouds as the roads were of traffic, the occasional scudding cloud or isolated rider coming the other way the only thing to mar the tranquil beauty of the day. The roads were in good condition, considering the recent rains. Willard's spirits lifted. He'd been unhappy to leave the millhouse, but what did a house or even a business matter when his wife had returned from the dead? Money, however, was a different story. They'd need money to start a new life, and Willard had invested everything in the millhouse. Still, that could not be helped. They would find another way, somewhere else.

In the late afternoon, Mary looked back at Willard and pointed to a line of trees in the distance. "I'll be back soon," she said.

"Where are you going?"

"To get supplies. I won't be long."

Willard nodded, and his wife disappeared into the trees. She returned barely a half hour later with a skinned rabbit for their supper. With unease, Willard noticed the absence of a bow and knife. Over the next few days, this pattern repeated. Mary would slip away into the trees or run across open fields to vanish somewhere among the long grass. She would return with game or tight bunches of vegetables. Willard never asked where she got them, perhaps dreading the answer. He ignored the growing discomfort, ignored the uneasy suspicions chittering at the back of his mind.

They were heading south for Dunedin because Willard had a brother there. The journey stretched more than a hundred leagues. Still, with a plentiful supply of fresh food, courtesy of Mary, and clear roads, they would arrive in a fortnight. Things would be better then. Everything would be alright.

That night, they set up a fire. It crackled between them, giving a sheen to Mary's eyes. Her hair looked like threads of molten gold.

"You are very quiet, Willard," she said.

"I apologise. It's been a difficult time."

His wife nodded. "Difficult. The loss of a child. That is indeed difficult."

"I feel ... I feel I should miss her more."

Mary tilted her head. "You cannot miss a person you never had a chance to know. I knew her, for she grew within me. They have taken much from us but not my time with her. Do you understand me, Willard? Do you understand me when I say that I knew Victoria?"

"I understand."

"I grieve for you, Willard, because you didn't have the chance." Mary looked to the stars twinkling above. "They'll pay for what they did to us. One day."

"Who? Who will pay?"

Mary shook her head. "Never mind. I talk idly. I am not even sure towards whom my anger is directed."

"What happened to you? In the time that you were gone? There was so much blood the day ... the day you disappeared. I heard ... stories of strange events in the city."

"Stories." Mary gazed into the fire. "It's all only stories, Willard. We choose the ones we like. I'll tell you my story one day."

"But I don't understand."

"Neither do I."

"You are a million leagues distant from me."

Her brows furrowed, and Mary remained silent for a long time. The stars dimmed and brightened again as clouds passed in the darkening skies. "I'm sorry," she said. "I have returned, but ... I feel the distance between us too. I'm changed, I know. But I'm still in here, Willard. Your Mary is still inside this shell somewhere. I'll find her and bring her to you just as soon as I can."

A reply would not come. Willard looked away. He sighed, fighting back the tears. Finally, he nodded and lay down beside the fire. Before he drifted off, he was aware of Mary placing a blanket over him. He murmured his thanks and closed his eyes. His sleep was restless, plagued by strange dreams of wolves and bears, of animalistic howling coming from dark cave openings. Dreams of soft flesh with striated claw marks.

In a small rural hamlet three days' ride out of Dysael, Willard approached a furrier and sold the rabbit skins they, or Mary more precisely, had collected along the way. The pelts were of good quality and gave them enough coin to buy basic provisions for the next stage of their journey. Mary made sure to keep her head under the cowl of her travelling cloak the entire time they stayed in the village, and Jess attended to her every step. Mary said that they should be away from the hamlet as soon as possible. Willard asked if Mary needed to take time to recuperate from three days' solid

CHAPTER 28 The Space Between

trek on foot, perhaps an evening in a comfortable bed. Mary needed no time to get her strength back, she said. She had all the strength she would ever need. Willard nodded, and, once they had paid for their supplies, the man, woman and dog set out on the road again.

But they did not set out alone. Three men followed behind at a casual trot; whether locals from the town or journeymen simply passing through as Willard and Mary had done, it was difficult to tell. The men wore sheepskin or tanned leather cloaks that spoke of quality, but the affluence of their outfits attested nothing of the nature of the travellers wearing them or their intentions.

Willard had no need to inform Mary of his suspicions. His wife was on edge, often glancing at the men behind. There was always danger on the road, but Mary and Willard had little worth the risk of taking. But even a little was much valued by desperate men.

Willard hoped those following them were not desperate men.

"I want them in front of us," Mary said.

Willard blinked out of his reverie. "What do you mean?"

Mary pointed to a grassy embankment. "We get off the road and rest until they pass us. I am uneasy with them at our backs. I don't trust them."

"What if they do not wish to pass us?"

"One horse will not outrun three. Whatever happens, let it happen now."

Willard nodded. They weren't far from the hamlet where they had sold the rabbit furs, and if there was trouble, perhaps they could ride back for help. Mary led the horse off the road at a casual pace, ambling as if she were quite untroubled by the three men following them, as if she were simply stopping to enjoy the cool breeze and green grass or a bite to eat.

Willard dismounted about thirty yards from the road, and he and Mary sat on the grassy embankment. Willard called Jess to heel. The strangers approached the point where Mary and Willard had left the road and stopped. They murmured amongst themselves, and then a large, grey-bearded man shouted in their direction.

"Hello, fellow wayfarers," he said, waving. "All health to thee."

Willard returned the traditional traveller's greeting. "All health to thee."

"Where are you headed?"

"Don't tell him," Mary whispered.

"Uh, Westport," Willard said.

"You're going the wrong way," the big fellow smiled. He pointed back the way they had come. "Westport's that way, a long way that way." The three men kicked at their horses and directed them towards Willard and Mary.

Jess growled, but Mary hushed her up. Husband and wife stood as the three men approached. Willard had not brought his axe, but he still had the kitchen knife. However, that implement rested out of reach in his saddle bag. He considered lunging for it, but that might be an inappropriate reaction to what could be a simple social interaction. Or this whole thing might be something more sinister. It was hard to tell until someone went for a weapon, but for now, the three men seemed to be unarmed and peaceful.

"It's a fine day for travelling," the grey-bearded man said.

"It is," Willard agreed. He edged closer to his horse and the saddle bag containing the kitchen knife, but one of the other men positioned his horse between Willard and his own animal. Willard swallowed.

"You'd better make haste," Mary said. She bit into a piece of rabbit meat and chewed. All eyes turned towards her. "Before the weather changes."

The grey-bearded fellow looked at Mary closely and then raised his head to the clear blue skies. "Do you know something I don't?"

Mary nodded. "Aye. I know things can change. One day, you're going about your business, and the next—" Here she tore another piece of meat and ground away. "—you're different."

"Different?"

"Dead." The three men stared. "Or alive but frightened and alone. Lost. A victim."

The large man frowned. "A victim of what?"

Mary met the man's gaze. "Who knows?" She took a step forward, and the man's horse snorted and shied away. The rider struggled to control his animal for a few moments. Mary took another step, and all three horses reared and walked backwards.

"You've no time for pleasant conversation," Mary said. "The weather is changing. Best be on your way."

The grey-bearded man looked from Mary to Willard and back again, seemingly contemplating his next action. Finally, he looked to the skies and said, "Aye. It's good travelling weather at the moment, and we'd best take advantage of it." The three men turned their horses and trotted away.

Willard let out a long breath. Mary spat a chunk of rabbit gristle to the grass.

That night, at Mary's suggestion, they set up a small fire far from the road. After the events of earlier in the day, Mary was unwilling to meet any more strangers, though Willard maintained that the three men on horseback had harboured no ill intentions.

Mary couldn't tell Willard that he was wrong. He would have asked how she had known, and she would have struggled to answer because she did not know herself. But those men had meant to rob them, or worse. Her instincts told her so, and these new instincts were to be trusted above all else. But how could she explain that to Willard? The man was like a leery cat, wishing to be stroked but on the verge of running in fright the whole time. Willard did not completely trust her, and Mary could hardly blame him. She had returned to him after weeks of unexplained absence. The rumours said that the wives had come to murder the husbands, and the rumours were quite correct. The fact that Willard had not run or attempted to turn her in to the law surprised and pleased her. He had shown loyalty despite his wariness, and she would do the same. She would not murder her husband. She had no desire to. The same could not be said for the others: they had been overtaken by a bloodlust that Mary did not, could not, share in. Whatever it was that drove them had failed to affect Mary in quite the same way. She often wondered why she was different. She was not one of them in desire or unfettered rage, and yet she was not like Willard anymore. He seemed like an innocent babe to her now, a helpless child who needed a guiding hand in a dark and violent new world. No, Mary was neither the sheep nor the wolf; she was something in between.

They had bought flatbread from the previous village, and Willard was now heating it over the fire in the only pan that they possessed. Such meagre possessions, but they would make do. The bread meant that hunting for rabbit or other small game would not be necessary this night, but she decided to do so anyway. Willard was still not comfortable around her, and giving him space might help. She needed it too, honestly. It was a struggle to chat with the man who had shared her bed for five years, a man with whom conversation had always been a natural thing but was now stilted and uneasy, forced. Mary sighed and moved away from the firelight. Willard did not ask where she was going. Poor Willard, there was so much he wanted to know, but Mary was terrified of telling him.

As she moved further away from the campfire, her senses sharpened in the darkness. The familiar sounds and smells of the night invigorated her. She removed her shoes and travelling cloak. She inhaled and let her breath out slowly. Slipping out of her garments, Mary padded up a slight incline between sparse trees out onto a landscape of tufted scrubland grasses and rocks. The soles of her feet were thick, unnaturally so, impervious to the small, sharply hidden stones among the grass. A canopy of stars shimmered overhead. Mary could almost touch the stars, so close they seemed to her now. A noise pricked her senses. Jess came gliding up behind her, ears pressed back against her head. Jess joined Mary and sniffed the air. Mary smiled. Jess wanted to join her and would not judge her for the changes she had undergone. Two animals giving reign to primal instincts. Two animals on the hunt. A small pack of females.

Mary transformed. Jess cocked her head and gave a small, puzzled whine. Then, the two of them were running across the scrublands.

CHAPTER 28 The Space Between

❋

A large hare and two possums: a good catch between Mary and Jess. They now had meat for a few days and more pelts to sell further down the road. Jess even managed to sniff out some wild sweet potatoes. Well, it was Mary who had sniffed out the local kumara, but she didn't tell Willard that. Bread, meat, potatoes. They ate like a King, Queen and royal pup that night. Perhaps it was the good food, or the beautiful vista of stars, or the mild weather, but Willard even smiled at Mary and for a moment did not seem afraid.

Mary sat on the other side of the fire and returned the smile. It was an odd thing, to strike fear in a man. The others revelled in it, sought to build it in their husbands before killing them. The power of fear was not something Mary had ever wished for. She didn't wish for it now, but Willard feared her anyway. That was only natural. Yet, he smiled as he finished his meal, and Mary's heart lit up.

"May I sit beside you?" Willard asked.

The breath caught in Mary's throat. "Yes, of course."

Willard moved around and sat down alongside her. "I'm stuffed," he said, patting his belly. "You see, I told you Jess is a good hunter."

Mary nodded. "Invaluable."

"You never used to like her."

"That's not true, Willard."

"Yes, it is. You'd always complain about the mud she'd traipse in. That's the word you used to say. *Traipse. Traipsing* in mud. You said it all the time."

"Willard, why do you speak of me as if I am dead?"

Willard frowned. "Sorry. I wasn't aware."

"You talk of what I used to do, what I *would* do on this or that occasion. I'm still here."

"I didn't mean to do that. I just meant that ... you went away, and things are different now. You're a different Mary."

Her heart went cold. "Am I? Am I a different Mary?"

"Would you not say that you are?"

The stars twinkled in the sky. "I suppose I am," she said finally. "I don't mean to be."

"Where did you go? It might help me understand if you … if you told me."

"I will. I will, but just not now. Not yet."

Willard took her hand, and it warmed to his touch. Could he be willing to take her back into his heart? Could things return to the way they were? She would even welcome a cheeky slap on her arse, anything to indicate that he had forgiven her for … for what? What did Willard have to forgive? What was Mary's transgression?

It was that Mary had changed without his consent. She had changed without her *own* consent, and she both loathed and loved her new state of being. She resented the strange force that attempted to control her but revelled in the power it gave her, not power to instil fear in men, but the power to run, to hunt, to be one with the universe. She didn't want to give it up, but she wanted Willard to take her back, wholeheartedly. Could he love this new Mary as he had loved the old?

As if to answer the question, Willard kissed her.

The kiss was sweetly familiar. Mary closed her eyes and kissed him back. They fell to a blanket that Willard had laid by the fire. She tugged at his tunic, and he pulled the cloak from her body. They lay together near the fire, close enough to feel its warmth but not so close as to put themselves in harm's way. It was a balancing act, this tenderness they shared between the cool night wind and the searing flame.

Willard paused a moment to run his hands over the scars on Mary's stomach, his freckled face creased in confusion. She took his hands away and placed them on her cheeks. She moved on top of him, and he entered her. Mary wondered if this would close the space between them or increase it, whether this event would heal them or break the tie between them and cast them adrift forever and finally.

❊

CHAPTER 28 The Space Between

A child's cries echoed from somewhere within the maw of the hole in the ground. Mary stood naked at the edge of the pit and scanned the grassy clearing, which was walled off by impenetrably dark trees. No one else was there to help the child. Only her. She had no rope to safely enter the dark hole in the ground, a water well, perhaps? Had the child fallen while collecting water? But Mary did not need the rope. She looked down as her hands morphed from her normal, soft pink hands to the long-fingered talons of a burrowing animal. A tail emerged from the base of her spine, and she leapt into the hole, using the talons to grip the earthen walls of the hole, her flexile tail gripping tightly to the tough, wiry vegetation growing in the darkness. She clambered down until a spark of light became visible somewhere below. The child's voice changed, becoming deeper, more resonant. She recognised it.

Willard?

Her husband's face loomed out of the darkness, an expression of terror on his face as he looked up at her. Mary gasped and opened her eyes.

The firelight crackled. She lay beside it with a blanket around her chest. Jess was asleep on her side, eyes moving this way and that under her lids, dreaming of the primal hunt. Willard was gone. She sat up and, with horror, looked at her right hand. It was transforming from one animal shape to another with great speed, from the hairy paw of a bear to the retractable claws of a feline to the long, nimble fingers of a monkey to the cloven hooves of a deer. One animal after another, though the rest of her body did not change. For a split second, her own human hand came into view. Mary squeezed her eyes shut and said, "Stop."

It stopped. Her hand resumed its normal appearance. She got to her feet and swung her head around. Where was Willard? Had he witnessed this?

She searched and found him kneeling in the darkness fifty yards from their campsite. When she approached him, he turned. Mary's heart dropped to the pit of her stomach. He'd been crying. He had seen it. He knew what she was.

"I … I'm sorry," Mary whispered.

He shook his head and looked away. A pool of vomit lay before him, the shock too much for his mind and body to take. Struggling to control his breathing, Willard wiped his mouth and gave another shuddering sob.

Mary's body chilled all over. The man she loved was repulsed by her. Could not stand to look at her. He'd tried to love the new Mary, but the truth had come down on the man too soon and too fast. They were now separated across an ocean of revulsion.

Mary backed away. Anger layered a coat of ice across her vision, freezing her sadness to icicles. She had lost Willard, forever. She had lost Victoria. They had taken everything from her. A murderous rage caused her hand to morph again. There was no escaping it, no escaping what she had become, so she would embrace it. Still, somebody should suffer for this. Somebody should pay for her loss, the numerous losses.

Mary Brown had a very good idea who that should be.

"You'll be alright on your own, Willard," she whispered. "You can start again. Goodbye. I love you."

She turned and ran. Willard did not call her back.

CHAPTER 29

Living Metal

Old farrier Jackson was pleased. Eight horses needed shoeing, and two of them required treatment for frog rotting before the metal shoes could be nailed in place. True, this work would test both his talent in forging and fitting horseshoes and his veterinary skills, but the money to be made was considerable. The stables out back were fully loaded before the sun rose that morning. This was going to be a day of great fortune in coin. It was also a stroke of luck that George Burridge was on the premises, for Jackson would need his help with the unusually heavy order.

Jackson had quietly hoped that George shutting up his business would direct more traffic his way, and this had proved to be the case. George was an excellent blacksmith, and while Jackson and he were, strictly speaking, competitors, or had been, they were also friends and had never let their business interests come between them. When George had approached Jackson and asked him to shelter young Douglas Partridge, Jackson had done so without asking any questions. Douglas was gone now. Something horrific had happened to him, and George had barely escaped with his own life: the big bushy-bearded blacksmith had scars about the throat. What had happened, old Jackson did not know and did not ask. In truth, he didn't want to know the lad's fate. It could be nothing pleasant, and George was not a man given to showing emotional weakness. When a man was in the shithole of his life's circumstances, it was better not to prick at the last thing remaining to him: his pride.

"Busy day ahead of us, George," Jackson said, resting his hand fraternally on the other's shoulder.

George nodded, stretched his back and said nothing.

Jackson employed two apprentices on a day-to-day basis: two brothers born a year apart and both tall with mops of unruly hard hair that turned them into identical wire brushes. They gave George a wide berth, as if sensing the unhappiness emanating from the man. The farrier's workshop was a hive of noise and activity: the forge fires were crackling, metal tongs and hammers were clinking together in preparation for a day's hard toil, horses were neighing. Jackson loved the industrious nature of his workshop on days like these. He was an important man carrying out important business in the hubbub of a large workshop in a busy city. There was nowhere else in Dysael, or all White Cloud for that matter, he would rather be.

When a big man bearing a hunting knife slammed the door open and stormed his way into the workshop, old Jackson's heart nearly stopped.

"George Burridge, you bastard!" the man shouted, pointing the blade at George.

Suddenly, old farrier Jackson could think of better places to be.

George picked up a long-handled hammer to defend himself. Garth had murder written all over his face, and George wasn't taking any chances. He didn't know what had gotten into Garth, but the nun's bodyguard was incensed by something.

"Put that down, Garth," George said, holding up his own weapon. The brothers glanced at each other and reached for weapons, one clasping an iron punch, the other a pair of tongs, though the Lord only knew what use they would be.

"She's gone, you prick," Garth snarled. "You put ideas in her head, and now she's gone!"

Farrier Jackson took a step towards Garth and held his hands up peaceably. "Steady on, man. We don't want trouble here."

"Stay out of this, old fella," Garth said. "This is between me and George. Step outside, George."

"No. You intend to kill me."

"I'll kill you if you don't. Sister Kempson has vanished. She's gone after them, and it's your fault."

George frowned. "My fault?"

"You put ideas in her head. She was about to leave this shitty town, on the very cusp of it, she was. Damn you to Hell, Burridge, damn you for leading her astray."

Despite the big bodyguard's outraged demeanour, hope fluttered in George's breast. Sister Kempson had gone to plead on behalf of young Douglas? There was a chance now, a slim one, but a chance that Douglas would survive.

"Alright, alright," George said. "We'll talk outside. Just put your knife away."

Garth hesitated, then sheathed his blade. "I intend to find her, and you're going to help me. Where is she? You said you know where the wives are, so tell me."

"Aye, I said it." George placed his hammer on an anvil and headed slowly for the door, keeping a wary eye on Garth the whole time. "I said it. Let's talk outside."

The two men maintained a distance from each other as they walked out into the still dark and quiet street.

"They won't harm her," George said. "I'm sure of it. She can get Douglas out, but if you or Thackery stumble in there, you're more 'n likely to set the whole tinder box off. Just … leave her go."

Garth shook his head vigorously, his breath steaming into the air. "I'm not letting her wander off alone into the lair of the Devil. I'm her bodyguard. You'd better tell me where she's gone, or by God, I'll kill you."

"Perhaps she has simply returned home."

"Not without me."

"Maybe, then, there's a reason she stole away under cover of night. Might be she doesn't need you."

"You've no idea what you're talking about. Where is she? Where are *they*? And how does the nun know where to find them?"

"That, I cannot answer."

"But you can tell me where they are. You mentioned some place called the Yard."

"I said I *think* they're in the Yard. The metal there has an odour."

Garth ground his jaw, speaking through gritted teeth. "That bullshit about dead metal. Not good enough, Burridge. You'd better start talking with a little more certainty. Take me there."

"If I do that, we're both dead. They let me go once, not again, and they'll strike you down should you show your face."

Garth unsheathed his blade. "Die now or die later. I don't care. Enough talk. Where is the Yard?"

Sister Kempson held Sage Schuman's bracelet in her hands. Oddly, the metal now pulsed different shades of darkness, from deepest black to lighter shades of coal grey. The streets of Dysael echoed the bracelet in its solemn and gloomy hues in the early hours of misty morning. Things moved in the shadows of murky side streets, but the nun ignored them, as she ignored her own instincts screaming to return to Garth's protection. She did not listen to that voice. A new voice drove her on. She had to do this alone. She had to prove herself. She had to save ... *somebody*.

Thrusting the band into a deep pocket of the cloak covering her habit, Sister Kempson scurried breathlessly on. Yes, the voice said, you can do this, you can do whatever you set her heart upon. You are powerful and only have to realise that fact, and then everything will change. You have the power to stop Death, to convince Keira Jack and her women that murder was not the right path. You can convince them to give up Douglas Partridge and let him face the consequences of his actions in a court of law. This was the righteous path. Yes, once Sister Kempson found them and put her case, they would see reason. The nun smiled. No more indecision; this felt good. This felt right. She had a cause, something to devote herself to. Her pleasure dimmed somewhat when she thought of Garth. The man was well-intentioned but overcautious. Keira Jack would do her no harm. The woman still had something worth saving; they all did. Garth would understand when she had the opportunity to explain. He would be disappointed in her, but it was better this way. Garth was out of harm's way, for while she carried no fears for her own safety, she could not say the same for Garth. He would not be a welcome sight to the wives. No, it was better this way.

The streets changed, became narrower, the houses more unkempt and rotted. Many of the dwellings were clearly unoccupied. A few blocks down, the streets widened again in cracked and uneven paving stones: a testament to the industrial nature at the heart of the city, yet no traffic of any nature had used this road for decades. Sister Kempson was not a native of Dysael, but she had heard stories of the Yard. Some kind of industrial accident had poisoned the central city over fifty years ago, and before the slow, insidious nature of the poisoning had been understood, many had sickened and died of malodorous humours.

A tingling at her hip alerted Sister Kempson to the needs of the metal. She stopped and frowned at the idea: the *needs* of the metal? What in the world could it *need*? She took out the bracelet once glowing in different colours, none constant in hue for long, as if the object had awakened from slumber.

Something clattered in the darkness between two sagging tenement buildings. Sister Kempson held her breath and reached for the knife gifted to her by Garth, but it wasn't there. In her haste to leave, she had forgotten to take it. Garth would be furious at her lack of preparation. She wished the big man were here to remonstrate with her as something came slinking out of the shadows. Defenceless and alone in the Yard. How could she have been so foolish?

"I am a holy woman," Sister Kempson said. "I am a nun here on an important business."

"This is a dangerous place to be, Sister, on important business or any other." The thin man that came forward seemed pale by the light of the fading moon, his face chalk white and sickly. He wore a peaked cap at an angle across his skull. "What is a nun doing here, of all places?"

She did not have time to stumble about in the darkness and thus took a chance. "I seek the Yard."

The chalk-white man raised an eyebrow under the peaked cap. "You're close, Sister. Very close. But that's a poisoned place. You don't want to go there."

"I must. Can you show me the way?"

"Aye, I can show you the way." The man eyed the bracelet in the nun's hand. "You're after the ladies, then."

Sister Kempson gasped involuntarily. She collected herself and said, "Yes. You know of them?"

"Everyone knows of them, least those who live around here. We see them wafting in and out of the Yard on carpets of mist, just like ghosts."

"Have you informed the Night Watch?"

"Not I. No benefit in it for me, Sister. And the law has never been a friend to us down here. We are … what's it called? Autonomous? Aye, we are autonomous, always have been. Besides, the ladies have done no harm to us what live in the Yard."

"Will you show me the way? I must speak with them."

"If that is what you wish, then who am I to refuse a woman of the cloth?" Without another word, the pale man made a come-hither gesture and set off at a sprightly pace down the cracked avenue.

The man seemed at home in the empty streets, as if he were sovereign lord over the area. Despite his sickly appearance, he maintained a jaunty speed, but Sister Kempson had no trouble keeping up. She felt strong and fit, fitter than she could ever remember. Under the cloak, her habit hung looser about her: she'd lost weight, and this pleased her, not that she'd ever cared about her weight, that was for others to fret over. The Mother Superior would often ridicule her for her size, which was ironic considering

CHAPTER 29 Living Metal

the Mother Superior was hardly a svelte woman herself. But she now felt like she could run forever and never stop.

You live in a man's world.

Sister Kempson faltered. "What did you say?"

The chalk-white man turned. "I? Nothing. Down this way." He pointed to a darkened alleyway where the half-light of the emerging dawn could not penetrate. "A short cut."

It's only a matter of time until one of them takes something from you.

Besides the man and herself, the streets were empty. Was the voice coming from inside her own head? Something about the words pricked at her memory. She knew those words, somehow.

The bishop, the king, the coppers or just some drunken bastard climbing in your window one night. You are powerless.

Sage Schuman. These were *her* words before she was burned and hacked to death. As Sister Kempson followed the pale man into the darkened alley, she realised her mistake. The voice was a warning.

"I am a nun," Sister Kempson said, "and I ask that you leave me unmolested."

The thin man turned, his chalk-white face split in a crooked grin. "And I," he said, holding out a glinting knife, "am a man of the blade, and molestation is my trade in calling."

"You would harm a nun?"

"I'd harm me own mum if it would benefit me. But she beat me to it long afore. Hand over your belongings."

"I have nothing."

"Nothing? What's that shiny shiny in your hand, then?"

"Oh, this …" Sister Kempson frowned at the bracelet. "I'd forgotten I was holding it."

The pale man snapped his fingers before Sister Kempson's eyes. "Hello? Stop daydreaming and hand it over."

"If you touch me, God will judge you."

"Hah. I have no soul to judge, Sister."

"It's never too late for redemption."

The man cocked his head and nodded. "Aye, never too late

for that." He leapt at Sister Kempson and drove his knife into her stomach. She screamed as pain shot through her belly, a lightning flash of agony shooting from her intestines to her skull. Time stopped. The chalk-white face of her assailant presented a horrific visage, teeth pulled back in a feral snarl around sharp, yellowing teeth, eyes wide in blood lust.

And in that instant, Sister Rose Kempson of the Holy Sisters of Conviction realised that not everyone is worthy of redemption.

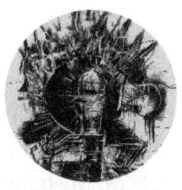

CHAPTER 30

Lending an Ear

Vincent E. Thackery stroked his moustaches. He was sitting on a worn chair in a dimly lit and cluttered parlour in a small house in the poorer district of North Quarter. The neighbourhood was less residential than it was slum. The houses down here attempted a kind of grandeur, but every structure had warped and collapsed under the weight of collective ignorance a long time ago. The people who lived here had homes at least, which put them one social strata above those who slept on the streets.

Mrs. Glaston was a middle-aged woman and, much like her house, presented a pleasant façade until one examined closely the mortar lines of her face, where the cracks began to show, and the seams of illiteracy and low breeding revealed themselves.

Two cups of tea sat on a table between Mrs. Glaston and Constable Thackery. The tea, like everything else, was an attempt at civility, but it failed to paper over the cracks. Thackery stared at Mrs. Glaston as she, in turn, stared, hands on her knees, at her cup of tea. Neither made a move to sup the now lukewarm liquids in the chipped cups.

Finally, Thackery cleared his throat and said, "You know, Mrs. Glaston, I'm starting to think that there is a conspiracy against me."

Mrs. Glaston raised her eyebrows but not her eyes, continuing to focus on her cup of tea. "Oh, is that right, Constable? What kind o' conspiracy?"

A low growl came from nearby. Sergeant Graham allowed his enormous mastiff to come forward, and the animal nosed at Mrs.

Glaston's lap, snuffling at her clasped hands. The woman closed her eyes tightly as the massive dog sniffed menacingly up her arms to her cheek. Thackery waved his fingers, and Sergeant Graham pulled the animal back, a half-smile on the handler's face. With trembling fingers, Mrs. Glaston grasped her cup and put it to her mouth.

Thackery gave his facial hairs one last twirl and leaned forward. "I am a man of the Law, Mrs. Glaston. I've spent my entire life enforcing it. I have worked tirelessly, as my father and grandfather before me, to ensure that every citizen in our fair city is nourished by that Law. And now I find myself betrayed by the very people I am here to protect."

Mrs. Glaston's yellowing teeth clinked against the edges of her cup, and tea dribbled down her chin. She wiped it away and said, "I'm sorry, Constable, but I don't reckon I follow."

"Sixteen unexplained deaths in the last fortnight, the coroner tells me. Sixteen dead men, Mrs. Glaston, all married, and each one, if one does the digging as I have, with a reputation for violence in the home. Now, the Law doesn't take kindly to domestic abuse, but we take less kindly to murder. You are the most recent widow on our books, Mrs. Glaston. The most freshly bereaved widow, but I see little in the way of grieving in you."

Mrs. Glaston flicked her eyes towards Thackery and then away again. It spoke for her guilt in the matter that she refused to hold his gaze.

"Henry, Lord bless his soul, died in an accident, and he never hit me, not once," she said.

"Come now, come now. A cursory inspection of your marital history would suggest otherwise. People talk, you know. Something very odd is going on in Dysael. Men dying left, right and centre, and their wives simply shrug it off as unfortunate accidents. I suspect foul play."

The woman opposite him sat up straight, raised her chin, and for the first time met Thackery's inquiring gaze. "I do not condone murder, Constable. My husband's death was an accident, a terrible accident, and not a moment passes that I do not wish to hold my dear Henry close to me once again."

"Accident? The man was found with a pear lodged in his throat. What man chokes to death on a pear?"

"My Henry was always in a hurry. Rip, shit and bust, as my old mam used to say."

Thackery raised an eyebrow. "The pear was uneaten."

"Obviously, he didn't quite get it down."

"No teeth marks were found on the lethal fruit in question."

"Then he were in more of a hurry than usual, weren't he?"

Thackery leaned back in his chair and smiled. "Mrs. Glaston, your artifice would be more amusing if a man hadn't lost his life. You're taking your husband's death rather flippantly."

The woman opposite sniffed. "Don't even know what that means. Flippantly whatsit?"

"You have heard the name Keira Jack, I take it?"

"I've heard the name."

"Could it be that a large section of the populace within Dysael now supports Keira Jack and her insane sisterhood? Could it be, furthermore, that these criminals have become folk heroes? A noble rebellion on behalf of women against … well, what? Men in general? Husbands in particular? *That* is a betrayal of common decency and the Law. *That* is full-blown conspiracy, damn it."

Thackery sighed, turned his head to Sergeant Graham and nodded.

The dog handler allowed the mastiff to move in on the widow once again. The dog slobbered large gobs of saliva all over Mrs. Glaston as it sniffed at her. She grimaced, the knuckles of her hands turning white on the teacup. The mastiff jostled her arm, and tea spilled from the cup over her lap. Fortunately for the terrified Mrs. Glaston, the tea had cooled.

"Did you seek out Keira Jack to do away with your husband?"

Mrs. Glaston squeezed her eyes shut and shook her head. "No."

"Did she approach you unsolicited?"

Another shake of the head. "No."

Thackery gestured to the big dog handler, his large-jawed face as savage as that of his dog. "Sergeant Graham believes his *boy* here, this rather ungainly dog, has found the scent of Harpy upon you. It would behove you to confess."

"I swear, I ain't seen them. I've 'ad nothing to do with them."

"The dog tells us otherwise." Thackery steepled his fingers. "I have my own confession, Mrs. Glaston. It's painful, but let me speak it. I was too slow to see the signs, too slow to react to the poisonous uprising currently underway in our city. I received potentially useful information early on in my investigation, but to my eternal regret, I failed to acknowledge the authority of the source of this information. I'll have to live with that. Eight men targeted in the initial attack are no longer living with it, but it would seem that eight murders are not enough for Keira Jack. Now, we have a further sixteen victims of cold assassination. I blame myself, in part." Thackery paused. "There, you've had my confession. Now it's your turn. You must know that Keira Jack will not stop until every married man in Dysael is dead. She is clearly insane. If you know where I can find her, then it is your civic duty to reveal this information."

"I have rights," Mrs. Glaston said. "Even us down here have rights."

"You're quite correct," Thackery said with a distasteful air. "Even the likes of you have rights. But remember, it's *my* family that gave them to you. And I can take them away. Where is Keira Jack?"

"Told you, I've not seen her."

Sergeant Graham's mastiff chomped down and tore off a large chunk of Mrs. Glaston's ear. She screamed, and the teacup flew as the woman toppled off her chair.

Thackery jumped to his feet. "Jesus Christ!" he shouted. "Control your dog, Graham!"

Sergeant Graham pulled the mastiff away. The animal casually swallowed a large section of Mrs. Glaston's earlobe and licked its sodden chops. Their hostess continued to shriek on the parlour floor, writhing around and clutching at the bloodied side of her head.

Thackery looked down at her in horror. "Damn it," he said, "someone, get me a cloth."

CHAPTER 30 Lending an Ear

❋

Thackery stepped outside and threw the bloodied cloth to the ground, where it disappeared beneath a layer of ankle-high mist. The act of violence perpetrated on Mrs. Glaston was not something that Vincent E. Thackery condoned. Sergeant Graham was proving to be as volatile as his mastiff. This was the second completely unnecessary act of barbarism the man had encouraged in his animals: Mrs. Sandhurst's small spaniel had been torn apart by Graham's *boys*, as he referred to the dogs, and now this. It may have been a mistake to recruit the man.

Except that Mrs. Glaston had, in her agony, blubbered something about the Yard, the abandoned industrial section at the heart of the city. It was not a confession of complicity, as such, but merely something she had heard among the salty gossip shared by those who enjoyed that kind of thing, middle-aged housewives mostly.

In the end, perhaps there was a method to Graham's brutality. Still, Thackery didn't trust the man's dogs to withstand the mental manipulations already demonstrated by the harpies. He carried a flintlock at his hip in the eventuality the mastiffs turned on their handlers or Thackery himself.

To the Yard, then, the toxic heart of the city. The lads weren't going to be happy, but the Law called them, and to the Yard they would go.

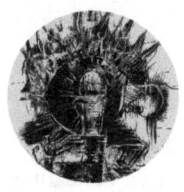

CHAPTER 31

Games in High Places

Douglas Partridge raced along the hallway, breathless. He brushed damp curls from his forehead and looked around. He could not remember how he came to be in the hallway. The only thing he knew for sure was that he had to run because *she* was after him and would kill him if she caught him.

Kill him again.

He remembered dying, more than once. The agony of his first death had overwhelmed him, but then he had entered what felt like a warm pool of water and the pain lessened until it finally subsided. Death wasn't so bad, almost tender in how it numbed the feelings. But then Helen Hardcastle had brought him back. Brought him back so Keira could do it all over again.

Where was he? How had he escaped? Was this another dream inside his own head?

He heard the howling wind from somewhere and the faint flapping of canvas like startled bird wings or a frantic dying heart. The pungent smell of rusting metal, faintly garlic, seemed everywhere. It was not an odour a young blacksmith was familiar with. Douglas was an apprentice, and his work involved the very conception of metal, its birth and formative hours and days. This metal odour, on the other hand, stunk of disuse and death.

The floorboards underfoot creaked, and Douglas stopped. The sound of rain somewhere above echoed through the warped timber ceiling. The hallway seemed to move in a slow, pendulous arc, as if the entire building were toppling one way then another. He retched and clasped his stomach. Douglas was hungry, but the desire for food had been submerged by a greater need: the need to escape, the primal urge to live past the next few seconds. His face was scarred from scalp to chin. Keira had cut him again and again, and even though Helen had resurrected him before he passed over forever, and the blood had ceased to pour from him, the scars of his torture remained. Not even Helen Hardcastle could heal those.

His breath back in his lungs, Douglas glanced behind him. The gloomy hallway was empty. He moved forward and came to a door partially open. When he leaned on it, the door refused to give. It had become jammed against the uneven floorboards long ago. Douglas squeezed through the narrow opening and came to another hallway. Left and right paths ended in shadows and probably death. It did not matter, then, which avenue he chose.

He turned left and arrived at another door. He entered what appeared to be an office. Documents, more dust than paper, lay on a sagging desk. He approached a small internal window and looked down onto a large dark space. He could make out a wooden walkway with a metal ribbing just outside the glassless window. If it did not take his weight when he stepped on it, he might fall. How far, he could not tell in the darkness. Perhaps it would be better to go back to the hallway and look for another way.

No, he was running *away* from Keira and the Wives. To turn around would be to go *back*. He had to go forward. Douglas took a breath and stepped out onto the walkway. The wood and metal groaned, long unused to supporting the weight of anything more substantial than dust and decay. A cool draught stung the scars on his face. He gripped the handrail and measured each step in the darkness. The sound of rain intensified; it came hissing down from above, echoing all around him. Clearly, Douglas was creeping through a cavernous space, only the next step visible in front of him.

He almost missed a staircase as he passed it. It disappeared over his head. To go upwards seemed counterintuitive, his instincts telling him to go down. It *could* be that he was underground somewhere, and the ascent might take him to the surface, but the rain would lose all significance if that were the case. Douglas sighed. All his ponderings meant nothing. He could either grope here in the darkness or take the new path offered to him. He was fooling himself if he thought he had any other choice. He crept upwards as quietly as he could. At one moment, the steps lurched beneath him in a vertiginous collapse, and Douglas suppressed a scream before the steps settled again. He clenched his jaw and moved gingerly upwards.

A source of light appeared somewhere over his head. He crept towards it. The steps came to a landing. The flapping of canvas ahead revealed light from outside. The sound of rain, more immediate now, less echoing. He was close to getting out. The floor beneath him comprised wooden floorboards that were missing in places to reveal metal crossbeams underneath, as if the boards had been removed or never set in place during the building's construction. This level had the feel of something incomplete.

Up ahead, canvas whip-cracked in a strong wind. Douglas caught a glimpse of a grey sky, late afternoon or perhaps early evening. He almost stepped into a hole in the floor in his excitement. *Close now*, he thought. *Don't fall at the last.*

He brushed aside the canvas and lurched into space. There was no floor. Douglas twisted and reached back. He managed to grasp a steel pipe jutting from the unfinished floor. He hung suspended a hundred feet above a desolate courtyard of cracked, weed-strewn stone. The metal pipe reeked of decay and began to bend and crack, altogether too fragile in its old age. Douglas didn't have time to scream as the pipe slipped from his grasp. But he did not fall. Something gripped him by the wrist and hauled him to safety. He lay panting on the patchy wooden floorboards. A woman stood over him, outlined against the darkening skies. Douglas moaned in his dismay. Better to fall to his death, a final escape, than to be taken by her again.

But it was not Keira Jack. At first, he did not recognise her, but then the name came to him. Jasmine Cox, Stephen's wife. The

CHAPTER 31 Games in High Places

milky-white woman stared down at him with the beginnings of a smile. Jasmine and Bessie had been friends: it was Bessie who tied Jasmine and all the other women together. Bessie had been a friend to all of them, and that was why they hated him. Douglas shifted his weight, preparing to roll over and fall to his death, when she held out a pale hand and said, "I'm not going to hurt you."

Jasmine was a slight woman but had hauled him to safety as if he were a babe. Clearly, she possessed unnatural strength, just like they all did, and an imperviousness to cold from the looks of it. The wind bit and stung this high above the ground, but she wore the same dress as she did the night of the absurd function at the butchery: a ball gown of blue silver off the shoulders.

"Don't take me back there," Douglas whispered. "Please, don't take me back to *her*."

Jasmine cocked her head in the growing darkness, stepped near the edge and looked down. The moon seemed to be rising over her bare, pale shoulder. "I found you. I'm the winner. The others will be so jealous."

Douglas' stomach lurched. Was this a game to them? Had they allowed him to run only to harry him down for entertainment?

"Please," he said. "I can't go back. Jasmine, have mercy."

"Oh, Douglas, what have you done? It's got us all. We're all in it now."

"Not I," Douglas whispered. "I didn't do it."

She waggled a finger. "Tut tut. You know you did. Your moment of insanity sparked this whole affair."

Douglas sat up and crawled a few feet away from Jasmine. "I'm not a bad person."

Jasmine shook her head and looked out over the abandoned square and empty tenements stretching away down the avenue. She sighed long and heavy. "No one is *bad*, Douglas. Keira's not a bad person. I killed my husband, sliced his fucking head off, and I do not see myself as a bad person. It's just what side you're on, who your friends are."

"Please, let me go."

She met his eyes. "There's nowhere for you to go. The lower level is cut off."

His breath was whipped away in the frigid winds. "Where are we?"

"We're in the Yard, in a factory and dormitories of some kind."

"The Yard? But … this place is poisoned. Aren't you afraid?"

"We ain't afraid of nothing. We're different now, stronger. You, on the other hand, may end up dying very slowly, but not before Keira has her fun."

Douglas gauged the distance to the edge. A quick lunge, and he would be falling, be free.

Jasmine followed his gaze. The wind flung her long hair about her milky-white face. "That would do it," she said. "Not sure even Helen could put you back together after a fall like that. But you don't want to jump, Douglas. Not really. Besides, I can't let you. Keira would be displeased with me. You don't want her on your bad side." Jasmine giggled. "But I think you understand that better than anyone." Douglas put his head in his hands and wept. Jasmine knelt and patted his knee. "Don't worry. Despite our power, we're a dying race. Only six of us remain. Sage is dead and Mary is gone, abandoned us she has. Keira is livid about that. Talk about being on her bad side. Anyway, sooner or later, the men will find us, and they'll do us all in, under the pretence of justice, of course." Jasmine spat. "Fucking justice, if you can believe that. But we'll get our licks in before that happens. So, if you bide your time and take your deaths like a good boy, you may wake up one day and be free. Free of all those deaths except the last one, whenever that may be. Isn't that worth hanging on for?"

Douglas wiped the tears from his face. "You're mad. You're all insane."

"Quite likely. But just you remember what I said. You brought this all down on yourself and dragged us down with you. If we're monsters, then you made us. When you killed Bessie, you made us."

"I am not responsible for your … freakish state."

Jasmine snorted. "We are not freaks. We're beautiful. The girls are unique. Every one of us has different powers. And me?" Jasmine tittered behind her hand. "You wouldn't believe what I could do if I told you. You really wouldn't."

Douglas shook his head wearily. "I'm in Hell."

A honeyed voice came from the shadows of the unfinished corridor. "You're not wrong about that, brother-in-law. Not wrong at all."

The young man whirled around, and there stood Keira Jack, Elsie Gallagher at her side. Douglas pushed himself towards the edge of the unfinished walkway and would have rolled off and plummeted to his death if Jasmine hadn't reached out to grab him by the shoulder. The crushing strength in her hand belied the frail appearance of the milky-skinned woman.

Keira nodded. "Well done, Jasmine. You found him first."

"What is my prize?" Jasmine asked coyly.

Keira smiled. "Power and pain. Whatever you choose to take or give. You're alive and dominant. That is your reward."

"I like it."

"So do I," Keira said. She held up a hand and clenched her fingers into a fist, admiring the power of her flesh. "We have transcended, and is it not lovely?" She knelt down, brought her fierce green eyes level with the pale blue eyes of Douglas Partridge and poked him in the chest with her finger. "You ... *men* simply do not understand. For all your talk of equality, you have failed time and again to deliver on your promises. Your public faces do not align with your private ones. Hypocrites, all. You walk around with cocks and a bit of muscle." She slapped Douglas on his upper arm. "And you think that makes you gods. You are not gods. We are the gods now. Have you ever wondered what a woman would do if she woke up more powerful than you? Have you, brother? *We* are the answer to that question. We are men's worst nightmare. We are power on the fucking rag." She stood and turned to Jasmine. "Are your potions ready? Are *you* ready?"

"Next purgation ain't for a couple weeks," Jasmine said, "but I've stocked up."

"Good because we don't have two weeks. I suspect they're onto us, and we'll be lucky to have two days." She turned back to Douglas. "But I reckon I can bless you with a few more deaths in the time left to us." Douglas began to scramble backwards, but Keira simply grabbed him by his blond curls and dragged him away.

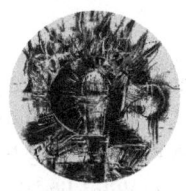

CHAPTER 32

Enter the Yard

Sister Kempson staggered against a mossy brick wall and collapsed, blood pouring freely from her stomach. She tried to staunch the flow, but she might as well have tried to hold back a river in flood.

The chalk-white man held Sage Schuman's metal bracelet in his hand. Anger flowed through the nun as blood flowed from her body. By what right did he take it from her? She was dying and all for what? A mere trinket? Outrageous. The villain stared at it as if mesmerised, a calm overtaking him where a moment before he had driven the knife deep into her belly with feral rage on his pale, skull face. So easily forgotten, this violence, when he had what he wanted, murder nothing but a simple tool of transaction.

Outrageous.

Muscles in her abdomen tightened and knitted together in fury, and the blood stopped flowing. She pushed herself to her feet. There was no pain.

"I've changed my mind," Sister Kempson said.

The pale man looked up sharply and frowned. It was clear from his puzzled expression that he expected her to be dead, but Sister Rose Kempson of the Holy Sisters of Conviction was in no mood to accommodate.

"What?" he said. The knife dripped blood in the first rays of the morning sun. "You changed your mind about what?"

"Redemption," Sister Kempson said. "Not everyone deserves it."

"Redemption," the man replied, holding up the bracelet, "is only for them what can afford it. The likes of us down here simply don't have the finances, but you'd be wrong to lay blame. It is society, you see, that thrusts its ills upon us, and we simply thrust back. We are products, if you like, of our circumstances. Now, why don't you fucking die?"

Sister Kempson raised her chin. "Why don't you make me, wretched arsehole?"

The pale man looked genuinely affronted and staggered backwards at the audacity of the comment. He screwed up his sallow face. "What kind of language is that from a nun? God damn bitch."

He stepped in to finish Sister Kempson with a stroke across her soft throat, but she grabbed his wrist and head-butted the man. His nose exploded, and this time, the fellow staggered under the ferocity of a physical blow: three unsteady steps where he sank to his knees, dropping the blade but holding onto the bracelet.

Sister Kempson clenched her fingers into a fist and smashed the man in the face, knocking out several teeth and causing his head to whip backwards where it bounced off the hard stone road. He did not move, and now it was his turn to bleed on the ground.

Sister Kempson pulled the bracelet from his still fingers and slipped it into her cloak pocket. "Cunt," she whispered. The nun spat on the pale man and set off down the street. The metal tingled whenever she turned in certain directions. It seemed to know which way to go, so she followed instructions.

The chalk-white man was probably dead, but that was not her fault: she had been defending herself, and God would understand. Indeed, her mission left no room for doubt or remorse. Her strength was a surprise, but again, nothing untoward. She'd picked up a little of Garth's martial prowess perhaps just hanging around the man. Besides, it felt good to punch the knave in the face.

She was holding the pale man's bloodied knife in her hand. Odd, because she didn't remember picking it up. She wiped the blood, her own, on her cloak and stowed the knife in the pocket with the bracelet. Things were looking up: she had protection now. The next fucking cocksucker to try something was going to get an unpleasant shock and no mistake, just like the last bastard.

She only wished she would stop using this vulgar language. Most unlike her.

❄

"Sister Kempson has a kind and noble soul," Garth said from the back of his horse. "A little headstrong but a good person. She is alone and in great danger. We must hurry."

"We're nearing the Yard," George said. The clip-clopping of both men's horses echoed along the lane with every step. "Not far now, but it's a bad place."

"Couldn't be worse than this," Garth said. The streets were dense and squalid. Desperation oozed from between the cracks in the cobblestones and the faces of passersby, many of whom cast sour looks at the two riders. Hopelessness permeated the stuffy atmosphere. It was hard to breathe down here. The houses leaned against each other, blocking out the watery mid-morning sun. Greyness dominated the skies as the rotting wooden houses dominated the streets. Eventually, foot traffic thinned until it disappeared, leaving the two men alone.

"The whole place is poisoned," George said.

Garth, hands on pommel, turned to the blacksmith and said, "Poisoned? What do you mean poisoned?"

George rubbed at his beard. "An accident, long ago. Three city blocks cordoned off. The Yard is toxic."

The tall structures looming out of the fog ahead of them now took on an ominous aspect. "Accident," Garth repeated. "What accident? What poison do you speak of?"

George took a deep breath. "The local government at the time commissioned the construction of a large industrial development at the heart of the city, factories, warehouses, even a cathedral, about fifty or sixty years ago." George fell silent. Garth acknowledged that the roads ahead were unkempt, with weeds sprouting here and there through cracked paving stones, but nothing indicated danger, at least to the casual observer. "Horses won't go much farther," George said. "They sense it."

"They'll go where they're bloody told," Garth said. "If Sister Kempson is in there, we're going in."

George shook his head. "Men discovered an odd metal in the hills around Dysael and thought to use it in the construction of the Yard."

"What's that to do with anything?"

"They found the metal but didn't understand it. No one had seen the likes of it before. In their wisdom, or lack of it, they decided to alloy the new nickel with iron to form a new kind of steel, strong yet flexible. The largest industrial project ever seen in White Cloud was underway, right here in Dysael, the new metal forming the very bones of it."

The wind whispered about them, and for a man who preferred his own company, Garth was uncomfortably aware of the lack of any other living thing.

"It did not end well, I take it," Garth said, gesturing to the desolation ahead of them.

George nodded and rubbed at his beard. "Aye, not well. At first, it was simply allergies and the like. Itches, red skin. That was all. Then, men developed coughs, bad ones. But things got worse. Many workmen started talking of seeing demons up in the scaffolding, burbling madness to their comrades. Eventually, several men leapt to their deaths from the height of their own unfinished creations. Others developed tumours of the lung and brain that killed them swiftly, if they were lucky. When the cause of the illness was discovered, the place was abandoned, the toxic metal dust settling on the dreams of many an entrepreneur. Nobody goes near the place, not those with any choice in the matter. Only the truly desperate."

"We have no choice in the matter," Garth said flatly. "And that makes us desperate. Damn it, this is why I avoid cities and fools with grand ideas. Civilisation and industry are the Devil's playthings. How long before the poison begins to harm us?"

"I am not a doctor, but the less time spent inside, the better."

"And you urged Sister Kempson in there on your behalf? Risking her life to save that of Douglas?"

"I wish no harm on Sister Kempson."

"You'd better hope none befalls her," Garth warned.

Within a few hundred yards, true to George's word, the horses began to buck and shy sideways. Try as he might, Garth could not force his animal forward. George's horse behaved much the same. Garth reluctantly tied his animal off at a rusting steel fence once bordering a front garden, home and garden long abandoned. He turned and was surprised to find George wearing a cloth over his mouth and nose in the style of a highway bandit. George handed a similar mask to Garth, who took it.

George shrugged. "Better than nothing."

Garth nodded. Things, apparently, were about to get a little rough.

"It grieves me, Sergeant Frood," Constable Thackery said, his breath curling into the frigid morning air. "It grieves me, truly."

Sergeant Frood raised an eyebrow and looked around, wondering what his superior officer was alluding too. The avenue upon which they stood stretched out until it disappeared into the mists. Frood shivered and tongued the gap in his mouth where his two front teeth had once been. Beyond those mists lay the Yard, a place he had never been nor ever wanted to venture into. Nearby, a small army prepared to enter the toxic fog: these men had marched an hour and a half through North Quarter to get here, and all the way, people gawked from windows or poked heads out of front doors as seventy men armed with short swords, longs swords, short bows, long bows, heavy crossbows, light crossbows, handgonnes, blunderbusses, muskets, musketoons, rifles, and even slings, along with three enormous mastiffs, stormed through their streets. Many of the onlookers had followed the small army's tail, never having seen such a sight, but even the most inquisitive had turned back here at this avenue, at the beginning of the Yard.

"What grieves you, sir?"

"All of this," Thackery said, waving a hand at the men checking their weapons. "That it has come to this. That we go to war in such a fashion and against our own people." Sergeant Jones came sauntering over from the main force to join Frood and Thackery. "It also grieves me, Sergeant," the constable said, watching the approach of the squat Jones, "that we had to call on the aid of West Quarter, that we have been unable to deal with this rebellion on our own. This shall tarnish our reputations for some time to come. But I had little choice."

"The men are ready, sir," Sergeant Jones said.

Thackery nodded and twirled his moustaches. "The city is an apricot, and the Yard its rotten centre where the worms attempt to hide from the Law, from judicial retribution. Today, we cut out the sickness. Today, we bring justice to the heart of darkness."

"Aye, sir," Jones said as he turned to go.

"Wait a moment," Thackery said. Jones turned back, and both he and Frood waited expectantly. Thackery lowered his voice, his eyes fixed on the three mastiffs and the men handling them. "Watch out for Sergeant Graham and the others from West Quarter. Constable Walters has sent us a bunch of immoral miscreants. Graham takes great pleasure in setting his dogs on practically everything in sight. I can't control the man or his animals, and I never trust a man I can't control. Watch your backs around him and the West Quarter men when things become heated."

Jones frowned but simply said, "Aye, sir," and walked away.

Sergeant Frood was less than pleased with the warning. As if they didn't have enough to worry about with the murderous harpies, now they had to guard against an enemy in their own camp. Fuck that. Graham was alright as far as Frood was concerned. A bit bloodthirsty, admittedly, but that was no black mark against him.

CHAPTER 32 Enter the Yard

In rough times, a man has no choice but to fight fire with fire. Anyway, Thackery had no right to judge a man's character because the constable really didn't give a shit about justice or morality despite what he said. He was as vicious as the next man. No, for Thackery, his concern only ever lay with the family name. Everybody who knew the man understood that.

Frood shivered again as he eyed the white wall of fog a hundred yards down the weed-strewn avenue. He wanted no part of that place, the slow death hidden behind that curtain, but with Thackery at his back, he had nowhere to go. He touched his scarred throat where one of the wives had nearly decapitated him with catgut. Frood had already guessed the name of the one that did it: Carlene Hickson, wife of Eugene Hickson, catgut spinner. She had been cloaked and hooded, but it was her. Had to be her. All the wives did their hubbies, and they'd come upon the catgut spinner too late to save him. Yes, Charlene Hickson was the name. If he could find her and kill her, then this whole thing might be worth it. Or the one who got in his head. The one who had made him a puppet. Elsie Gallagher. He wanted to slay her, too. If he could kill *any* of them, it would be worth it.

"Move out!" Thackery called.

Frood joined seventy heavily armed men and three large dogs bred for murder as they marched down the avenue towards the blanket of toxic fog and the Hell pit hidden behind it known as the Yard.

The streets had been designed for industry: broad avenues of sturdy paving stones allowing for the movement of goods and services. That they were now abandoned and carried no traffic, industrial or otherwise, only added to the ghostly desolation of the Yard.

Sister Kempson's footsteps echoed across the cracked paving stones and played among the twisted and rusting iron fences and crumbling concrete facades that lined the avenue. She came to a large intersection and stopped. Several tall structures loomed out of the fog in different directions: a cathedral spire here, the high windowless wall of a redbrick factory there. The bases of these structures were invisible through the mist and so appeared as oddly constructed ships floating on a sea of vapour.

She pulled the metal bracelet from her cloak pocket and held it loosely in her hand. One of her fingers was bleeding. She must have brushed it against the blade in her pocket. That was careless, but the small cut sealed in an instant. Come to think of it, that was not the only injury that had healed of its own accord with shocking speed. She ran her hands over her lower stomach where the pale man had stabbed her and lifted her habit to get a closer look. Dried blood on her undergarments, but she was not currently bleeding and felt no pain. Extraordinary. She should be dead.

No time to think on that; the metal was tingling with varying intensity depending on which way she turned. The stronger vibration seemed to indicate the correct path forward, so she continued to follow the singing hum of the metal band. This time, it urged her left, away from the cathedral spire and towards ... well, it was impossible to tell just where the metal was leading her. The only course of action, however, was to trust it. *Trust.* How odd, to trust in a lifeless thing such as this. But was it truly lifeless? Sister Kempson was beginning to suspect otherwise.

She followed the insistently vibrating object. Garth would scoff at her for putting her faith in the bracelet. The woodsman would also be livid with her when he discovered her gone. He would feel betrayed, but she could not worry about that now. If he had known of her intention to meet with the women and plead for Douglas' release, he would most certainly have refused, and no persuasion on her part would have changed his mind. No, this was the only course of action remaining to her. Garth was safe, and whatever happened to her did not matter. This was God's work, and sometimes God's work was a frightening and lonely endeavour. Besides, if she could just meet with Keira Jack and the others, they would see reason. Peace would prevail in the end. She was sure of it. Sage Schuman had maintained that Keira Jack was immovable, a cold heart living only to avenge her sister, but why then gift her with the metal bracelet? It was a sign, a sign that communication *was* possible, that the future was not fixed.

Or it could be a trap, and the metal simply a lure.

It didn't matter either way. She had to try. She hoped Garth would forgive her. He was a good man, an attractive man despite his gruffness or perhaps because of it. He pretended to be hard, a killer, but the fellow had a soft heart. She wanted to touch that stern face. She wanted to kiss those grim-set lips.

She stopped, the mist dissipating around her, revealing the base of an enormous brick wall, but Sister Kempson was too shocked by her own thoughts to notice. She put her hands to her mouth. She shook her head and turned around in a circle as if looking for something she'd dropped.

She wanted to kiss Garth? No, she could not allow such a thing to happen, nor even give voice to the idea. Her face reddened despite the lack of witnesses to her treacherous thoughts.

But it was alright to desire such a thing, quite normal in the greater scheme of what it meant to be human.

True, but to even conceive the notion was forbidden.

Yet why should she be embarrassed by a kiss? Or even the thought of it? She was only flesh and blood, a creature of want and lust, after all.

Stop saying that, she thought. *I'm a nun. Physical intimacy is forbidden.*

Hah. You can't forbid a thought. No one controls your innermost self, not even God.

Sister Kempson breathed in sharply. *Stop, stop. I won't unbridle my mind or body to lust.*

Stay bridled then, Bride of Christ. Bride. Bridled. Controlled. Dominated. All women are bridled in the end, to a man, to God, like a horse is bridled. Chattel, all. But not Keira Jack. She's free. She knows what she is. That's why you're here.

What do you mean? Keira Jack is a murderess. She has strayed from the righteous path. I'm here to help her, to guide her back before it's too late.

Bullshit. You're here to join her. To become free just like she is, the way you've always wanted to be.

No, no, no. That is not my intention. I serve God. Sister Kempson put her hand to her temple. *Who are you? Where are you? Are you in my head? I demand you identify yourself. Who are you?*

She could hear a smirk in the voice when it replied.

I'm God, bitch.

CHAPTER 33

Trouble with the In-Laws

The killings of Douglas Partridge had proved a bore in the end. A tedious, repetitive bore. Kill him, only to have Helen bring him back. Kill him again. Bring him back. Keira had enjoyed the screams and the pleading, the begging for mercy, at first. Yes, she had been delighted the first few times, but even that joy wearied in the end. Douglas was nothing but an ashen shell now, his mind and body almost inured to pain and suffering, if that were possible. The pleasure of killing the man had begun to wane.

Even death lost its charm after a while.

The wind whipped at the canvas forming one wall of the small room. Douglas lay leaning against the back of his chair, shirtless, his handsome face carved beyond recognition. Keira clenched her teeth and thrust a vicious knee into his stomach, but Douglas barely stirred. He didn't even moan anymore, just sat there dribbling, his body scarred where it had been opened several times. How he managed to live without some of his vital organs was anyone's guess. Well, that was Helen, no doubt. She was keeping him alive, but it was taking its toll on her.

Keira turned to Helen. "He is unresponsive. Is he dead? Is he trying to escape me again?"

Helen Hardcastle started from a standing doze and shook her head wearily. She was pale and tired. "No, wherever he's gone, it isn't to the other side. He's alive."

"I want him here," Keira said, "I want him present. He needs to *feel* this."

Helen shrugged. "Maybe give the man a day to recover. Let him get some of his strength back."

Keira balked. "What are you suggesting? That I feed him? Bathe his wounds? That I nurse him back to health?"

"If you want to hurt him all over again, yes."

Douglas was a wreck, a human carcass that yet breathed, but no sympathy did she feel for him. "I can't do that," Keira said. "I can't let up, even if I wanted to."

Helen moved away, her body almost as deflated as that of the bloodied man in the chair. "Then squeeze what you can from him and quickly. You won't get much more pain out of the man. I need to sleep."

"Alright, love. You get some rest."

Keira considered crushing the man's balls in her fist and then dismissed the idea: too little after everything else she had done, like a peck on the cheek after fucking hard enough to break the slats on the bed. She'd have to come up with something better than that to get a reaction from him now. He was disappearing from her. Escaping. She could not allow that. He'd died a dozen times, but a dozen deaths were not enough recompense. Not enough. A hundred deaths would not be enough to avenge Bessie.

You bastard, Partridge, Keira thought. And *you stupid little fool, Smudge. What did you ever see in the man except for a square jaw and cute blonde curls?* Was that all it took for a woman to fall in love with a man? A stupid grin and the unearned confidence of youth? They were all fuckers. All of them.

The tall, green-eyed woman leaned in and whispered. "Bessie was my little sister, but you know that. You know that all too well, brother-in-law. She used to wet the bed, which you probably didn't know, and Dad would give her such a hiding for it, a beating like you wouldn't believe." Keira looked up and down Douglas's broken body. "Well, maybe you would. Anyway, Smudge was always such a scared little thing. She had no temerity, not one ounce of it in her body. I tried to instil boldness in her. It was me that encouraged her to ..." Keira wiped a bloodied hand over her eyes. "It was me. I told her to give you a chance when you came sniffing around all moonfaced. So that's on me." Keira gently slapped Douglas' cheek. "Are you in there, dearest brother-in-law? I'm not done, do you hear me? I'm not done. I'll find you and bring you out. Just when you think you've escaped me, I'll be there to drag you back from the pits of Hell if I must, for you see, *your* Hell is here, with me. You belong to me, and I to you. Our pain is one."

"Keira!"

She turned to see Samantha and Jasmine standing on either side of a cloaked figure, holding the newcomer by the elbows as if she, an oddly familiar woman, was too tired to stand on her own. With a jolt, Keira realised that it was the nun, Sister Kempson, though much less chubby than Keira remembered. The woman was noticeably sharper-cheeked. Helen stood behind them, a frown on her weary face.

"We found her wandering around outside," Samantha said. "Said she's here to ... save us. I believe those were her words."

Keira approached the nun and put her hands on her hips. "Sister Kempson, welcome. I'm not sure you'll be saving anyone today." The nun's horrified gaze was fixed on Douglas Partridge. Keira looked from the nun to the man lolling in the blood-slicked chair and back again. She smiled and said, "Care to give him a kick in the bollocks, Sister? Go on, you know you want to."

CHAPTER 34

The Female Seed

"You must set Douglas Partridge free," Sister Kempson said. She had discarded her cloak to reveal her habit, but the religious nature of her garments held no weight in present company.

Several tallow candles on a long rectangular table shed a smoky light that did not reach the corners of the small room. Around the table sat the Harpies, for so Keira had come to think of them: her Beautiful Harpies, creatures of great feminine power.

Of all the women present, Keira felt closest to Elsie. It was to Elsie that Keira confided her secret fears, but Keira loved them all. Each woman was distinct and remarkable in her own way. But there was one of their kind that did not appreciate the gifts given to her. Mary Brown had not returned, and the news had come that Willard Brown had disappeared. The betrayal was implicit, and it hurt Keira, angered her. There would be a reckoning for both Willard and Mary someday when her work here was done.

"Douglas must be set free," Sister Kempson said again. The only sound that accompanied her voice was that of a distant wind whistling somewhere. Not one of the women sitting at the table met the nun's imploring gaze.

Keira examined her bloodied fingernails and said, "If you've come here seeking compassion, Sister Kempson, you've wasted your time. We won't be turning other cheeks. Retribution, yes, that is our stock in trade now."

"Has there not been enough death and blood?"

CHAPTER 34 The Female Seed

"Not really. Girls? Has there been enough death and blood?" A round of head shaking greeted the question. "You see? We're only just getting started, Sister."

"Getting started? Surely, this will end with the death of that poor man in the other room. But I urge you to release him before that happens."

Keira bristled. "That poor man in the other room murdered my wee sister. I have nothing against you personally, but any more talk like that may bring consequences."

The nun was not to be cowed. "I understand that the man is guilty of a heinous wrongdoing, but I think, it is fair to say, when you consider the multiple deaths of men in the city of late, that you may have overreacted."

The urge to slap the nun fought with the urge to laugh. The latter won and Keira chuckled. "Fair enough, Sister. Aye, we may have taken things a little too far, but there's no turning back now. We are past the point of no return."

"God will forgive you if you but give yourselves up."

"It's not God that worries me. It is the townsfolk, the men, that concern me. That prick Thackery and his cruel henchmen. They seek our destruction, but we won't lie down to die. We won't choose forgiveness and compassion as we know none will be afforded us in return. Things are in motion that cannot be stopped, not by you or anyone else."

"You still have a choice."

"There's no free will in these parts, love. It's all predestined. All part of God's great plan, or so we are told."

The nun seemed lost in thought, as if searching for a coherent rebuttal to Keira's declaration of war. Keira frowned at the nun's hand rummaging around frantically inside her habit pocket. Sister Kempson seemed awfully preoccupied with whatever was in the folds of her habit.

"Care to share something, Sister?" Keira asked.

"What?" The nun's eyes were wide.

"I wish to see what is in your pocket."

Sister Kempson blinked and removed the fine metal band.

Several of the girls gasped and shifted in their chairs, but Keira Jack did not move, not a hair, her eyes locked on Sage Schuman's bracelet. Her mouth suddenly split into a smile.

"Ah," Keira said, "now this begins to make sense. You have heard the call. Clever Sage. My clever Sage. You're here to join us, Sister. You've heard the voice."

Sister Kempson rubbed at the metal nervously. "Voice? Whatever do you mean?"

"Don't be ashamed," Keira said. "We've all heard it, and none of us are mad. We are all sisters, not of God, mind you, but in a deeper sense." Keira stood and lifted her lush green dress, exposing her leg all the way up to her short undergarments. Around her smooth, muscled thigh stretched a band of metal pulsing different colours along its length.

Sister Kempson rose from her chair and stared at the object. She held up her own band. "The same? The material is … it's the same as this one?"

Keira nodded. "The same. You've lost weight, and I believe you could manage it."

"Manage what?"

"That band is not designed for the arm, much too obvious, and we have our secrets to protect, don't we ladies? It goes around your upper thigh, like mine, like we all have." Keira waved around the room. "Think of it as a symbol of sororal chastity. We are bonded now, and no man shall cross our borders." As Keira said the word 'borders', she caressed the strangely glowing metal around her thigh. She laughed and let her green dress fall over her legs.

"You misunderstand," Sister Kempson said. "I am not here to join you. I am here to plead for morality."

"Hah! You'll find morals in short supply in Dysael." The tall woman raised her hands. "But I will not force you to join us. We are not here by dint of subjugation, either at the hands of man or woman. We're here because we have shrugged off the yoke of that other life, the life of mores and decency and slavery to obligation, in whatever form obligation takes. You, Sister, have given yourself willingly to your God, but you can take yourself back just as easily."

"No, no. I will never do so. This is …" Sister Kempson turned this way and then the other. "This is quite …"

"This is our new reality, Sister Kempson, and yours too. Come with me."

Keira abruptly swept from the room, Elsie and Charlene right behind her. Jasmine and Samantha gently guided the nun outside and into a chilled, dark corridor. Soon, they entered the room containing the bloodied and broken Douglas Partridge. The man was no longer in his chair: a crimson trail led along the floor towards the canvas sheet forming one wall. Douglas had lost consciousness before he could pry the canvas loose and attain his freedom. Keira Jack laughed bitterly and dragged the comatose man back towards his torture chair by his blond curls.

Sister Kempson shook her head, anger vying with distaste. "Is it really necessary to drag the man around by his hair? This is obscenely cruel."

"I'm only dishing out what was dished to Smudge. Bessie, *Smudge*, we called her. Don't ask why. It doesn't matter. Nothing matters now."

Charlene and Elsie hauled Douglas back onto his chair and tied his hands behind his back.

"You can't condone this," Sister Kempson said, addressing the room. "There must be a shred of pity in someone's heart. You cannot all agree with this … this violence of the soul, this sickness, this travesty against God!"

The nun spoke with such vehemence that every woman in the chamber stopped and stared. Keira folded her arms and glowered. "Save your sermons for those who believe in your bullshit."

"A travesty, I say," Sister Kempson said, waving her arms around, becoming more agitated. "God shall reach down with his righteous hand and smite all of you!"

"Steady yourself, Sister." Keira's voice was low and growling, an implicit warning. "We want no fire and brimstone theatrics here."

"Smite you, I say!"

Keira exploded. "You're a fool! You call on a male God to come and lay blows to the women gathered here?! An unwise supplication for the present company, I would suggest. We don't take beatings anymore, not from man and not from your God." Keira swept upon Sister Kempson and pushed her roughly to the floor. The nun swiftly bounced back to her feet and hurled a knife. The blade stopped a mere inch from Keira's nose and slowly rotated before clattering to the floor. Keira blinked in surprise at the swiftness of the attack. She turned towards Charlene, who nodded. Keira nodded back. "Thanks, love. You saved me a nasty scratch there." Keira kicked the knife away. "Well, Sister Kempson, what happened to your doctrine of non-violence? Something's stirring your blood; that is plain to see."

"I'll thank you," Sister Kempson said, "not to touch me again, whore."

Keira pursed her lips and whistled. "What kind of talk is that from a nun, eh?" She smiled. "I like your spirit, Sister. You're one of us, no doubting it now. Only one who can't see it is you."

"Stop saying that!" Sister Kempson put her hands to her head, as if an unbearable noise assaulted her ears. "Get it out! Get it out!" The nun sank to her knees and began to hammer at her own head. "Get it out!" She collapsed on the floor and began to writhe.

Charlene and Samantha moved to offer aid, but Keira waved them back. "Leave her be."

"What's happening to her?" Elsie asked.

"Just stay back," Keira said. "We've all been through this. It is rebirth, though what form it will take, I cannot say. Stay back."

Blood appeared to pool under the body of the nun, but at second glance, one could make out that it was not blood but rather fluid shadows spreading from under the spasming body of Sister Kempson, quickly covering the warped floorboards like water escaping from a broken bathtub. Each woman backed away, but the shadows enveloped their feet with astounding speed. Charlene jumped but could not evade the darkness coursing up her legs.

Jasmine screamed as the entire room filled with darkness. Charlene called out in fear, her voice adding to that of Jasmine.

"Silence!" Keira shouted. "Be quiet, be still."

Sister Kempson no longer cried out in pain. The room was deathly quiet and black. Then, small pin pricks of light began to appear somewhere above their heads. Stars, some so close that you could reach out and touch them, some seemingly a million leagues distant, began to slowly rotate on an indistinct axis. A massive galactic map in three dimensions surrounded them, swirled about them. The stars stopped rotating, and a sun sparked into being, burned bright and then accelerated out of sight as the stars whirled past with increasing speed. Orbs of varying colours came and went. Another star burned bright, the sun of a distant galaxy, until it, too, disappeared.

"Christ," whispered Elsie. "What is it?"

"It is everything," Keira said. "The universe beyond our reckoning. We are taken somewhere. Or something comes here."

"But what?"

"I can't say. But this is beautiful."

"I'm scared, Keira," Jasmine said.

"Do not be afraid. It speaks to us. It communicates."

"What speaks to us?" Elsie said.

Keira did not reply, and a hushed silence ensued until the darkness began to fade, and the gas lamps began to glow again. Then, the stars disappeared.

To everyone's surprise, Sister Kempson had regained her feet and stood among them. Her eyes were black, the pupils dilated so that they had become orbs of pure liquid night. She simply stood on the spot, swaying slightly and staring into space. Everyone backed away from the eerie sight. Then, the nun blinked and turned her head to take in all those in the room. She smiled slowly.

"I have watched you," Sister Kempson said. But it was not Sister Kempson who spoke. This voice belonged to another. It was a rough, masculine voice, like grit under foot: the bearer of those black eyes. "You have done well. I commend you all."

Keira and Elsie exchanged glances. Keira cocked her head. "Thank you," she said. "To whom do I speak?"

"Your master."

"You are mistaken. We have no master."

"Everyone has a master, even I."

"We have none. What are you?"

The shadow within Sister Kempson laughed, a brittle laugh like distant stars colliding. "You are quite right. You have no masters. Consider this a final test of your will. I am pleased with you. Bow to no man, no representation of God, not even me."

"What do you want? Where is the nun?"

"The nun is indisposed. She will return shortly. What we want is to see you succeed. To see you *seed*."

Keira paused. "Generous of you. Why do our fates concern you?"

"We want you to take seed where the others have failed."

Keira frowned. "There is much to ponder in that statement. We? There are others like you? What *seed* do you speak of? Who failed to take *seed* before us?"

The shadow within the nun simply shrugged and said, "Did you know that only the female cottonwood trees produce seeds, which float on currents of air? We chose the wrong gender. We understand that now and have corrected our mistake. Consider us the winds of the universe and you our cottonwood tree. Spread your seeds, *our* seeds and together we will flourish."

"You are responsible," Keira said, "for what we have become?"

The shadow nodded. "We are the conduit, yes. Your gifts have taken different forms, as they do among all those whose blood they inhabit."

Keira stepped closer. "I am trying to understand. What do you mean when you talk of blood?"

"The metal that you possess is in your blood, now, but this you must know."

"I suspected as much. Where does it come from? Where do *you* come from?"

"You would not understand, nor do we have the time to explain.

Know this, that our fates are tied. Our survival depends on yours. But first, you must withstand the assault that comes."

"Assault?" Keira looked around. "What assault?"

"They are coming to destroy you. You must survive. The tether between us weakens, and I cannot remain in this form. I leave you now. "

"That's a shame. I would have enjoyed further cryptic conversations. Will you return? Will you fight with us?"

"We wish you to flower, we wish you to blossom, but I can offer you no further aid than to forewarn you. Remember, we are never truly gone while you carry the metal." Sister Kempson's eyes rolled up in her head, and she collapsed. Keira caught the nun and lay her gently on the floor.

Keira stood to find Douglas Partridge giving her an accusing look. Between split lips and in a cracking voice, he said, "What have you done? What evils have you invited into our world?"

"Shut your gob."

"What was that thing?" Charlene asked, a horrified expression on her face.

"Our benefactor, I would suggest," Keira said. "What is this about an assault?"

Elsie put her fingers to her temple, squeezed her eyes shut. She took a deep breath, and another. Then, she nodded. "They're here. Men have entered the lower levels. Many men."

Keira turned back to Douglas. "Well, brother-in-law, if these men destroy us, you live. If we kill them all, then you and I will have a final chat. One way or another, this is the end for somebody. Your life and ours are in the hands of ..." She glanced at the unconscious Sister Kempson. "... powers beyond my understanding. Still, that is the way with us mortals, isn't it? Do not fear, girls," Keira said, raising her voice and addressing the gathered women. "Now is the time to fully express yourselves. We are prepared. We have laid our snares. And if you die today, remember one thing. Remember to take as many of those pricks with you as you can. And above all, enjoy yourselves."

CHAPTER 35

A Gentlemen's Accord

Sergeant Frood climbed through a window that had never been glazed and onto a large factory floor containing rows of dusty looms. Whatever had caused the building's construction to stop all those years ago had come late in the process. The place looked almost ready to open for business. Frood shivered as he recalled just what had halted the building's fabrication: the poisonous metal. Frood coughed and cursed. If he lived through this, he expected an increase in wages.

The desolate wind had entered the abandoned factory along with the scrawny sergeant and whistled mournfully among the virgin looms. A darkened doorway, lacking a door, lurked in the shadows to his right. He didn't fancy going into the stairwell beyond. Frood cursed the ill-light. It was late afternoon, but the gloomy conditions of the Yard did not allow for decent visibility on the streets and no visibility at all within the stairwell, yet he had been tasked with searching the place top to bottom; there was no avoiding it. Through the doorway and up a set of stairs to the upper levels, he had to go. Perhaps he should fix up a lantern.

A hand grabbed Sergeant Frood by the shoulder, and he nearly shat himself. Frood turned as Private Wilkins leaned closer to whisper in his ear.

"Sergeant Frood, how are we to fight a woman who can become invisible, who is nothing but air? She could creep up behind us and stab us in the neck before we were any the wiser."

CHAPTER 35 A Gentlemen's Accord

"Startle me like that again, boy," Frood said, "and I'll stab you in the neck myself."

"Sorry, Sergeant. And what of the woman with the power of flame? That's not natural, sir."

"You fucking idiot. You and the other West Quarters have been briefed and should know that Sage Schuman, she of the flame, is dead."

"Oh. Still, they have the invisible woman and the one who gets in your mind. And what of the others? What strange powers are we up against?"

"You've had a complete run-down of the supernatural faculties that we know about, and if you are ignorant of them, you only have yourself to blame. Where's that god-damned dog? Get it in here, and get a lantern lit. We need to dispel some of these shadows." The young private peered into the darkness as if the Devil were waiting somewhere unseen. "Hurry up!"

Private Wilkins scarpered, and Frood backed away from the doorway. He was going to wait for the light and the dogs and the other men. He was no hero. Wilkins had spooked Frood with his inane questions, the younger man's fear catching, as fear often did. The young private seemed unprepared, his questions coming too late in the day. All the men had been informed to beware of invisibility, mind control, random animal attacks and lethal objects flying at them with no apparent source of locomotion. Frood touched the scars around his neck. He was personally familiar with three of the dangers, being a victim of Charlene Hickson's attempt at throttling him with catgut and Elsie Gallagher's temporary control of his mind. And then there was the vile-tempered alley cat that had torn his face to pieces. That event was no random attack: the animal had been set on him by one of the women. Now that he thought on it, Frood had been the victim of an unpleasantly varied array of violent assaults: garotted, clawed, turned into a marionette and punched in the head, twice by the same man. Frood nervously tongued the hole in his face where his two front teeth had been before Garth knocked them out. He hadn't forgotten the broken nose from their first encounter, either. Bastard.

Scuffling noises, a dozen men, along with Sergeant Graham and his bristling mastiff, approached him. Frood breathed easier. Constable Thackery had decided that the small army should be split into three groups with roughly equal numbers, and each group would be spearheaded by a mastiff. Ostensibly, this was to cover more ground, but more likely Thackery was afraid that if one of the harpies got to the dogs and turned them, one dog would be more manageable to put down than three feral animals at the same time, each the size of a small horse. The square-jawed Graham swore that the dogs would stay under control, but he had not witnessed the murder of Yohan Schuman. Whoever controlled animals had a strong enough hold to drive them to suicide.

On one hip, Frood wore a short sword. He checked the one-shot flintlock pistol on his other hip. The projectile within the pistol would do for the dog if aimed directly at the brain, or it would do for Charlene Hickson or Elsie Gallagher if he had the chance. Hell, it would even do for himself if it came to that.

Private Wilkins returned with a glowing lantern. Frood snatched the lantern and turned his back on the young man. "Wilkins?" Frood said a moment later.

"Yes, sir?"

Frood handed the lantern back. "Be a good lad and go first."

"Me? But I'm a … I'm just a private."

"Second class, if you survive this. I'll see to it. Off you go. Don't worry, I'll be right behind you."

Wilkins cast a nervous glance at the dozen men milling around. The young private must have been reassured by the look of sturdy resolve on his comrades' faces and the equally sturdy mastiff and its handler. He probably wasn't convinced by the expression of fortitude on Sergeant Frood's face because the sergeant was moderately sure he wasn't wearing one. He hated the idea as much as the private.

"Yes, sir," Wilkins gulped.

CHAPTER 35 A Gentlemen's Accord

The young man entered the darkened doorway, and Frood followed. Graham and his monstrous dog came close on Frood's heels. The lantern swung in the young private's grasp, casting a sickening light around the molding stairwell.

"Hold it steady, boy," Frood said.

"Sorry, sir."

"And keep your voice down. We're meant to be surprising the harpies, and they mustn't hear us coming should we wish to do that."

"Yes, sir. Sorry. You think they're in here, sir?"

"It's a search," Frood said irritably. "Could be, might be elsewhere. The dog will tell us, hopefully. Now shut up and move." Several men at the rear of the party tripped over each other on the musty stairwell, and the mastiff began to growl.

"Nathan is unhappy," Sergeant Graham murmured. "Too many people crowding him."

What kind of man names his dog Nathan? "Your precious animal is just going to have to put up with it," Frood whispered.

Private Wilkins reached another doorway opening out onto a landing running around the upper level, some kind of walkway with rooms on the west side. Visibility was better up here, several windows on the east side allowing a filtered light. Frood peered over Wilkin's shoulder and saw movement on the far end of the landing. He grabbed the young private by the collar and hauled him back inside the stairwell.

"Extinguish the lantern," Frood hissed. "I saw something." The young fellow did as he was told. Nathan began to growl and pull at his lead. "Sergeant Graham, keep your dog quiet. Give me a musket, quick, quick." One of the men handed Frood a rifle. Two men came forward carrying identical weapons, and Frood bade them position themselves on either side of the doorway. Frood gestured at the far end of the walkway. "Fifty yards, directly that way. Get ready. As soon as we've fired, rush them, don't give them time to react." Several men nodded and jostled each other as they nervously drew bladed weapons. "Sergeant Graham, let your dog go on my command." The big dog handler nodded. "Wilkins, get downstairs as quickly as you can and get the others in here." Wilkins didn't bother to nod as he scurried away. The idiot was more than likely to break his own neck in the darkness of the stairwell, but Frood could not risk a lantern alerting the harpies to their presence.

Frood crept low to the doorway and peered down the long barrel of the musket.

"Shouldn't we wait for the others?" someone whispered. Frood shook his head. He had no intention of missing the chance that had presented itself. Hesitation could see him lose it. There, two figures walking along the walkway in the distance. Frood squinted but could make out little about them other than they wore masks over mouth and nose. Which one did he want dead the most? Who did he hope to see at the end of the musket, Charlene Hickson or Elsie Gallagher?

He lowered the weapon and frowned. These figures were male. Had two of his men somehow found access to the upper floors by another route and wandered into his line of fire? He cursed their idiocy and was about to hand the musket back when he realised that one of the men was Garth. He could tell from the shape of the man and the way he walked with that arrogant swagger. Suddenly, and to his own surprise, Frood realised who he most wanted dead.

He raised the musket to his eye once more and made the necessary calculations. Forty yards now and coming closer. He'd only get one chance at this, only one chance to make it look like an accident.

"Sir?" One of the other musket men said, "I don't think—"

Frood squeezed the trigger, and a sharp retort echoed around the factory.

"Shots fired, sir! Shots fired!"

Constable Thackery didn't need the young private running out of the mist at him to know that shots had been fired. He'd heard the

CHAPTER 35 A Gentlemen's Accord

distant crack of muskets, two shots in quick succession.

"The textile factory, sir, judging from the direction and distance," the young man puffed.

This information proved more useful. "Well done, Private," Thackery said as he broke into a run. "Men, on me!"

Thackery sprinted into the fog, several armed officers at his heels. He'd memorised the general outlay of the Yard and hoped that he had accurately recalled the location of the textile factory. The last thing he needed was to lead his men in aimless circles within the fog, to be picked off one by one by the murderous harpies. His spatial memory proved faultless as the large windowless structure loomed out of the mist. The shouts of agitated men echoed and bounced around the brick walls within the factory. Something was happening, some kind of battle. Sergeant Frood and his men had found them.

Thackery hurdled through an open window and onto the factory floor, pulling out his rapier as he did so. A group of men were standing in a semi-circle, looking at something, but were otherwise not engaged in combat. A man was shouting; Thackery could hear the deep bellowing and just make out the top of the man's head over the gathered soldiers. The constable shouldered his way past the gawking men, and there stood Garth, several muskets and swords pointed at him. On the ground beside him lay another man, his hands clutched at his side, blood seeping through his fingers.

"What is happening here?" Thackery demanded.

Garth turned angrily on the constable. "That fucker," Garth said, pointing at Sergeant Frood, "fired on us, got George in the stomach."

"Is this true?" Thackery turned to Sergeant Frood.

Frood shrugged and said, "It was dark up there, sir. I thought it was them. It was an accident."

"Bullshit!" Garth exploded. "This is the second time you've fired on me, Frood, you prick. This was no accident."

"We're all on edge," Frood said more to Thackery than Garth, "we thought you were the harpies."

Garth clenched his fists. "Do I look like I'm carrying around a pair of tits? You tried to murder us."

"That is an unsubstantiated accusation," Thackery said. "Who is this man?" He pointed at George.

"George Burridge," Garth said, "blacksmith and master to Douglas Partridge. He's hurt. He needs medical attention."

Thackery put away his rapier and pushed down on the musket barrel of the closest man. "Stand down, put your weapons away. This man is … if not a friend, at least he is not the enemy. What the hell are you doing here, Garth?"

"Never mind that now. George needs a doctor."

"I don't have time for this. I can't afford to spare the men. You'll have to get him out of the Yard by yourself."

"I'm not leaving. Sister Kempson is in here somewhere."

Thackery screwed up his face. "What?"

"She's gone after the ladies."

"But I thought she agreed that … that she would leave. The woman is insane. Why?"

Garth sighed. "Her crusade to make the world a better place? I don't know, but I'm not leaving 'til I find her."

"Christ's balls, are you telling me she is now a hostage?"

"I don't know. Perhaps she found them, or they found her … I just don't know."

"God damn it!" Thackery kicked at the ground. "God damn it! I hold no responsibility for her welfare, do you hear me?" He waved a finger at Garth. "No responsibility! I warned her several times, you were witness to that. I urged her to get out of Dysael. If she dies, I'll have the bishop crawling all over me."

"That's all you're concerned about?" Garth snarled. "A complaint from the bishop?"

"I'm concerned about a great many things at the moment. The nun has made her own bed. I will not be held accountable."

Thackery's rage seemed to quell Garth's somewhat. "George has a musket ball in his side and needs a doctor."

Thackery sighed angrily. "Alright." He turned to two men

behind him. "Get a stretcher and get him out of here. Return as soon as you can." The two men nodded and ran from the textile factory.

Garth knelt at George's side and patted him on the shoulder.

"I'm alright," George said through clenched teeth. "I must go on. I have to save Douglas."

"No, no," Garth said. "You leave that to Sister Kempson. If she's found them, then your boy is safe. She could talk the ears off a donkey and change the mind of a mule. Don't you worry about Douglas."

"I'm sorry I dragged the sister into this," George said between painful breaths.

Garth smiled sadly. "She was already in, George. All the way in. Headstrong, our nun." The woodsman's smile faded. "You should have let Douglas face the consequences of his actions, George."

The blacksmith's breathing quickened with the pain. "I'm sorry. I'm sorry. Forgive me."

"It's not my forgiveness you need to ask for."

The men returned and eased George onto a canvas stretched between two poles. As he was hauled away, Thackery stepped closer to Garth. "I must talk with you in private."

Garth turned to eye Thackery suspiciously. "You going to shoot me where there are no witnesses?"

"You have misjudged us."

"Not all of you." Garth glanced at Sergeant Frood as he was pouring gunpowder down the muzzle of the musket and lunged at the scrawny man. Frood shrieked and raised his arms over his face. Garth grabbed the musket and walked away, ignoring the sergeant's protests. Thackery followed him to a quiet corner.

"I could do with a man like you on my side," Thackery said. "There are certain … elements within my own force that I, quite honestly, do not trust. You're an idiot but an honest one. I sense no artifice within you."

Garth glared at Thackery. "Artifice? If that means what I think it means, then you're right. I'm a plain man and I speak plainly.

I'm not here to kill anyone." He held up the musket. "I'm here for the nun. That's all."

"I hardly think you're in a position to refuse our help. We have many men, well-armed. We'll get your nun, if she's still alive, but I want your word that you'll help us fight those creatures. We are stronger united."

"United? You argued with Sister Kempson the whole time. She came to you in earnest with valuable information, but you are an arrogant prick and publicly rejected the woman, tried to shame her. Now you want to unite? With me?"

An uncomfortable feeling of guilt crept through Thackery. "I may have erred, then. But a man makes mistakes. I am prepared to acknowledge them. Do we have an agreement?"

Garth leaned in and bared his teeth. "I'll lend my strength to yours because the Green Gods know you are currently in charge of a group of corrupt, incompetent cunts, and you need my help. But as soon as I find Kempson, I'm out." Garth swung the musket at the wall, and the weapon splintered in several places. "Fucking guns."

"I hope you feel better, but don't do that again. I suspect we are going to be thankful for the new technology before this is over."

"I don't like them."

Thackery shrugged. "Noted. Then we have a gentlemen's accord?"

"Aren't no gentlemen around here. And by the way, what the hell are you doing bringing dogs in here? They'll turn against you."

"You may be right, but I'll personally put them down if they do. However, they are useful for the time being."

Garth grunted and walked away. *Another hound*, thought Thackery. Another big stupid, slobbering hound, but he needed the man, just like he needed the mastiffs. For now.

CHAPTER 36

Bath Night

Sergeant Robert Jones of the Night Watch did not have the will to put up with all the emotional bullshit that went along with having a wife. He preferred the friendship of his fellow night watchmen or the carnal benefits of the occasional whore. At least with whores you didn't get all the grief and the backchat and the general impositions a wife placed on a man. Part of him was quite smug about all the murders, all those wives doing in their husbands. You see? He'd been right to keep himself free. At the age of thirty-two, it was not yet beyond him to find a wife; he was still young enough, and his career, if not blossoming, had proved steady. But why would he want to? His newly married friends had boasted of sex on tap, but after a couple of years, those boasts had turned to sullen looks at the merest mention of their wives. He had to laugh. But witnessing his friends grow old and bitter prematurely was not always amusing. No, indeed, it wasn't worth the trouble, a wife. God damn wives.

Jones watched as Sergeant Hardy and his enormous mastiff approached a redbrick building. Hardy was a big, powerful man, as were all of the dog handlers, for they had to physically control their animals. Hardy pushed on a door, which fell from its hinges and collapsed inwards. The dog handler and his mastiff disappeared inside, several men right behind him. Jones was supposed to be directing the search in this area of the Yard, but Hardy's dog seemed to be on the scent of something, so, for want of a better idea, Jones had allowed the handler and his animal to take the lead.

Jones followed them into an interior no less eerie than the misty streets outside. The place was odd. Gargoyles lined the walls, each artfully designed to look different from the other, dozens of them, and where one might expect to see them high on the outside of a building, these were low on the walls and facing a central nave containing rows of splintered pews. It was unlike any place of worship that Jones had ever seen. Perhaps it wasn't a church, after all. It didn't feel like one, and there was no obvious alter, no crosses or religious symbology, nothing of that ilk.

"What is this place?" Sergeant Hardy said, echoing Jones' own thoughts. His dog sniffed at the floor and broke into a fit of sneezing.

"Don't know, mate," Jones said. "But it's big." He looked up but could not make out a ceiling in the dim light. "Spread out, fellows, look for ways to go higher. If they're in here, they'll be somewhere up above, probably hanging upside down in a belfry." Several men cast Jones confused glances as they began to search the floor, and the squat sergeant laughed under his breath at his own joke.

"We need light," Hardy said. Jones called for lanterns. Several minutes later, three gas lamps shed light in nooks and niches around the walls.

"Found something, sir," a young soldier called out.

Before Jones could respond, Sergeant Hardy said, "What is it? What have you found?"

Jones' ire rose. *This is my command, West Quarter*, he thought. The stocky sergeant was further aggrieved when the young soldier, a North Quarter man and one of his own, answered the dog handler, thereby giving weight to the bastard's attempt to usurp his authority.

"A way up, sir, but it's sealed off. I guess there's nothing up there."

"We check everything," Jones said angrily, taking back control. "We leave nothing unexplored." He walked over to where the young private was holding a lantern to an archway containing several steps that ended in a cement wall. Jones had to admit that nobody could possibly have used this way in or out. "Must be another way up," he muttered.

But no other way up existed despite a thorough search of the ground floor. Jones returned to the cement wall and rubbed at his jaw. Sergeant Hardy came to stand beside him.

"Anything from your dog?" Jones asked.

Hardy led his mastiff to the concrete partition and waited. The dog sniffed at the base of the seal but otherwise did not react. "Nothing," Hardy said.

"I don't like it," Jones said. "Who closed this off and why?"

The dog handler shrugged. "Can't have been recent. Perhaps upper levels are unsafe, and they blocked it when they abandoned the Yard."

Jones shook his head. "Seems like a lot of work for nothing. Something's not right. Sledgehammer! Get hammers in here, something, anything and knock it down!"

Nobody had thought to trek through the heart of Dysael with a sledgehammer on his back, but several smaller tools were rallied and set to chipping away at the concrete. Jones frowned as he thought he saw movement after the first few blows against the wall.

"Stand back," Jones said. "Get back." The men stepped away, and the squat sergeant moved in. "Give me a lantern." Jones took the proffered lantern and checked the seams where the concrete seal met the original walls of the building. He stood on his tip toes and leaned on the seal with one hand. The wall flipped on a hidden hinge and nearly collected the sergeant under the jaw as he backed away. They could now walk bent over under what was not a wall but a revolving door on a central hinge. A moment later, Sergeant Hardy's mastiff barked and leapt forward, the leash flying from his hand before the handler could react.

The dog bounded up the stairs and disappeared into darkness.

❦

A box of rusted nails and an iron bar. Not much in the way of weapons, but Keira Jack and Charlene Hickson would just have to make do.

"Are you alright?" Keira asked. The two women stood in the darkness at the end of a long hallway. Keira clasped the metal bar in her right hand. The object felt comforting, weighty.

Charlene gently kicked the decades-old box of nails at her feet, and they rattled. "I'm good as gold. First bastard along this way gets an extra peehole."

Keira patted Charlene on the shoulder. "Remember, we strike first, but we do not linger. We retreat to the welcoming embrace of our sisters. We do not allow a pitched battle to form because their numbers will overpower ours. We rely on surprise and movement and the narrow confines of this place. They will stumble and fall over themselves. We are more of a lure than a first line of defence."

Charlene gave a shuddering breath. The woman was nervous despite her bravado. "I understand. I have no wish to die this day. We stick and run. It suits me."

"Good. Quiet now. It's almost time."

The two women waited and listened intently, the only sounds their own anxious breathing. And then, before long, a scuffling noise, a snuffling and scrabbling. Keira could see better in the dark than most nocturnal animals, and she made out the shape of something large and low at the far end of the dusty hallway. Charlene shifted nervously beside her; several nails levitated from the box and rotated slowly in the gloom.

Keira raised a hand and whispered, "Wait."

The mastiff came down the corridor, its blocky head swivelling this way and that. Then, the animal saw them. Its hind legs scrabbled for purchase in its eagerness to rush at them, to tear at them with its powerful jaws and teeth.

"Keira," Charlene said, fear in her voice, "Keira, do something."

Keira put out a hand, and the mastiff came sliding to a halt before them and rested on its haunches. The dog cocked its head, its tongue lolling from its mouth. "There, there, love," Keira said softly. "You calm down and be a good boy." The dog stared at Keira. It growled and jumped backwards, only to crawl low towards her and roll over. Then it twisted back to its feet and ran in circles, chasing its tail and letting out a high-pitched whine.

"What's it doing?" Charlene asked.

"The dog is perplexed. He fights against his training and the new mistress that he senses. I have not seen this before. He fights me. His former master has a deep hold on this animal."

"Can you break it? Can you control the dog?"

"Yes." Keira knelt to bring her face level with the mastiff's. She reached out gently and allowed the dog to sniff the back of her hand. Soothingly, she said, "Well, well. Such a fine animal they have recruited to track us down. Such a strong young fellow." She scratched the animal under its ear, and the dog's hind leg quivered. "But I have a better suggestion. You serve me now. Is that agreeable?" The dog whined and licked Keira's hand. "Good boy." Keira reached under its thick neck and rubbed. "I have a task for you, my friend. A very important task."

Sergeant Robert Jones cocked an ear. The distant, frantic barking of a dog echoed from somewhere. It could only be Hardy's mastiff, the West Quarter man apparently in agreement because he set off at a run along the darkened corridor.

"Wait!" Jones called. "We stay together." But Sergeant Hardy was proving to be as obedient as his dog, which was not at all, and disappeared into the gloom. God damn it. Better to stay together. Who knows what they might find in this accursed place. A dozen men followed at the stocky sergeant's heels: a dozen lives that he was responsible for. They had no choice but to trust each other, to back each other up. Dead men all, otherwise. He didn't need a weak link in their armour, for that would place them all in danger. Hardy and his dog were proving to be a volatile combination. He remembered Thackery's warning about the West Quarter crew. Jones cursed again. There was little he could do about it now.

"Over here!" Hardy called. Jones held out his lantern, squinting. Where the fuck was over here? He could see bugger all in the narrow confines of the hallway. It had to be late dusk outside; the only light now came from the pools of lantern light. Where was Hardy? What had he found?

"Over where, you idiot?" Jones called.

"Over here!" Hardy replied, not at all helpfully. The dog barked again. Hardy shouted something indistinct. The dog sounded angry. Christ's shit, had one of the witches turned it? Was it having a go at its handler?

Several doors stood ajar along the hallway, and in one room, Jones found Hardy and his mastiff. The room contained a window that still allowed a modicum of light to filter through. Early evening then, not dusk, but it would be completely dark soon, and the lanterns would be their only means of visibility. He hoped they didn't run out of fuel, for blindness now would mean death, either at the hands of their enemy or tripping over each other and blasting holes in a friend by accident.

Sergeant Hardy was looking down into a steel container on four squat legs, his dog panting beside him. The room contained a pungent chemical odour that set Jones' nerves on edge. He approached the container and peered inside, a dozen men joining him. It held a purple liquid and several rags floating on the surface. The ceramic floor tiles were cracked or missing in places, but the functionality of the room was unmistakable.

"We're in a bathroom of some kind," Jones said.

"Anyone fancy a dip," a joker nearby guffawed.

"Not in that shit," another said. "That's kerosene."

Kerosene. That was it, kerosene. But there was something else, another smell coming from the liquid, something metallic. Jones hurriedly pulled his lantern away.

"Why would anyone fill a bath with kerosene?" someone said.

"Just don't get too close with the lamps," Jones said. He turned around just in time to see Sergeant Hardy's dog disappear into the hallway outside. The dog's handler had not appeared to notice his animal's absence. "Where's your dog gone now?" Jones said angrily. "If you can't control your bloody animal, Hardy, get it out of here."

CHAPTER 36 Bath Night

Hardy turned with a frown. "Eh? Travis?" He put two fingers to his lips and gave a sharp whistle. "Travis, get back in here."

Jones had nearly made the door when the dog returned carrying a lit torch in its mouth. It trotted right past him and towards its master. Where had the dog found a burning torch? Jones poked his head around the door, and there at the end of the hallway stood two women. One he recognised as Keira Jack. Jones inhaled sharply to scream a warning when he realised the true danger.

He pointed at the mastiff and shrieked, "Get that dog away from the—"

But it was too late. Showing surprising nimbleness for such a large animal, Travis playfully evaded the hands of several soldiers and leapt into the bathtub.

In a blinding flash, the explosion obliterated the mastiff, shattered the steel bathtub and blew Sergeant Hardy's head off, taking various limbs of other men nearby. The nails that had been laid in the bathtub pierced flesh in a radius of a dozen yards.

Jones was knocked off his feet and out into the hallway. When he awoke, dazed, a few seconds later, he found himself shredded, several nails having passed right through him, others still sticking from his chest and legs. Keira Jack stood over a moaning man lying close by. She raised a metal bar and viciously crushed the man's skull. Jones' hands were broken, useless, and he could not find his weapon in any case. He tried to crawl away, but his legs would not obey. Keira Jack was upon him.

Sergeant Robert Jones screamed.

Constable Thackery turned to witness a roiling cloud of flame burst through the mist in the distance somewhere up high. The ground shuddered under his feet, and several men exclaimed and pointed skywards.

Thackery started running in the direction of the explosion.

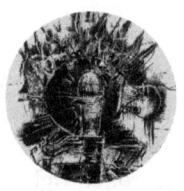

CHAPTER 37

Ballroom Blitz

When you hunted, you counted on two things: weaponry and experience. Foremost among that experience was knowledge of your prey's territory. The men that had entered the Yard seeking to slay the harpies had weaponry hanging out of their arseholes. What they didn't have, from what Garth de Silva could tell as he pushed through the mostly frightened young men cluttering the stairwell, was experience. And they sure as Hell had no idea of how to fight in the narrow spaces that penned them in single file, turning them into docile sheep in a race, funnelling them straight to the slaughterhouse.

Garth squeezed his way to the front of the milling soldiers. Many of them were cut and bleeding or had singed eyebrows and angry scald marks on their faces. The sickening reek of burning flesh and kerosene hung in the air. He tiptoed a few more steps and warily eyed the corridor. The men behind him were rooted in fear and did not follow. It was almost completely dark, but Garth's night vision, honed from years of living in the True Wilds, allowed him to see well enough, and what he saw was carnage. Bodies littered the hallway, many of the men still breathing but dying slowly from wounds received as they had attempted to run. Garth grabbed the ankle of a young soldier lying on the floor a few yards in front of him, his clothes smoking, and dragged the man back into the stairwell. He was still alive but unresponsive, staring into space.

"Soldier, what happened up here?" The man's teeth began to

chatter. Garth wanted information, needed to know what was out there, what had caused the explosion and the likelihood of another. "Soldier, talk to me." The man opened his mouth, and blood spilled from his lips, half his tongue missing. He had pissed himself and probably bitten his own tongue off in fear, or the explosion had caused him to bite it off. Either way, Garth would get nothing from him.

"What do we do, sir?" A soldier in the stairwell asked. It took Garth a moment to understand the man was talking to him.

"I'm not your commander. But I would advise you extinguish that lantern, right now." The man with the lantern compressed a thumb lever and blew the wick out. Garth heard a commotion on the stairs below and a familiar voice. A few moments later, Constable Vincent E. Thackery barged his way through the men to join Garth, Sergeant Frood right behind him.

Thackery eyed the half-tongued soldier trembling in shock. "What has happened here?"

"A loud bang," Garth said. "That's just a guess, of course."

"Why are we waiting?" Thackery said. "We must move forward. Show some spine, man."

Garth raised his eyebrows and then waved a hand towards the hallway just above them with its sprawled dead and dying. "Be my guest, fuckhead."

Thackery cast a disdainful look at Garth and stepped up and onto the hallway, albeit clinging to the wall like a creeping vine. The man was a preening fop, but he didn't lack courage. The big woodsman followed the constable, and the two men edged their way past charred and bloodied remains that once were men. Bolstered by the bravery of their commanding officer, Sergeant Frood and several more men joined the silent procession.

"This is ridiculous," Thackery whispered. "I can't see anything. I can't even make out your hideous features, and you're right next to me. I'll get a lantern."

"Don't do it," Garth whispered. "You'll make yourself a target."

"I'm a target anyway. There's nowhere to hide."

Thackery was right; there *was* nowhere to hide. The women had chosen their lair wisely: they could not be outflanked, and numbers meant nothing when they could defend such narrow avenues. The men of the Night Watch and Garth were at the mercy of whatever bizarre powers the wives possessed. It was attrition, that was all. Men would fall and die, and others would take their place until the enemy had exhausted themselves. It did not augur well to be the next in line at this early stage of the fight.

"I can't stumble about in the dark anymore," Thackery said. He crept back and whispered to Frood. The scrawny man nodded and melted into the soldiers behind him. Garth gripped his hunting knife and waited. Three lanterns began to glow and move forward.

Thackery uttered a lunatic call to battle. "Charge!"

Garth took a breath. He had no choice but to join the dozens of men now careening down the hallway, lanterns swinging crazily among them. Shadows flickered on the floors, walls and ceiling, disorientating him. Garth expected to be shot, stabbed or blown apart any moment. But the hallway was clear. All the rooms on this floor were clear. The harpies had moved up another stairwell, for they had not slipped by the nearly forty men cramming the hallway. Up, they had to be up.

Sergeant Frood cried out. He was kneeling by the corpse of Robert Jones, a pool of blood forming a halo around the man's bludgeoned head.

"Fucking bitches!" Frood screamed. "Fucking bitches! I'll fucking kill them bitches!"

"God damn it," Thackery said. "Damn it. This whole building is a trap, but we're not backing down. Lanterns to the front! All firearms to the front. Get up those stairs, now!"

Garth sighed and tagged along at the rear of the mad crusade.

They came rushing headlong up the stairs. Men. Young men. Men full of bravado and semen. Men who'd never fucked a woman

CHAPTER 37 Ballroom Blitz

without offering coin and some who had. Flesh in male form, in all shapes and masculine sizes. Somewhere, two dogs barked, also male and eager to establish their dominance. The stairs upon which the men stumbled over themselves led to a small corridor and then an antechamber which opened onto a spacious room: a hall or ballroom in days of old. Keira Jack was waiting within the ballroom, an iron bar in her fist. The weapon lacked any character, a simple bludgeoning tool, but it would suffice, for it was the hand wielding it that made it a fearsome weapon.

"It sounds like our dance cards are full up, girls," Keira said. "Any moment now."

Charlene Hickson stood at Keira's side, and at Charlene's feet was a box of rusting metal: nails, bolts, screws, anything that could be used as a projectile. Samantha Burgess carried three small vials containing a mixture of kerosene and Jasmine's menstrual blood, the last of the same mixture in the bathtub on the floor below.

Samantha brought a vial of the deep purple liquid to her eyes and winked at Jasmine. "I always said you was an explosive beauty."

Jasmine raised a knife and a tin container of kerosene. She smiled and said, "Plenty more where that came from."

Keira turned to Helen. "Go and wait with the nun and my brother-in-law. If we die here, I want you to cut Douglas' throat."

Helen's eyes were pleading. "I can stay and fight."

"No, love. You're a healer, but the last task I assign to you is to kill. I'm relying on you to do right by me and Bessie and all of us. Off you go now."

Helen nodded and backed away. She disappeared through a door at the far end of the room. Keira took a deep breath. Now, they would be tested. This would be the critical battle. If they failed, they would all perish.

Samantha slipped out of her blue-silver dress and prowled the floor, her voluptuous body fading from sight, the incendiary vials now apparently floating of their own accord. Elsie Gallagher crouched in a darkened corner of the room behind a sagging piano, her fingers to her temple, seeking her first victim. The antechamber took on a faint glow. The men were almost here, but Keira and her girls were ready.

The first men through the door carried muskets, pistols and crossbows, but whereas these weapons could only fire single shots, Charlene was capable of much more. The first few soldiers walked into a hailstorm of rusting metal. Four men dropped, but two others got off a shot, both missing by a wide margin. Elsie, still hidden behind the piano, clasped onto a single mind among the throng, and this man stabbed a colleague in the back with a short blade and punctured the heart of another. In the wild clamour to enter the room and attack the Harpies, and in the darkness created by so many bodies blocking the lamp light, Elsie's puppet killed a third man before someone shouted a warning. The infiltrator went down under a series of hacking blows, and Elsie instantly switched to another man, and the process began again. Elsie's rapid mental infiltrations had the desired effect of distracting the soldiers, turning them inwards in confusion.

Charlene continued to pump corroded metal shards into living flesh, making it dead. Samantha threw a glass vial into the midst of the soldiers, and it shattered and exploded. The lethal cocktail of Jasmine's menstrual blood and kerosene ripped open bodies and burned others. Men tripped on the dead and fell and, before they could rise, joined them in death.

Another musket fired, but again, the ball flew wide of the mark.

The charge halted, and men took cover on either side of the antechamber door, huddling out of range of Charlene's lethal projectiles. Samantha hurled another vial, but it shattered and burned out harmlessly against the wall. The men were, however, not safe from Elsie's mental probes. She found a new target, and the man lunged at an ally with his sword, but he was instantly disarmed. Elsie tried again, but the men were on guard now and at the first sign of puppetry, the target was pinned and his weapon removed. Elsie began to tire as she searched again and again for a new target.

Samantha, last explosive vial in her hand, crept close to the door, intending to throw it within the antechamber and into the mass of male bodies. She was too close. Keira could see the vial floating through the air, and if she could, then so could the enemy. She was about to cry out a warning when she realised that she would simply alert the men to Samantha's presence. She held her breath.

"I'm out," Charlene said. The pile of metal detritus at her feet was gone.

Masculine shouts of command came from within the antechamber. The men were organised now, the initial surprise of the audacious ambush gone. They would be reloading, preparing for another assault, and this time, Charlene could do nothing to stop them.

Samantha walked up to the doorway and was about to hurl the vial into the antechamber when Constable Thackery shot her in the face. Samantha fell, and her naked body became visible as the vial rolled harmlessly from her hand, spilling its contents onto the floorboards. Half her face was blasted off. Keira could not reach Sam in time. The men fell upon her, hacking and slashing, destroying the beautiful curves of her once warm body: the butcher's wife now cold cuts of meat.

Jasmine screamed Samantha's name. She doused herself in kerosene and ran towards the men murdering her closest friend. Keira tried to call her back, but Jasmine's rage made her insensible to her own welfare.

Sam's head was cleaved from her neck. Jasmine shrieked and leapt into the throng of male bodies, swinging wildly. The men left off their destruction of Samantha and turned their attention to Jasmine, but she fought like a lioness, killing several men before the enemy managed to lay a blade on her. But she was soon cut and spurting blood.

"Charlene," Keira said. "Can you set Jasmine alight with a lantern?"

"Oh God, no. I can't." Charlene said.

"You must. Jaz is gone. She's doing this for us."

"I'm too far away."

Keira ran forward as Jasmine fell. She ducked under a sword strike but took a rapier to her shoulder in the frenzied melee. Ignoring the pain, she grabbed a lantern from a startled soldier and hurled it at the men surrounding Jasmine. The lantern shattered, and the kerosene on Jasmine's body burst into flames. In a chain reaction, the kerosene sparked Jasmine's blood, and the resulting explosion blew limbs off torsos in a swathe of spraying blood and burnt flesh. Keira was knocked off her feet but had retreated quickly enough to survive the blast. Blood poured from the rapier wound in her shoulder, but a tingling sensation indicated the healing process had already begun.

Survivors staggered, clothing on fire in all directions. Keira moved in clubbing with her metal bar. One stroke here and a man died, another there and another life extinguished. But still, more men poured into the ballroom.

Keira backed away as more men lunged at her, hacking and thrusting. *Not enough*, Keira thought. Not enough. Our strength is failing. Sage is dead. Samantha is dead. Jasmine is dead. Mary has betrayed us. We are weakened, exhausted. Not even my power, nor that of Elsie and Charlene, can delay the end.

Then, Keira heard the barking of dogs. She smirked. These stupid men still hadn't learned. The dogs could buy some more time, and that might be all they needed.

Keira gave a sharp whistle, and Elsie and Charlene sprinted from the room, Keira on their heels. They ran along a corridor, the sounds of pursuit thumping and scrabbling right behind them. They burst through another door, and Keira slammed a deadbolt into the locking arms. Seconds later, the door almost erupted inwards off its hinges. It held, for now.

"Where are Sam and Jaz?" Helen asked, her eyes wide beneath the kohl eyeliner.

"Dead," Keira said. The room contained a bloodied chair where Douglas had sat, but the man was gone and the nun with him. Keira put her hands on Helen's shoulders as the petite woman shed tears. "Where are Douglas and the nun, Helen?" Helen looked up, only to shake her head. Keira gripped her shoulders tighter, causing the small woman to cry out in pain. "Where are they? Did that nun turn you against me? Don't listen to her poisonous talk of redemption and forgiveness. No one cares for us but us. Do not betray me."

"No," Helen said. "I would never … she just …" A banging and rattling came at the door.

Keira released Helen and approached the door. "For Smudge," she whispered and closed her eyes.

CHAPTER 38

Crossing Over

Most of Thackery's forces lay dead. Only two dozen lived of the masses that had come storming into the Yard that day. How Garth, himself, had managed to remain alive, he did not know. Men pounded at the door while Constable Thackery shouted unnecessary orders to knock it down. Sergeant Frood paced the corridor with a flintlock pistol. Garth still didn't trust the scrawny prick not to put lead in the back of his skull. Several other men were in the process of reloading their weapons. Among the throng stalked the two remaining mastiffs and their handlers. Both dogs were yapping and snarling, turning in circles, as eager as the men to burst the door in. When one of the animals stopped barking and backed away snuffling, the skin on Garth's arms prickled a warning. Garth shouted and pointed. The men stopped hammering on the door and made a circle around the mastiff, eyeing the animal warily.

"It's alright," Sergeant Graham said. "Nathan is with us, aren't you, boy?" The dog snarled and bared its teeth at its master.

"Control your dog, Graham," Thackery said. "Or I'll put it down." The constable grabbed a freshly reloaded musket from a nearby man to make his point.

Sergeant Graham waved Thackery away. "No, no. Nathan is alright. He's alright. No one's going to break my bond with him, no one, and especially not a woman. Isn't that right, boy? We've been through too much, you and me." Sergeant Graham smiled and moved slowly towards his dog, his hand held out, palm down.

CHAPTER 38 Crossing Over

He stroked Nathan on the head, and the dog blinked, whimpered and rolled over. "You see? We're solid, Nathan and I."

Graham rubbed his dog's belly, and the men turned back to the door, preparing to finish the task of smashing it in. Nathan flipped back to his feet and clamped down on Sergeant Graham's balls. The sergeant shrieked as his testicles popped between the mastiff's teeth, and his scrotum was torn open. The other animal attacked its handler at that same moment, clamping onto the man's shin. Thackery aimed the musket at Nathan as the animal ripped a large chunk from Graham's inner thigh, but he couldn't get a shot without risking hitting the handler. Garth lunged and used his hunting knife to cut the dog's throat. The animal tried to turn on him, its breath rasping through a severed windpipe, but Garth's grip on the animal's neck was too strong. Other men hacked at the second mastiff. Amid the cries of the panicked soldiers, the agonising screams of Sergeant Graham and the death gurgles of the dying mastiffs, a cacophony of pain and chaos slapped off the walls.

When it was over, the two mastiffs and Sergeant Graham were dead, the loss of blood a fatal wound. The remaining dog handler had turned white. Bandages were wound tightly around the man's lower leg, and he was dragged through pools of blood and bollocks to the rear of the group. Men looked at each other in horrified silence.

"Knock that fucking door down!" Thackery screamed, breaking the growing unease among the men and rallying them to their duty. "They must not escape!"

As if on command, the door, already broken off its hinges, splintered and opened down the middle, allowing the deadlocks on the inside to be shoved away. The door fell inwards and men rushed inside.

A single candle illuminated a small empty room with a fireplace and sash window, which opened out onto an ornate façade. Garth poked his head outside. Perhaps a proficient climber could scale the exterior wall, but there was no sign of anyone clinging to the face of the building.

"Here," Frood said. He was kneeling at the fireplace. Steel rungs embedded in the bricks within allowed for secret passage up the chimney. It would be one at a time, then. Who dared go first? Thackery strapped his musket to his back and disappeared inside. Garth followed, and Frood entered behind him. It was an effort to climb with Thackery blocking the light ahead of him and the reek of Frood's body odour behind, though the scrawny sergeant's lack of hygiene was the least of Garth's concerns right now. The ladder led to a gabled roof of mossy and broken tiles. Garth took a deep breath of air and immediately regretted it. The fog seemed to glow a strange amber colour, providing a dim light by which to navigate the roof, but Garth remembered the stories of the toxic nature of the Yard and shivered.

Sister Kempson carried Douglas Partridge, supporting him under one arm. The man wore only thin leggings and a tunic, both items of clothing so dark with blood that they appeared tie-dyed in the man's bodily fluids, but at least he had some clothing to protect him against the bitter winds whipping across the gabled roof. The moist, chilling atmosphere had coated the roof tiles in a layer of mold, creating a slippery surface on which one misstep would see them both plummet to their deaths.

Douglas was not heavy; his corporeal frame seemed hollow. His torture at the hands of Keira Jack had broken the man to the point where his body seemed to have melted like a wax candle. Or was it not that Douglas was a ruined and lighter version of the healthy young blacksmith she had first encountered a few short weeks ago? Could it be that she, herself, had changed? She was leaner, faster and fitter—that much was obvious. She suspected that her newfound strength may not be a natural consequence of her recent physical endeavours. Something was rummaging around inside her, something powerful, but was it friend or foe?

No time to think on that. Douglas, for all his sins, had to be saved.

She had to get him out and answer to God and her conscience later.

Somebody, somewhere, said, *Let him die. Let chaos reign.*

For a moment, the nun wasn't sure she had heard it. She *hadn't* heard it, for the voice had not come from an external source, but rather within. The voice in her head. Ignore it. Keep going.

They came to a rope bridge. Judging by its rudimentary construction, this had to be some kind of escape route should events not work out in Keira Jack's favour. The far end of the bridge remained beyond perception out in the fog. Lightning flashed through the grey clouds overhead, the sharp crack of thunder following soon after, and a strong wind whipped at the nun's habit. The rope bridge was a potentially fatal obstacle for the awkward of foot, but Sister Kempson was no longer graceless and now possessed a fledgling strength and agility. If the two of them could cross over, they might encounter friendly forces or hide themselves from Keira, somewhere.

Hah, there are no friendly forces here, nun, and nowhere to hide. Let the bastard fall.

Ignore the voice. Ignore it.

"Come on, Douglas," she said. "We must cross this bridge." The young blacksmith swayed but did not respond. He seemed unaware of his surroundings, so Sister Kempson decided to piggyback him across the chasm for fear that he would stumble and fall to his death. Sister Kempson bent at the hips and eased the blacksmith onto her back. Her legs remained strong, and she took the first step. The wooden plank flexed and lowered under their combined weight but did not crack or splinter. The makeshift footbridge was only two handspan wide, but, thankfully, the depths below Sister Kempson were hidden by the fog, and she did not have to deal with the vertiginous glimpse of her awaiting death. She breathed slowly and put one foot in front of the other. One foot in front of the other. A simple task, one foot in front of the other. One foot in front. Something splintered, and Sister Kempson froze. Douglas began to stir on her back. "Stay still, Douglas."

Surrounded by a sea of murk, fog behind and in front, above

and below. Lost, the two of them, suspended high above an unforgiving pavement, one slip short of death, but Sister Kempson walked on.

The planks began to tremor underfoot: someone, or something, had stepped onto the walk bridge behind them. Sister Kempson increased her pace as fast as caution would allow and a little beyond.

Out of the fog came a wall. The nun stopped, unsure of where to go. Above them, a balcony railing provided a tethering point for the rope bridge. Douglas was in no condition to jump the gap and clamber the five feet required to the safety of the balcony. She would have to do so with the blacksmith on her back.

"Douglas, hold on. We're almost there."

Sister Kempson took a deep breath and jumped. Her hands clasped onto the base of the baluster and she pulled. Her wrists and elbows ached, and a burning sensation ran up her forearms, but she found purchase with her feet and straightened her knees, propelling them both up and over the balustrade. She lost her balance, and the two of them tumbled to the ground. Sister Kempson lay panting for breath on what appeared to be a wide upper landing of a massive cathedral: arched windows and coloured glass towering over her.

Sister Kempson scrambled to her feet but could find no exit. The landing curved around and disappeared from sight. They had to follow it and find a way down quickly. She grabbed Douglas and hauled him upright.

And then Keira Jack came leaping out of the amber fog.

CHAPTER 39

Angels and Demons

Keira landed catlike on the balcony, and her anger flared. She had caught the nun in the act of trying to get Douglas to safety. Did she not understand the man was guilty of crimes against all women everywhere? The nun was a traitor. Keira snarled at the Bride of Christ and then kicked Douglas in the stomach. The man's breath left him with a whoosh, and he curled into a foetal position.

"Leave him alone!" Sister Kempson cried.

"You disappoint me, Sister." Keira reached over the balustrade. She pulled Elsie onto the balcony and then reached back down for Helen. Charlene came last. When her sisters stood by her side, Keira pointed at Douglas with a disdainful sneer. "He isn't worth your efforts. You can't redeem him." Keira turned to the others. "Cut the ropes."

"No, you cannot do that," Sister Kempson said. "There may be men on the bridge."

"I'm counting on it," Keira said.

"That is murder."

"This is war. Nobody murders anyone in war."

Keira approached the rope on the left, Charlene the rope on the right. Charlene closed her eyes and the rope began to shift of its own accord, working itself free of the knot tying it to the balusters. Keira took a more physical approach and began to hack at the thick twine with her sharpened fingernails.

Sister Kempson grabbed Keira by her long black hair and jerked her away from the rope. Keira cried out in pain and backhanded the nun, who staggered but did not fall.

A crossbow bolt whizzed past Keira's head and narrowly missed the nun.

"They're almost on us," Elsie cried.

Charlene's rope slipped free of the balusters, and the bridge collapsed on one side, dropping and tilting. Screams came through the fog: men had fallen, but many remained clinging to the bridge.

"Keep the madwoman off me," Keira said, moving in to finish cutting the left rope while Elsie and Charlene attempted to subdue the nun, but Sister Kempson was not without a supernatural strength of her own. She threw Elsie aside and landed a punch to Charlene's jaw that knocked the spiky-haired woman backwards. Helen put her hands to her mouth in surprise and backed away.

Keira snarled, lowered her head and tackled the nun to the ground. She raised a hand to strike Sister Kempson. Douglas punched Keira, and the ratcatcher's wife turned her attention to her brother-in-law.

"Leave her alone," Douglas said.

Charlene and Elsie hauled Sister Kempson to her feet, one on each arm, and this time, the nun could not break free.

"What's this?" Keira smiled through clenched teeth, rubbing her jaw. "Helping the nun? Helping a *woman*? You're the hero now, Douglas, is that it?" She swatted aside Douglas' next punch and grabbed him by the collar. "No. I will not allow noble sacrifices from the most ignoble creature that has ever lived." She dragged him to the balustrade and lifted him from his feet. "Give my sister and your wife all my love." She headbutted Douglas in the face and hurled him over the balustrade.

"No!" Sister Kempson screamed, but Charlene and Elsie held her tight.

Keira Jack backed away from the edge and looked at her own hands. She had finally done it, had avenged Smudge. Keira looked to the tumultuous heavens. *Bessie,* she thought. *I did it for you.*

CHAPTER 39 Angels and Demons

❊

Constable Thackery leapt onto the balcony, his musket pointing straight at Keira's chest. "You cannot escape judicial retribution! You shall be punished for your crimes, not least of which is the murder of the man you just threw to his death."

Garth jumped to the balcony, and Frood fell onto his face right behind him. Other men scrambled over the baluster, but of the survivors, only a handful carried firearms.

"Garth!" Sister Kempson called.

"Sister, are you alright?" Garth took a step towards the nun, but a warning look from Keira stopped him.

"In the name of the Law," Thackery said, "I carry out your execution."

Keira waggled a finger. "I fear your weapons are currently useless, Constable. They are without powder and shot."

Thackery glanced at his musket briefly, and as he did so, it jerked from his grasp and twisted out over the balcony, disappearing into the mists. The other soldiers lost their firearms in a similar fashion or threw them away voluntarily. Keira laughed and clapped her hands. Before the lawmen could grasp rapier or short sword, these weapons too hurtled from scabbards over the balcony.

Thackery and his followers were now without arms of any kind. They had come within the radius of Charlene and Elsie's mental powers, a fatal mistake. Garth still had his hunting knife, hidden at the back of his hip, but he chose to leave it there.

"We still outnumber you," Thackery said. "Give yourselves up."

Keira smirked and nodded to Elsie. "Let's even those numbers."

Elsie touched two fingers to her temple. One of Thackery's men leapt over the balcony. Frood attempted to join him, but Garth hauled the sergeant back as he climbed the balcony. Garth slapped Frood's face, breaking Elsie's hold.

Thackery and the remaining men attacked Keira Jack with their fists. Garth lunged for Sister Kempson. Charlene and Elsie released the nun as the big woodsman came at them. Garth had one duty:

protect the nun, no complications, and whatever reservations he had about killing a woman had to be suppressed because, by the Green Gods, these women had no reservations about killing a man.

He pulled his hunting knife from its scabbard, and it immediately tugged in his grip, wanting to be free of his hand. Garth buried his blade in Charlene's gut. The woman's eyes grew wide in pain, and the hunting knife no longer resisted him. Charlene went down, clutching her stomach. Elsie came clawing at him. Sister Kempson grabbed her and pulled her away from Garth with such force that Elsie spun through the air to land ten feet away, the contact with the hard balcony stone knocking her senseless. Garth had no time to stand there astonished at the nun's strength. Two more of Thackery's men lay sprawled on the ground, either dead or unconscious. Garth had to get Sister Kempson out. He grabbed the nun by the hand and headed for the stairs but could find no such path.

Keira dodged Thackery and his men. She kicked out and slashed with sharpened fingernails, tearing flesh and causing hesitation among her attackers. She felled one man with a kick to the balls, but another grabbed her by the leg, and she nearly fell. She twisted free and backed away, kicking and slashing as the men pressed her backwards.

Charlene Hickson still lived. Sergeant Frood took the opportunity to kick her in the head as she lay writhing on the ground.

"Fucking try and strangle me, will you, bitch?!" Frood bared his teeth as he again drove his steel-capped boot into her face. The sergeant kicked again, and bone broke with a sickening crunch. The spiky redhead, however, was not powerless. She grabbed Frood by the ankle and took his legs out from under him. She pulled herself on top and began biting his neck with her remaining teeth, getting her own taste of bloody revenge. Frood shrieked and struggled but could not get the feral woman off him. All the time, Sister Kempson was shouting for everyone to stop fighting while struggling against Garth, who was trying to drag her away.

When Frood stopped struggling, Charlene sat up, wiped her mouth and then toppled forward, senseless, onto the man's chest.

CHAPTER 39 Angels and Demons

❊

Helen Hardcastle stood against the balcony railing, a witness to the battle but unsure of what to do. She had no desire to kill or maim but could not allow her sisters to be hurt. She weaved her way through the melee and dragged the limp body of Charlene off the sergeant. Charlene was bleeding out, her abdomen sliced open, and her face a mess of purple pulp. Helen sat with the unresponsive woman, hands on her stomach and cheek, closing the gashes, but the grievous nature of Charlene's wounds challenged her powers of healing. Charlene was on the cusp of death.

Helen heard someone call her name and turned. She gasped. Mary Brown floated down out of the amber mists. She was naked but possessed large wings like those of the field hawk. Mary cradled the broken, bloodied and unconscious figure of Douglas Partridge in her arms, as if he were the crucified Christ released from the cross and she a winged angel. Helen called out in awe, and the fighting stopped as all eyes turned to see Mary alighting on the cathedral balcony.

Keira Jack stared and, in a dead voice, said, "You have returned."

"I have returned."

"Of all the men to save, why that one?" Keira asked.

Mary looked down at Douglas. "I did not know who he was when he fell into my arms, but it seems that fate placed him in my care."

Keira turned the edges of her mouth down. "Your care? You should have let him fall. And Willard? Tell me that you come with news of Willard's death, and all will be forgiven."

The wings slowly retracted until they disappeared, and Mary lost her angelic aspect, mortal woman once more. "I do not. I come with news of your own demise."

"Hah, you'll have to wait your turn." She smiled at Constable Thackery. "My demise is quite the prized commodity."

"What's going on here?" Thackery said. "What witchcraft is this?"

"I think we're better off staying out of this," Garth whispered. "Just walk away, Thackery, while we can."

"Never. I have come this far and will see justice served." The constable, his eyes still flicking from Keira to Mary, knelt at the side of Sergeant Frood, who was gurgling and rasping, but the man yet lived. "These women are murderers, all of them."

"You've lost," Garth said, indicating the three soldiers remaining at the constable's command, huddled together with fear in their wide eyes. "Your forces are spent. Let it go."

Thackery stood. "We fight, Garth. To the end. Where's your honour?"

"Suicide is not honourable."

Keira wiped her bloodied hands on her green dress and stood tall. She gestured towards Thackery and Garth. "You see, Mary, how they squabble among themselves? Men are frail, capricious creatures, lacking true solidarity, but we women, we have each other's best interests—"

"Silence," Mary said. "Where are Jasmine and Samantha and Sage? Where are they now?"

"Dead at the hands of these bastard men."

"No, dead at *your* hands. You are the reason they are gone. Charlene and Elsie are hurt. All of this is your doing. They all trusted you, and you led them to their destruction."

Keira shook her head. "No. We only sought to avenge poor Smudge."

"Bessie would not have wanted so many to die. This is senseless."

Keira's eyes narrowed. "How would you know, betrayer? You have turned your back on us. You do not belong. "

"I, too, have lost," Mary said.

Keira's expression changed. She raised her hands in a pacifying motion. The anger disappeared from her face to be replaced by sadness. "I know, love. You're angry about your baby. I understand that. I empathise, I sympathise, of course I do. We are sisters in this pain. Listen to me. These men are defeated. We have won. I'm sorry for what I said. Join us again, join your family again, for in this new life, we only have each other. Let me soothe the wrongs between us."

CHAPTER 39 Angels and Demons

Mary Brown gently lowered Douglas Partridge to the balcony tiles. "You've gone too far, Keira. You've been driven mad by the poison within you. You are the victim of something that you do not understand, a power that seeks to use you, bend you to its own will."

Mary's words pricked at Helen. So many of the girls had died, and beneath Helen's fingers, Charlene trembled on the precipice of the abyss. Had they erred? Yet Keira had always seemed so sure, so strong in the force of her spirit, and true to that spirit, she would not be swayed now.

"I bend to no one's will," Keira said. She nodded at Douglas. "How dare you save that man's life? You make a mockery of everything we have been through, the sacrifices we have made. You have spurned me for the last time. You're disgusting, a traitor, a betrayer. If you've come to kill me, then have at it, love, and don't hold back because I will surely not."

"Stop!" Sister Kempson cried. "Stop this madness."

"Sister, keep out of this," Garth whispered. "We can still get out while they're at each other's throats."

"No, no. This is ... no more death. There must be another way."

Garth shook his head. "No one ever bloody listens."

Keira threw her head back and laughed. "Sister Rose Kempson, the biggest fool of them all." She waved her hands at the cathedral. "Here we stand high upon this majestic structure, a hundred feet above the streets, clinging to the side of the Lord's great phallus. But He won't come to your aid. He didn't come to ours, after all. You are a worse hypocrite than most, nun. You pretend to be chaste, to be better than the rest of us, but you walk around with His cock all the way up you, a blind whore who doesn't even know what she is. But I know what you are. You're one of us."

"You've had your say," Sister Kempson said. "Now let God have his."

"God can lick my cunt. You try to protect my sister's killer, foolishly believing him still capable of remorse and restoration. I won't have that. And you," she said, stabbing a finger at Mary, "are guilty of the same crime. You have betrayed me, both of you, betrayed the sisterhood that binds us. But I offer you this one last chance. Douglas killed Bessie, and he deserves to die. Cast that man to the pits of Hell where he belongs. Throw him over the side."

Mary shook her head. "No. You no longer control me. I have taken myself back."

"I never asked for anything," Keira said, "but solidarity."

Keira leapt at Mary and raised her hand to strike the other woman dead, but Mary struck first. The hand that laid a resounding blow to Keira's cheek was not human but rather that of the mountain bear, its sharp claws tearing shreds of flesh. Keira shrieked and cursed. She backed away, holding her hand to the ruinous injuries on her face. She narrowed her eyes, and a bat flitted out of the amber fog to scratch at Mary's eyes, but this was little more than a nuisance to the other woman, who swatted the pest from the air. Then, with a cacophonous chittering, a thousand bats erupted from the amber fog, a dark cloud of tooth and claw cutting at Mary's flesh. She swung her single paw at them but this proved ineffectual against so many winged assassins. Mary screamed, her voice starting out human but ending in the roar of the mountain bear as she completed a transformation to that gigantic creature of rending claw and tearing muzzle. Mary was now a bizarre amalgamation of woman and bear, recognisable features of both evident in her anatomy. The bats fluttered and clawed at her, but Mary lunged for Keira, determined to stop the attack at its source. Keira Jack was too quick, the ratcatcher's wife slipping under a murderous swing from Mary's paw.

Helen sheltered Charlene's body with her own and looked over to where Elsie still lay unconscious, fearing that the helpless woman may get hurt in the battle between Keira and Mary, as each hacked at the other in a mad bloodlust, apparently oblivious to their surroundings. Charlene moaned and shook, and Helen whispered for the injured woman to hang on.

❇

CHAPTER 39 Angels and Demons

Garth dragged Sister Kempson away, looking for a means of escape before they found themselves sucked into in the deadly maelstrom between Keira and Mary.

"We must get Douglas out," the nun said, resisting her bodyguard.

Garth had no time to explain all the reasons why that was a bad idea, not least of which was the man probably deserved everything he got. He settled for pulling harder at the nun, but she twisted away from his grip with ease.

Constable Thackery, meanwhile, was screaming impotently for both women to give themselves over to the Law, a farcical demand that two combatants ignored, locked as they were in a struggle for supremacy of life over death. A wayward bat flew into the constable's mouth, and his calls for obedience ended in a choking cough as he spat the flying mammal from his mouth and retched.

Bats clawed and shredded the massive body of the mountain bear. Mary waded through them, heaving her heavy arms this way and that; many attackers fell, but more remained. Keira continued to back away and dodge and weave the cumbersome blows, yet her opponent showed no signs of weakening.

As the two women battled, Garth had a chance to run with Sister Kempson, but to his horror, the nun broke away and jumped on Keira's back, wrapping an arm around her throat. The manic cloud of bats dissipated momentarily, and Mary swept forward, raising her paw with a roar.

"No!" Garth called. "Do not hurt the nun!"

Mary hesitated, and Keira pulled at Sister Kempson's fingers, snapping them and freeing herself from the other's grasp. The nun cried out in pain, and Keira hurled her to the floor as if she were discarding a lemon rind. Garth cursed and dragged the sister away by the habit collar. Mary brought her raised paw down in a killing stroke. Keira rolled, but her back erupted in striations of red gashes, the fabric of her green dress torn to pieces. Keira tumbled to the ground and, for a moment, did not move. She lay at Garth's feet, the blood spurting from her back. The woodsman, still gripping his hunting knife, had a split second to act. Strike at

Keira in a vulnerable moment or try again to extricate the nun. In an instant, Garth made his decision. *Let them destroy themselves*, he thought. Garth had one duty. No complications. He went for Sister Kempson, who now knelt at Douglas' side, and Garth stood over them both, hunting knife poised.

Keira staggered to her feet, ashen-faced. The gashes in her back were deep. Any mortal woman would be cut in half, but she somehow lived. Keira had suffered a punctured lung and, without sufficient time to heal, could no longer evade her enemy or recall her bats. The bear moved in for the kill, but Mary's own strength dwindled as the blood seeped from her body. Keira stood tall and raised her chin.

"Stop this," Keira said in a wheezing voice, blood bubbling at her lips. "It's not too late. Let Helen heal us both. This is … just a spat between siblings, between sisters. We love each other. We do."

Mary did not respond as she swayed, her body slowly resuming its human aspect, shrinking, diminishing, the bloodied fur disappearing to reveal the torn and ripped flesh underneath. Mary sank to one knee and bowed her head.

Thackery screamed and hurled himself at Keira. She turned as the enraged lawman barrelled into her, driving her against the balcony railing with enough force to break the balusters and send them both over the side, where they fell through the fog and disappeared.

Helen shrieked, her cry of dismay absorbed by the amber mists.

Sister Kempson gingerly peered over the edge of the balcony. "They're gone," she said, shaking her head. "Gone."

Garth did not sheathe his blade, the threat ever present while any of these women still lived.

Sister Kempson turned to Mary. "You must flee. You and the others. This is not over for you. There may be more men, stragglers or a second wave on the streets below. You must avoid them, for they will burn you like they did Sage. Your transformation is evidence enough of damnation in the eyes of these men," she said, gesturing to the three soldiers still standing. "Leave Douglas and save yourselves, quickly."

CHAPTER 39 Angels and Demons

Garth was disquieted by the nun's suggestion, for Elsie Gallagher, Helen Hardcastle and Charlene Hickson had committed multiple murders. Of Mary Brown, he could not say. The three men of the Night Watch did not speak but were clearly as confused by the nun's eagerness to help the harpies as Garth was. Still, they were probably just relieved to be alive and made no move to intervene.

Mary stood slowly. "I am not strong enough to carry more than one."

"Then take Elsie, go," Sister Kempson said. "Helen, you must get Charlene out, quickly."

Helen nodded and pulled Charlene to her feet, the spiky-haired woman wincing in pain. Helen supported Charlene, and the two stumbled along the balcony, searching for a way down.

Mary gestured to Douglas Partridge. "What of him?"

The nun crouched beside Douglas and put a hand to his chest. "He yet lives. He is saved. Leave him with me. I will see that he receives medical attention."

Mary, cradling Elsie as she had done Douglas, closed her eyes and, a moment later, her wings slowly emerged from her back in a display that caused the three remaining night watchmen to gasp and shake their heads. She approached the spot where Keira and Thackery had plummeted to their deaths and spread her wings. She stepped out into the amber fog, her powerful wings propelling her and Elsie out and away.

Garth knelt by Sergeant Frood. The scrawny lawman, too, still sucked in rasping breaths. Say what you liked about the man, but the bastard had a will to live. Garth tore strips from his tunic and stemmed the bleeding at his throat as much as possible. He eyed the three soldiers of the Night Watch standing by. These men were witnesses to Sister Kempson's abetment of the fugitives, and while Vincent E. Thackery was dead, man's Law was eternal. Garth shook his head. Just what in the Green Gods had gotten into the nun?

CHAPTER 40

The Wind

"You will be returning to the True Wilds, I take it?"

Garth looked up from where he had been staring at the floor. "Aye. The bishop has absolved me of any further duties here in Dysael, and I have missed the tranquillity of the woods and the companionship of my kind of people."

"What kind of people are those?"

"The four-legged kind, mostly."

Sister Kempson smiled and placed the palms of her manacled hands together. "I thank you for everything that you have done for me or tried to do. I am at a loss to explain my own actions and … well, I'm at a loss. I was carried away by emotions that I had not expected to feel."

Garth sat back in his chair and nodded. Outside, the wind howled and flung anything not tied down in protest. "I have informed the bishop of your situation. I am certain he will send someone of more authority than I to get you out of here."

The nun smiled sadly. "I fear the bishop may be under a certain amount of political pressure to distance himself from me. I expect little aid from that quarter. But I still have God on my side."

"Aye, you still have him. How are your fingers?"

The nun slowly flexed her bandaged right hand. "Healing very well. I barely notice the pain."

Garth sighed. "I don't like to leave you like this."

Sister Kempson looked away. "But you must. They will not hurt me, Garth. I'm a nun. Have faith." She touched the crucifix at her chest. Despite her current circumstances, Sister Kempson did not wear the gown of the prisoner but rather her customary habit. The powers that be had allowed her that modicum of respect, for now.

"Do you still carry it?" Garth said.

"Carry what?"

"Sage Schuman's bracelet."

The nun shrugged. "It must have fallen by the wayside somewhere. I lost track of it, and there was a lot going on."

"Aye, that there was." The big man cleared his throat and shifted his weight from foot to foot. "I'll hang around the city a bit longer."

"No, no. Off with you. When you tire of your precious animals and trees, come see me at the Sisters of Holy Conviction, for I fully expect to be released." Garth grunted that he would and turned away. "Civilisation is not all bad, Garth. There are good people."

He nodded and attempted a smile. It did not take.

Outside, the wind had set up shop under a grey canvas sky. It was selling chilled bones and chapped lips, but Garth was not buying. He strode through the streets alone, for no other soul dared brave the shivering winds that howled and shrieked like harpies.

Sister Kempson squeezed her fingers into a fist. The manacles about her wrists allowed her just enough freedom to peel the bandages from her right hand with her left. Fading yellow bruises discoloured her knuckles, but otherwise, the hand and fingers were in perfect working order.

The small room within which she sat had once been a bedroom for prostitutes. Construction of a replacement for the Law Courts was underway, but it would be some time before that structure was completed, and so the drapery-cum whorehouse continued to function as the centre for law and order in Dysael, North Quarter. She approached a window which had been boarded up to prevent detainees from escaping. It was entirely unnecessary. The nun

CHAPTER 40 The Wind

giggled at the ludicrous thought of her attempting to jump from the second floor to go on the run from the law.

Sister Kempson heaved a sigh, and the board that sealed the shutters clattered to the floor. The nun raised an eyebrow and waited for an officer to rush inside and seal the offending window, but none came.

She leaned closer to the window and scanned the windswept streets. She sighed again, and her breath fogged the windowpanes. She raised a finger to sketch something in the tiny droplets of misted breath and, to her surprise, the windowpane melted away under her touch and disappeared, allowing the chill winds to blow about the cell. Sister Kempson stood back from the window, wide-eyed. An idea struck her. She raised her arms and puffed on the manacles at her wrists, and they dropped to the floor with a barely audible clink. She breathed on her hands, and a tingling sensation danced along her fingers. Sister Kempson ran those same fingers over her habit, over the subtle ridge where the metal band encircled her thigh. Suddenly, the jump to the street below was not such a ludicrous prospect.

Suddenly, anything was possible.

Love Your Book

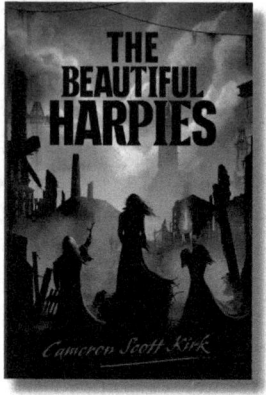

The Beautiful Harpies

TIMELINE

DECEMBER 2023

Soft-back book printed from paper that has been carbon offset through the World Land Trust Scheme.

PRINTED by Hobbs the Printers Ltd
at Southampton, United Kingdom

PUBLISHED by Cybirdy Publishing
London, United Kingdom

SPECIAL EDITION
Autographed by the Author

[signature]

CAMERON SCOTT KIRK

WHO are you?	WHO did you obtain the book from?	WHEN did you obtain the book
FIRST GUARDIAN		
SECOND GUARDIAN		
THIRD GUARDIAN		
FOURTH GUARDIAN		
FIFTH GUARDIAN		

Cameron Scott Kirk (Christchurch, New Zealand) has published many short stories, won a Best of Fiction award and is the author of the novel *The Mad Trinkets*. He has been published in over a dozen magazines including *Antipodean SF*, *Aphotic Realm*, and *Alcyone* magazine to name but a few.

Cameron has been known to slay dragons, fight off invading aliens and match the hardiest dwarf in a drinking competition. When he's not doing that, he's writing about it.